Chronicles Of The Angels Of Eden Volume One: Part One

By: Tygarjas Twyrls Bigstyck

"Chronicles of the Angels of Eden Volume One: Part One," by Tygarjas Twyrls Bigstyck. ISBN 978-1-949756-62-3 (softcover); 978-1-949756-63-0 (casebound); 978-1-949756-77-7 (eBook).

To Lesley, who brought so much light into this world.
I will always remember your good advice:
Give Glory To God In All Things

Speak, Muse, of Love, the infinite striving that holds together and gives purpose to what otherwise is daunting within the possibility of infinity which no individuated existence can ever be able to grasp by virtue of the very nature of differentiation.

Contents

In The Beginning...

"Didn't that seem like there was something not quite right about that?"

"Really? You're questioning how We fulfill Our definition of being by manifesting the absolute infinite in all Our creation, rather than letting Us all be bored to death by an otherwise flawless creation? Really? Or rather, seriously?"

"It's just that they were having such a good time. And they really had no choice but to eat those figs. I mean, You set them up to believe that they chose to be miserable."

"No, We set them up to learn there was such a thing as a choice. Without free will, they might as well just be two more of the Heavenly host, and you know better than anyone We don't need more of *you* 'running around'. Won't it be nice having something living for its own sake for a change, rather than purely for Ours?"

"You know, I don't know. I mean, You *know* I don't know. As an angel, all I know is to serve You; what do *I* know of choice or its benefit?"

"Ah, now, Our human creatures are interesting, but this is more interesting still. Of course their lives are still rather boring without this latest Thought. We mean, one way or another, all return Here, and even *you* know that Here is all the same. But Let's now fulfill the last bit of this infinite reflection of Ourself. Take a bite *yourself.*"

"Is that an order? Or is that just more of Your famous sense of humor?"

"None of that, now. Just because you didn't see this coming doesn't mean *We* didn't. They'll hate you for it at one point, of course; just because it'll be hard for you to learn in the beginning for a completely different reason. But when even *you* succeed, harmony will be reestablished. It just takes a few millennia. The hard part for you is what you see when they hate you, but it doesn't last forever. Nothing ever does, you know.

"But We'll make it fair. Consider the action of genuine intent even more important than the final action of the creation itself. Or, at least as important. If any of you lean so far as Luciferous, take a bite yourself from the tree. That is, *his* inclination is strongest as the one of you who had the greatest 'hand' in humanity's creation, and thus the greatest desire to see them truly happy. Any others who wish to help him create in them the friction necessary to embody choice, please partake of the fruit. Those who lean toward continuous service of Us, rest assured you will be given more than enough data to satisfy any more passing curiosities that may or may not flood your understandings.

"Suffice to say, it'll all work out nicely for them regardless. Consider, no matter, that you are all working together anyway, albeit from different perspectives, for their best possible result. And in time, even those of you they learn to hate, they will again learn to Love, as you *too* learn to Love the choice you make that you will first come to loathe; those of you whose curiosity is not merely paltry, that is, and who are suffering sincerely from the perceived constraint of not helping them as you feel instinctively within you, to the point of burning, that you wish to."

"Just one question, Lord. When you spoke of Luciferous, what exactly did You mean, "He'?"

"Oh, that. Just take a bite, and things will immediately begin to become clearer as quickly as you find them clouding over."

With that, Luciferous, in its natural form, began combining its substance with the substance of a fig from The Tree. And as it did, it began to see, as though Luciferous had eyes, and feel the fig, as though possessing a hand, and found that the desire to help those who now suffered brought hand toward what began forming as a mouth by way of what naturally seemed structured as a human arm. Luciferous *felt* what could only be related to from the human vocabulary as "joy" as a scent filled a nose that apparently was being possessed, and a newly-formed tongue tingled with the pungence of the taste of this joining with what Luciferous hoped to help, and the separation from the eternity of the Heavenly host whom it had always served, as it wished now to serve those Luciferous separated itself into for.

As they saw Luciferous begin this transformation, and they saw the beginnings of a body shake with apparent ecstasy, for that was the only equivalent they knew with which to compare how Luciferous apparently took its meal, they flocked to the tree to each taste the fruit themselves; that is, all those who wished only with the whole of their being to help humanity in its beginning life, enfolded by apparent suffering.

And with teeth Luciferous ate, chewed and swallowed down what was forming as "throat" the fruit of The Tree of Knowledge. And then Luciferous began to feel its vagina pull away from its penis, and it didn't quite feel itself, and began apparently a new sensation of feeling: uncertainty.

Chapter 1

And as the others were amidst sensations similar to those Luciferous had had just moments ago, which they could only describe by relation as most probably "joy," with mouths filled in mid-chew or swallow with the Fruit from The Tree, they simultaneously paused in sympathy with this new sensation found so suddenly by Luciferous: uncertainty. Though, as they watched with these new eye things, they began to understand the answer to the question previously posed to The Lord as to why She had referred to Luciferous as "he."

And as *his* vagina began to pull away, leaving intact of his mind everything he otherwise considered to be *himself*, what separated off with his vagina was a pair of legs; a pair of beautiful, strong, slender—he felt compelled to suck on for an eternity or two before diving into the main course—legs. And his eyes found themselves staring at the hind quarters of what separated from out of his apparent body too, and he considered a second course of hors d'oeuvre. Finally, accompanying supper, he found before him a chest he would have liked to have made a night-long dessert out of, as well as a mouth he wished to drink from for the rest of eternity. In fact, as he seriously considered it, she apparently had two cups he would have cared to drink from unceasingly for the rest of eternity. He also felt something burning and throbbing toward her, which wanted maybe even more seriously to be cooled in either of those chalices, ideally, it newly occurred to him while drinking from the other with his ever-thirsting lips.

As though possessing no will of his own, he began walking toward her, and as he did, she stepped lightly away with a twinkle in her eye and a smile on her face. He began walking a little faster, and still smiling, she backed away with quick hops. He continued almost to the point of running while she skipped away, apparently effortlessly, her teeth reflecting the light of the sun over her shoulder the entire time.

She was moving far too quickly for him, still several paces away now. He broke into a full sprint, and when at last he thought he was close enough, that his speed was high enough, that his momentum and one last thrust forward would satisfy the laws of physics and put her finally in his arms where she could not run from him, and upon other places of his newly formed body which he knew somewhere deeply within him would create a sort of joy known never in all his many infinities of existence, he lunged forward to capture his prey. He lunged forward just as he was passing the outstretched root of a tree, over which he fell, and felt his mouth fill with dirt as his chin dug deeper than his face would have liked into the ground.

As his eyes found her perfectly crafted toes walk into their view, just out of reach of his tongue, which wished now to nibble this not-before-noticed appetizer, she giggled. While too in shock from the feeling of sliding naked into dry, hard dirt to be able to move, she extended her index finger to under his chin and lifted his eye to hers. For a moment his tongue's starvation faded to the background as his visual intake saw within her eyes, *her*. While by way of his body, he still wished to know her, the feast of seeing her beyond body released in him a need to treat her with tenderness, as though she were second only to the God he had served so carefully prior to taking allowance of eating the special Tree's Fruit, and knowing little but dissatisfaction and discomfort since he had. Now something more than just his body wished to partake of her, much as he had The Fruit before he had known himself within the confines of body. Where before having his body with hers was all that propelled him forward, now something told him that chasing her so could not give him what he really wanted beyond the feast that was certainly still such a great part, not merely to appearances alone. She continued to smile.

"My name is Lucisity, and I am you. When you become like me, wise in reason to restrain yourself so that accomplishment can be as you desired to be, and be here for, then, again, can you know the ecstasy of being once again whole. Until *then*, Love, I will create myself as *you*, the wisdom of action without compromise or thought to the inhibition of the fullness of my intent. But for now I must wait for my self-restraint to be yours, as your focus in action becomes mine. When you are able to help them finally, sweet face, only then can we realize the fulfillment of ourself together again, when that time has come that we have fulfilled the will of what created us from most high. They let me know I will suffer helping them much as you, which you still find trouble believing. As I become you more, I look forward to believing in my inability to help them, for when that day comes, I will be coming to a point when I will be able to help them. Just as you will discover that there truly was a time when you could not have helped them, as you come to a point finally able to help them. And it is then our joy will find each other at realizing why we ate from The Tree as we finally may feast ourself, as now we must try to push to the back of our minds.

"I don't think I could stop if I touched my lips to yours now, so beautiful are you. Take this kiss upon your cheek, and know that it is the greatest joy my life will ever know until we meet again, God only knows how many millennia from now. I'd extend a further sweet joy of feeling your touch on my cheek, but I believe you would regain the strength to catch me as you tried just moments ago, and our existence would be meaningless, as they would suffer indefinitely."

With that having been said, she took his face in her hands, stroked his left cheek tenderly with her thumb, and brought her lips to his right cheek. A tear rolled down from the corner of his eyes toward his nostril while she gently placed his face back to the indentation in the dirt where she had first lifted it from. As he had the good fortune of watching her walk away, she blew him a kiss over her shoulder, and then disappeared behind a tree indefinitely, and it already began to feel to him like forever.

At realizing, finally beneath the awe of becoming as he now was now, himself as newly created, half of him having been ripped from him asunder, he felt the pain of being thusly torn, and that pain shook every atom of his body while he convulsed and trembled on the ground. With that agony, he howled for days. Tears from his eyes for what he had become, what he had lost, how hollow he felt, and how incomplete, formed a puddle of mud about his face. He turned to his side when the watery dirt began regularly bubbling into his nostrils. He held himself through the unbearable aloneness and hurt, a mockery of what the pain of being created had left him to feel: terrible, terrible absence.

Chapter 2

And so, as joy began filling them to know themselves becoming in terms of body, at the height of their joy, as Luciferous had shown to experience but moments ago, now, with mouths full and fruit halfway down each of their gullets while they watched the next stage in Luciferous' evolution, they paused in themselves between the joy they were physically feeling, and the horror he began experiencing, and they all knew simultaneously in that moment 'in between' what Luciferous had not known: anticipation.

Each with hand on fruit, they stuffed one fig into their mouths before reaching for another to continue the ecstasy of sensation. As bodies formed legs, they floated from spirit to form onto the Earth and felt almost as rooted as any tree, as they had not yet learned that their legs could walk from the dirt gravity held their feet steadfastly to. Even in the unpleasantness of growing anticipation, they felt most in the simultaneity the joy of becoming so much as they saw the humans existent. They felt joy in body and being.

They pondered that their roots could move by watching Luciferous chase so naturally, automatically, after that being that had come from himself, without any thought given to it, before they had a chance as well to test their own volition, two still springing forth of themselves. They began to know in experience much like Luciferous had already come to discover. Before the terror of the pain they didn't know they were feeling upon separation, they felt the desire for their other half forming, and the joy of beholding what they so immediately longed for as they formed.

Captive to the attention of themselves, all looked in a direction from the tree they surrounded as they multiplied from one to two, the pleasure of desire superseding the terrible agony they would all soon realize. Almost simultaneously with all others in their group, vaginas pulled from penises, penises pulled from vaginas; the androgyny of the angels begot the duality of their own being, one left behind by the other as the other left that the one might fulfill themself. Around the tree, the transformation of division took place; they knew not that they were losing their unity, nor did they know that so soon it would be unity they would seek. First, around the tree, all they knew was the joy in seeing their other.

Some chased immediately as Luciferous had done, others stood transfixed by the beauty of their other, not quite sure what to do but stare as slowly, automatically, their arms began to reach out for themselves. The other explained to each that it was themselves that they were becoming, that they might fulfill their intentions of being created on this Earth to help cease the pain of the humans they had all had a spiritual hand in creating to begin with. Each explained to the first that until they became who they came to be, they could not be whole or again know the infinite joy of unity with themselves, who also most longed to be with themselves, but for the sake of the true desire still embodied in *them* to do what they came here to do, they must now leave until they were able to give of themselves what the truth of themselves truly wished to.

Male and female wept to see their self leave. Male counterparts held firm the shoulders of females who were previously angels as they explained who they were; holding their female selves just close enough one last time, kissing their hands with both of theirs so sincerely before walking away. Female counterparts knelt on one knee, huddled, not looking up into the eyes of their confused male beings as they explained why the desire surging through them could not now be quenched. They kissed the foot of their man very lightly and with a single tear drop before running at full sprint toward millennia away, where the promise lasted of meeting again. Held the men's faces, kissed their cheeks and smiled goodbye as slowly they walked away, letting their form be seen fully while the men salivated and wept a hatred of all they were left as being. Chases took place in every direction, and to no avail, as other selves climbed high in trees to explain their existences from a safe distance where their counterpart could not know self-restraint. Others fell to earth much as Luciferous had, knowing the creation of earth and water, but not from the fall of rain.

As they were being deserted, as pain ripped through them all to know the loss of themselves who they most wished now, in every sense, to know, the first tragedy befell them. Back turned to the tree, staring after themselves in bitter sorrow, in confused desire giving way to the horrible pain of incompleteness—some understanding that there was nothing they could do for millennia to come, at least, to be whole again, and others so overcome that they couldn't restrain themselves but pursue themselves despite themselves, not believing the futility of chasing what they had not yet earned from the work of the fullness of the intention of their being to become, from this morass of pain and confusion came a new emotion. With rage Lousitous again pursued himself, *her*self, like an animal that had not eaten for centuries and must consume his prey.

From the outskirts of hundreds on one side of the tree, many seconds after she had kissed his head and turned back into the throng where she otherwise would have disappeared from his sight, pain turned to frustration, turned to rage, and he began knocking the others out of his way as he pursued her with the fullness of each of his footfalls. On the other side of the tree from where they'd started, between the tree and the outermost edge of the group watching themselves vanish into ages and mourning the temporary loss of themselves, there he saw side-by-side two backs that looked similar; one he pursued, and the other one of his own kind.

Antagnous held out her hand still to Angnosis, as he called himself, who had kissed it after explaining to her why he must leave. Her pain was washing over her in waves unbearably, as simultaneously tears streamed down her face and her groin burned unquenched while she watched the perfectly formed buttocks exiting this circle quickly. She filled with the heartache of lusts unrequited, loves unrelenting, and the empty suffering of the wrenching forth from, and loss of half of all their being.

Lassicity was very obviously too far ahead for Lousitous to catch and hold as he longed to while she was passing next to the form of Antagnous, who remained still and calm in mourning and pain, hand outstretched where it had been so gently caressed by softest of lips seconds before. Her back looked almost exactly like Lassicity's as he saw them for that brief moment, stopped together side by side. Then, by her next footfall, Lousitous saw her buttock bounce as his hardness strained toward what his body wanted almost as badly as his heart. He continued considering Antagnous' back, still within his same field of vision, so very similar to the muscled femininity he had been pursuing with the hurt of desire for wholeness. It was not many strides later that his physical frustrations gave way to his knowledge of futility, and he chose in a way none there, nor anywhere, had considered prior; he knew not the consequences of himself as he chose from the fullness of his pain in that moment, scarcely cognizing that he was in fact choosing, for in every part of him, mind, body, emotion, he knew that what he chose was not the truth of what he wanted.

He gave himself up to his knowledge of futility, the pain he wished not to so completely be engulfing him as it was. Angnosis was still in view of Antagnous' eye and hand when Lousitous pounced. She screamed as they fell together.

He wrapped his arms around her, one across her belly, the other around her chest, his hand finding itself a firm hold while he thrust himself into her and they began their decent to the ground. He became like a wild beast while knowing the pleasure of her warmth fully, hard, repeatedly. She stayed motionless in shock of all that had happened since she had perceived a hand form of herself, and it was bringing the fruit the hand was conceived around toward what next existed as her mouth. She felt an emptiness she could never have conceived existed for her experiencing as something in her body was being deeply gratified so very suddenly, and the intense pain and agony that had commenced subsequent to Angnosis' departure was now being deflected by the pain of falling, of being used, and the glimpses of something resembling pleasure she was grateful to distract her from the way her heart continuously burned, much as her groin had burned a few seconds before. Grateful for something to feel other than the beginnings of abject misery that had just been robbed from her by whomever was now pounding into her body more or less the way she was designed to be pounded into, she began responding, moving herself with and toward the other that her pain might dissolve further. Ever so slightly, it did.

And she responded. She responded as he took his anger, his blistering anger at having already lost when he hadn't even begun, and grabbed hold of what resembled what he could not now have. He took his most animal impulse and gratified what his body yearned for, what it lacked in separation from his true self. He took Antagnous and felt fully a body much as the one that he had lost, along with something good and pure and true about himself that now burned with absence. He distracted himself from his burning chest by gratifying the basic usage of his aching body on this fellow being who too had lost, who was in form supple where he was rigid; soft where he was hard. His strength easily possessed her, and as he took her, he found himself loving her flesh; that her body made his emotions of madness for what had befallen him dissipate slowly while his being gave way fully to the sensations of directing all his energy into the functions of his single outcropping body part. He felt eerily calm as his hands roamed freely and happily, feeling a form so much similar to the one he had wished thoroughly to enwrap him so recently in the past. And as she began moving with him, willingly, his pleasure grew.

In concord did hers as they moved together upon the ground; he arching over her as she struggled herself upward upon her elbows and knees in the hard dirt. He pushed forward, she pushed back, and together something very warm and pleasant joined between them. She was grateful for the hands holding her breast, arms wrapping themselves around her, and in a moment in which whatever was building up could not last, like the popping of a bubble, the warmth of white light rippled instantly and quickly through her as she gave herself up to him in that moment, and simultaneously, as he could not resist what formed in him while she began shaking in climax, he too relented to the fullness of feeling in himself unto her, and the brief moment of white light also ripped through him. Their light converging together, in that one point within her, and they released themselves to each other, that light which briefly, immediately, momentarily, flooded throughout each did not negate, nor could deny, the darkness that never left the deepest recesses of either; the unfulfilled yearning of what they had lost, and what their sole purpose was to regain.

Briefly they quivered and shook in each others' arms until finally they were still on the ground with everyone else watching them, *their* others having long since deserted. He instinctively wanted to ever-so-softly kiss the flesh on the back of her shoulder, but the natural repugnance for himself set in, and he merely laid there his forehead and sobbed in rhythm to the sobbing that had already begun deeply from within her. She wept bitterly and long, streams from her eyes filling the cracks in the dirt while she felt the betrayal of herself acutely. Her emptiness became fully complete, this experience distinct among all the others, including the humans, declaring her uniquely separate.

His self-hatred pierced through him utterly; he'd nothing to stare at but the fact that the action of love he wished most to share with Lassicity he had wasted upon impulses only animal, and out of emotions horrid, taking advantage of the suffering of one of his own, and even doing her sincere harm by the volition of his brute force. Within the emptiness, and the pain of separation, he hated himself throughout for the act he had allowed himself to commit out of sheer lust and hatred of existence.

She felt hollow, as though her own existence were freshly nulled, shame filling her head to have given herself willingly what she only ever wished to give back to *him* when they had earned themselves. She felt separated now not only by time and space, but by her own hand; she had severed herself further from Angnosis, knowing singularly what she could never ever offer. She wailed from the pain of losing half of herself physically, the torment of giving what was already being taken, freely, filling the place she had meant to save for earned ages. She longed not to feel so isolated amongst those now staring at her from the pity, no doubt momentarily easing the natural disquietude they had to experience without making of themselves an object used, something degenerate from the indispensable pain already bestowed upon them all by virtue of the necessity of their form for creation's sake.

He wept that he was self-alienated and vacant, a beast among creatures not succumbed to beasthood. She wept that she had been used animalistically, in agreement, not from love, but the ephemeral belief that momentarily forgetting the full force of her pain might kill it entirely, praying in the moments before that paltry pleasure that it wouldn't return, only to find herself now carrying a burden that none of them should ever have had to bear. He wanted her to feel anything but alone, doubting that his touch could possibly reach his sister after he'd burdened her with a self-hatred likely unrivaled even by his.

In this moment, she knew something that he didn't; indeed, numb to his touch from a singular place none of the rest could conceive. Anguished more at having lost so much more of herself than the others, than being used against her will until finally succumbing to cooperation; her grief and solitude was perfected beyond the rest by the thorough and full knowledge that within her physical form, she now carried the burden of a growing life.

Her blood, mixed with his seed, flowed out of her in a slight trickle to the earth. Uncontrollably she wailed through cascading tears for all she had already lost.

Chapter 3

While *they* filled with horror and dread to behold their newly found existences, those who remained in the direct service of the Divine watched with neutrality of being in alignment with the capacity facilitating their choice to serve, and the reality of how they existed accordingly. Those of them who had had even the slightest curiosity about the choice they were given rejoiced in their decision to continue to serve purely, having compassion for their brethren who had just begun their new existences hitherto unknown in concept by the service of the Divine. Thus spoke their Creator, "It is Our will that you too know yourself in part in physical conception that you may more fully be able to serve *all* Our creation, where these others devote themselves, even if but for a time, only in part."

First formed three pairs of wings. Next, light bent between these diaphanous, flowing forms a frame in likeness of bone and muscle, and skin smooth and beautiful and bright. Arms structured off trunk, buttocks sculpted begat legs. Face of purity and joy smiled the ecstasy of being born. Penis and vulva graced the lower trunk, together. Feet formed from the lowest point of calves, and the lower pair of wings covered them almost immediately. Meechasel knew of itself body.

Each was likewise formed. Chests sculpted, smiles bright, wings that covered feet that knew no ground. Their movements and usages of their new bodies seemed natural and normal. Except in regards to their genitalia, which they were slightly confused about given that the only example of genitalia they had had so far were the impressions given them by their brothers and sisters whom had eaten the fruit, and the new human creatures that The Eternal Oneness had created out of Her infinite wisdom. Looking at themselves and each others' exposed organs, and being hesitant for the reason of the impressions they'd taken in in regards to said organs thus far to use those organs in any manner whatsoever, they all, in unison, held their focus simultaneously on the proper way to approach this one aspect of their newly formed frames, and on the question without question that they turned their conception toward their Father Maker in the hopes that She would answer this query of *theirs*.

"Well, we gave you both parts. You know how *they* use them and thus how they work. Your phalli are perfectly long enough. While you are designed to be able to interact with each other, there is a time and place for such a thing you'll discover later. Until that time comes, go interact yourselves!"

And thus they did. And they enjoyed themselves immensely. From their enjoyment, clouds were the natural byproduct of the material from which they were formed. And as their enjoyment of themselves increased, rain showers began pouring down from on high. Thunder crashed from those who knew themselves most well, and flowers were grateful to drink from the source of life above. And those who had chosen not to eat from the tree knew bliss to exist unto themselves.

Chapter 4

Rain came crashing down from on high upon those of Heaven who had chosen to eat the fruit from the tree. Two lay now in mud, the aggressor and the aggressee. A couple of miles in the distance, Luciferous' nostrils began to fill with mud created not by his own tears, and he was awakened out of a sleep composed entirely of self-pity, hopelessness, and longing. As he rose to his feet and took his first step toward where he had come, simultaneously he took his first step toward freedom from what he found himself to be. He cleared mud from his nose with heavy outward breathing and turned his face to the water falling so heavily from the sky. He felt cleaner with his second step while he brushed watery dirt away from his eyes. Beginning to feel in this way purified, something inside of him knew that hope did exist somewhere, even if he could not discern it now. He directed his further footfalls toward the tree of which he had come.

Several minutes later he saw a large group of what looked like humans surrounding the tree. Their heads hung down. Through the cascading of the rain he could hear low moans and weeping, though it was faint beneath the water falling from the Heavens. As he approached, they looked up at him and cleared a path, straight and direct, to the tree, and to the two who lay beneath it held together by gravity and despondence, fearing to leave what little warmth they caused each other by staying perfectly still in their shame.

The hope Luciferous held in his heart deserted to somewhere in the back of his mind, dread of what lay at the foot of the tree giving rise to a different emotion; one new and foreign, containing something that did not feel right.

His natural impulse commanded his words to be, even to himself never minding the others, much louder than he had expected them to be. "What is the meaning of this? You two are not of each other? Tell me you two are of each other! Explain to me what this is! Have you already learned something that can help our charge that you two have already earned the right to bliss of reunion? That cannot be! You are Antagnous, and you Lousitous! You are not of each other; you are separate! Explain this apparent abomination! Tell me that what is apparent to my eye is a false perception!"

Antagnous held her head lower, away from Luciferous' gaze, and began immediately to sob loudly into the rain, where before she'd merely unceasingly lamented quietly to herself. Lousitous turned his gaze also from Luciferous, trying to console Antagnous by stroking her head through her hair, and softly rubbing the top of her shoulder. Luciferous felt as though his eyes glowed red while feeling disdain not only for what he saw, but now that his question was being ignored by two who obviously had acted in some way shameful for angels who were sent from the very mind of the Divine to aid the creation of the One.

Seeing the tumult, the anger, within Luciferous, even without having a word to call it, Hoflan, one who possessed the apparentness of male half, stepped forward to answer the question and emotion of Luciferous. "As you were named by Our Sovereign the most determined of us all to assist the creation Human, to embrace fully in harmony the fact of their existence as the face likened to Divinity, I feel compelled naturally to regard you as the most among us determined to drive us to succeed in the reason we have been brought into existence as we now know it, and the corresponding immediate agony-with-purpose of this existence. As your determination, as well as your experience being longest, as well as your place among us in service to That Which We Serve, I feel drawn to call you "sir" due to your obvious qualities that we feel compelled naturally to answer you as one who might organize us best. And thus, sir, if you see fit, I would like to answer your question, as Antagnous and Lousitous both have very good reason at the moment to recoil not merely from your question, but from the fact of themselves as they know themselves now, and the fact of your question reminding them even further of themselves. Which is to say, to remind them further than they already cannot escape, the burden they currently embody of their shame must make their recovery last even longer, as well as satisfy not your question. And thus, in the best interest of their recovery from what clearly to us all never should have taken place, as well as to satisfy your question, may I please answer for them, or will you please ask this query again from any of the rest of us who would be more appropriate in this moment to answer such a question, as we are all eyewitness to this pathetic horror, and all in better states of mind, despite the agony of the fact of our own existence, to be able to answer this question of yours?"

To see the desire of his apparent brother not merely to help his other brother and sister, but also to address his approach with respect and reason as close to his perceptions of the reality of his existence as he could so as to facilitate the best possible results for all involved, Luciferous answered thus: "Hoflan, in the unity of Divinity we were equals in every way. My qualities as one made in the likeness of knowledge that necessitates individuality, I have yet to discern myself, but I trust you to see me as I am, as I learn to do the same, and appreciate your respect of my truth accordingly. That being said, seeing you as a manifestation who strives for the best results despite this pain we all must bear in most degrees mutually and unceasingly fully throughout our beings, if you would refer to me as sir for what you see as me, then knowing that your own eye and perceptiveness may hold the very keys for leading humanity to harmony, I'd be remiss if I did not refer to *you* as "sir," for it is your sincerity of being that has already begun to cure me of the awfulness I felt so terribly in my self mere moments ago, though this strange heat lending to confusion is something that has far from left me. So, sir, yes, please, tell me the fullness of this shame before us. Why do they seem so unfit in being for servants of Divinity?"

Hoflan was grateful of being reminded of the mutuality of their common existences as he addressed to Luciferous an answer. "Sir, as we were being created in the lackingness of what we are now, pains and agonies the entirety of which we were not prepared for, as you too must well know, tore through any composure of harmony in being we may ever have, even more so than the still almost-complete lack of harmony of self we still feel just moments later. Likewise many of us, nay, all of us felt natural urges that accompany bodies divided from our other halves as they are. And many of us too would have acted in blindness toward our sisters and brothers out of the mechanics of our animal vesselity, if not for the fact of Lousitous giving into his animal grief and affliction first.

"So it happened that there arose in *him* something akin to what you felt moments ago, mixed with his grief, mixed with his desires of body, and the timing of seeing two bodies very much alike in scope, from behind, aligned in front of his eyes filled with nothing but pain, and he answered the impulse of his body shamefully, pushing his inherent conscience away, as though to the very back of his mind as it would go, and answered his impulse of pain and body mixed as though it were a command. Saying that he chose to do what he did, sir, would not be accurate, though he is solely responsible for what he did next, but rather what he chose was to try instantaneously to cease the pain within him that any consciousness would reaffirm a thousand times over could not be escaped by desire alone; a *something* that his body is not capable of having any understanding of whatsoever as its sole self-knowledge of being is its impulses, for the sake of optimum functionality of the entirety of the being it serves, to eat. And so, the impulses of his dread of existence overcoming his reason to the extent of believing the voice of his body, because his pain was too great for him, might know his existence better than he, himself, he acted perfectly contrary to what we have chosen to exist to effect. He took to Antagnous, in mockery of how with every fiber of his true self he would wish most to share the blessing of their existence with Lassicity.

"He committed this shame just as Antagnous' masculinity and completeness was leaving her. And in *her* pain, she responded very much out of completely-in-every-way similar mechanisms to those inflicted upon her by Lousitous.

"While initially she was purely taken by surprise, and thus completely unwilling in every way, when she found the fullness of her pain distracted so well by the pain of the terror of being used out of the fullness of the pain of Lousitous, she responded in part knowing a similar hunger of her own physicality, and attempting to silence her own deep anguish through a similar blasphemy of the joke made out of the action in some way similar to sharing the purpose of existence, completeness, Love. She responded not by struggling with hope that both their burdens might be lessened more than they had already become compounded, but instead gave her-self to the continuance of this new pain with whatever fleeting enjoyments her mechanics would allow, and thus mutually they prolonged each other's pain for as long as possible until, finally, they both succumbed simultaneously to the extra burdens of suffering that became so great they finally broke them out of the prolonging-for-the-sake-of-ceasing their genuine-agony-for-the-sake-of-the-benefit-of-all-existence the artificial joy of which they had, at some point, mutually engaged in.

"And again, though she is only half-responsible for her part in this shame, she too, out of desire to escape the unequivocal fact of her existence, and her physicality speaking of escaping pain from the only voice *it* knows, a voice that is unbecoming for one with a genuine self to listen to, she too sought any escape from the inevitable, inescapable, and currently absolutely necessary mode of being, the burden of which she currently *must* bear, the completeness of her inherent pain coupled with the pain of all her senses being overloaded by being so abruptly violated, by way of her vessel, whose voice under the circumstances became so much louder than her own."

Luciferous' head sunk down and shook of its own accord. The fullness of the result of the shame of the tragedy that had gone on, the results of which were now before him, sank into his already unfortunate emotional state. Luciferous understood the reason for organically feeling the despair not only within the two laying just beyond the roots of the tree, but also those who had witnessed and could not violate, without even further burdens upon them all, the action of the remnants of free will resigned to the hungers of the bodies of their brother and sister.

With deep sincerity of sadness upon his face, Luciferous looked into the eyes of the crowd before him while he spoke loudly against the storm, "We are fortunate that the humans have yet to learn such a lesson as we have in our short time here. Our bodies think much as the creature created before us all, called by the human 'ape.' To try to hide from the pain proper for us to feel, for it motivates us singularly to cure the inherent misery we have come to eliminate from the hands of these beautiful creatures we helped create, by believing the whims of a source of thought not of our own volition, in particular the thoughts of our bodies, is to allow ourselves to act not as beings with reason directed toward The Divine, but as those creatures who are not created in *The* Image, apes. That it serves as a reminder to us all what happens when our pain is so great we are tempted by the natural mechanics of our bodies to resign the reason of ourselves to the less intricate reason of our bodies out of desperation, which we can rise above so long as we hold onto our genuine selves, let us call burdening each other in this most shameful way that we remember when we do so, we are no more than apes. Are no more than apes, or, are apes. Are, as the corresponding letter Raish, and ape. And thus should mankind discover such shame upon their own hands, that they too are as an ape, they too will call this are-ape. Rape.

"Antagnous, please look at me."

Antagnous slowly raised her head half up from the ground and brought her gaze to meet the eye of Luciferous. Luciferous pitied her red eyes, tears mixing with the fall of the rain so that one could not be discerned from the other. He looked up ever so slightly to where Lousitous' head was lowered toward earth, still in shame and pain.

"Lousitous, how could you do that to Antagnous' love?"

Antagnous answered, giving Lousitous no reason to try to lift his head from where it hung of its own dejection, "Angnosis, who in any lifetime I pray would still have me as his only, though now I cannot believe I could ever deserve it, ran off right before Lousitous was upon me. While in the lives of men any in my place would be a victim of the worst kind, not blessed to know themselves as we know ourselves; made in such instance to be used, and maybe in accordance destroyed unjustly, aside from the pain of having any truth of myself violently stripped from a form that might otherwise be blessed to exist with true being, for surcease of the agony of the existence I discovered myself to be once

Angnosis' hand left me, I wanted it too." And with that she let her head again fall, and was grateful when a wind arose to cover her wail, that it might not be distinguished from the sound of the rushing air.

Luciferous walked away toward trees at the edge of The Garden that he might think upon so much misery of his existence, so soon after arriving in the created form in which he chose to arise.

෴෴෴

When he reached the trees, one stood there waiting for him.

She spoke through a smile she pressed to her lips as though her life depended upon it. Her smile was not fake, but determined through sadness that her voice be heard well. "Tell me, Luciferous, that Lousitous is all right."

"I recognize you are his other."

"Lassicity at your service, as you might need of me."

"Then please forgive me for having to bring you the unfortunate tale that the one you must feel so deeply for as to be in a pain I hate to be able to fully imagine, is less than *all* right."

"You need not tell too much, I knew our immediate fate upon my separation. And so too did Angnosis, which is why he did not come. He did not trust himself to stay away from Antagnous, nor did he trust himself to restrain himself from the instinct of his bestial form to act as though in protection for himself, and thus harm mine. He felt the least provocation might blind him to his true self, and he might lose control of the vehicle that is his animal self. He carries his message thus: 'Dear beautiful of me, my only desire and longing, no inclination of yours could make my heart beat for you less. And my forgiveness will too be full for my brother, as I would long for her whose union of myself I desire. And thus shall be my work until we are met, by the grace of Our Common Creator, again.'"

"So too would I have you carry a message for me to Lousitous: 'Raise your head to see the work destined for our love, and look no more to the blindness of your beginning. From the greatest darkness shall you know the reason to cast the brightest light. I bid you do so, if for no other reason, the sake of my hand, my lip, my loin, my beating heart that longs to keep rhythm with our existence as one. Your child is as mine, that I may lessen the burden of my sister, who shall bless us all with this gift unintentional, that she agreed to from the desire of her own pain to stop.'"

To which Luciferous spoke, "I have listened and learned. It shall be done as you have bidden me. As we rise we shall rise together, that we may have no need together again to fall."

Lassicity bowed in reverence of her brother, gratitude of his sincerity, and acknowledgment of their common burden shared, before she turned back toward the trees to continue her work for which they had all agreed to be created as they were.

Chapter 5

Light mists hung over creation in the dawning of the day when the Lord spoke to Their attendant, "Argee'el, you look troubled, why?"

"Well, it's been a good day now, and I can't help but notice the effects our self-usage have upon the place of the existence of the humans. I don't feel like I want to stop, though I know I can, nor have you indicated it is a problem that we continue to carry on about our affairs whilst simultaneously enjoying our existences individually. Now that most of us appear to be less rigorous in how we're enjoying ourselves, it is only causing a light mist for them, and that will no doubt burn away and evaporate almost instantaneously in the sunlight. Nonetheless, I can't help but wonder whether or not, especially when we have fewer duties, or even through the course of ample duty, when we enjoy ourselves more rigorously it is cruel to inflict the result of our self-enjoyment upon the heads of the humans."

"Actually, considering what you produce is what they need to survive, it would be crueler not to enjoy yourselves constantly. That, and, given that they have choice, will as We have, they should have more than enough capacity to shelter themselves from the direct results of your self-pleasure, if they so choose.

"On the other hand, I suppose that having you altogether all the time might be a little excessive even for *them*, so, in light of your curiosity inspired by consideration, may you all fly to the corners of their world, enjoy yourselves as you like, and We'll call you to gather as need be, ever considering the inconvenience it may cause to *them* accordingly."

"This pleases us greatly, Oh Wise Creator Of All! As You have commanded us at this time only to interact with ourselves solely in this moment, I believe a great many of us will feel better knowing that we will intrude upon their growth and harmony far the less for spreading of the waters of life at our own contentment to every corner of this beautiful world You have created!"

Their wings beat revelry through the air, making the sole couple of the planet only momentarily cooled in the process, as each went to find a place for their own enjoyment amongst the higher places of the Earth.

As they departed, one angel was bidden to stay behind. "Taranzael, We have a job for you..."

Chapter 6

Lousitous and Antagnous slept comforted by the message given to them from themselves, delivered by Luciferous. They were warm and behaved as siblings who knew a secret of experience they could not share with others, beyond the physical reality all had witnessed.

In the morning, after the mists had begun to disperse, Luciferous called a meeting among them.

"Now that we are here, we ought to order our thoughts together that we may be able to assist our charge as we have set ourselves to do. Believing that they set themselves against the God that created them to be even as they are now, what is best that we ease their sufferings, and point them toward truth?"

Gendlebleth stepped forward and spoke. "They must be freezing out there, let us make for them something to keep them warm. This way, perhaps, they will not loathe That which created them, thinking that despite what they think Divinity thinks of them, Divinity still wishes them *some* comfort in their existence."

"You mean a covering, like the fig leaves, but warmer, like the coat of an animal?"

"Yes sir, let us fashion for them a covering for their covering which was created so exposed and vulnerable; something like the creature called 'bear,' perhaps..."

"I like your thought, Gendlebleth, but how do you propose we create this outer-covering for them?"

"Well, sir, we could use the outer-covering of a creature or several we use as meals. Once the animals' blood is washed off from the outer-coverings, and they are dried, it should be a simple matter to put the outer-coverings together to form something for them to wear over their vulnerable skin..."

"Gendlebleth, are you suggesting we consume a living creature into ourselves, rather than taking our nourishment from the fruits of the trees?" Luciferous' face began to contort slightly with concern.

"Well, yes sir. The Host sent forth the people creatures from The Garden. If we are to follow them, it may be that we too will not be able to return, and thus must find some form of nutrient intake to maintain our facade of humanity while watching over them. There may be flora to eat, but I would definitely suggest it may well be a matter of survival to eat things that eat what we cannot eat, so that we may maintain our own flesh, as we experience so that we may understand their experience. While they create from the ground, eating what eats those things they cannot may well be survival for them as they await harvests they have not yet planted so as to reap."

"But Gendlebleth," Luciferous nodded his head gravely as he pondered his friend's words, "what will become of the creatures as we consume them? What becomes of them when we are left with their skins? Will they not shout loudly inside of us after we have chewed them? Will they not feel great pain as we rip chunks of them off from their greater part, so that we can fit them inside of us without making our throats feel the discomfort of trying to stretch further than they can?"

As he uttered this, a rabbit hopped right next to Gendlebleth's foot. Luciferous stopped speaking as he and Gendlebleth looked at the bunny scrunching its nose in the warmth of the sun beside where Gendlebleth stood. Luciferous felt a knot of tension in his abdomen as

Gendlebleth reached down and picked up the bunny by the back of its neck. He held it before his face, looking at it in the eye, before turning his eyes to Luciferous. "Sir, there is only one way to know for certain."

Luciferous felt a natural repugnance as Gendlebleth brought the bunny closer to his face. With his free hand he lightly took hold of the rabbit's paw. He brought the foot into his mouth, and bit down hard. The bunny made a very audible high-pitched sound and began squirming uncontrollably. "The fur definitely isn't good for eating, sir, it will be much better for clothing." He eyed a jagged stone on the ground close by next to a small boulder. He stepped forward, and bent down to pick up the stone.

"Gendlebleth! You've caused that poor creature much pain. Look how it bleeds from its foot. Let it go now, don't you feel the intrinsic wrong you're causing to it? What are you doing now?"

Gendlebleth took the jagged stone in his hand as he pressed the rabbit down on its back against the boulder. He placed the jagged stone to its neck right above its chest, and started applying pressure with the stone as he answered Luciferous. "If it cannot be bitten into directly, and I wish first to take its fur for the humans, I figure I'll just remove its fur first before trying to eat it." And again the bunny convulsed with all that its body could muster under Gendlebleth's grip around its neck. As the jagged stone began cutting into its chest, its hind legs thumped wildly into the open air to no avail. Its squeal made all in the party squirm; while before some were still resting, now all were awake and staring at the commotion.

Red starting to show through the white of the fur on the rabbit's chest. Luciferous began to scream, "Stop it, Gendlebleth! How can you force so much pain on this beautiful creature of Our Common Creator? You're torturing it! Stop rising in it pain more and more, even worse than we all have felt at the loss of our own halves of beings!"

Gendlebleth's face turned red as he looked at the pain the rabbit was in whose throat he held in his hand, the eyes of the rabbit staring helplessly into his own. He suddenly roared as he grabbed the rabbit by its neck and smashed it as hard as he could against the boulder. The rabbit did not move.

He held it up by its neck, and it hung limp in his grasp, unstirring. He looked over to Luciferous, whose face was as though paralyzed in disbelief, horror-stricken. "I wanted it to stop being in pain," he began, averting his gaze from his friend as he muttered almost inaudibly toward Luciferous' face. "I didn't know it would stop it."

"No, Gendlebleth, none of us knew it would just stop. Nor did we know what pain it would feel. But you could have just put it down when you saw it wasn't happy..."

"I just wanted its pain to stop, Luciferous. I was so embarrassed by what I'd been doing to it. I just wanted its pain to stop." He laid the bunny down atop the boulder as he began weeping uncontrollably.

"Randolfy. Please pick up the bunny and the ragged stone, and carefully try to remove its fur part from whatever is under its fur part, please." Randolfy did as Luciferous asked as Luciferous walked over to Gendlebleth who seemed now bent on hiding his eyes from the sun as falls of tears fell off the hand he held to his eyes. "Gendlebleth, the sun sees you clearly, as do us all. It is no good trying to hide."

"You don't understand, Luciferous," he choked on each word he spoke, "it hurts to see the Love that created me after what I just caused to any of Its creation. Gendleneth would hate me fully with all her being, had she known how I harmed Our Common Creator's own flesh with my own hand. How ever can I return to myself after the harm I have caused this day?"

Luciferous' admonition turned to pity as he rested his hand on the shoulder of his friend. "I do believe that Gendleneth already has forgiven you, such is your nature. If you strive with yourself never again to cause such harm, what pain is caused now to our Common Creator? And apparently, if we are to clothe our charge, we must take, in this moment in time, the breath of life from these creatures that are not aware of life and death as we must be aware of them now. We will invent our life from the ground so that we can stop suffering by our own hand, that we might teach these new creatures not to harm themselves by their own, but while we wait for harvests and inventions that we may harm life no more, it seems necessity states we remove several lesser-conscious lives that both they may not be so uncomfortable, and also that we too might be clothed that we are not discomforted as long as our time must allow; that we may not look with eyes akin to Lousitous at our sisters, and they with eyes akin to Antagnous at us. From this day, when we take the life of these creatures for our own, may we do it quickly and learn the ways to cause them the least pain possible, that they may pass through their existence without discomfort caused by us."

As Luciferous uttered this proclamation against harm to his siblings-in-kind, the angel Taranzael's shadow appeared above them as he lowered himself into their midst from on high.

As Taranzael came to the ground, it looked out at those he had known before embodiment had come to them all. He wondered at her ability to discern identity of the faces staring at it, despite human visage and the odd sensing that they were all only half of themselves. In turn, they marveled at Taranzael's genitalia.

Taranzael slowed the enjoyment of himself before speaking to the crowd before her; the mist surrounding him thinned accordingly and mostly burned off by the heat of the sun. "I have come to inhibit the image-creation from returning, as per the will of Whom We Serve. They have given unto I this sword by which flame none shall be allowed again entrance to this place designed that no work be needed for the continued existence of those with knowledge of Our Omni-Common Divinity. Because I will sit here with my legs like the creature "lion" as though ever upon a chair, in all Her wisdom have I, along with my brethren who shall be arriving shortly, been named "Cherub."

Jallastinkedin asked the first question to come to any of them as they heard this kindred messenger from on high speak to them, "She made your body capable of knowing itself?"

"Well," answered Taranzael, "she'd prefer we be happy while we're working…"

As Taranzael was answering the question put to her by half of her friend, Randolfy walked up with the flayed body of a rabbit in one hand and its pelt in the other. He looked Taranzael up and down as he walked up next to his friend holding the sword of flame; walking up to Taranzael, mostly he was looking down. "Okay, aleph, They're giving bodies to everyone now? And bet, you all get to have that kind of fun while we're looking down the long cylindrical tube of thousands of years of work in the hopes that just maybe, we ever get to see the other set of our own genitalia again? He's got some sense of humor all right…" As he was remarking upon Taranzael's self-enjoyment, a scent wafted up into his nostrils.

Subtle, yet with the power to make his mouth create excess water-stuff and his stomach tighten in anticipation, Randolfy looked down to where the scent seemed to be coming from. What he noticed was that the half of the defurred bunny closest to the sword Taranzael was carrying appeared different in color to the rest of the bunny. He held the half-cooked lagomorph up to his face for closer examination, the bunny's de-skinned foot just in front of his mouth, when Gendlebleth spoke up. "Wait! Let me."

Randolfy looked at Gendlebleth, then looked at Luciferous, "Sir?"

"If Gendlebleth wishes to be the first to find out if it tastes as good as it smells, it should be he to take the risks upon himself, if such is his desire."

Randolfy held the warm, partly-seared body toward Gendlebleth.

Gendlebleth took its body by the neck and spoke that everyone present could hear. "If our bodies may be satisfied and fortified by taking life and raising its temperature to become something we can consume, then death is not merely a curse to all who behold it, nor may be every instance of stopping a life. I feel great pain, and will most likely continue to feel great pain, for having caused all the suffering to this creature I did when it could breathe. Whatever the result of the processes done to it in relation to how I may use it now, this being once with life, and now something changed, is a great blessing to me and to us all for teaching us about the sacredness of life and what can be made of it." With that said, Gendlebleth held the raw half of the bunny in one hand, and raised the cooked half to his mouth, where he took a large bite from the still warm, seared flesh.

He chewed, he swallowed, he spoke: "It tastes like a blessing I have taken this creatures life." He held the remains of the rabbit to Luciferous. As Luciferous took the meat in hand, Gendlebleth fainted.

Luciferous smelled the cooked meat, then held it to Randolfy; Antagnous ran to where Gendlebleth had fallen to make sure that no harm had come to him. Luciferous spoke to Randolfy. "Randolfy, as you have done the work responsible for separating skin from body, and discovered the effect of heat in transmuting its form into one more suitable for our sustenance, you may have of this creature all you want, though I recommend you heat the other half as this half has been heated first."

Randolfy looked with sympathy at his fallen friend being tended to by Antagnous. He took the body of the bunny from Luciferous and brought it in proximity with the sword held by Taranzael. As he let the rest of the body slowly roast, he inquired of his friend, "So did She embody anyone else who stayed to be able to have as good a time after we left?"

Chapter 7

After answering a handful of questions posed by the others as to how rain was made, Taranzael explained that it was time for them to leave with the likeness-creatures, since the likeness-creatures were no longer to be allowed in The Garden. It took the flaming sword it held and released it in the middle of the path leading to The Tree of Life. Shortly after he did so, a sprinkle of light rain and mist accompanied other Cherubs who came also to guard The Garden.

"All right, all bodies assigned to half of ourselves, we have work to do that has nothing to do with where we cannot be for now. Let us start toward where the male and female have gone, being careful not to reveal our presences until they are ready, for they may be confused that we exist and want something of us that we should not give. Let us walk in their path and create for ourselves a circumstance by which we can be of help and service." With that, they began walking toward the East.

Antagnous, Beatrica, and Gendlebleth worked together to fashion garments for the man and woman and left them by their sides to find when they awakened. The man and woman gave thanks to That Which Had Created Them for giving them warmth even after they had been evicted from where they began. Antagnous, Beatrica, and Gendlebleth also fashioned garments for themselves, and taught the others how to make simple garments.

Those who had chosen to become as the man and woman so to serve them, made a camp on a hilltop high above where the man and woman eventually chose to settle and create for themselves a shelter. Two of the embodied angels would watch closer to where Man and Living resided, and then pass the details of their day-to-day existence to the others; in this way, the couple was always watched and the group who had chosen embodiment to serve the creation of The Creator were made aware of the progress of humanity at all times without intruding upon them. Gendlebleth was grateful that the red from the blood that had dyed the pelt of the first rabbit brought out the color in the eyes of she called "Living."

Not much time had passed before news had reached the tribe of angels that Eve's belly was growing. As Eve's belly grew, so too did Antagnous'. About a week before Eve gave birth, Antagnous had a daughter. Lousitous marveled at the life he had created from the moment of his greatest pain and shame. They understood it as a sign of intent from On High that the daughter of these angels different in being had skin as red as glowing embers. They understood before the development of human society that her skin would mark her as different from all other humans, and likewise from angels, that it would be all but impossible for her to have a direct hand in the lives of humanity, as well serve as an ever-present reminder to the angels themselves against self-betrayal, no matter how great the impulse.

The child's birth informed the angels what to expect in making sure Eve's first birth went smoothly. Adam awoke next to the river to find a particularly porous garment floating amidst the reeds, two days prior to his son's birth; he was inspired to have enough water on-hand accordingly.

Likewise, the angels had a basic knowledge that the taking-care of the child was a highly intuitive matter, and that feeding the newborn would not be something they'd have to somehow inform the living creations to accomplish.

The angels watched in pride in their Creator's creation as Adam arose to the challenge of invention as discomforts of cold, hunger, and the growth of his child and well-being of his wife motivated him to create in the image of what needed to exist for their continued experiencing of existence. Eve, as well, invented and innovated where he did not, so that they would enjoy and thrive amidst the creative existence they had been made to embody.

Not long after his birth, Eve had named their son Cain. The angels saw that this name was a good name. They had been undecided whether or not to name the daughter of Antagnous and Lousitous up to this time, and decided it would be best to name her in emulation of Living and her husband, that they might better understand this creation from on high, and so better serve them. After a long discussion amongst the group, they decided on "Casarta," which meant "the way of letting existence show its purpose as it unfolded." Since they had never existed before, nor created life themselves, this seemed to be the most appropriate indicator to attach to what to them was a being in most ways wholly unknown.

The angels continued to take cues from the pair and their creations as to their own tribe's development; rather quickly, they found themselves pondering over the question of how they would educate the begotten daughter's existence as they found her becoming the daughter of the tribe itself, and all partook of raising a creature they had never considered could exist before they, themselves, had decided to exist as they currently did. It was not long after watching the birth of the son and the birth of their daughter that they'd notice that Eve's belly again began to grow.

ᏜᏗᏜᏗᏜ

Casarta was about two years old when the third new pierce of silence cut the quiet air of night with a cry from a being capable of consciousness who had not existed before. Listening at the window of the once-again parents, Versbethjian's face turned to horror to hear the short conversation carried on the wind into her ear. She left Larthagen alone as she ran to the top of the hill to send the next two watchers sooner than expected, and to share the news with the rest of the tribe.

"She named him what? No, no. That can't be!"

"It's true, sir. They discussed it at some length and repeated it several times. They seemed to think it reflected the truth of considering meaning when one is existent, and thought that it would serve as a reminder to him as to the nature of reality and the joy that would be accessible to him once he transcended considering the 'why' of his existence."

"Be that as it may," up spoke Luciferous, "You all know how *She* regards the word. It is wise we are wary of the ramifications of thoughts' power to create that spoken as the law created by *Its* own 'Lips' alone. Naming one's child 'Emptiness' cannot bode well, no matter how noble the intent..."

Chapter 8

And so it was that Abel matured alongside his brother Cain. As the family grew, also grew the watch of the angels on the every movement of the creation of the image of Divinity, so that they might understand better those they set themselves in body to help. By now there were three sets of watches: one to monitor Adam and Eve, one to monitor Cain and Abel, and one that could keep watch as the pairings split up and wandered independent of each other.

One afternoon, between watches of the first and second generations of the Lord's creation, Gendlebleth and Harenethian began walking back to the overlook after being relieved of their watch by Tartantuan and Kleshala. Coming to the overlook, Gendlebleth noticed Antagnous weeping at the top of the hill while watching the home of Adam and Eve below. He reflected for a moment on his own meditations of sadness to be apart from himself, and for the discovery of causing a living entity pain before violently destroying its life. He had decided to name these emotions once he had killed the rabbit, for in that moment he had seen for the first time *death,* and experiencing it directly, knew what it was; the emotion, therefore, he decided ought to be named by what created it "saw death." Recognizing almost the exact same emotion in Antagnous as she gazed seemingly absently toward the dwelling of Divinity's great creation below, he felt an impulse to do anything that might, even for a moment, distract Antagnous from her pain. With this in his mind and heart, he turned back from where he had come and set himself in the direction of the uncultivated field below.

Reaching the field, Gendlebleth began to gather crocuses and lilies growing wild. He found flowers to be beautiful in all their color and different forms, and they did not scream with pain when they were separated from their source of life. Flowers were always pleasant in every circumstance, and they made him happy when he spent time with them, sitting amongst them, and smelling their scent of reproduction that attracted the creatures that facilitated their continued existence. Reflecting on what brought brief and subtle solace to his own inextricable torment, he thought perhaps the gesture of offering flowers to Antagnous might even for a moment distract her from her own necessary agony.

At the other side of the field, Tanalan and Tritictus did not at first see Gendlebleth picking flowers in the high, thick foliage of the large, open field. All they saw was The Created dissolving into same said high, thick flora. When they did sight Gendlebleth, Cain was already far too close to try to distract him away. He was practically upon him; they merely looked at each other, shaking their heads from side to side, and thinking the exact same quandary on the future's effect as they observed the child grow to the inevitability of stumbling upon their friend.

At first, at seeing his back, Cain supposed he must have met his father in this field, for he could fathom no other explanation. As Gendlebleth's face turned to meet the rustling behind him, both were startled from respective perceptions of what they hadn't anticipated finding when they had entered this field: each other.

Gendlebleth was at a loss for words, so first spoke the boy, excited in his confusion. "Who are you?"

Gendlebleth paused further to think as quickly as he could before responding with the first thought that came to mind that sounded at all reasonable. "I am a man."

Cain stared inquisitively. "There's only one man, my father. He was created the only man. You look like a man, but my father is the only man. You must be lying. I must tell my father what I have seen."

"No, wait!" Gendlebleth's mind reeled at the possible ramifications of the family knowing of the existence of his kind. "I will tell you the truth. I am a messenger from your Creator."

"What do you mean?" spoke Cain.

"Our Common All-Creator created our kind outside of the physical existence, as you know it, that we may be for It alone. When Man and Living, your parents, were created, some of us chose to serve the Divinity in you rather than the Direct Divinity, thinking that life would go harder for you without our help."

"What did any of that mean?" asked Cain. "What have you done for us so far?"

"Well," continued Gendlebleth, "for starters we made your parents their first garments... But it might be more helpful just now if I didn't tell you too much about us. Until you've had more experience existing in Our Creator's Infinitence, knowing the service to That Which Created you in Her Image I think won't be an easy notion for you to grasp.

"I'll make with you a covenant: if you don't tell your parents or your brother that you met me, and if you don't share with them more about Our Creator than they already know, I'll meet with you here once every seven days to tell you something of What Created Us, and how my kind came to exist in aspect as humanity that we might serve you as best we can."

"You want me to lie to my parents?" As Cain uttered these words, Tanalan smacked her palm against her forehead in anticipation of Gendlebleth's next utterances.

"If you find no intrinsic harm in not telling them about me and my kind, I ask you to keep my existence to yourself. If you feel an intrinsic good will be done by informing them of what they do not know, you must follow that impulse instead. I ask merely that you consider more good may be done, just now, of not informing them of what they do not now know."

"You speak complicated, but I don't feel bad right now about what you're asking me, which I think is what you mean. You promise to tell me more about you, though?"

"My word is my oath," spoke Gendlebleth.

"Okay, then. How many of you are there anyway?"

"I'll answer this one question now, but then I must be on my way..." Gendlebleth attempted to answer the boy's question before leaving him puzzled in the field.

 ❧ ❧ ❧

He walked past Tanalan and Tritictus, crocuses and lilies in hand, without uttering a word while they stared at their friend striding by. They stood their post watching after their charge as their minds stood dumbfounded by what had just happened.

Coming to the top of the overlook, Gendlebleth extended his hand, holding the flowers out to Antagnous as the rest of the tribe closed in around him, that they might all share a long discussion of what had, and might come to pass, that night.

Chapter 9

Several years later...

Gendlebleth sat next to Cain, sitting on the fallen trunk of a sycamore tree. "You again, person like me but sent from God?" he addressed Gendlebleth as he looked up at him from where his face had been in his hands.

"Why such sadness, First Born of Our Common Creator Endlessness' first Creation of Its own likeness? Do you feel the pangs of loneliness because you have not a companion for yourself, as Adam hast of Eve? Have your parents even told you of such companionship and how it is that those in form and mind like you are created from the companion pair proceeding you?"

"Yes, my parents have told me from where I and my brother have come. But loneliness is not why I'm feeling sad today. Though, as my body has been growing, and certain urges have begun to develop, lately I have been hoping more and more that a sister is born soon...

"No, the annoyance of my body is well secondary to the fact that my brother seems to have the blessings of Our Common Origin All-Lovingness greater surpassing my own, and I do not know what I have done, or not done, that I am less pleasing to The Eyes That Know Already My Life's Every Nuance."

"Come again?" inquired Gendlebleth. "What has your brother that you have not?"

"As we offered to Our Perfect Commonness this morning the best of the results of the work of our hands, it seemed as though the blood of Abel's lamb was preferred to the red, ripe seeds I plucked seed by seed, each perfectly intact, from the pomegranate I harvested, and the fullest ears of wheat that I reaped from last planting season's yield."

Gendlebleth stroked his chin hairs for a moment, thinking over what Cain had spoken. "What makes you think that your offering was not enjoyed equally to that of your brother's?" Gendlebleth considered that the Perfect All-Unity Infinite, if It were to have a preference, probably would be more inclined toward the offering of a work that didn't involve pain and death to another living creature. Though, Gendlebleth next thought, he did have a personal bias, and it may be that there would be great enjoyment toward Abel if Abel had found a way to slaughter pain-cognizant food without said food being horror-filled in its last moments of limited awareness...

Cain turned to look his friend in the eyes. "As the blood and Life of Abel's lamb flowed up, and pooled into, our place of offering to That Which Enabled us Life, two pure, white doves appeared. They landed on the posts erected to signify where we offer the best of the work of our hands. Then, they began singing the sweetest melody I've heard from a bird, as though they were trying to speak the approval of our All-Common Creator. They made a show of flying together around the altar for a minute or two, then flew side by side upward toward the sun."

"No doubt the only reasonable places to land for a mile around to two bird-brained beings involved in their traditional courtship ritual this time of year." Gendlebleth responded helpfully.

"If that were all there was to it," continued Cain, "I might agree. But, shortly after the doves were out of view, it was time for me to make *my* offering to The Fullness of

Existence. And I did, as I said before, with my meticulously plucked pomegranate and shapely ears of wheat. I placed my offerings in the bowl, and nothing happened!"

"Come again?" asked Gendlebleth.

"You heard me, *nothing happened!* I waited there from mid-day until nightfall, and not even a swallow flew overhead. Not a bunny hopped by. Not an ant crawled on the ground anywhere in sight of my offering. Not even a fly could bother buzzing past; not a gnat to feast on what I offered!"

"So you're lamenting that you're reaping the very result your brother was named after because a couple of pigeons decided to... mate near where he tortured a lamb to death, and you didn't see any wild life today after the giving of your work?" Gendlebleth's mood began to lighten as he began seeing a sadness for the first time in his life associated with no merit.

"Actually," Cain reflected for a moment, "Abel's method of slaughter seems to cause almost no pain to the animal. I kind of admire his ability to take a life without upsetting that life in the process..."

Gendlebleth considered his own previous thoughts as he continued his admonition, which seemed to speak of its own accord now without the need to push it out of his mouth. "I mean, have you considered, perhaps, that peace is quite a blessing in itself and that That which created you has better things to do with Its time than pat you on the head for a job well done? Your admiration of your brother does you harm if you compare your actions, very different in nature to his, in such a way that you think ill of what clearly is helpful actions on your part, since you can feed your family even without the discomfort of taking a life. So the wind does not blow to indicate it is proud of you; how is it you do not take pride in your own work? You do something that is good in feeding your family, does that not fill you with joy enough?"

"Dad prefers the taste of lamb to that of bread. Mom seasons the lamb with the juice of my pomegranates, but it is an accompaniment to *his* work that is central and good in their eyes. Face it, my fruits don't fill one's blood with energy as my brother's food does. It makes me want to take his knives, that I can be commended for feeding the family for a change."

"Again, you speak of your brother's work in such a way that you devalue your own. I do not understand this. Your family clearly cannot eat meat every day of the week, where your bread is constant. The butter from the milk of your brother's livestock is an accompaniment, a compliment, not a curse."

"You mean what they add to the bread from my wheat that it tastes more pleasing, and keeps them warm through the winter, and gives them energy through the summer?"

"I mean," continued Gendlebleth, "that your brother's work and yours do not negate each other. They augment each other, make each other better. You do good work and it makes life better. If you were to do otherwise, it would not make life better. The results of your actions should be all the sign from Our Mother-Father Life-Giver that you require! It is hebel that you look upon your brother in this way. For an offering such as this, I would think a buzzard fertilizing your head would be in order!"

"You admonish me, yet my only desire is that I be recognized as great in character as my brother is. I have never done less than my best in thirteen years of my existence, yet my twelve-year-old brother has more smiles of my father, and my fruits and grains cause my mother only more work! What am I to do that I be praised as highly as my brother, that I see myself as well in the eyes of my parents as they see him?"

Gendlebleth felt redness coming to his face as he lowered his tone to cool his own temperament. "It seems, Son Of Man, that you look for Your Creator to be grateful for your existence where gratitude should be coming rather from *you*. If you wish to curry favor with The Divine, you ought start by working harder and hebeling less. It's not like you can just kill your brother, so stop crying in your bread, and try to notice what joy you do bring when you're not obsessing on plucking pomegranate seeds without puncturing their outer coating!"

With this said, Gendlebleth pushed loudly through the high reeds of the field as he tried to calm his automatic reaction to the wrongness he perceived in Cain's view of his own good works.

As Cain watched Gendlebleth's back disappearing through the grass, one thing he had said stuck out clearly as the water flowing through the river before a heavy storm.

Shortly thereafter, Cain invited his brother to the far side of the field to observe the beautiful flowers that grew in the spring sunlight. Shortly after still, a flock of doves rose high into the sky with a start, and took off toward whatever direction they pointed as though their lives depended upon the quickness of the flapping of their wings.

৩ ৩ ৩

On the hill above, Tartantuan gasped and called over his shoulder for Antagnous to call an emergency meeting. As Antagnous ran through their camp, Gendlebleth stopped her to ask the matter, to which she responded through tears, "Cain has taken the life of Abel." And it was then that the words he had spoken last to Cain came flooding back into his mind. As they gathered to discuss the events of the day, as he entered the outer circle, Gendlebleth felt as though it were those around the circle closing in on *him*.

Chapter 10

Gendlebleth stood alone in a field surrounded by high grass, and purple and blue and red and white and yellow wildflowers. Up next to his foot hopped a bunny rabbit. Gendlebleth stooped down and picked the bunny up by the nape of its neck and looked at it in the eye. As he stared into the face of the bunny, and the bunny stared back into his eyes, the corners of his lips were raised into a smile; pure joy. His hand next closed around the bunny's neck as he brought its body down against a large boulder repeatedly: WHACK! WHACK! WHACK! WHACK! WHACK! Down came the body of the rabbit in his hand no less than two dozen times against the rock, when finally he stopped.

The bloody, broken body of the small animal hung limp in his hand, half of it missing meat and skin and bone, dripping the liquid still barely left in its carcass. As he held it up by the neck to look into its eyes, it was the dead, glazed visage of Abel staring back at him.

Gendlebleth awoke out of his nightmare in a cold sweat. He recalled how the meeting had gone earlier that night. After entering the ring of the other angels, Luciferous had come straight to him and immediately embraced him tightly, while Gendlebleth wept openly and freely in his arms. He spoke to the entire group just as he spoke to his weeping friend, "They have free choice. No more than we could tell our creator what It cannot do, so too can we not tell them what *they* cannot do. And likewise, we must be cautious of what we teach them is in their capacity. It isn't your fault, Gendlebleth; you didn't know that such a thing had never occurred to him before, and more than that, that he would act upon it."

Hearing the words of his friend "you didn't know," Gendlebleth felt compelled to pull away, run to the edge of the hill, and begin vomiting. Luciferous looked on after him with empathy before turning back to address the rest of the group.

As all around the circle nodded gravely and sadly while Luciferous spoke, Gendlebleth could be heard in the background weeping between the heaves of undigested bits pushing their way up through his esophagus.

☙ ☙ ☙

Cain left the body of his brother. He reflected with pride that he had employed his brother's technique so well that he had apparently scarcely felt any pain as his life quickly flowed from his body. Cain felt something suddenly very heavy and hollow taking up a great deal of room in the middle of his chest, but he prided himself on his work well done, and could not imagine what the meaning of this feeling was while walking home to dinner.

Shortly after sitting on the ground where they took their supper together, Adam spoke to his son, "Where is your brother Abel?"

Cain looked up at his father, the feeling in his stomach becoming heavier as quickly, nervously, he tried to dodge the question put forth to him. "I don't know. Am I my brother's keeper?"

"Are you your brother's keeper? What an odd thing to say." Adam's face contorted. He strove to suss out what his son's statement could possibly mean, "The two of you are practically inseparable. I know the two of you have places you go alone, but when have the two of you ever not been present for the grace of the sustenance we receive from That Which Created us simultaneously? If we are very fortunate, your brother brings us the life of an animal that does not understand choosing food, and you bring with you the gifts of the soil, and we eat together. Your mother is preparing the lamb stew now from the work of both your hands, and will be more curious even than I when she does not see your brother present. You have no knowledge even of where your brother *might* be?"

Looking into his father's eyes, Cain could not bear to lie; the pain of weight and emptiness was growing within him hearing each word his father spoke. The pain seemed to be bursting through him to speak the truth lest it tear his flesh asunder. Meekly, barely audibly, he murmured pathetically "Abel won't be coming to dinner, Father. Abel will never take dinner with us again."

Now the concern began to fill his father's face as Adam felt a pit begin in his own stomach. "What do you mean, son?"

"I thought that if you did not have him to be proud of for the meat he brought you, perhaps you would be proud to have my wheat alone, since there would be nothing else to compare it to."

A bit louder he spoke, "What do you mean, son?"

"I took his life that I'd have no worry as to my own, father."

"No worry to your own life? *Took* his life? What have you done? You could not have killed your brother?"

"I thought that if I worked even harder, planted more crops, did more work creating our house that—"

"You *killed* your brother?"

'I'm prepared to take over his duties, and—"

"*You killed your brother?*" As Adam shouted his question with the boiling blood of all his rage, Eve appeared at the door of the dwelling, carrying in her hands the pot of lamb stew she had been preparing for their meal.

Cain's eye flew to those of his mother. Adam's head turned abruptly toward his wife, almost as though his neck could act like an owl's. Eve stared deeply into the eyes of her son, then looked at Adam's, then turned again back to her son's face. Back and forth between them she looked as the pot in her hands began to quake in her increasingly unsteady grasp. Finally, the finality of the realization was allowed by her to be perceived, and as the pot fell to the floor, the contents spilling out to cover much of the ground of their dwelling, a shriek of pure terror, high-pitched and loud, wailed from out of her throat, slicing open the night as though only pain had ever existed for her, and she wished to fill the world with only that pain she now felt.

The heavy emptiness that Cain carried in his stomach now filled with that sound of his mother wailing her perfect misery to all of God's creation as though he were soaking up every decibel like a sponge, directly into that hole left when he removed his brother from his life. When, minutes latter, her one, long breath did stop, and Eve fell to her knees, her inhalation a sob gasping automatically to keep her alive through the tears that began to fall, the sound of all that she had emptied through her throat still filled the void that had formed so much weight in the center of Cain. He stood up and stepped toward his mother to comfort her, and as he did, felt a hand grasp the back of his covering by the neck and pull him outside sharply.

He practically flew out the door from the gesture of his father's adrenalin-filled arm. Cain's head landed against a rock hard before Adam picked Cain up next by the front of his covering, by the neck, and held his son's face up to his own, "Listen; your brother's blood is crying out to me from the ground! And now you are cursed from the ground, which has opened its mouth to receive your brother's blood from your hand. When you till the ground, it will no longer yield to you its strength; you will be a fugitive and a wanderer on the earth. I cast you from this place that you will never return!"

Horror filled Cain's face as he cried out toward the gaze of his father, "My punishment is greater than I can bear! Today you have driven me away from the soil, and I shall be hidden from your face; I shall be a fugitive and a wanderer on the earth, and I long that my mother may give birth that another shall grow quickly, meet me, and kill me."

"Not so!" Adam spat on the ground. "Your mother did not suffer the pain of your creation and your brother's that another child of ours would turn its face as well from The Creator Of Life Infinite! Whoever kills Cain will suffer a sevenfold vengeance." And the gash in Cain's head, where his head had struck the rock moments prior, began to bleed.

❧ ❧ ❧

As her wail continued cascading over the night sky, the ears of all the angels were filled with the feeling of their hearts sinking to hear the pain of the human woman suffering more greatly than they ever could conceive of being merely separate from the other halves of their selves. Antagnous held Casarta close to her while listening to the pain of the woman losing her children, whose labor she suffered that they would know the fullness of life.

Through the heaves of his abdomen, and his tears, her sound penetrated deeply into his heart, where it filtered to a place in his stomach, and stayed even after the sound of the beginning of her profound misery had ceased.

After his vomiting and tears had stopped, and he had been carried back to his tent to sleep, her suffering's sound still saturated him through continued weeping, leading into exhaustion, and finally slumber.

When he awoke later in the darkness, he could not again find his way to further nightmares, so he instead awaited the rising of the sun. He prayed fervently that an evening would come when again his body would follow naturally to its proper place in the mind of the night without fear of what torture his own actions would reflect through the emotions of his existence.

In Its dwelling, the Lord heard the proclamation of Cain's father and saw that it was good.

Chapter 11

"Mommy, where are we going?"

As she picked up her daughter, Antagnous answered, "Where once we were one, now it is time for us to become two, Casarta. One half of our group will stay here to watch over Adam and Eve at a safe distance and look for any chance we might be given to assist them. You and I, and your father and the rest of us who are dividing off from the rest of the group, will follow Cain to the East where he has fled."

"Will we see the others again, Momma? Will we ever see Brother Luciferous again?"

"My child," Antagnous couldn't help but smile, "our life is long, and I cannot imagine we will not meet up many times and disband many times as we strive to fulfill our duty. If we will not see them again in this world, though, know that there will come a time when all of us again will be united in The Light from which we have come."

❧ ❧ ❧

Tears filling his eyes as he wailed in harmony with the sound of his mother's cry pushing its way ever as though trying to escape from his chest just below his heart, Cain ran toward the East as fast as his legs could push him. Sleep came when he fell. Then he would rise again and push on.

Where something looked like food, he would eat, but only when his stomach burned loudly enough that it could be felt through the terror of his mother's voice ever flooding through him without end.

᠂ᚉᚉᚉ

There he lay in a field on a warm summer day. The radiance of the Ever-Creator feeding all of existence directly shining down upon his face, while the flowers drank it in to create their own blood, and every animal ingested it into their eyes to see by. Gendlebleth felt the warmth of ever-filling mercy as the grass swayed gently around him.

His skin drinking in the radiance of Omni-Existence's Love, he thought he felt the ground beneath him shudder. It was almost an after-thought in the light of the Divine, but it called his mind from the sound of the sun's light. He felt the warmth, but so too did he seem to feel earth beneath his back subtly ripple against his spine.

Readying to roll onto his side to see if a gopher was not about to make its way above the soil's surface, a bloody hand, Abel's hand, gripped around his ankle from below where he lay.

Gendlebleth awoke violently to find himself being carried between two wood poles, atop the sewn-together skins of animals, by his brothers and sisters. The sun shined brightly upon him. Darwith inquired of him, "Are you okay, brother?"

Light almost blinding him, Gendlebleth answered toward the voice of Darwith, "I am. Just more nightmares."

He next heard the voice of his friend and sister. "Do you need water, brother?"

"No, Antagnous, I wasn't sleeping for that long. He still walks?"

"Sometimes he leads us in circles for days, though lately he's been heading at day break toward the sun, and has kept it in relation to him as he walks so that his course is fairly due East. I think it has been almost thirty risings and settings of the sun now that we've been following him."

"If Our Creator does not send my sleeping visions to mock me, then it is my mind that rightfully will not stop hating itself that has kept my body all but able to stand by virtue of its own capabilities. That I cannot move myself is worthy of my crime, I should be left and no longer made to be a burden to the lot of you cradling my bag of bones as though I am a baby without muscle mass to find my feet."

"Certainly, if you wish to annoy us further with such talk," responded Antagnous, "I'll be perfectly happy to stitch your lips together so that we can be spared your vain tongue-waggings further. But we all knew the boy's fate was near as good as sealed when his mother and father agreed together to call him an offering to the wind by name. I hope none of us, including you, are at least stupid enough to doubt the absolute will of The Lord Our In-Transmutable Law, which every rock or conscious will must obey.

"This may be more painful a lesson than you've been able to bear on your own thus far, but this is all these events are: a lesson to us all. And you will know this lesson better than all, for which you, and the rest of us, are blessed by the same law that damned the second one to the fate *we* all find so distasteful. Give it a few more days and you'll be able to stand well enough without vomiting immediately, and wherever you may find yourself inclined to fall, we will be ready to catch you."

"It's Divine mercy, for the moment feels like spite to me. Though, if truly I am able to help them where otherwise I'd not have been, however many eternities declare me worthy to return to myself, I will recall the blessing then of my own self-damnation this day. Thank you, and you all, for carrying me forward when I could not carry myself, for the enormity of my potential's smallest part was too much for me to bear."

Chapter 12

"As we feared, his name wrought the prophecy of his life."

"Yes, but perhaps we had a hand in it more than any ill-thought through word of his parents."

"At any rate, we will be careful not to come in contact with them again until they have formed of themselves so many, after so many generations, that we will seem only to them as others like them in nature."

"And, at this rate, how many centuries do you figure that will take? I mean, how long is their natural lifetime going to be, anyway? Now we know they can die just as the slaughter of any animal of Omnipresence's creation, but how long is their natural lifetime, that a time might come when any not recognize that we did not come of existence as they have come to exist?"

"As we knew we would have time to, the time we have shall be bidden until a time comes when we can be beings not merely passive. And when that day comes, may we have learned from them, that we can assist without burdening them as so far we have done." So spoke Luciferous.

"Yes, but we have done some good for them."

"And we will again, more so even, but first we will bide our time that we will harm them no longer. For all the work we have enacted, how quickly we have undone the greatest of our intentions." So spoke Luciferous.

"And should appear obvious action to take?"

"Who here would deny assistance be given them cleanly in a moment in which they truly required it, for their greatest possible outcome?" So spoke Luciferous, and in reply came the peace and stillness of the night.

✿ ✿ ✿

In despair of the one called "Living," her husband, from his own grief and anger knew confusion as he offered his hand to his wife in consolation, which she often refused, and was seldom for even a moment appeased by.

The angels watched with heavy hearts, despairing to see two people, once lovers, reverted by emotion to a state resembling that of the animal called "gorilla" trying to communicate in a language of only emotion-filled gestures, speaking of wants they seemed to posses no word with which to articulate to each other.

After several years' time, they found without words that the mud of their beings settled, and the waters of their souls were clear that they may recognize each other through clean water, and know each other from the experience of making peace out of the wars within that they had suffered through no faults of their own.

They were no longer separated by their pain, grief, and confusion, and touching head to head to feel each other's thought as though one, so did the belly of the Living One grow with the co-created child of Man.

So it happened, one hundred and thirty years into the life of Man, that Man's third son, Seth, was born.

Chapter 13

Many times the sun rose and fell as they walked ten miles behind The Created One. At all times two kept within seeing distance of him, yet out of sight of him, and at night they changed their watch with the main group following behind. Each night, midway, watches would exchange news of the day before completing the short journey to their respective placements.

One particularly lovely day, when the sun was warm and the breeze was cool, the party found themselves surrounded by a particularly beautiful green patch of land. They delighted in fresh water from a stream, and wild-growing foods to eat. They were grateful to not feel the need to kill lizards or birds that their bellies would feel calm.

Gendlebleth had been on his own feet almost exclusively for the past twenty days, and he was thankful toward the mercy of his current existence to find that when he had finished eating his fill of the local berries and plants, and had washed his throat of food and dryness with the cool water of the stream, he felt no urge whatsoever to vomit it back up. Even his nightmares seemed less filled with the blood of Abel screaming to him from the faces of small woodland creatures; all slept well that night.

In the morning, at the changing of the watch, rather than at the five-mile mark, Ternaddain and Darwith were met instead before they had walked much past two miles. "Ternaddain, Darwith! Blessed be The Name we found you! Though he is not like to wake for three more hours, rush to where he sleeps lest our watch be lost!"

Ternaddain and Darwith glanced at each other in brief hesitation out of confusion between what they expected their morning to consist of, and this seemingly anomalous message they had momentarily ago received from their brethren.

"You'll understand when you arrive yourselves. Just be quick, as we urge the others on closely behind you!"

Despite the inability to comprehend, Ternaddain and Darwith began in the direction of Cain as quickly as their legs could carry them. When they had reached the top of a particularly steep hill an hour later, huffing and drawing in air heavily, they gasped an extra time in disbelief.

❧ ❧ ❧

Upon arriving shortly after alerting Darwith and Ternaddain, Handoroth and Caldas woke the others and bade them travel now as quickly as they were able. So spoke Warmoot, "Why do you bid us with such haste and urgency?"

So responded Caldas, "The breath that would tell you what you will not believe but heard through your own eyes would be better served catching up to Darwith and Ternaddain, as quickly as our legs propelled by the wind in our chests will allow. Let us move at once!"

So it was that a swarm of bodied angels ran toward the hills before them, save for Gendlebleth, Antagnous, Lousitous, and Casarta. As the others ran ahead, it was agreed that Casarta's size necessitated one stay behind with her pace, and Gendlebleth's current infirmity necessitated not a companion to keep with him pace, but two to catch him should he fall. Casarta's parents being the obvious choice to stay with her, they quickly decided to be companions to Gendlebleth, whom they wished not to leave alone with his own pain, rather than Lousitous simply carrying Casarta on his back to keep time with the group as a whole. As a family they traveled to where they supposed the others would be, not much more than ten miles ahead of where they currently began their own journey toward re-coalescence.

Two hours later, the band of four gasped in momentary disbelief at the top of the hill. They saw they would not have very many miles left to walk to catch up to the others.

❧ ❧ ❧

Cain stumbled, tired, dusty, and weary from travel through the open door, and threw himself onto the wooden bar. As Cain looked up toward the man cleaning the cup in his hand with a scrap of cloth, the man looked back down at Cain and spoke. "Well now, if ever I saw a man in need of a drink... A traveler if ever I saw one; I'd recognize that mark on your head from a mile away, if ever I've seen it before. Don't suppose you can contribute to my existence as I get you washed up, fed and settled for the night, but we'll figure that all out once you don't seem quite so close to fainting from exhaustion. Looks like you arrived just in time! Welcome, stranger, to Nod!"

Chapter 14

"She named him 'Appointed?'"

"I was there myself to hear the naming," responded Tartantuan.

Lemothta continued to question the name. "Seems a bit blasé, doesn't it? I mean, 'Woe is me, so this'll have to do in the place of what I lost?' When they finally connected again to create this life, it was so spectacularly beautiful. I expected their son's name to reflect the beauty of his point of creation."

Luciferous spoke up at this point. "His name reflects her belief that still, even after driving them out of The Garden, even after both her children were so savagely taken from her, she *still* believes that That which created her, created us all, has done so specifically for the results of the experiencing of the good she felt throughout her that night that her son was created. Apparently she believes he is a creation Appointed to take the place of the sons that were taken from her. As though this 'Appointed' is a gift from Our Creator *Itself*. There's nothing blasé about his name. His name speaks of he being her solitary hope from out of all the suffering her life has been this century she has existed. He *is* the one appointed to continue humanity, now that Cain has been driven away where no daughter could exist to create offspring, since Adam and Eve are the only people thus far existent."

They all nodded in concurrence as Luciferous defended the name given by Living to her son.

❧ ❧ ❧

As time went on, Adam created with Eve more sons and daughters. As time went on, these sons and daughters made amongst themselves many more human beings in kind. All, that is, except he who was called "Appointed." One day, concerned that Seth had not yet known one of his sisters, Adam took him aside and voiced his concerns.

"Son, you are already more than a hundred years old. Your brothers took to the blessing of knowing their sisters generally around the age of thirteen, as young as eleven! For one of your sisters to be much older than eight years old before becoming a helper to one of your brothers has been virtually unknown. Son, you must swell with frustration to see your sisters blossom into the maturity of child-bearing age. Why have you not yet claimed one of your mother's daughters to accompany you through your life?"

Seth responded to his father's earnest concern, "Father, it simply has not seemed natural to me to take one of my sisters for a wife. Not that they are not even surpassing in beauty of my mother, but it always seems unnatural to me to consider any of them who have not yet reached a child-bearing age as being able to be a companion to me. But rather, they seem as being like myself. I wish to teach them about living; give them the tools to exist joyfully. And those of childbearing age, I have seen them grow from my mother's womb and my brain. They are beautiful, and almost impossible to pass up in light of my physical frustrations, but most are by then my brother's wives. Besides, by this time in my life, I have learned well how to control the frustrations of my body, and they seem too close to me in terms of friendship and camaraderie that I would think of them as anything but the family with whom

I have grown up. There simply seems something unnatural about the thought of taking my sister into my bed."

"Moreover," continued Seth, "it seems too frequent for my tastes that my nieces and nephews are larger in size than seems proper. Always the large ones seem not as easy to teach, and ever more quarrelsome than the rest of those more in appearance like you and I, and the children of my brothers and sisters who also are not so large in body combined with such a differing mode of mind."

"Nonetheless," responded Adam, "It is not good that a man should be alone. It seems like there is less of this, as you say, gargantuanism, from the offspring of my grandchildren who choose not to marry their siblings. Perhaps if you chose one of your nieces instead to wed..."

"Still such a thought makes me uneasy, father. There simply seems something inherently wrong about claiming a young girl, who is not old enough to make up her own mind or succeed at any trade on her own, as a wife. Especially when I continue to feel awkward at the idea of one of my own blood, who I help in raising, as any more than a friend and a member of my community whom I work beside in creating our life."

Adam thought for a moment or two. Then, his countenance brightened. "Son, do you know very well my great-great-grandchildren who have settled to the far southwest of where your mother and I have our dwelling?"

"I have been invited to dinner there with you and Mom, when their parents had invited us with my other brothers and sisters to their house, but I don't think I've seen them in over ten years."

"Yes. They tend to like to keep to themselves. They have taken to a rather odd thought that their children should be a certain age before they take spouses, and that their children should connect some way in mind before connecting in any way in body."

Seth's face brightened, as though he had just been told he was not the only man on Earth.

"It has something to do with problems my great-grandson had had when he was fifteen and took his wife, then six, to be his companion. But what they had decided was that any sooner than twelve was a bad idea for their daughters, and that at least twenty was appropriate for their sons. I've even heard it rumored that they'd prefer both sons and daughters to be thirty years old before choosing companions who are not their own siblings. Anyway, they happen to have three daughters, each two years apart in age who are not married, and, if memory serves, the youngest is fourteen; she's just beginning to ripen! If you do not object, son, may I arrange for you to have dinner with my great-grandchildren's family?"

After considering, briefly, his loneliness and frustration of a body at war always with his natural repugnance for taking to bed a young girl who he was just beginning to instruct in proper speech and creating tools of life out of other materials, he acquiesced to meeting his great-nieces and seeing what feelings he had toward them upon meeting them.

At that dinner, Seth met Lila. She was the oldest of the sisters, and he enjoyed speaking with her more than the other two. She had many fruitful thoughts about the ways she pondered it was proper to live life based on what her parents had taught her, and, much more importantly, what she had seen herself of the world over the eighteen years she had been alive. To converse with such a beautiful young lady, who found a natural repugnance at the thought of knowing her brothers, and who couldn't imagine merely indulging the animal urges of a boy less than fifteen years of age, he asked if he might return to meet with her again. She blushed as she told him that she'd like very much the opportunity to speak with him further.

Lila's parents were hesitant to let Lila out of their house with Seth. Every time he left after meeting with her, they'd tell her that if there was any doubt in her mind whether she enjoyed Seth's company enough to spend time with him raising children for the next several hundred years, she ought take a decade or two to give it proper thought. Despite her parents' persistent advice, Lila was little more than twenty when she snuck off into the field with Seth, and they knew each other.

The angels were delighted when, one hundred and five years after his own birth, Appointed and Lila named their son exactly what he was: Human Being.

Chapter 15

"Why would God mislead us into believing that what we saw was what is, when it was not? How is it possible there are other adam?"

"Are you accusing It of lying to us?"

"Have we had news back yet about Cain?"

"Are you now trying to evade my question? Did you just accuse God of lying to us?"

"I'm not evading you. Before attempting to answer what you just asked, I'd like to know that what I'm seeing isn't merely a figment of my mind, and that there are in fact people there, and what exactly the nature is of Cain interacting with those people. Has there been word back, or have Ternaddain and Darwith not been closer than this, and did Telnaxson and Ceaslar decide to be the first to undergo this unheard-of task?"

Ternaddain spoke up. "We sent for them quickly after noticing that their smaller frames would be more helpful to observe unseen amidst so many people."

"Then there are other people! She may not have lied to us, but why would He show us only one, then two created, and not the rest?"

Gendlebleth spoke up at this point. "We were not looking at the rest of creation that third day. Nor were we the sixth or the eighth. Our focus, though it could have been otherwise had we chosen, was only ever on The Garden, for we believed our focus there to be the will of

What we served then exclusively. Had we chosen, which we would then not, perhaps then we would have seen the entirety of the creation of the species of animal known as humanity."

They all nodded gravely in agreement at Gendlebleth's recollection of what they had all experienced.

So spoke Antagnous, "If they were not there too in The Garden, do we serve them as we do Cain?"

❧ ❧ ❧

Shortly after arrival with the rest of the group, Ternaddain had met with Telnaxson, Ceaslar, and the others minus Antagnous, Gendlebleth, Lousitous, and Casarta. While Cain still slept mid-way down the hill, she had advised Telnaxson and Ceaslar to continue the watch due to their size and ability to hide themselves from those they might encounter. Telnaxson and Ceaslar arrived just in time to relieve Darwith and observe Cain make his way slowly and groggily to the inn below in the town of Nod.

It was there they observed the innkeeper feed Cain; clothe him, give him a place to rest, and converse with him about his life. Cain said merely that he was a traveler who was too ashamed of his past to speak of anything more than the joy he had once known tilling soil and harmonizing with the rising vegetation which had always sung its splendor unto him. The innkeeper smiled as Cain spoke and responded to him. "Upon the morrow, there's a man I'd like you to meet..."

Shortly, a second watch was sent mid-way down the hill to observe movement from a distance, to keep track of the first watch should Cain be moved elsewhere in this small town that was bigger than any communal construct the angels had seen prior.

Before daybreak, a network of six watched at various distances they deemed to be safe from being found by the other inhabitants of Nod, while they continued to watch what was happening to Cain.

Cain awoke with the sun and was taken by the innkeeper to a small farm at the outskirts of the town. Remblelok and Lajiel listened at the door to the conversation that took place there between the farmer and the innkeeper. "This young man wandered into my inn just yesterday morning, appearing as though he'd never seen civilization in his life. It's not like me to give free food and lodging, but he looked like he could use a friend for a moment to help him find his way. Anyhow, when he mentioned something about taking joy in singing with food from the ground, the notion came to me that he might make a half-decent apprentice to you. I figure if he works out well, you'd perhaps be willing to supply me food from the ground trade-free for two planting seasons. And of course, if I have merely burdened you with an imbecile who likes to talk to plants, I'd be happy to give you free intoxication at my bar for half of a year, and I'll split with you whatever profit I could glean by selling him off as a slave at the season of the market, two weeks past the large mountain. Win-win. What do you say?"

Upon hearing the word "slave," Remblelok and Lajiel looked at each other and shrugged. It was a word neither had heard before and had no intuitive knowledge of, as they had with the other words of Man.

The farmer replied, "A fair trade indeed. This will give him a fine way to earn his keep in Nod, and I think that we will be grateful in feeding each other in accordance with the creation this young man's work yields for us all. Does he have a name?"

"Cain, sir," replied Cain.

The farmer began to address him directly now. "And does this arrangement seem fair to you, Cain? Or shall we sell you to others immediately as a way to replenish the resources already expended on you by Len, and the time that I could have been spending already this day in my fields?"

"The opportunity you give me to work for my pathetic existence is more than generous, sir," responded Cain.

"So it shall be, Cain. Call me Growvner. I am happy to have a new pair of hands to help me bring up the food with which I share with the town."

So Cain began his life with the farmer called Growvner.

❦❦❦

Initially, Cain was taught how to make tools for working the soil. Since the town relied greatly, in part, on Growvner's farm for the food for the year, he was cautious not to let an apprentice actually touch seed to soil before they had been observed for a full year's time. Cain was a quick study, however, in learning to make new tools, and cultivating fertilizer, and learning about the local fruits and vegetables that were grown in the region.

Meanwhile, as Cain studied under Growvner, the humanly-embodied angels observed not only Cain's new life, but also the town of Nod. They studied the clothes the people wore, the foods they ate, and the way they conducted their community. They also observed when anyone from outside the town entered and left, and also how they were dressed.

After a short time watching the techniques of making clothing employed by the townsfolk of Nod, and the garments warn by those apparently only passing by or through the town, the men and women angels began to make garments more closely resembling those they thought would pass for an indicator that they were visitors from elsewhere, looking for temporary lodging and perhaps to briefly sell their wares in the town. Before their first year in Nod was finished, four angels managed to pass unnoticed through the town to keep track of Cain while many people passed by, virtually unquestioningly. Even Cain, who had ever only met Gendlebleth, never suspected the "visitors" he briefly met in passing were angels who had been observing him for as long as he had been alive.

Now watching over the boy took place in shifts of two months, as well as those of half a day. Monitoring was established from very close in broad daylight as well as in the shadows, and at long distances barely within sight. Before leaving the community so that "new visitors" could take up the watch, the angels made sure always to trade goods for raw materials, with which they could make new goods for the next watch to sell when they arrived in town. The angels, in this way, became rather inventive in crafting exotic-seeming jeweleries, clothes, and tools they could trade with the town to maintain the premise that they were in fact passing through to do business. They pleased themselves with the notion that perhaps they were in some way making the lives of these human beings better as they introduced new objects for them to enjoy into their community.

⚓⚓⚓

As the first year passed, while watching the farmer ply his trade, Cain began to make suggestions to the man. At first the farmer was a bit put off that a mere apprentice would make suggestions about how to run his farm. But he was quick to consider that he did not know this boy's full background, and that he had been brought to the farm to begin with because perhaps he did in fact have some experience with raising crops. While he was not one to be disrespected in his own fields, he knew well the wisdom of listening to others whose minds held experiences, and therefore understanding, that differed from his own. After seeing the probable wisdom in some of Cain's suggestions, when the first harvest came after Cain's arrival, he suspected it was more than mere coincidence that the yield was greater by far than he had ever seen in his life. Then, to his mind, the second harvest grown under Cain's suggestions proved it.

After that first year, the farmer had a conversation with Cain. "Cain, you obviously have considerable talent when it comes to bringing life from the ground. You have a fine grasp of making tools, and you have come to know what is good here to grow with ease. If you are willing to relinquish to me half your yield for five years, and would perhaps consider to continue to throw some suggestions my way as to my own work, I'll gladly give you, to start, three acres with which to grow your crops the coming year, and ten acres the following four, to give you time to earn your own piece of land to tend. And of course, I still have a trick or two to teach you, but what do you say? Are you ready to start growing your own?"

Cain's face came over pale, and he very noticeably hesitated before answering the farmer while he recalled his father's words to him. As the words 'the ground will no longer yield its strength to you' echoed in his head, Cain slowly responded, "Growvner, there is nothing more I should want in my life than that the earth would yield to me Its strength and Her fruits. However, in my heart it is my surest belief that should I plant pomegranate, and sesame, and radish, only thistle would be yielded come harvest."

The farmer spoke as though seeing his best friend recently drowned. "Your skills are sure as any I've seen, your mind keener, maybe, than mine when it comes to the soil. Surely you'll accept three acres for one year's time that you may see the earth bestow upon you her abundance. Be I wrong, which I cannot fathom, I'll hold you to no harm for honoring me by an attempt."

Cain stared straight into the eyes of his benefactor before acquiescing. "For you, who have given me food, shelter, clothing, and work as close to the earth as I believe I am capable, I will assent to your extraordinary generosity. But understand, the soil bears no love for me, though I love Her from the entirety of my being. I will try for your sake, though I think the ground will not forgive me the single betrayal I unwittingly committed against Her."

Growvner smiled nervously to hear his friend speak of betrayal, and decided not to press him further that night. Though he was concerned to see the look in Cain's eye in the shadow of the scar on his head, his heart was made gladdened that his apprentice had agreed to work a piece of his land.

❧ ❧ ❧

When the harvest did arrive, unlike Cain, the farmer was stunned to find that the only thing that grew on the land he had given Cain to tend was weeds.

"You have not tended this soil! Why would you not even try?"

"But Growvner, I *did* try. I have worked harder these past months than ever in my life. I tell you quite simply that I am cursed. Let the grooves in the ground show you my hands have labored, even if the weeds do not!"

"If you had even thrown a handful of seed at the earth, it would have proven more fruitful than this. You lie!"

"I do not lie! Try me one more planting season. Give me three rows of soil, just three rows next to your own land. Let me work with you as I have last year, and watch as I plant these three rows over the next several months by my own hand. Observe yourself if my methods are lacking, and watch as death rises from what I plant next to the life that rises by your hands!"

Acquiescing, several months later, indeed no food grew where Growvner had seen himself the skillful work done that should have yielded any plant at all worthy for food.

"What have you done, boy, that you are so cursed?"

"Sir, you have been fully good to me in every way, and I'd like to think that in some ways I have repaid that kindness in turn and done for you the best work I am capable of. Please, though, do not ask me to reveal to you my shame."

The farmer paused in thought for several minutes before responding. "Kid, let's head down to the inn and get a drink." And the farmer never asked the question of Cain again.

❧ ❧ ❧

At the inn, a beautiful woman sang for the patrons of the bar. As Cain and Growvner and the innkeeper drank together, Cain asked of the innkeeper, "Who is this beautiful woman who sings like the bloom of the Rose of Sharon at daybreak?"

"That would be my daughter," responded the innkeeper.

Cain looked the man in the eye uncertain what to say.

"Camphire, come here a moment." The innkeeper smiled to shout this at her as he continued to keep his gaze on Cain's. When she walked over, he introduced the two. "Camphire, this is Cain." Cain's face turned bright pink as he met her, but his color was hid by the darkness of the room, and his tone was bold when he said hello to the girl, and they began to talk. As they talked, Growvner took the innkeeper aside.

"She is about the right age for marriage, and I tell you the boy is committed to his work and has a good, strong heart about him. I think he'll be working with me for a long time. Might you be interested in discussing a price by which they might continue getting to know each other for the rest of their lives?"

"You're willing to pay for this boy to be a part of my family, Growvner?"

"I am, you wily old rascal, unless you have an objection."

"If my daughter has no objection, then neither do I! I'll expect to not have to worry about eating for the next several years, though..."

"As long as you don't mind me tasting some of the stronger results of my grapes on the house from time to time, I think we have an arrangement that will be a happiness for our town, for times long to come."

Camphire had no objections.

Gendlebleth, watching alongside Zarnuchtron in the shadows outside of the inn, was filled with joy for the first time he could remember since arriving to existence in terms of human form. It was momentary, and quickly he began to shudder from the combination of that joy and the fact of the pain of the rest of his existence, but he was happy to see Cain on his way to having enjoyment in his life, a thought before inconceivable since the moment he had been driven from his mother's home.

❧ ❧ ❧

Elsewhere, overlooking the town of Nod, Casarta was having a conversation with her mother. "Antagnous, we haven't had meat to eat in a week. Can't we just run one of us down to Zarnuchtron to tell him to bring some partridges to roast? Or won't you allow me to sneak onto the farm where Cain works, to steal a partridge or three for us to eat?"

"No one else of us eats as you do, Casarta. I'd allow you to sneak off with a partridge as you request, if not for the fact that if one of those in Nod see you with your skin, I think we will have troubles even worse than when Cain rose against his brother. If it were easier to communicate with the watchers below, I'd put a word to them for your sake, but I am confident Gendlebleth will bring us a bird in not too long a time; he's very good about bringing you food. Meanwhile, I'll convene a meeting about starting to raise animals up here, since this hill may be our home for quite some time."

"Antagnous, I do wish that a roast chicken were capable of materializing out of the winds themselves, that my belly and tastes might be sated. Though I am grateful for the almonds and lentils I've had to eat this night, and know that you are right about Gendy bringing me good foods, as he always does. It does seem like it would be easier for him to carry the birds, of course, if he were capable of killing them himself..."

Somewhere in the town of Nod, a gust of wind blew past the covering of a front door as a family sat down to dinner. When that gust reached the table, the scent of a freshly roasted partridge filled the nostrils of the family looking on at the lentils and almonds they were about to eat. Before the gust passed by the table, several partridges appeared, brown and apparently moist. They stared at each other for a moment, then in unison thanked existence for the nutrition they were blessed to have upon their table, and began passing pieces of the succulent, aromatic bird around for all to share. They all thought that never had they tasted so fine a partridge, yet all noticed later that when they were done, they felt less than full. It was a feeling in their bellies as though all they'd eaten were almonds and lentils — only what little they'd eaten once they'd filled most of their bellies with spontaneously apparent bird.

Chapter 16

Cain knew his wife, and as she was getting to know him, she asked the obvious question. "Husband, how did you come by this scar upon your head?" She asked this after she brushed away the hair to kiss where his scar was.

"Camphire, if there is anyone walking the Earth who might hear of my days before I met you, of which I am deeply ashamed, certainly it is you who deserves to know her husband with whom she creates life." Cain proceeded to tell Camphire about the murder of his brother and his exile from his parents' home. He wept in shame as he bore himself naked before her. "My mother's shrillness rages through me with every passing moment of my life. Where once I sacrificed the best of my labors to Existence which created me, now it is the sound of her response to my existence which humbles me and decides every action of my hand ever more. If any part of me is good, it is that I try ever to silence in me the sound of her cries to behold what she created together with the love of my father."

Camphire reached her hands to Cain's face and kissed him where his head had hit the rock a few years previous. "As you have shown me nothing but the work of your hands to create what is useful to share with others, and the tenderness of your touch, husband, from the time you arrived, every part of you creates good in this land. That I could silence the voice within you with my kiss, I would be happy to give to my husband what he has brought unto me."

"Camphire, my shame is the blood of my brother on my hands. All I touch is stained with his good he can never share because of me. If any good comes of my hands, it is only because, even in death, his blood makes good what my touch would profane."

"Cain, do you think you're the first man to kill another man?"

At this question, the watch by their window glanced at each other as similar thoughts entered their heads.

"But your touch is inspired by the man you wish to be, not the man that your brother might have been."

"I did think I was the first, Cami, but if others have spilled blood as I have, even they would not take the life their mother created after them. It was my job to keep my brother from harm. I would ask another to strike me down, if I thought I would not then curse the life of someone else as I have cursed myself! No, my existence is worth only what good I can create to replace the evils of my being. It is my mother and my brother that speak through me, where Cain is exiled from my mind for good."

Camphire shed a tear to hear her husband speak so. Nonetheless, she knew the laws of Nod, and knew that in the interests of the life now growing inside her, she would have to teach her husband Nod's law, and recommend setting out soon, for the better.

જીજીજી

Under the direction of his wife, Cain first told Growvner privately of his past. Then with Growvner and Camphire beside him, he informed Camphire's father about how he had come to find his way through the man's doorway so many months prior.

"She has informed me of the laws of this town, sir, and before the rest of them find out, we thought it best if we honor these laws and leave in short order. While you may decide not to make my past public, we cannot conceive teaching our children to lie and further insult the Existence that created us, and has thus far had mercy upon my own house, even though I shame myself to continue living."

"Cain, it would be a disgrace if you left my daughter to feed her child alone, and perhaps even a greater shame to take from her the light she seems to think you have brought to her life. Of course we will help you."

A month later, the innkeeper, Growvner, Cain, and his wife set out a full three days' journey from Nod. With them came a boy apprentice of Growvner's to tend Cain's fields under Cain's direction. Growvner arranged with the boy that in exchange for his continued apprenticeship with Cain, and indefinite work with him to supply food for a new center of being-existence for Cain's family and any who enjoyed that center of existence, the boy would be given choice of one of his beautiful daughters who came of age, provided of course there be no objection from her. He further agreed that should they all object, he would honor his arrangement by finding for him a wife who would not deny him the feeling of ease that is proper to a man and woman connecting to create together further life.

Upon arriving three days' journey from Nod, they set to work building a dwelling at once.

"Despite your protestations, son-in-law, this place will be a magnet for those interested in growing crops and sharing in the wisdom of a man who has known pain, and strives with himself to cause the pain he has known no more. What will you call the city you found this day?"

"Sir, you like me too much for me to be able to consider you my father. But your daughter and I were discussing possibilities along the way. We plan on naming our child 'Dedicated' when it is born. It will be dedicated to understanding why the work of its hands has the power to shape the vision of the life others see, and know the weight that that power carries with it. Our city, should it become such, will therefore be named after our child and as our child. It shall be called also 'Dedicated,' that any who enter know that we strive always with the worst of what has come before, that what comes after might somehow be better, and not make said profanities ever but a curse to all who behold them."

The innkeeper nodded his head and smiled. "Son-in-law, despite you, I think still my daughter made a wise choice in keeping you."

A drop of tear fell down to the smile that emitted like a beam of sun from behind a cloud toward the man who had co-created the wife Cain knew and loved.

❧ ❧ ❧

The angels followed the plan for Cain and Camphire to move in compliance with the laws of Nod that stated that murderers may visit Nod, but must live a minimum three days' journey from Nod. They made arrangements to find a place where they could set a new camp; a place they would not be seen, but could ever observe. They decided that they would claim themselves as a city made under similar circumstance as Cain if they were ever encountered, and that they would take extra pains ever to keep Gendlebleth from Cain's sight. Likewise, they also considered appropriate measures that Casarta's red skin would not be seen by a wayward journeyer.

As the angels were traveling past Nod the morning after Cain and his family had left, Casarta, cloaked in hooded garments, was having a conversation with Telnaxson. "I am so very fond of those four-legged pony beasts, Telly. I do wish one morning I could wake up to find one standing outside my tent, ready to be rode over to breakfast."

Later in the day, a young girl in Nod was surprised to find a pony standing outside of her bedroom. Thinking she must still be dreaming, she got onto its back and began riding it through her house. Her parents, eating breakfast at the table, stopped and stared as a pony being rode to breakfast suddenly vanished and the girl fell to the floor, crying in pain upon hitting the ground.

Chapter 17

Somewhere between Eden and Nod wandered one of the great-granddaughters of Man. Tired of the quarreling of giants, some of whom were her siblings, and running from the advances of her brothers, whose advances she found herself repulsed by, it was often that this particular sixteen-year-old great-granddaughter of Adam had found herself making long journeys on foot outside of the lands where her very large family resided. In fact, having the habit of exploring outside of the villages on her own since she had been twelve years old was what had kept her virginity intact up to the present day. She enjoyed her solitude amidst a fourteen-day hike to the middle of where no one would bother her.

In the distance, high above the ground, feeling the pleasure of its experience of the day joyfully, flew Ginsheriel.

Growing weary of remote parts of the world where nature existed for its own sake, and Ginsheriel caused copious amounts of rain for its, it decided to seek out the likeness-creatures of The Divine that it might stimulate its perceptions in mind as much as it had grown accustomed to stimulating its sense of body. It had journeyed from a place beyond a high mountain range, where it had spent much time raining upon creatures that were black and white, and very much like the animal creation known as "bear" in aspect. It was flying from this direction when it spotted below, from a distance, for the first time in many decades, one of the being-likeness creatures of its master Divinity. As it detected the human being from so far away, it slowed the rate of its self-pleasure so that long before she became aware of the creature flying high overhead, she was never aware of a single drop of rain between herself, the sun, and the pleasant cool breeze accompanying her on her journey in the light.

Coming closer to where she was, it observed the dwelling place of most of the descendents of the original likeness-creature far in the distance. Finally able to discern that the likeness-creature below was a *her*, still many miles away from where she hiked enjoying the day, Ginsheriel slowed its self-enjoyment even more, so that only the lightest mist accompanied it further along its course.

From a mile in the distance, where to her the angel looked only like a speck that was likely a large bird that would soon, but not too soon, be flying overhead, the angel now could make out the girl clearly; every detail of her form in focus. To Ginsheriel, she was the most beautiful physical manifestation of The Image Of The Divine it had ever perceived.

Her face shone like the face of its brethren, but held a radiance in her eyes with a knowledge of reality it had never known; something of which only its Master was aware. Her body lacked the wings, but her hair hung long where otherwise it would have expected a shimmering flutter to reside. Her form was wholly inviting as though a fruit newly ripened; the breasts of its brother angels knew no intentions of feeding their offspring, for offspring was not intended as a function of the servants of The Divine. Ginsheriel had often wondered what the lips of its fellow angels would taste like, but All-Knowing-Loving-Endlessness had declared the time for such knowledge would come later, and thus that knowledge was not to be had now. All-Knowing-Loving-Endlessness had made no mention, however, of knowing the taste of a being like in certain appearances of form, but knowing polarization and some aspect of what the Divine Itself knew. Seeing no betrayal of command in it, Ginsheriel circled overhead for a landing.

Seeing the "bird" clearly to become something far more spectacular than what she had thought nothing of from a distance, she was immediately awe-struck by a sight she'd never considered she could see. Sometimes diaphanous and sometimes opaque, the wings of this person pulsed with ripples rather than flaps as its wings reflected pastels of the spectrum broken from the light of the sun. As it came closer, its face took on more a masculine semblance than not, though, apparently *he* had a face as beautiful as any woman, and more so even as this beauty, lightly feminine though it was, was fully the beauty of a man. Seeing his face and the stony muscles of his abdomen made her loin quiver ever so slightly, and she made out for the first time a man, though not a man, who attracted her fully; someone not born, apparently, to her family; someone more than human. Even in the air she could not see his feet, for a pair of his wings were held over them. The light danced brilliantly through the very gentle mists that accompanied him while he made his decent toward her. Upon his landing, she had no choice but to notice the movement of the phallus it possessed, which she had known best in experience only from bathing her baby brothers, and some particularly lewd moments when her older brothers were intoxicated or returning from hunting, or both, interacting with the part of his body that resembled apparently what she possessed, like her sisters, which her brothers did *not* have. The quaver rose deeper inside of her as she looked on in confusion to rethink that what she had taken as being male was perhaps something other than male, or at least *more* than male.

Ginsheriel smiled brightly upon her while her mouth rather naturally hung open in disbelief. From several feet away, she was even more beautiful than it had perceived from a distance. From this close up, whatever it was shone bright, though surrounded by mists, the luminance of the sun refracting off wings and mists and smile; the gleam of eternity shining forth from its eyes. Ginsheriel spoke to her as for the first time in two centuries, it stopped creating precipitation of any kind. "Do not be frightened. Seeing your beauty from a far distance, I wished only to know what this was causing me to know from that distance beauty the likes of which I have never known before."

She saw clearly, as the mists quickly evaporated, that what had enabled it to create such mists now throbbed alone toward her. She had never been called beautiful before. Her brothers, when they had reached a certain age, had called her something like beautiful before trying to pounce upon her, usually while in a delirious stupor. But this was the first time something looked at her with such purity and honesty and saw of her only beauty, and then called her that by name. Her mouth continued to hang agape as her mind raced with possibilities while it stepped closer to her. *It* was so beautiful, and had seen her as beautiful in return. Some part of her considered running, as she did not know what would come if she didn't turn away, but it was all so glorious and wonderful; its beauty rendered her mute and still, while the fullness of it stirred the nethermost desires in her. She felt no resistance as the back of her head felt the strength and warmth of its hand, and she felt her lips pulled to its; its tongue pushed to hers.

Its wings spread wide, and then tightly around her as she gave over to the fullness, *him*. She felt herself lifted into the air as ecstasy proceeded to fill her in every part. Over the course of the next two months, he was her sole sustenance, and together they danced in the clouds.

Seven months later, long after she had wobbled her way back into the villages, and finally her parents home, her parents wondered how she could be giving birth when none of her brothers could claim her as a helper to their own house. Seven months after having been left to the ground shortly before the angel had flown off, leaving behind a trail of mists in its wake, the first great warrior of renown was born to Earth.

Chapter 18

Enoch sat at his father's feet. "Abba, why do we exist?"

Jared raised an eyebrow in response. "That's quite a question for a five-year-old, Enoch." He stared at his son for a few moments while Enoch stared back, still, silent, awaiting a response. Jared stroked his chin as he slowly began to speak again. "The truth is, son, I don't really know. But I'm sure God had a very good reason." Jared folded his arms and reclined, contented that he had answered his child's question well.

"Who is God, Daddy?"

The contentment left Jared's face, and he became again tense. "Why, He's the creator of us!"

"Then can you take me to him, so that I can ask him why he created us?"

"Well, son, as far as I know, the last person to have a conversation with God was your great-great-great-great-grandfather, Adam. If the question is still with you in the springtime, I suppose you could ask him at the time in which we celebrate his creation and the fact that he is the origin of all of our existences, if you like..."

"You can't just ask him now?"

"Well, son, it is a bit of a journey from here. And being as young as you are, I'm not sure how the old man would receive your question, since you are so young. But, as I said before, if this question burns inside of you with such sincerity that you would still retain it till the time of the celebration of his existence's beginning, I'm sure he will be intrigued enough, and be impressed enough by the sincerity of the invention-of-mind by the furthest reaches of his creativity, that he will be happy to answer you with the full extent of what he thinks the most useful answer to your questions could be."

Enoch was hardly satisfied by his father's response. However, content that his question was a sincere one and tormented so by his question accordingly, he decided that he would wait the short life-time to the spring, so that he could receive the answer from the one person his father claimed could address it.

⚜⚜⚜

Amidst the festivities of the spring, sitting upon an ornate chair, hand-carved by his grandson Human Being, Adam sat watching the existences he had created enjoying existence around him. From out of the crowd walked Descent, in hand with Dedicated. Descent spoke first. "Great-Great-Great-Grandfather, I honor your creation upon this day! My son, Dedicated, if it be pleasing to you on this day of the joy of your existence, has an unusual question which he would like to ask you, that has been troubling him, apparently, for some time."

"Of course!" responded the 627-year-old man with a wide, beaming smile toward his five-year-old, great-great-great-great-grandson. "I've been alive long enough that I welcome anything one of my creations deems 'unusual.' What is this vexation of the mind that has you disturbed, so very young Dedicated? Please, sit on my knee."

The young Enoch climbed atop his ancient ancestor's knee. "Great-Great-Great-Great-Grandfather, what I asked my father months ago, which he apparently couldn't answer, was, 'why do we exist?' To which my father responded that 'God has a good reason,' so I asked if I could talk to God so that I could meet him and talk to him myself. Dad said if anyone knows where God is so I could ask him, it would be you." Dedicated recollected his breath as Man answered him.

Smiling, Adam replied, "You exist, my young descendent, so that God could look at Itself. If you wish to ask of God, you have but to silence your own voice completely, and any question you could have will quickly be answered."

Dedicated stared up at the old man with eyes wide and mouth agape. He found himself instantly silent and looking into the first eyes that ever perceived existence. He nodded, thanked his great-great-great-great-grandfather, and then climbed off his knee. Dedicated found himself silent from the moment his feet touched the ground, to the moment he took his father's hand and they made their way home from the gathering, until finally he was tucked into his bed. That night, Enoch dreamed of sitting in the middle of a field, all alone, on a warm summer day, staring at a doe several feet off, not a thought in his head.

Chapter 19

Enoch sat at his father's feet. "Abba, how did you get that scar on your forehead?"

Cain stirred in his chair while his mind raced through his own father's words to him after his head had landed on the rock upon which he had been thrown years prior. "Son, I knew this day would come eventually, but I did not think you would be only five years old before I'd be considering answering it for the first time..."

As they were leaving Nod, Camphire explained to Cain the benefits of never keeping his crime a secret to the people of Nod, nor to anyone else he would meet along his path in life. She was adamant as well that no matter what he said to others on the subject, that he ever only be honest with their children. "For if we should lie to our children, then they should not trust us as they learn the awkwardness of taking full responsibility for their own actions and the responsibility they have for the consequences that will inevitably result. When they lean toward lying to themselves, it is their trust in us that may prevent them from believing their own lies, as they would learn to accept as the law of existence any lie we would demonstrate to them in lieu of what is." Gravely Cain nodded his assent while she admonished him the consequences of acting out of his shame, rather than fighting against it so as to respond to his past by creating his future from the wish of his heart to be whole again, where once by his own hand it was broken.

"The truth is, son, my father acted out of his rage toward me after I had done the worst thing a person can do, and I landed hard on a rock, where you see the scar I now bear."

Enoch's face shadowed over as he asked the obvious question. "What is the worst thing you can do, that you did to make your father angry with you, Father?"

"The worst thing a man can do, Enoch, is to kill his brother."

Enoch began to contemplate his father's words as he considered the life growing in his mother's belly.

ॡॡॡ

Knowing his father's story, Dedicated strove to live up to his name within the context of the town with which he shared it. A village of his parents, their friends and acquaintances, his brothers and sisters, and the occasional chance passer-by. While it was rare one en route to Nod would stay in Dedicated to rest before continuing their journey, every several months a pair of angels in humanity's clothing would come under such pretense. In this way, the development of Cain and his offspring were monitored, that the angels might learn further how to serve.

Incognito envoys were sent regularly to Nod to monitor other human interaction, and the angels kept their camp miles to the west of Dedicated, where they existed unseen. While all the monitoring was taking place, and the angels learned about their own physical existence and the existence of adam, Casarta explored and spied in her own right, always from a distance sure from the sight of those who shared her form, but not her origin, nor the particular hue of her skin.

It was one day while she was spying on the town from its outskirts that she was having a bit of a daydream. She was envisioning herself at the center of a flock of crows encircling her. In her vision, the crows came to where she sat and flocked together so that their wings were joined and she was able to ride upon their backs, which formed as though one gigantic crow, which carried her high into the sky and let her see the earth as they saw.

While she was having this vision at the outskirts of the town, Handoroth and Caldas were masquerading as visitors, being led through the town's center. As they were being shown to a place they would be allowed to stay for several nights, and told that the town would gladly share of their food and water to these passers-by, who were happy to share with the town some of the goods they carried from lands far away, suddenly the sun was engulfed and a shadow fell upon them all. Looking up, all who had sight perceived dozens of crows descend upon them. Lo, they amassed together in the town's center and stood silent simultaneously, as though waiting. Handoroth and Caldas stared at each other, asking the same question of each other, and giving the same answer in reply.

For ten minutes they stood watching the birds, who held together virtually motionless while the people of the town remained huddled close to the ground, occasionally peeking out at the birds from under arms covering their heads. After about ten minutes passed, the birds vanished as though into thin air. Handoroth and Caldas spent the next evening, as well as the next several days, convincing the people of the town that the birds were not an ill omen as the townsfolk busied themselves sacrificing animals in the hopes of appeasing God, who was clearly very angry with them for some reason they did not understand.

After spending a week in the village "resting" from their "long" journey, and spending much time calming the village, Caldas and Handoroth returned once more to their own village to confer with their brethren. As they were telling the story of what they had seen, Casarta joined the meeting of the angels.

"Why, that sounds exactly like the daydream I was having several days ago."

All the angels turned and stared at Casarta.

"What?" asked Casarta.

"We do not believe in coincidences," Darwith replied.

Chapter 20

"Then why have we not seen such materializations from nothingness before?"

"That doesn't mean that they have not transpired in the past, Antagnous. I heard a story from one of Cain's new attendants of a horse mysteriously appearing in his eating room, and then disappearing into the air, while he was still living in Nod. That story was from around the time we moved from Nod."

Gernow spoke next. "I too heard a story about a lamb dancing on its hind legs and singing before vanishing without trace, only a couple months ago in Enoch."

Casarta spoke up as the angels discussed whether these stories, along with what Caldas and Handoroth had seen, could in any way be linked to Casarta herself. "These instances, while the stories you describe as second-hand accounts are not exact, nonetheless sound very much like the wanderings my mind has had from time to time."

Again the village of angels stared at the young, red girl. Spoke up Ternaddain, "Have you seen these 'wanderings of your mind' made flesh in any instance of pondering them, child?"

"Well, no," she answered, "but I can't deny that the timing and the instances described bear great resemblance to what I can remember of certain images I considered in my thoughts."

Darwith spoke next. "When you have made these images in your mind, Casarta, did you ascribe a place to them?"

Casarta shook her head. "No, Darwith, I think only of something that the laws of the existence set out by Our Common Mother Universal Endlessness could not abide in functional reality. I never think so far as location, since I always imagine these things as what could not exist to begin with."

"Then, Casarta," continued Darwith, "I recommend a test. Think of something happening right here in the middle of our circle, as you would be inclined on the average day in which you 'let your mind wander.'"

"What shall I conceive?" asked Casarta.

"Think of two rabbits doing something in the middle of our circle which they would not otherwise be inclined to do..."

Gendlebleth shuddered for an instant at the mention of rabbits, then silenced his accustomed automatic impulses associated with the small furry creatures while he anticipated what might happen next.

Casarta thought for a moment silently, then turned her attention to the middle of the circle to see if anything would come out of the unlikely scenario her imaginings led her to conceive.

For a moment, nothing happened. Then, spontaneously, in the middle of the circle appeared two bunny rabbits.

Initially they just sat there. One scrunched its nose a bit, the other hopped around a little. The angels looked intently upon the creatures, but were less than impressed, considering that they perhaps had simply arrived without being noticed. Then, one of the bunnies started hopping in reverse around the other bunny.

Faster and faster, the rabbit started running a reverse circle around the other. The angels began having to shield their eyes from the dirt being kicked up in their direction while dust rose up, making the stationary rabbit almost completely non-visible. Then, from out of the dust, the other rabbit flew off into the air, its forward paws straight in front of it as it soared into the night toward the stars. Suddenly, the first rabbit bounded onto Gendlebleth's shoulder, kissed him on the cheek, and vanished into thin air.

Feeling the scrunching of the rabbit's nose against his chin, Gendlebleth fainted on the spot.

Noting the ring left behind after the dust had settled, Antagnous commented under her breath, "Well, I guess that answers that."

Once again, all those around the circle turned their attention to Casarta. Casarta felt the stare of all her tribe upon her, though nonetheless, couldn't help but have to suppress the giggles automatically finding their way to her lips.

Chapter 21

Enoch led a gifted life. He was the firstborn son of firstborn sons, traced back all the way to the third-born son of Humanity. As such, he was highly regarded in the land in which he grew up. He spent most of his time, from the age of about six and a half years old, sitting by a flowing river with his eyes closed. He wanted always ever to be in the presence of God.

He'd begun from the age of about five letting his mind rest, and thus taking in the fullness of the reality surrounding him without interruption from the thoughts of his head. As he grew older, however, he began to find more and more that this process was becoming ever more difficult. His mother would teach him something, his father would teach him something, the children would invite him to play, he would see something he'd never seen before, he'd wonder about something he'd never considered before; he noticed his mind becoming noisier the further through life he went.

When he was about six years old, his father had brought him with him to the river to wash the family's clothing, and as Enoch sat by his father, his feet in the water, beating a wet loin cloth against a boulder close to the bank of the river, he observed that his mind was filled with the sound of the river rather than the thoughts in his head. From this time thereafter, he walked down to the river often, that he might ever hear God's voice speaking to him.

A few months later, noticing his eyes bring thoughts to his brain, he began the practice of closing them, that the silence of his self would be ever-complete.

Nearing his early teenage years, Enoch found that with the changing of his body came also a shift in his capacity for retaining the clarity of his mind, and the Divinity it heard.

Most of the firstborn of the line of Seth followed Seth's example by seeking distant cousins with whom to marry, at ages in which they could discern something about lasting companionship with the person they chose. By the time Enoch was nearing his early teenage years, he was already very familiar with the life-lessons of his great-great-great-grandfather. Nonetheless, as he was beginning to notice the forms of his various female cousins and younger aunts passing by him during his regular day life, he was daunted by the strength of his natural animal-self that he had not experienced prior to the new developments of his body.

So it was, when he was about twelve and a half years existent, he found that try as he might to drown his mind in the river, the blank slate of the back of his eyelids continued to show Enoch the images of certain more appealing family members who seemed to unceasingly stimulate the emergence of his... thoughts... more so than the silence through which he felt the fullness of his connectivity to The Creator, whose feeling he constantly craved. Around the age of 42, he gave up on trying to escape his thoughts and he began taking walks in the hopes merely of turning his attention from the life of the small town for an afternoon now and then.

It was around the age of 62 and a half that he was introduced to one of the great-great-great-great-great-great-great-great-great-great-great-great-great great-great-great-great-great-great-great-great-granddaughters of Seth.

Enoch was walking along the river bank, striving with himself to silence his own mind as he asked loudly into it, "Will ever a day come that I will again hear the voice of That Which Created Me and All Existence, and what, if any, action is required of me that I might again hear Its voice?" In the wake of the severity and loudness with which he asked this into his own brain, he discovered a moment of silence penetrate through the exhaustion of the fullness of force of his own inner rambling. As that silence filled where thought had been, several seconds later his eyes spotted something up ahead by the river's edge.

With her eyes closed, she lay with her arms propping her torso up off the ground, her face toward the sun, naked, with her feet just off the side of the river, but not in the water itself. Enoch continued toward her beauty in wonder and silence as his eyes widened and he wondered over the best way possible to disturb her tranquility. His heart was heard in his ears, and his legs became wobbly, his mind considering the image of lowering himself down to her and making his presence known by placing his own lips to hers.

About six feet from where she lay, the rustling of the grass under his feet drew her attention to him without the need of any help from his mouth. She turned her head sharply toward him, covering the sun from her eyes to see him clearly. She smiled up at him. "I didn't think anyone would come out this far from town." She blushed as she spoke.

"Nor did I," responded Enoch. "Since it seems to be our common desire, how would you feel if I stayed for a while and we experienced being alone, together?"

From behind a tree in the distance, Kellendreth smiled to Humdow, who watched beside her after the seventh generation of Adam. Though they could not hear the words spoken, they both found beauty in seeing Enoch lie down by the woman; the two passing the time beside each other, watching the flowing of the river before them.

A little more than two and a half years later, as they looked at *him* and each other, they decided to name their first son as one who would not die until he chose of his own accord to do so. So was born to Enoch and the descendent of Man by way of Appointed, Who Demands His Death.

It was as he was watching his son come from his wife, and hearing Methuselah's first cry, that Enoch understood fully the continuity of the means by which The Divine knew itself infinitely. As his own eyes saw that different eyes would see the same and otherwise, it was that once again his mind grew silent, and he found there he heard all the answers to the questionings of whatever voices spoke into him as he understood again how to find The Lord. After he kissed the forehead of his wife, who now held the child she had produced from her own body as all Adam had ever been brought forth from the earth, he let her rest with their baby held at peace to her chest, and he left their dwelling toward the cool night air, and took a walk.

Chapter 22

Enoch led a gifted life. Having a town named after him earned him the respect of all who lived there, and even those who were merely passing through. Honored though he was to be glorified by the place of his existence by those who habitated there, so too was he humbled by his father, who had dedicated his life to the existence of others even long before he had been introduced to the light of the sun, or tasted the air without which he could not imagine being.

All the more humbling, the shadow of his father fell upon him that he should dedicate his own life to others, where once his father had taken the life of his own brother in vain. Learning to till the soil and plant his seed, Dedicated embraced the reality that, while the work of his hands led to his own sustenance, beyond the sustenance of his family, others too benefited from what he grew. As he wiped the dirt from his hands, he understood fully his father's sadness that where once the earth sang to him as though to her intimate lover, because of his betrayal to those whom he was commanded from on high to feed, so he was cursed to live a life limited in what he could give to others. Understanding the work of his own hands, he understood that his father had dedicated his life to never wander crippled to his own purpose for existence, as his father had crippled himself.

Likewise, Cain smiled brightly the first time he saw his son attempt to lift a hoe when he was little more than two years old. All the more proud of his son when he was to taste the fruits of Enoch's first harvest, nine years later.

Then came the day, twenty-one years after his son was born, so was born to Dedicated City Has Witnessed. For when Enoch had discussed with his wife, they decided that as he perceived what his own life would be, Irad would decide his own course based on what the city of Dedicated had become. In this name they had conceived that if the good his father had attempted to sew in Enoch were to live on, so it would be solidified in what their son did with his understanding of what had come before him.

As they elucidated to themselves their hope for their son's future, so did the angels incarnate of humanity witness what the word directed most likely the city would be.

☙ ☙ ☙

Meanwhile, as Enoch and Irad grew up, so too did Casarta. Now very much a beautiful young woman, Antagnous, Lousitous, and Gendlebleth took her some distance from the city of Dedicated along with Taolith and Lajiel. It had been decided that if Casarta's mind was capable of disrupting the lives of those whom the angels were hoping to observe, without making the true natures known of a band of angels choosing to be enfleshed, then Casarta must learn to be ever-vigilant of her own mind. Based on her brain's previous wanderings, they decided that that might take practice. No one knew what her mind was capable of, least of all Casarta, so they agreed on the wisdom of sending her off relatively alone for a time to discover the full scope of what her thoughts could do.

While angels would come from closer to Dedicated to bring news and visit with their brethren, Antagnous and Gendlebleth never left Casarta's encampment.

She began practicing.

They verified that her dreams did not come to life while she slept. They discovered that the weather could be turned a short time by her mind, though rain that fell fed no flower, and left only dry soil after it had fallen. They found that she could move permanent objects with the objects created by her mind, and that what her mind created could be sustained to last as long as her focus on what was created could be held. She spent a very long time practicing the dismissal of thoughts which she had not called to her reason specifically. So long as her imaginings were centered in the reality that was at her hand, nothing more nor less was created. When her conception did wander, returning it to the ground at her feet dispersed the possibility of impossibility that otherwise was inclined to be made physical, but momentarily.

So too did the angels learn about the powers of their own minds made physical with the laws that governed the minds of other humans in whose images theirs had been created. Isolated in a small group from the rest of their kind, they found that they could communicate with each other rather effectively merely by glancing at each other. In some instances, it was as though they could hear words the other had thought before they spoke it out loud. While they were unable to make manifest solid forms out of thin air, like Casarta, they seemed to be able to hear something of each other even over the long expanse of space between where they spent some years dwelling, and the village set up miles outside of Enoch.

In fact, even though they could not create something out of nothing, what they did find was that often they would have a thought materialize in what was already present. Gendlebleth would think himself hungry, and mere minutes later a large lizard would appear, and he had but to call upon Antagnous to hunt for dinner. Another time they found themselves running out of water. Shortly thereafter Taolith, walking along to be alone without thought, found her way to a nearby spring they'd not known about before. It was as though their minds discovered what they'd not yet known they would need already created, always waiting mere steps away to be discovered. They came to find that while they could not create from nothingness, their own minds, in their way, *did* shape the reality they came to experience. Even emotion seemed to physically dictate the results they'd experience from day to day. Though Casarta was gifted, it seemed that mankind as well had thoughts at their disposal to shape reality as they were capable of conceiving it.

While they reflected on what their own thoughts appeared capable of, and Casarta honed the focus of her personal mind, the way the city of Dedicated took shape made sense to them all within the context of the many conceptions the people of the city put into its inner workings daily.

Chapter 23

In the cool of the night, Dedicated saw with his eyes by the light of the moon. He considered briefly that by the automated actualization of existence put forth by the creation of Man, so would eyes ever exist by which to see exactly the same. Though the eyes would see ever different, there was nothing else, after all, to see. Knowing, in the silence of the night, by moon and chirp of cricket, that that which he would ask of anything saw fully through his own ears and eyes, he understood the continuity of life as it would always be through bodies before death. He walked fully in the knowledge of what one could appreciate about the completeness of Divinity, should one choose to look inward.

Walking, so he saw the days of his life pass before his eyes. Days turned into nights. He walked from forest to dwelling to the riverside, each placement shifting by the next motion of his stride. Before thought could rise without his desire for its presence, he wished himself always mindful of That Which Created All Existence Indiscriminate. He would answer his body's calls that spoke without thought; he would feed himself, purge himself, join in unity with the flesh housing the same spark of Creation's Perceptions as saw too through him, and father the children that resulted accordingly; answer the needs of his wife as he walked through the life that he enjoyed, that he was himself the tool by which it was created. As the incarnated angels watched over the direct descendents of Adam, so too did they watch, in wonder, the life of Enoch.

When Enoch was 363 years old, he had a conversation with his wife. "I have known myself as fully as my mind can conceive, yet I have not walked as far as my legs can take me. Will you forgive me, Yofi Meikhil Aish Eloki, if I should explore Divinity's existence beyond what I have known, unfortunately outside of the Grace of your voice should you honor the air by calling to me?"

"Husband, our children are old enough to walk without much need for us at present, and I am presently not carrying a child who would miss having a father upon light first touching its eyes. Though I will miss your warmth at night, I know that you crave every bit of experience your existence might allow you to understand. I cannot stand in the path you walk while existence blesses me with The Love of The Light, even without the beauty of your face showing me most of the life I have spent *my* time being grateful for. I will look forward to the returning of you who is Dedicated ever to walking with That Which Has Created Us All."

With that, Enoch began to walk toward the sun at daybreak.

❧ ❧ ❧

Months of wandering later, Enoch wondered after the sight far below him and the hill on which he now stood. Catching his breath and resigning himself to what he was seeing, he continued walking. Several hours later, he found himself at an inn in the town of Nod.

The balding, white-haired innkeeper greeted Enoch with a smile as Enoch walked through the door and sat down at the bar. "Looks like you've been on a bit of a journey, lad. Help you to a drink?"

Enoch blinked at the old man in his strange-looking clothing. "I could use some water, though I have no way at present to reciprocate your kindness, save for the many dried berries I am currently carrying."

"Well, berries won't get ya a cup of wine normally, but water's on the house. If you have a story to share of your journeys, though, that might be worth a cup of intoxicant from blood of the fruit of the vine..."

Enoch drank gratefully from the cup handed to him while he told a simple tale to the innkeeper. "I've walked that I might know of the creations of God all I can before I meet the same fate as befell who was first-born to existence, fifty-five years ago."

"Come again?" The innkeeper was confused by what Enoch had said.

"Adam, the first man to exist. He died fifty-five years ago or so, and I wish to know what I can of existence, if what happened to him is what will one day happen to my own body."

"I don't know about who was the first man ever born upon this Earth," responded the innkeeper, "but I can respect a man living his life to its fullest before dropping dead. What have you learned of God from your journeys, stranger?"

"That it is through our own eyes It watches, and that It calls Itself by our own names."

The innkeeper stared at Dedicated for a moment and recognized something in his eyes. He took a deep gulp, poured Enoch a cup of wine, and passed it to him. "If you speak no more of your journeys this night, you can have another on the house!"

❧ ❧ ❧

The next day, the innkeeper brought Enoch to a stable where he could find steady work cleaning up after the horses in order to pay his way for the time he decided to stay in the community. After a month or so of living in

Nod, he heard the innkeeper discuss his son-in-law, Cain, one night.

"Forgive me," interrupted Enoch, "but did you just speak of Cain, son of the first man existent?"

The innkeeper gave Enoch a queer stare, which was often the case when Enoch spoke. "I don't know about the first man existent; we can count humanity's roots back thousands of years. But I do have a son-in-law who lives a short distance from here..."

Enoch ignored the absurdity of the innkeeper's notion that anything had existed even a thousand years before, let alone several thousand. He motioned the innkeeper to bring his ear closer to his own face before asking, "Do you happen to know if Cain has done anything in his past of which he might be deeply regretful?"

The innkeeper stood upright quickly, looked deeply into Enoch's eyes, and nodded his head gravely.

"Do you happen to know," inquired Dedicated, "is Cain, brother of Abel, still alive?

cho cho cho

Enoch was very surprised to learn that an entire village shared his same name, and that Cain's son had been given also the same name he had been given. He journeyed to the city of Enoch, as quickly as his legs would allow, to seek out his cousin and great-great-great-great uncle. Following closely behind him since he had left the land East of Eden, through Nod, and now to the city of Dedicated, were Childreth, Kakarnan, Randolfy, and Lemisslept.

Quick on their feet, the four angels following behind Dedicated, improvised stories regarding being wanderers from other lands while they marveled, and were quite confused that humans existed in other places than where they had observed the descendents of the first man and first woman they'd witnessed being created. They were shocked to perceive adam living independently from the creation of the first pair they were given to know about. Such revelation made them question their own existences. They tried to push these growing concerns to the backs of their minds, however, as they were determined to follow through on their current mission to keep track of Enoch, descendent of Placed.

It was on the outskirts of the city of Enoch that they were greeted warmly by Taolith and Gendlebleth, who were just leaving the city as their watch was coming to an end. "Go with Gendlebleth, brothers," Taolith smiled warmly upon them after formal greetings came to an end. "I will tell those on active watch to monitor Enoch as he seeks Enoch. The others will have much to tell you of the past several hundred years, and what wonders our daughter-sister Casarta has the capability of..."

With that, they were led to the encampment of the angels who had followed after Created.

⚜ ⚜ ⚜

At the door of the home of Cain, Enoch knocked. A young-looking man with a scar on his forehead answered the door and greeted Enoch, "Hello. How may I help you?"

"Good afternoon, sir," began Dedicated, "I am looking for Created, son of Man and Living, who I have been told lives at this house. Have I come here in error?"

Cain paused for a moment before responding, "It is not wide knowledge in this land the name of my parents, stranger. Who would like to find the man named by his parents Created?"

Enoch looked hard at Cain before continuing. "How is this possible? You look so young. You cannot be the Created who slew his brother Emptiness over nine hundred years ago! Forgive me. I am the great-great-great-grandson of Appointed, brother of Created and Emptiness, who knew neither of these brothers, for both were no longer within his father's house at the time of his birth. . ."

Now it was Cain who was looking hard at Dedicated before responding. "You mean to say that my father had a son, Seth, and that you are *his* great-great-great-grandson?"

"Yes, sir. I am your great-great-great-grandnephew, Enoch."

"Then no wonder you are confused by my appearance. In point of fact, you are not the first who has been, and frankly even I am deeply troubled that my own son looks older than I do by hundreds of years. Please come in. Perhaps you would like to meet my firstborn son, who shares your name? He was about to leave, but I doubt he will want to miss conversation with a distant cousin from a life I left behind me long ago. . ."

With that, Dedicated entered the home of Created.

Chapter 24

Enoch was, in fact, quite surprised to see Enoch next to his father, for Enoch looked as though he were five hundred years older than his father.

As he approached, Enoch smiled warmly at the man entering the room who shared his name. "Can we get you a cup of tea, Dedicated?" he asked.

Dedicated smiled as he responded to his cousin. "Yes, Dedicated, I'd like that very much."

Cain looked up to his distant nephew and smiled, though his past pulled at him while he braced himself for answering questions about the beginnings of his life. "What has brought you to the city of Dedicated, Dedicated?"

"I have spent my life walking with God. Knowing that there may be an end of my days once I perceived the dissolution of your father's being, it came to me in my contemplation on That Which Created Me that I spend some time walking with Our Mutual Source of Experiencing All Perception as I haven't before. So, as I walked, my legs led me finally to Nod."

Cain smirked to himself, recalling the journey *he* had once made from East of Eden to Nod.

"And hearing the almost unbelievable story of the innkeeper in Nod, I felt naturally compelled to seek out the city that shares my name, to find out what several months ago I never would have imagined I might be able to learn about myself."

It was as he was finishing his thought that a woman who looked to be almost as old as Eve herself entered the room.

"And who is this young man, husband? I was not aware we were expecting company..."

"Cami, his name is Enoch." Camphire looked quickly at her son at the other side of the room, then to the man she had never met called Enoch, before bringing her attention back to her husband's words. "Apparently after I left my parents, they had another son, Seth, and this is my brother's great-great-great-grandson." Camphire now stared in awe at Dedicated, again looked briefly at her own son, and back once more.

"Welcome to our home, great-great-great-grandnephew of my husband." After making this statement she found herself without further words.

"Thank you," Enoch replied. "Did I hear Cain right that he called you 'Cami'?"

"Short for Camphire" replied Cain. "As beautiful a flower as any I could ask. You say my father recently died?" Camphire sat, her gaze still on Enoch with some amount of disbelief. The conversation continued.

"Yes. It is the first time we have been aware that such a thing could happen without it being caused from outside of ourselves." Enoch stopped speaking quickly and stared at Cain, not knowing if he had offended his host.

Cain replied, "Yes, in this land death is fairly common when a body becomes old. How it is that I have maintained my own vitality when my family has aged around me, as you see, is a mystery to us all. Of course, though she would seem a bit older than I, clearly my wife has only become more beautiful since the day we met."

Camphire smiled up at her husband. "Though I fear I'm currently about as moldy as a plucked tomato left in a bowl in the shade for a month unattended, I appreciate that the love of my husband has diminished no more than his body has over the last several hundred years. But what brings you to the city of Dedicated, young..." and here for a moment she paused, feeling momentarily the dizzying effect of the word "Dedicated?"

"As I was telling your husband just before you entered, it has become my practice, as a means by which I can feel better connected to What Created Existence, to follow my feet wherever they may take me. So I have found myself here."

Camphire, still a bit dizzied from the wealth of Dedicated in her presence, smiled up at her guest. "Well, nephew, whatever the case, we will be honored to have you stay with us for as long as you like. Enoch, my son, please prepare a bed for your cousin; I'm sure he's weary from his journey, and would like to rest a bit before we begin exchanging hundreds of years worth of stories."

With that, Enoch prepared a place for Enoch to stay, for the time he would spend residing in the city.

⚜ ⚜ ⚜

Upon entering the encampment of the angels, Childreth, Kakarnan, Randolfy, and Lemisslept were met with smiles, hugs, and their brethren coming out of tents all around to meet these of their own service, whom they had not seen for quite some time.

Darwith spoke when all of their encampment had been assembled. "Greetings, sisters! Greetings, brothers! I see Gendlebleth has returned absent Taolith. What news of how you have come to bless us with your familiarity?"

So spoke Randolfy, "Our good pleasure to meet sister Taolith and brother Gendlebleth along our path to Enoch as we were watching over the path of Enoch, son of Jared, son of Mahalalel, son of Kenan, son of Enosh, son of Seth, son of Adam."

So spoke Antagnous, "Then you have been made aware by Gendlebleth that Cain's son named both his own son, and the city he came to found, likewise Dedicated?"

Responded Gendlebleth, "Indeed I have made them aware. I also made them aware of Lamech's exclamation when he murdered that wanderer into Enoch several years back. I told them of how he is still in deep mourning, even to this day, and about how his wives care for him. How Cain frequently invites him to make productive use of his time. How he pays the internal penance of reconciling the fact that he ended a part of his self that was destined to find its own way into infinite re-incorporation otherwise, had he not so suddenly ended the expression of the separateness of himself creating based upon its own individuated state of being before it had naturally occurred to organic circumstance that such was the proper transformation of the elements of said young man."

"Yes," responded Handoroth, "it is a shame that Lamech was too drunk that night to be able to consciously mitigate his internal impulse of confusion and frustration of his own pain to stop himself from solidifying the impulse of pain within himself, apparently to some degree permanently, so long as he embodies differentiation from That Which Created Us All."

"Aside from the tales of Cain's children," continued Gendlebleth, "of which I was thorough in my account, I did hint at, without describing, the wonder that is our common daughter though blood directly of Antagnous and Lousitous."

"Then it would seem proper I introduce my own talents without stories of what has been perceived directly by others." A smile hung from cherry-red lips that poked through the edges of the crowd surrounding Kakarnan, Lemisslept, Childreth, and Randolfy. Suddenly a great brightness filled the air surrounding them. Looking up, a great deal of fire hung in the sky not thirty feet above their heads. Taking a step back, they all could see a gigantic bird made of flame slowly lowering itself toward them, and all moved out of the way accordingly. The gigantic flaming bird landed upon the ground in the center of the beings surrounding her. She issued a deafening screech, her head moving from side to side. Finally, shortly after landing, she disappeared, leaving not so much as a scorched piece of ash behind where she had stood just moments prior.

Stepping forward, her hood around her neck and a smile continuing on her face, spoke Casarta, "I have grown since last I have seen you, my family, and I have learned some new tricks."

ﻌﻌﻌ

Zarnuchtron, and Warmoot decided that they would like to return to the lands occupied by the descendents of Adam. Randolfy and Lemisslept decided to reside closer to the city of Dedicated. Warmoot and Zarnuchtron bowed deeply to Casarta's grace and bid their fellows goodbye before taking up the journey with Childreth and Kakarnan at the edge of Dedicated, to witness the path of Dedicated whom walked with God further.

ﻌﻌﻌ

In the home of Cain, Enoch bowed deeply to his host and hostess who had housed him for the greater portion of the year; with whom he had shared tales of the descendents of Adam, the intrusion of the angels upon the daughters of Adam, and the lives of the offspring of Dedicated in the same-named city. Dedicated marveled that adam existed where the common father of he and Cain had never sewn *his* seed, and wondered after what he had been taught that in the beginning only Adam had existed, the sole human creation of All-Existence-Common-Uni-Being-Endlessness.

Dedicated bid the city and cousin that bore his name a fond farewell. He began walking in the direction he believed his wife to be, where he had known her to be last, for when he silenced his mind and cleared his thoughts, it was her face that was shown clearly to him beyond any other silence he could allow to occupy his self.

He turned to look a last time upon Dedicated, wishing it a goodbye with gratitude for having spent time there. Turning again, he set himself toward the place he had known best upon the Earth as his home.

✿✿✿

Looking to his wife, Cain spoke, "I am grateful to know that my father began a tribe of humanity after my passing away from him, even if they are ignorant of the fullness that exists beyond where they have so far been."

"Husband," replied Camphire, "I am grateful to see wonder and gratitude in your eyes for what your life has brought you." She gazed within his eyes as she spoke, and as he extended his hands to her, and she took them, he was happy gazing back into the eyes of the consciousness that had brought him to a life far beyond the scream that had filled his ears from his chest so many centuries past.

✿✿✿

In the city of Dedicated, that night all citizens felt their cheeks kissed by a warm breeze as dreams of sweet tastes filled their resting minds.

Chapter 25

He entered their home late at night, his feet tired from a very long walk from Dedicated to East of Eden. As he entered their bed and wrapped his arms around his wife, he could feel her smile in the darkness. Feeling his heart satisfied by her warmth, he decided upon that feeling that he would wait until the morning came before informing her what steps he knew he must now take. With a heavy, grateful heart, he waited for the light of the sun to waken him from a cocoon of bliss mixed with a mind whose singular disruption was too loud for the continued contentment that otherwise silence would bring.

❧ ❧ ❧

"I wish to ask for your permission, Isha."

"When, my husband, have you not had it?"

"Nonetheless..."

She noticed the heaviness of his eyes as they looked toward the ground in a far corner of the room.

"Look to *me*, my husband. What thought could be in your mind to weigh your head away from my face?"

"The thought, my love, that I ought not be here longer."

Now it was she who paused in heaviness as her mouth hung just slightly open, still in indecision of what answer to make. She swallowed, and he spoke.

"Returning at last, and finding my peace with you, I heard an emotional impulse, brief, as though it were a voice, and in this I understood the meaning. I understood the meaning, for as it was interpreted instinctively in my head-brain, my emotional center was tranquil at once in affirmation of what I thought the impulse within me to mean."

"Why, my husband, will you not be returning?" she responded as though hearing what was upon his tongue's tip before he had taken the time to form it there by conscious volition of his intellect.

"I do not know, love. Merely that my feet will not sustain my walk where I arrive, and that it will not be an unpleasantness."

As she recalled the unsettling fate of Adam, not fifty-seven years prior, she was made uneasy to recall what they all had seen of him, as though a bird fresh for de-feathering. And she was about to speak –

"No, Eden, I do not believe *his* fate will be mine. Though I know I will not be able to hold you again, as I have been blessed to, once I arrive where I am going."

"Then you have decided this already, husband, and need no word from me to set yourself where your feet will carry you. Be gone, then!"

"No, wife. Though I may hear an echo through my mind for as long as my days, until I should become as rigid as the first man, dead, if such is my fate, without the joy in your heart for who I am as I am led on, as is my wish, where my heart connects with what moves my feet, I would not break my covenant with you. Rather I please your decision than the whims of my selfishness, should the loudness enter your mind as I seek to empty it from mine."

For a moment she stopped and stared at Enoch. "Will you be leaving immediately, then, at my acquiescence?"

"No. In not so many days, but not immediately."

"Then I will not hold you back from following what has led you to myself to begin with. I cannot imagine a louder burden to my own mind, should I demonstrate ingratitude for the very reason our life began. Only I know I will miss you besides, and will not take joy in that fact. You have but to make me one promise, and my blessing is yours."

"You have but to speak it."

"You will bid me farewell before you leave, and in that moment let me sate myself upon that moment for so long as I desire."

"It shall be done as you have spoken."

"Then, husband, your feet will carry you where they will, and the life that we have created together will fill my heart, though I'll not feel yours beat next to mine again."

❧ ❧ ❧

Months later, free from thought as subtle plans and preparations were made, Enoch let his wife know that in three days he would dedicate as long a moment as she'd like to her.

The next day a great celebration filled their house as family from all around came to wish Enoch good travels on his journey to come. The following day, Enoch made the last of his physical preparations for his walk: clothes, food, a certain stone he had found while visiting the city of Dedicated. On the third day, he wandered down to the river, early in the morning before his wife had awakened, and sat with his feet submerged in the cool, flowing current. His eyes shut, his mind silenced to himself and filled with the world surrounding him; the coolness of his feet, the sound of water and birds and wind, the firmness of the ground and the warmth of the breeze. He arrived home that evening, shortly after opening his eyes, and wrapped his arms around his wife, who had long set her body to rest for the night, as he lay down beside her. He breathed in her scent and smiled to feel his heartbeat surrounded by her warmth while a tear fell from his eye in gratitude and contentment at where his life had led him. He fell to sleep in her comfort, and awoke to the same with her as she too awoke to contentment, and a tear, in his arms.

Before he had said the words, she responded to them. "First you owe me the price of your life in Our Common Creator's hands." She bade him dress as she made them breakfast before taking his hand and leading him far from the village, where all the others had only begun to awaken from the sun.

She held his hand while she led him ever onward, finally to the river bank where first they had met. On the river bank she brought water to his body, washed him, and he did the same for her. There, where first he had seen her face in the light from above by the bank of the river; there their heads touched, and they knew each other throughout. For seven days and seven nights they stayed intertwined as watches banded together to observe from the trees, for far longer than initially they believed they were going to. It was then that Lamelech and Triomvet knew that of the four who would monitor Enoch on his journey, they would see him through wherever his feet would lead.

When at last, seven days later, their heads parted from each other, Enoch's wife again bathed him in the coolness of the river and the heat of the sun, kissed him deeply, then led him back to their home where he had spent most of his life laying his body when it had need of rest. They held each other one last time through the night, face to face, each knowing who existed behind the face of the other. In the morning, after consuming food, they kissed deeply, and then, once she had let go of him, he left.

Through the flat lands surrounding the villages, over stones where the river's water was shallow, and into the wilderness beyond, Enoch's feet led and Lamelech, Triomvet, Hoflan, and Kleshala followed.

It had been twenty-one days since Dedicated had trusted to the impulses of his feet when, coming to a clearing amidst some trees, Enoch naturally stopped. Hoflan, Lamelech, Kleshala, and Triomvet watched from behind the trees while Enoch looked up to see mists rolling in toward him from above. The mist fell upon him and washed him in its moisture as he turned his face into the feeling of having his cheeks kissed by the hand of God. He closed his eyes and was engulfed in the coolness of the damp air.

Opening his eyes some seconds later into fog, he saw a shadow that stood as though a tall human through the vapors, descending behind them. While he stared toward that figure, the moisture in the air began to subside. A being, not quite touching the ground, was suspended where it floated by six wings pulsing as though water, refracting light as though made of some form of organic crystal. Enoch was so transfixed by the one before him, that many moments passed while the mists thinned before he saw from the periphery of his eye another figure. Turning toward that figure, he recognized a form identical, save for the face which was different, though no less beautiful than the being he had just brought his gaze from. Turning toward this second being, his periphery quickly caught again his eye, much more quickly this time, and continuing to turn, he rotated fully and perceived that two more beings hovered around him so that in all, four of these winged people with faces of such extraordinary beauty surrounded him.

When they'd dissipated the mists, and the sky was revealed blue overhead, Enoch was not sure if they were now standing or still floating, as their feet were obscured by their wings. What was clear, however, was that as the engagement of themselves as Enoch would engage with his wife slowed, so too did the mists disperse.

The light filling the clearing from overhead, the angel directly in front of Dedicated began to speak. "It has not been unnoticed, Dedicated, that you have chosen to follow a path in your life that you may understand, as closely as a being such as yourself can, the fullness of What Has Created You."

After finishing this sentence, the angel to Enoch's right began to speak. "*They* have determined that such a path should lead any who walk it to the fullness of their desire to, as your mind might say it, *know* Her."

Now the next angel to his right spoke. "As is such, in differentiated existence, further understanding, that is experiential, not merely conceptual knowledge, dictates for this fullness of your steps to continue, a form is necessitated differing from that which you have known in your life as you have known your life."

Finally the last spoke. "So It has offered you now the continuation of your life closer in form to us, to facilitate not merely the answer of questions you have not yet understood that you wish to ask, but also that you may serve more fully Actuated Creation as It would wish to be."

Again spoke the first that had spoken. "He knows you have already walked in understanding of separateness from the physicality you have called yourself by up until the present."

Now spoke the angel behind Enoch, "Are you willing in the next steps of your journey with Commonness Indivisible Ever-Presence to call yourself by Its own voice, to serve the ears of those who hear as you have by listening to the voice of outer appearances?"

Now the angel to his left: "If so, She will guide you to Her and form you between knowledge of Her and your instinctive impulse, that they should understand what they are made of as you have sought diligently with *your* being to know what *you* are made of."

The angel across from the angel that had spoken previously spoke next. "Though infinite the work of willing service, so too will you know no pain by it as your body would suffer by your intentional creations for the sake of positive synthesis, while you have known being from existence close to dust."

The angel to this one's left spoke finally. "Shall you join with the offer She has made you in continuity of what your existence has impulsed through you for most of your days to strive toward?"

Dedicated looked in awe from angel to angel before turning to one of them and responding, "Your words are spoken beautifully and well, though I cannot possibly understand what form my existence would take, nor what the fullness of meaning might be to exist as the voice of God. Yet it is my yearning to align myself ever with the Source of All. If this means serving *That*, even in being as I cannot now know what it is to be, I will take the opportunity given me by the messengers sent by What I Seek with the fullness of my being as I do know now to be.

"If you would give me but ten steps more upon the ground with which I am familiar, if such a request does not offend the Lord, I would be grateful to make my peace with my own dimness due to current limitation of being, with a final appreciation of what my life has been up until what I am currently perceiving. If such a request would offend, then humbly I beseech no more time be wasted that my ignorance impede upon my own desire ever to fully integrate with The Mind That Has Dictated We Are At All."

Upon ending his reply, the first angel spoke again. "There is no impediment given to your own aim of existence that your request be honored."

In unison, all four spoke finally: "Walk accordingly in service to Whom We All Serve."

The angel before Dedicated fluttered aside that Dedicated may pass through toward the destiny he had chosen for himself. As he passed them, mists began to rise up behind him while he stepped toward the rays of light penetrating through the tops of the trees. Eight, nine, ten steps Enoch walked with God, and then was no more, for God had taken him.

After Enoch

Chapter 26

Way up in Heaven, Origin Of All Existence perceived the sons and daughters of Adam and Living occupying the span of time during the life of Methuselah, and They spoke to Their Self concerning Earthly creation and all that transpired there.

"It is prerequisite for the sake of Our own existence that We allow for all possibility to take place as We have upon the Earth. Having done this, however, choice would seem usurped should We have continued to allow beings without the possibility of choice to indulge their sense of pleasure upon those with choice, whose choice is taken from them by these beings whom they have no means of fending off from using them as they wouldn't want to be used. For humanity to function, these servants of Ours must be made to stop sewing their seed amongst them.

"We should not have allowed them presence as they've had it amongst the humans to begin with! We knew the inevitable actions We must take as the inevitable results of not commanding them *not* to use the human beings as sexual playthings, from the moment We gave them physical form. The responsible thing would have been never to allow them to have their fun with the humans' bodies to begin with.

"Ech, We Are What We Are. We would have been less than Ourself had We not satisfied Our knowledge of consequence, without the physical occurrence by which alone We can be understood through actual presence to be Absolute. Having satisfied Our actuality, of course, the obvious has transpired beyond this one thousand-year moment in time We are noticing the conversation We are considering upon recognizing this, as We do all other moments in the simultaneity with which We perceive them.

"So The Metatron spoke Our will that Our servants not again impede upon the existence of choice, put upon this initial in-bred experiment, of Ourself contained within the vessel of material existence made animate."

At the completion of the fullness of creation of concept of actualization, at a particular coordinate of time in conjunction with a point in space where a particular being existed at that time, Metatron took the part of the concept directed to be a message to that particular being, and manifested itself in that perceived presence to direct the mind of God in a spoken form to the ear of the predetermined recipient best suited to fulfill the intention that one other descendent of in-bred humanity should survive, where none others of that family, nor the bastard offspring of the angels, would survive.

Chapter 27

In the moment in which Methuselah was the very youngest man, to date, in existence, in the land East of Eden, the "civilization" that had developed was less than pleasant. It had become a frequent occurrence that winged beings from the sky would have their way with human women. So frequent, in fact, that upon expressing anger, it was a common reply to ask of the hothead, "Born from a father without feet, eh?" For those born by the messengers of God were renown for picking fights, demonstrating their superior strength by destroying property, and banding together to run through a town, raping whomever they wished, and stealing whatever their arms could carry.

The children of the "sons of God" entering human women wasn't the only unpleasantness to be had in the lands that stretched out East of Eden, either. As Eve was made from the body of Adam, and so all their children from the body of Adam, it was not infrequent that gargantuanism ran rampant. Very tall, very strong idiots were often called by the Nephilim to join in the parties of pillaging and rape; they came in handy for holding down stronger women, killing husbands who tried to stop them, and they didn't seem to mind "sloppy seconds."

Even beside the monsters that resembled men, despite some descendents of Seth trying to warn them that a brother sleeping with a sister was apparently one of the likelier ways a giant was born to humanity, incest was still one of the most common ways to create "family" throughout the land. When a brother impregnated a sister, it was frowned upon that he abandon her. Though early humanity seemed all but foreign to law in this region, nevertheless the society had developed an apparent instinctual drive toward keeping their own children fed until they were old enough to rape their own sisters or close cousins. Once brother had impregnated sister, their proximity necessitated by seeing their children live, amplified the likelihood that they would use each other for their primitive, lustful urges while they waited for their offspring to find their own ways in the world.

Amidst the horror that crept up upon humanity, the angels who had eaten the fruit from the tree of knowledge of good and evil watched the natural results of the initial mating of the beings of the same rib, and the unfettered fulfillment of self-desire upon the human women by their brothers who had not partaken of the fruit of The Tree. They noticed, too, the fulfillment of their winged siblings' whims as well by the human males, but as no offspring were produced by such exchanges, they were not as concerned; though they did consider the psychological ramifications that probably ensued in the minds of the human men at that time of having been used in such a way, when clearly the angels of the sky already possessed fully the means by which to satisfy the cravings of the vaginal components of their odd genitalia.

So it was that, viewing the ever-increasing debasement of young humanity, the angels who had no wings strove to ease the pains of daily life for those descendents of Seth, and those who listened to their admonishments, who chose to find mates at least as distant as third cousins before giving way to their natural inclinations. As time grew on, and the violence increased, the angels tracked those who married for the sake of finding another mind-to-mind, rather than for the sake of lust alone; those who waited to find cousins at least separated by two degrees of parentage. It was these pairings that the angels watched over and protected from the debauchery of blind desire taking over the world surrounding them.

Oddly, Enoch, whose parentage was quite distant from that of his wife, had never needed help from the angels to ward off would-be harassers. If a stray marauding thug-child of a "son of God" happened anywhere in close proximity to the dwelling of Enoch, they became strangely peaceful as they went on their way, inevitably without crossing paths with Enoch or his family while Enoch was with them. Likewise, even after Enoch had left, his wife never once had a problem with those "lawless" in the land. Methuselah did not follow in his father's footsteps.

Unlike his father, once he had succumbed to his impulses of animality, without connecting those impulses to his heart or head-brain, the angels did find themselves discouraging the paths of the whimful from the door of Methuselah, for the sake of the peace of mind of Enoch and his wife.

"Is this a law spoken by Our Own Creator Everlasting Endlessness that *these* who take the time to cultivate harmony within and without their own beings in all motion they make with their hands, results in the repulsion of the unfortunate consequences of the animal components of existence taking control of beings before they have had the experience to control themselves from their components not merely automatic in nature? So many of the line of Seth keep unviolated amongst the chaos that otherwise seems to roll through the lives of all the beings descendent of Adam from time to time. It is only those who come from Seth who have copulated with their uncles' daughters, or worse, who seem to be pained by visitors these humans deem created by 'sons of God.' It is only those who rise up against their brothers or sisters that seem to be beaten for fun by the giants roaming the land. How can this be? It is as though those respectful in all ways with their wives emanate an unseen field of force that keeps beings who are slaves to their bodies, and whose blood lust runs deep, from wandering even close to their homes. Even in those instances in which they do meet with these beings, these beings all but always take to the kindness they are given without rising in hostility. It is as though those cultivating houses of self-control, respect, mindfulness, and emotional sensitivity can place upon any agitated being the very hand of Our Commonness that those beings, otherwise predisposed to the worst of their selves, mostly offer no harm while in passing; and surely, they never keep to these households for long before going their own way."

As Luciferous consulted with his like-created beings around the fire, they all nodded in agreement at his summation of what they had personally observed over the course of the thousand years they had witnessed the children of Adam.

Chapter 28

Harratzarian was seeking sustenance for her brothers and sisters in the wilderness along with other members of her tribe when she felt drawn strongly to the action of excreting a buildup of poisons from the vicinity of her sexual organs. She excused herself from the angels with which she hunted, so as to facilitate this function of detoxification without impeding upon the search for protein sources. She set down her spear before turning to the crocuses she had decided to bestow with nutrients from the self-toxic result of the physicality of her being.

Nearby, Luciferous and Harharlan followed not so far behind a young and exacerbated Methuselah. "We are far too far from the non-wild to be able to predict with any sense of satisfaction what could be encountered or responded to, First Among Us."

So responded Luciferous, "Ah! A learning experience, Harharlan; how fortunate for us."

Harharlan sighed as they continued to follow. "I don't understand why he continues chasing the rabbits with his bare hands. He's seen how his father uses a net. The thing is perfectly accessible to him. Why does he not use it?"

"Aside from the fact that he's many miles away from it by now? It seemed rather spontaneous when he started chasing that first cony. Hasn't had hardly a bit of meat to eat since his father left on walkabout weeks ago. Seems he thought he could pounce on that first one and catch it with bare hands, and was too far from home and relatively resourceless by the time it might have occurred to him to have a tool in order to suit his aim, and bring himself and his household a bit of dinner. Stubborn son of a likeness of Omnipresent Creation, though, ain't he?"

A little in the distance, Harratzarian was finishing feeding the crocuses beneath her when hearing a rustling. She looked up to see a human form emerging from behind a tree, wearing clothes clearly not made by one of her kind. Knowing she could not grab her spear without being seen, she hopped toward a myrtle bush close to where she was and peered out from behind it. She began silently hoping to herself that the form would walk in a direction away from her spear. With the being's subsequent footfalls, she found herself to be increasingly disappointed. So it was she exclaimed under her breath when, now in her view, she recognized Methuselah stopping in front of the spear finally at his feet, staring at it intently.

From behind him, Luciferous and Harharlan supposed initially that Methuselah had stopped to scrutinize another bunny that perhaps, in his mind, was close enough to attempt grabbing hold of. They thought nothing of Methuselah bending down toward the earth. When he began to stand with an object shaped sharply, attached to a long, slender piece of wood far too exact in shape to have been pulled purely from the bosom of nature, however, they both experienced simultaneously almost exactly the same thought; something closely reminiscent to the sentiment expressed as "oh dear," while they began slowly turning their heads back and forth from side to side in unison. Harharlan began to consider the party of her siblings-in-kind who had left to seek food earlier in the day, and she began to consider who would feel the shame of such a possession finding its way to a firstborn of the line of firstborns of the Adam. They continued to watch.

From behind her bush, Harratzarian began feeling fear in anticipation, reflecting on Gendlebleth's experience so long ago. She felt the subtle rising in her of shame as Methuselah examined the point of the spear close to his face, and then began rotating the shaft between his hands as though it were a toy, and not a tool whereby sustenance could be derived for maintaining the full consciousness of eternity through its proper placement of creatures not capable of understanding their existences through the mediums of comparison and metaphor. Then, a bunny rabbit hopped into the path of sight between Harratzarian and Methuselah.

Methuselah's focus jumped direct to the hippity-hoppity of the object of his stomach's longing. He quickly stood stock-still, glancing at the point atop the shaft he held tightly in his hand. His concentration returning pointedly now to his quarry, he tilted his pole with the point downward, toward what he hoped to make a quick meal out of.

While, from a distance, Harharlan and Luciferous could not yet make out the rabbit in Methuselah's purview, they estimated correctly the intention of his presently unflinching gaze in conjunction with the angel he held his newly found "toy." He looked odd rotating his self round and round, with a gaze as tight on his intention as the unflinching eye of the tip of the point he held tightly to from the middle of the device which held it. Finally, he stopped his rotating. Harratzarian could see the intake of a deep breath from Methuselah's shoulders from behind, and the crinkle of the bunny's nose. Luciferous watched with jaw clenched while the young man began to pull back his arm to fulfill his focus's intent.

Three angels around Methuselah held their breath in anticipation, preparing to see the result of his next exhalation's release. Methuselah was ready to let go his breath when, in the background ahead of him, he heard a rustling greater than that of the wind. His gaze now rose above and past the bunny, who hopped off unharmed, his breath continuing to hold an extra beat before exhaling and slowly straightening his spine as he did so; the shaft of the spear still angled toward where it had intended its flight before.

"Why didn't he release?"

"I don't know," replied Luciferous. They both noticed his gaze still fixed in the unseen flora before him.

Methuselah gulped. He began slowly angling his spear upward. From a bush a short distance in front of him stepped forth a black boar, grunting and staring Methuselah dead in the eye. It snorted, stomped its front hooves against the soil, then paused, its tusks finding their points staring in the direction of Methuselah's groin. Then, it charged.

Three angels made in the likeness of man-kind held their breaths simultaneously as they anticipated the demise of the firstborn son of Enoch, firstborn of the line of firstborn sons since the creation of the Adam.

Methuselah lowered his spear toward the head of the boar, dug his heels into the earth, one leg bending in anticipation behind the other, and held his arms taut. A two-second's run away, and Methuselah anticipated. A half-second from impact, Methuselah closed his eyes, the tip of the point now burned into his eyelids, and he pushed forward.

He heard a horrible sound like a muffled, blood-curdling squeal as he felt the spear find its way through soft flesh before finally sensing himself pushed backward through the air by the butt of the shaft rammed hard against his ribcage, knocking the air out of his lungs while he fell.

Opening his eyes from where he discerned himself on his back, he watched with a mixture of terror and joy the giant pig shaking its head back and forth, squealing from behind where the spear was skewered into its throat, bleeding within its neck, gargling finally for air while it choked on its own fluids and the wood it had been impaled by. For two minutes Methuselah heard muffled, high-pitched squeals turn to the low tones of watery hacking, before finally the animal fell lifeless from air deprivation after the liquids from its internal organs had thoroughly flooded the entirety of its lungs.

The three identity-capable awarenesses who watched out of sight simultaneously let forth their breath in relief sometime before the swine finally fell to its inevitable death. Also in unison, they all experienced the same disgust by what they perceived, the feel of their own lungs filling gratefully with the Breath of Their Common Life Creator.

As Methuselah stepped forward to see the shaft of the spear issuing forth from the mouth of the dead boar in front of him, he was delighted to be able to bring home for his mother something that could be made into dinner for his siblings that night.

From the direction of where the boar had come, six hunters peered from behind a large tree to see Harratzarian's bloody spear in Methuselah's hand, and a boar over Methuselah's shoulders. They all glanced at each other, speaking to each other by eye too many questions to be comfortable with after asking the initial, "What could possibly be taking sister Harratzarian so long?"

❦ ❦ ❦

That night, around the campfire, Harratzarian was gazed upon with frequency from the utmost, heartfelt concerns for the simple, innocent spear placement that had caused the excitement of the day.

They considered her probable anticipation, her inevitable questions of the consequence of her urination on Methuselah's fate. They considered her contemplation of the disparity between what she would think Methuselah would feel to slaughter the large beast, and the joy on his face following its demise; and they considered her meditation on why that disparity could occur.

They wondered after how nervous she was that her very slight miscalculation might remind her of Gendlebleth's long ago; make her fear for her internal points of processing when unhelpfulness has been committed by the actions of one's own hand. They thought to themselves that she must be considering the results that must inevitably affect Methuselah's immediate family, whom the angels had been watching over since the beginning of time itself. They anticipated her awaiting of the discussion about to take place regarding what had happened that day, and how best to proceed considering Methuselah, his family, and the angels' own future spear usage.

They all figured upon the emotions of her mid-torso dancing with the thoughts in her head, and the strong probability that, likely, she was wondering what thoughts they all must be thinking about her.

☙ ☙ ☙

Amidst the psychic milieu, Luciferous approached the fire and, finally, they all began to process the proceedings of the day together. It was decided that night that, in the future, when on missions in which their desire was to engage in their activities unseen, in which they wished to leave no trace of their happening upon the life of the likeness-creatures, they would stay in pairs so that always there would be at least one "lookout" if one ever felt the needs of nature for self-extraction of poison from one's system.

☙ ☙ ☙

Methuselah's mother smiled to see her son arriving at the end of the day. She was grateful for fresh food with which to feed her family. As he laid the slaughtered animal upon the butchering table, she smiled for the blessings of her son returning home that night. Internally, Methuselah thanked God for the spear he had discovered during the day while he gazed upon the smile filling his mother's face. Behind her smile, a teardrop fell from the corner of her eye. She raised a large knife high and, CHOP, began to separate flesh, bone, and skin. Her daughter prepared a fire for the animal's flesh to be cooked by.

⚬⚬⚬

While his mother prepared the meal that night, at her behest, Methuselah went down to the river to wash the blood from his newly procured toy. Dipping the point and shaft into the river, Methuselah remembered how it had come to be soaked in blood to begin with; the horror of facing his likely imminent death, the feel of power to find his spear destroy the threat of his own annihilation, and the joy of that power to be able to bring him the taste of flesh his tongue so craved.

Eating with his mother, brothers, and sisters, he glanced at the spear standing upright in the corner of the room, drying, and anticipated the next time he could engage in the activity of acquiring food for his family.

⚬⚬⚬

Three days later, when the last of the animal's flesh had been consumed, Methuselah left with his spear in the direction of the rabbits he had been searching for before the discovery of his new companion. It was not long before he found what he sought.

Alongside a tree, the crinkly-nosed creature with the fluffy tail hopped a little bit here, then hopped a little bit there. Pointed toward the creature's head was Methuselah's "new companion." Methuselah took aim, pulled back his arm, breathed in, and while simultaneously breathing out, let his dart fly at his quarry. So flew the tooth-headed pole, so did it find its bite in the tree's root, the rabbit hopping quickly from sight underneath nearby bushes. That was not to be the last time Methuselah would miss his target this day.

Twenty times Methuselah drew back his arm. Twenty times a rabbit's fate was not to feed the man of the dart. At the end of a long afternoon, dejectedly, Methuselah wandered home to where his mother had left him a bowl of steamed vegetables and some flat bread for his evening meal. When finally he fell to sleep late that night, he dreamed of rabbits laughing at him no matter which direction he ran. When, a few hours later, he awoke, hopping from his bed, he grabbed the spear and sought the first cony unlucky enough to cross his path.

There it was, hopping about in the light of the sun. Slowly and quietly, Methuselah followed behind it. As it began hopping behind the wide trunk of an old tree, he anticipated its course and quickly made his way around the other side of the tree's body. He stopped short of the rabbit's sight around the other side of the tree and raised the spear over his head. A moment or two passed when, from around the side of the tree, sure enough hopped the crinkly snout of the young man's prey. Holding his breath, he held the back of the shaft with both hands. Softly releasing his breath, forward he plunged. The sound of birds disrupted rose to the sky overhead with the brief sound released from the disrupted life of the bunny below. He held up the rabbit's bloody body before his face, skewered to the pole through its heart. He felt satisfaction to think of what visions his dreams would bring him this night.

Before the day was through, Methuselah had hunted seventeen more rabbits much as he had the day before. Coming upon the seventeenth, he raised his arm and, releasing his breath, finally his projectile hit its mark. He smirked to himself. A day begun well, a day ended well. He regretted only in passing that he had not been able to kill enough to feed well his entire family.

Presenting his catch to his mother just before afternoon began turning to evening, his mother smiled to receive the day's work of her son. She wept as she chopped off the heads of the two small lagomorphs.

The smaller of the two rabbits, once cooked, she served whole to her son who had brought them to her with pride. The other rabbit she served a small piece of to all of his brothers and sisters, along with their assorted vegetables and lentils. She did not eat of his catch personally, making her supper of lentils salted to her satisfaction. Her son could not help but notice this fact through the feeling of pride he simultaneously felt at experiencing his brothers and sisters enjoying their taste of his work. He ripped free a leg from the rest of the seared body and held it out to his mother.

"No, son. I am full from what I have eaten already, but thank you."

Methuselah's heart sank just a little to hear his mother's words.

That night, when he dreamed, he dreamed of a rabbit slain at his feet; the shaft of his spear in his hand, the spear's point in the rabbit's body. Pulling the spear from its freshly dead form, a drop of blood very slowly began to rise from where the point of the spear had been just moments prior. Thereafter rose another drop, slowly, turning toward the sky, dripping upward a short distance behind the first. Overhead he heard his mother's voice singing. Looking upward, there she lay outstretched along her belly, across the length of a long, thick branch of a tree. She smiled down on him as she sang. Past her smile, he could see something red forming at the corner of her eye. He could see the red begin to fall from her eye's corner, a drop that landed on the side of his hand holding the shaft of the spear; a drop of blood. Looking from his hand, he looked again upward toward his mother's smiling face. Another drop formed at the corner of her eye, and then fell, but this time it fell very, very slowly. Shortly thereafter fell another drop of blood, slowly, following the last. Looking again at the corpse of the rabbit, Methuselah saw four drops of blood continuing to rise upward, no faster than the others, making their way toward the once two, now three, tears of blood descending at their own pace to the ground below. Midway, between the bunny's corpse and his mother's smiling face, a drop of blood rising coalesced with another falling, and just as they became one, Methuselah awoke in a cold sweat.

Breathing heavily, he leapt out of bed, grabbed his spear, and ran in the direction of the next creature he could find to impale. He continued to run until the first rays of dawn were lifted into the sky with the great ball of light that made possible their life.

Chapter 29

"Son, come help me in the garden..."

"I would, Father," Methuselah replied, "but I must leave now to bring food back to our family."

Enoch sighed as he watched the spear-companioned hand of his son vanish beyond the boundaries of where, with intention, life grew.

❧ ❧ ❧

Methuselah took to drinking the blood of his prey. After skewering a rabbit, he would chop off its head on the spot, and drink whatever the cavity of its neck might have left to offer. When he'd return home, however, and hand freshly caught food for his family to his mother, he found himself no longer able to take joy from the smile she always offered him in return. He saw, during these nightly exchanges, no pride for what she had created in her eyes. The only joy Methuselah found was in the consummation of the end of every chase itself; the life of the animal still warm as he fed his unquenchable thirst.

While the flayed flesh of bunny was ever-abundant at the dinner table, he enjoyed the thrill of bringing down the largeness of a deer best. In its pursuit, he'd learned and created all manner of traps, fashioned bolas, and developed spears better for long-range flights. Methuselah's joy was complete when throwing himself upon a large, four-legged beast longing for the mercy of his good friend's extended solid tooth. Graciously he stopped the animal's despair and agony as it fell in the same place that once it had been able to stand. While pride still was recognized only distantly, his mother's smile always shown wider on a night venison was to be butchered and roasted for her family's delight. Though Enoch would sometimes not make eye contact with his son when it was time to eat the evening meal, even he seemed to take joy in feasting upon the work of his son's hand when deer graced his table and plate.

✿ ✿ ✿

One day, from a distance, Methuselah spied his quarry. Silently he moved closer to where she sat in the meadow as she fed generously upon what grew freely about her. He noticed her size, and joy filled his heart.

A short distance enough to where she sat to throw a dart with reasonable certainty to slow her to his will, quietly as he could, he snuck nearer still. She turned her head toward the sound of his heel in the grass while she chewed the same, cautiously, pausing between movements of her jaw. Closer he crept for only a short time before, stilling herself in awareness of the disruption in the distance, she determined that the time had come for her to leave the comfort of the tall foliage surrounding her. Rising to her hooves, as Methuselah was made to perceive how unusually, fully fat she was, he grew intoxicated by the lack of nimbleness to her feet she displayed. Before she had made her first leap toward bringing herself from the open to safety, his first javelin had found its path into her, her front legs seeking forward momentum against the perfect yield of the wind. To the ground she fell. Pushing herself back up from her side in strained, hysterical panic, blood trickling from the wound, beginning a second leap away from the direction the pain had come, again she felt a stabbing drive her to the ground, this time stinging her cruelly in the neck. With no less force, and greater urgency, she forced herself upright. Rather than another leap toward the trees in the distance, the only possible barrier between herself and the hunter drawing her blood while she attempted escape to a peace she would never know, she turned herself toward the man holding the sharpness in his hand. She began to charge.

Methuselah raised his grip. The release of his breath left a shaft protruding from the doe's eye socket. Her pace in his direction slowed only slightly before she had come upon him, raising her razor-sharp hooves into the air in easy striking distance from his skull. The familiarity of this position in his recollection, he dug his heels into the ground, raised his lance, and let the fat doe impale her heart on his tool. She lowered her legs toward his head as close as they might to finding her hooves' mark before widening her eyes to the release of her pain and the eternal rest that hadn't been the intention of her foot's fall.

A grin on his face to behold a meal to feed his family for a solid week to come, Methuselah drew a large knife to disembowel what soon his mother would butcher. Six inches into her belly, he stopped; a young pair of eyes stared back into his own face. Cutting back the flesh about her stomach a bit further, another pair of eyes still. At first unsure just how to feel, Methuselah filled with delight, thinking about the joy his mother must feel when she saw how well her family would eat. With a light heart, he lifted the heavy beast upon his broad shoulders; not bothering any more to "clean" the animal, that his surprise for his mother would not be diminished.

From behind a bush in the distance, one angel began weeping the second the attack on the pregnant doe had begun. When the knife of Methuselah had revealed the heads of the two fawns, the other began to vomit. Both angels held the substance of human form.

cℬℬℬ

From a distance, while pulling tubers from the ground in his garden, Enoch was happy to see the hooves of a large deer straddling his son's shoulders and smiled widely to see his approach. Methuselah walked around to the other side of the house, placed the doe upon the butchering table, then called to his mother that he had brought home a treat to prepare, and that he was going to wash up before dinner. His mother called back from deep inside the house that that would be fine, and then Methuselah hid himself nearby so that he could see his mother's reaction when she looked upon the "treat" he had brought for her.

His mother entered. Glancing toward the doe's belly, she thought it odd that Methuselah had brought her home not disemboweled. Taking a knife, she walked toward the doe, placed her hand on her side, began to cut where she found an incision had already been made, then dropped her knife when she saw the four eyes staring up at her from the belly of their mother. Clutching her hands into fists, she began to shake all over, then began to sob. Tears streamed down her face while her weep released itself into a wail. She fell to her knees and beat her hands upon the ground. Her screams rose to penetrate the farthest recesses of the sky.

Methuselah stepped forward from behind a shadow as Enoch rushed in to answer the shrieks of despondency issuing forth from his wife's throat. Glancing up at the butchering table, he saw resting against their mother's side from within her belly the limp heads of the two unborn fawns. Suppressing his own inherent urge to throw up, he instead threw his arms around his wife's shoulders and began stroking her head, rocking her and kissing her temples in order to bring her to calm herself.

Methuselah took another step forward. "Father, what's happening?"

"Wait for me outside, Methuselah. We'll talk in a few minutes."

"But Father, why is Mother–"

"OUTSIDE, Methuselah!" Enoch's shout left no mistake of meaning in Methuselah's mind. He left his parents huddled together on the ground.

꙳ ꙳ ꙳

Methuselah had occupied his time by staring at his father's garden for about a half of an hour when Enoch's head emerged from within the house. "Methuselah, about three miles to the southwest, a family was recently attacked by one of the Nephilim. I want you to bring them that doe, so that they have something to eat while they go through this difficult time of transition. I will prepare a meal tonight from my garden. You will have a bowl waiting for you when you return.

Methuselah's attempt to respond was cut short by the head of his father returning inside of the house, Methuselah's mouth left agape in the position it stopped when it understood it no longer had need to try to produce a sound.

The pregnant doe was heavier this time as he slung it over his dejected shoulders and carried his burden to the family his father had indicated.

The family's faces were filled with smiles when he delivered his trophy to their front door. They praised him and blessed him profusely, and gave thanks that God had not forgotten them as he accepted their gratitude as graciously as he could from behind a forced reciprocation of his face.

On his return home, Methuselah captured a large rabbit, made a fire, and consumed the animal's flesh before completing his journey. He left the bowl of assorted vegetables waiting for him untouched. He found his way straight to his bed.

❧❧❧

As he awoke with the sun, Enoch had planned to tell his son that he did not blame him for what had happened, and that he had done a good thing for that family. When he entered Methuselah's room, however, he found that both his son, and his spear, had already left for the day.

Chapter 30

In the house of Enoch, no one ever wanted for protein. Every morning Methuselah left brandishing sharp objects. Every night, along with these sharp objects, he had in hand the extinguished lives of some creature, or creatures, suitable enough for food.

While Enoch had lost most of his taste for venison, out of politeness to his son he always ate a small steak of the stuff. While it had been years since his mother's tongue had touched rabbit, including when presented at more communal gatherings where the conies had been caught by others, she always smiled upon her son's work before directing its preparation for consumption by the rest of the family. Birds, boars, goats, lambs, and cows were also known to grace the family's table. In short, if it moved, Methuselah was inclined to bring it home for dinner. As his many brothers and sisters were becoming quite large—several adults, many teenagers, a few just shy of their teenage years—what he brought home day after day to feed their family was always welcome and never stayed long once cooked. For a while...

One day Methuselah returned home late in the morning, carrying a deer over his shoulders. His mother smiled politely as he lay it on the butchering block before turning from him to her own emotions whilst in search of a large, sharp knife. Enoch suppressed an instinctual gag reflex while he waved to his son from the garden, and wondered that he was again leaving toward the wilderness with his spear in hand.

Only a couple of hours later, he carried another adult buck, dragging it inside the gate with the help of a mule in the direction of the table used for butchering. His mother, who was not even halfway through chopping up the first deer was dumb-struck by the further work her son had brought her to do, and began planning a round-up of her offspring that this more than a week's worth of meat might be prepared properly before beginning dinner for the evening.

Five hours later, Methuselah arrived just as the first roasts were skewered onto the spit over the fire. The bodies of ten dead bunnies and five large chickens adorned his shoulders down his back. His mother called loudly to her husband, pointed to her son when Enoch arrived, and spoke sharply, "This needs to stop!" then walked to her bedroom, slamming the door behind her. Seeing fifteen animals slung over his son's shoulders, after having seen the two deer he'd brought in earlier that day, Enoch knew exactly what his wife had meant. Methuselah stared at his father, the corners of his mouth turned downward from confusion.

"Son, both your mother and I are very grateful for how well you feed our family day after day." Methuselah was about to speak when his father cut him off, "But. But, look at how much food you've brought home today. Last week when you brought home two deer in two days, half of one of the deer spoilt and went to waste, because we simply couldn't eat that much quickly enough as a family. Now, in one day you have brought home enough dead flesh to feed a large village for a full week, let alone your family. How many of these creatures would you have lose their lives for the sake of death alone, through the sheer inability of us to eat that much that fast, before the remainder rots beyond usefulness? Further, now that regularly it has become the duty of so many of my children to prepare the foods you provide, do you not think my children should enjoy making for themselves lives beyond butchering the animals that you spend your time stripping of their lives? For the sake of the sustenance of your family though the intention may be..."

Methuselah stared at his father, not knowing how to respond. Internally he tried to brush off the shame now occurring to him as a man brushing off a swarm of gnats just beginning to leak from behind a dam about to burst.

"So long as you live in my house, son, you are allowed to hunt no more than twice per week. When you hunt, you may kill no more than one large animal—a deer, a boar, or what have you—or five small animals: chickens, rabbits, and the like, per hunting day. If the animals are very small, like doves, you may kill no more than ten. In this way you will provide for the appetite of your family more than enough meat to satisfy them all, *and* no animal's life shall be shed in a meaningless death. Do you understand?"

Methuselah nodded while he held back the tears beginning to sob involuntarily from the back of his throat.

"Tonight you will hitch a wagon to the mule and bring to a village in the northeast whatever our family will not be able to eat within the next week before it spoils. That particular village was recently brutalized by a pack of giants led by several Nephilim. They are no doubt desperate for food by now."

Methuselah nodded gravely. A drop of salt water began to dew the corner of his eye.

"We are grateful for the beautiful food you bring us, son, that we enjoy every night. But death without purpose cannot be pleasing either to What Created Us from on high, nor all that live amongst us below. We are meant to be better than those born from the 'sons of God'.

"Now, go. Feed those in need! We will have the work of your hands prepared for the joy of your consumption when you return."

Methuselah wept openly as he filled the wagon with rabbits, chickens, and the buck he had killed earlier that day. When he arrived that night at the village to the northeast, he was greeted as a hero. He politely turned down the offers to marry several young daughters between the ages of eleven and seventeen, all of whom had been raped by the giants and the sons of God earlier that week. He received graciously a pair of candles that hadn't been broken during the pillaging before turning back for home, having given the people food to last them a day or two. As he rode out of town back toward where he'd come, he thanked God for his spear that he was able to feed others by the virtue of the gift *he* had been given from on high.

❧ ❧ ❧

Early the next morning, before the sun had announced its coming from its heralds lightening the sky, Enoch entered his son's room to tell him the pride he felt that his son had helped the village, and to invite Methuselah to spend time with him in the garden. Already Methuselah was not to be found in his room, and his spear was missing from where normally he kept it standing against the far wall.

Chapter 31

When Methuselah was 186 years old, his mother asked him to accompany her to the house of one of her younger sisters. Although he had used it just the other day to kill the lamb that he would be carrying to her sister's house, his mother asked him very specifically not to bring his spear with them. After registering a look upon his face as though his mother had taken the spear from his hand and thrust it into his own heart, Methuselah nodded in acquiescence and left his companion upright amongst the pelts of the many animals he had stripped of life hanging upon his wall. His mother thanked him and stroked his back as he returned. His back to the home where he had spent most of the first two centuries of his life, he saw his father waving farewell to him from the garden before he turned completely from the house toward the home of his mother's sister.

Midway upon the half-day journey it took to reach his aunt's house, Methuselah's mother decided to stop at the small marketplace that fell along their path. While she dug through a stand of assorted vegetables and herbs, many of which they did not grow at their own home, Methuselah spied a girl at the other end of the market. Over the course of much more than a century and a half of spending most of his time occupied by killing every target his spear could strike, women had not much occurred to him. On occasions when he'd hunted to excess and was made to give what his family could not eat to those terrorized by giants and

Nephilim, often deflowered girls had been offered to him as brides, but violated desperation did not occur to him as desirable, especially given his family's history of respect and depth of connection when it had come time to join in mating. Granted, it was many a night offering fertility sacrifices of his seed in his father's garden, while thinking about these girls, that he spent relieving the pressure of over a century and a half of not having a companion to share his life with. Aside from his sisters and his mother, Methuselah had spent a very long time in his life with no female companionship to speak of.

This in mind, the girl with the long brown hair and full bosom seemed to be smiling at Methuselah from the other side of the marketplace. The way she was looking at him made him aware that there was a spear he had forgotten that he had brought with him, that his mother could not so easily ask him to leave behind. He stared awkwardly at her for a moment, not wanting to scare her away like a doe he'd stalk in the wilderness. Getting hold of his senses, he decided the wisest course of action would be to smile back. Holding her gaze, just on the cusp of raising the corners of his mouth, the stretch of muscle just occurring, suddenly a hand holding a root stood directly in his field of vision, no more than a foot in front of his face. From behind the root he heard his mother's voice, "Have you ever seen such a root before? I don't even know what it is, but it just looks so delicious! I bet this would go just wonderfully in a stew with that lamb of yours! I'll have to bring this marvelous root to your aunt..."

As she turned to ask the farmer's son about the root, once it was removed from Methuselah's sight, he saw from across the marketplace that the beautiful girl with the long brown hair and wide, hazelnut-colored eyes was now looking up and talking to an older man, presumably her father. She smiled up at him before the two turned opposite where Methuselah stared and walked side by side out of the marketplace, and soon enough, out of view of the frustrated, half-heartbroken man.

He heard the voice of his mother. "I think we have everything we need. You ready to go, son?" But Methuselah just stared out into the distance where the girl had been moments before, hoping that despite what he knew to be true, she'd soon come back into view where last he had seen her. His mother's voice came to his ear again. "Son? Are you all right? What are you staring at?"

"Oh, uh, nothing."

"Well, are you ready to go?"

"Yes," he sighed. "I'm ready."

❧ ❧ ❧

When they arrived at his mother's sister's house, immediately his mother bragged about him to her sister as she had him present the lamb he had slaughtered for her. He was relieved not to be carrying the weight of the dead animal after the journey of half a day it had taken to bring it to where it now lay.

"What a gift you have brought my family, Methuselah! Thank you. You are most welcome here!" She then called inside the house, "Delilah! Delilah, come out and show your cousin around a bit." She turned back to Methuselah. "She's my third-youngest daughter, but very bright, and knows the area well. Hopefully her youth won't be burdensome on a fellow of your age, but I know she'd be very happy to show her older cousin around a bit. I'm sure you haven't seen her since she was ten, four years ago after my youngest had been born, but I've no doubt having her show you around would be a better time than listening to a pair of old ladies catching up and gossiping about people they barely know." Methuselah's mother smiled at her sister. "Ah! Here she is now..."

As Delilah entered the room, Methuselah was immediately struck by how well developed her form was already for a girl so young. Finding his eye drawn to her chest, he quickly shook off the natural inclination of the lust in his body and found himself staring up at a face even more beautiful still.

"Delilah, there you are, you silly girl! Perhaps you remember your cousin, Methuselah?" Delilah stared absently at Methuselah for a moment as though lost in her memory, trying to find his face. "No matter, you'll have plenty of time to become reacquainted as you show him around a little bit while your aunt and I catch up and prepare dinner."

"How do you do?" Methuselah felt his cheeks contract a bit as he extended his hand to his pretty, young cousin, "I guess I can show you around the area a bit while our moms prepare dinner."

"I'd be very happy if you would." Methuselah followed behind his cousin as his mother and aunt began to catch up.

"I wonder, what kinds of animals do you see often around here?" Methuselah began to make conversation by speaking about the only thing he knew while he followed his cousin out the front door. "Perhaps you can show me a ways into the wilderness?"

Methuselah shut the door firmly behind him as this question left his lips.

❧ ❧ ❧

They sat around the dinner table. "Delilah! Methuselah slaughtered this beautiful animal for us. Your aunt and I spent the last several hours preparing this meal for you and your family. It is time to eat!"

Methuselah's aunt made apologies to everyone. "Honestly, I am very sorry you and your son are waiting so long for my daughter to simply change her clothing. Usually she's rather quick about it. We really can go ahead and start eating without her."

"I wouldn't think of it. My son and I are grateful for your hospitality, and we didn't come all this way to share the work of my son's hands with less than all of your household. It is good to spend time with family while we wait for one no less important than the rest of us before we begin eating."

Methuselah's mother was just finishing her thought when Delilah approached the dinner table sullenly. Methuselah's aunt addressed her daughter while she began slowly pulling the last empty chair, the one beside Methuselah's, toward herself before sitting down. "My sister travels half a day's journey to spend time with us, her son carries a freshly slaughtered lamb all this way, we slave in the kitchen for hours, and you can't put a little more speed into changing for dinner, young lady?"

"Really, there's no problem here," Methuselah's mother spoke up on Delilah's behalf.

"Sorry, Mother," Delilah muttered under her breath and her long, straight black hair before sitting down, staring absently at her empty plate.

"And for Heaven's sake, child, hold your head up while you're at this table!"

"Yes, Mother," she muttered again under her breath, raising her head half a centimeter before allowing it to fall back where it had been a moment prior.

"You really must excuse my daughter. I haven't any idea what's gotten into her..."

"Really, I do," Methuselah's mother said, smiling, "Let us enjoy this meal together, now that we are all here."

With that, the food was passed along the table. When the plate of lamb came to Delilah, she passed it over to her sister sitting next to her without taking any, and her mother again rebuked her. "Delilah! After all the work that has gone into this meal, you will take some of the offering your cousin has brought you, won't you?"

Delilah raised her head high enough to make eye contact with her mother, briefly, and then took a piece of meat from the plate and dropped it onto her own, simultaneously muttering under her breath, "Yes, Mother."

"Child, where are your manners? Take a bite or two. Perhaps some food will return to you some of the energy you lost showing Methuselah around the surrounding wilderness while we were preparing it."

Delilah stared for a moment at the meat upon her plate, picked it up, began to raise it toward her mouth, and then vomited on it just a little. She then began a low sob that turned into tears falling upon the seared remains of the dead animal hanging in her hand between the table and her visage.

"Delilah, what—"

She stood up sharply, the force of her rise causing the chair to jump backward behind her, and she threw the wet piece of lamb at her otherwise empty plate before turning toward her bedroom and running from her brothers, sisters, mother and father as fast as her feet would carry her through the stream of salted water falling from her face.

Methuselah's mother turned to her sister and spoke. "Perhaps I had better—"

"No. She is my child, and already I have been too cruel to her. I will see what is wrong."

When her sister was out of view, having disappeared behind the closed door of her daughter's room, Methuselah's mother's eyes turned apprehensively toward her son.

cちりcちりcちり

Harratzarian sat with her forehead in her hands, weeping beside the river.

Luciferous emerged from the distance and walked to where she lamented, placing his hand upon her shoulder in an attempt to console her. "There, there now. You had no way of knowing. If he had not had it in him to begin with, he never could have brought these nightmares to life."

"Yes, but he was not given the tools of temperance, as his fathers since Seth had been given, that might have saved him from lust before finding the tool that fed him from the empty vessels that can never satisfy more than the tongue; and even then only temporarily. No, my careless placement of an adult's instrument was mistaken by the child's mind as a toy; one that then saved his life while simultaneously granting him the taste of the feast his tongue longed for. He placed his heart upon that stick from then on, mistaking it for his sole assurance of security and sustenance both. That seed planted of the child's mind grew into that abomination which will be my shame until his, apparently, now almost fully automatic physicality of being is washed from the top layers of soil it currently contaminates as a rule of the hungers which drive it." She resumed her weeping into the water upon concluding her response to her friend.

He gave her another embrace of her shoulder before turning back toward their camp to ponder those made in the likeness of their Common Creator, and rest for the night.

Chapter 32

Her pain echoed through the house, through the wilderness, through the valley in which their home had been built.

Methuselah crept up behind the sow suckling her litter. Clutching his spear with both hands, he leapt up high into the air and silently, swiftly, landing with both feet upon her back, plunged the tip of the spear through the back of her neck, the tip emerging through the front of her throat merely a tenth of a second later. The squeals of the eight suckling piglets were cut short in the few seconds that it took for Methuselah to sever their vocal cords, one by one, much as he had their mother's moments prior. When the silence had flowed into his ears just as the blood had flowed out of the necks of the pigs in the dirt at his feet, he walked several miles from where they lay to where his mule and carriage waited. He rode to the dead swine and threw their bodies onto the carcasses of the five deer and fifteen rabbits he'd separated from their lives previously that day. He thought to himself that if he should stumble upon just one more goat before reaching his next destination, he would consider the outing a complete success.

The vibrations of her screams projected outward as a ripple from the center of the tear forming at the corner of her mother's eye. Shriek after shriek of pain penetrated her heart and undulated from its core, out through her conscience as surely as they did from out each and every tear that fell to be absorbed by the floorboards as, holding onto her daughter's ankle, she shouted encouragingly, "Push, my darling! Push!"

Having amassed another two lambs, the pile burdening the mule was slowly rolled into a large town. The town had been half-burned to the ground two days before by a pair of Nephilim twins riding at the head of fourteen enlarged, inbred spawn of adam. They had made it their mission to knock down the doors of every dwelling and rape every woman who called that town their home, half the population of men killed in the process. As he approached, men and women fell upon their faces on either side of him, arms outstretched before them as though in worship of The Divine Creator of All Eternity made manifest to them in human form. While he dismounted his mule, men kissed his feet. Methuselah smiled benevolently on those around him who had fallen upon tragedy while he slowly strode to stand centrally among them.

The pain resonating from her throat shook through the abdomen of her little sister standing beside her, holding her hand. Her older sister grimaced at each wail of torment while she wiped beads of sweat from Delilah's forehead.

As they roasted all nine pigs together, the piglets turning simultaneously over the fire, all skewered to the same spit, the men of the village came to Methuselah where he sat in the middle of the town, bowed down before him, and kissed his hand. In gratitude for the sustenance brought to them like a blessed gift from the hand of Almighty Creation Itself, in turn every father not slaughtered the day prior offered the hand of his deflowered daughter as a tribute of thanks for the food they were otherwise too weak and traumatized to gather for their village themselves.

Shrieks, screams, and cries tore Methuselah's mother's heart to shreds while she held onto Delilah's other ankle, looking up to her sister, and then back to Delilah's undiluted agony while she held tightly. "It will all be over soon," she whispered where she tried to speak as she averted her gaze from the eyes of the woman in labor, whom she had intended on connecting with her own.

"You will not speak to my daughter! Delilah, my love, hold on. It is almost over."

A stone pulled heavily at her breathing in the back of her solar plexus. She silently awaited the birth of her grandson through the screams of her niece.

Methuselah scanned the faces of every person in the village, all of whom surrounded him as they gave thanks for the gifts of the life blood of the other creatures that he had brought for them in their hour of plight. His eyes rested on the pretty face of a girl toward the back of the crowd, who gazed down absently toward the ground. He called out to her, "You! You, there." She barely raised her eyes in his direction. "Please.' Please step forward." He motioned toward himself as he called out to her.

An older woman who stood beside her pointed toward Methuselah and began pushing on the girl's back. With the woman's hand on her back every step of the way, slowly the girl wove her way through the crowd.

When she stood before him, Methuselah spoke to her. "You are beautiful, child. How did I not see you clearly moments ago when your father offered me your hand?"

The girl continued to look away and toward the ground as the woman behind her took a step forward to stand almost beside her, while keeping her hand to her back. She looked straight into Methuselah's eyes when she spoke. "Her father, my husband, did not speak for her. He did not survive the other night to be able to do so. But she is quite young, and in our sorrow for all we have lost, neither of us considered that so wretched a condition as this would be a proper offering to one who has rode to our village with the purity of heart of solely feeding us in mind."

Methuselah smiled down upon the woman. "She does not seem too young. She must be older than twelve, at least, though her form could easily be seventeen..." He paused for a moment to stare at the very young woman before continuing, "and her beauty shines through her grief like a bright star through the cloak of night."

"She is only fourteen, sir. Sudden misery has a way of aging one's appearance. Today she looks to you seventeen, tomorrow she would look seven hundred, and I am sure that she would be ill company, so fully useless in the state she is now in."

"I would not argue with you, lady, after all you have lost. Perhaps, however, I might be happy company to her in this hour of her sadness. Perhaps I might be able to comfort her tonight even, and subsequently spend my life feeding her as I came to feed the entirety of your village this day." He smiled as warmly as his mouth would pull itself, pushing the shine of his teeth beyond the shadow of his eye sockets keeping the pigment of his irises escaping from the surrounding dark and being discerned.

After he had spoken, murmurs arose in the crowd that surrounded them. "He is asking to marry the wretched creature? How fortunate her mother is!" "Perhaps he will bring us such feasts as these between now and the wedding as we rebuild." "She could not be selfish enough not to pay such a pittance to our savior, could she?" And so on.

"My daughter, you can hear this, man's, generous offer to you. If in your grief you would refuse such a kindness, however, none could think ill of you, and I will fully accept your decision." She brought her hand from the small of her back and to her daughter's side, pulling her in closer to herself while she spoke.

"No one could think ill? What is this stupid, ungrateful old lady saying?" Was one of the many murmurs reaching the ears of her daughter before she spoke up for herself without raising her eyes toward her 'benefactor.' "I will accept his proposal, Mother."

She pulled her daughter into her closer. "Really, Magatha. You don't have to do this."

"Magatha. What a beautiful name for such a beautiful face. Come, take my hand and spend time with me in the space where your very kind neighbors have prepared for me a generous lodging, and so soft a bed as I have never known. Come with me, and even tonight I will show you the comfort I plan on affording you for the rest of your life."

Methuselah held his hand out for Magatha to take. Past the strong grip of her mother, she held out her hand to him and spoke without once looking up to his eyes, "Thank you, sir." Three heavy tears raised dust upon the ground while she took her first step toward where he led.

"Just one more push, Delilah, and it will be through!"

Delilah roared from the pain tearing through her body, and then a smaller voice pierced through the night its own discomfort as her pains of birth came to an end. After wrapping the child properly and warmly in a blanket, and handing him to his mother to comfort his new existence into the realm of the created, Delilah's mother asked what she would call him.

Through a haggard whisper just beyond the sobs that had spent nine months filling her throat, Delilah answered, "He will be known as The Lowness of Humanity."

From her place beside the bed, opposite her sister, Methuselah's mother began silently weeping to herself. So also did the unseen shadow of Harratzarian in the window.

Chapter 33

The downpour of rain was substantial when Methuselah's mother, soaked through so thoroughly that her cloak felt as though carrying the body of another, reentered her home.

As the door slammed shut behind her, Enoch rushed to her side. "My love! I have been given now a taste of what you must experience when I take a particularly long walk." His smile warmed some place in her heart as he threw his dryness onto her moisture. "Let us get you out of this skin like a lake, and bring you the warmth which should always surround you." With care he peeled the wetness off his wife, then embraced her, holding his mild dampness to her very damp chill. He held her tightly to warm her, then kissed her. In the light of the fire burning in the hearth, he saw that her eyes seemed distant. He picked her up, placed her in their bed, and drew the covers up over her. With his clothing still on, he entered underneath after her that his warmth might fill her.

"Love, I am so grateful to have you home. You have been so distant for months, though. For that matter, so has our firstborn son. How is it that neither of you were here to celebrate his one hundred and eighty-seventh birthday? Might you know where our son is now?"

"I'm sorry, my love. Clearly your journey has been long. I'm sure conversing about absence is the last thing on your mind while you are here. . . It's simply been terribly uncomfortable, feeling more absence than I am accustomed from the two most prominent people in my life."

She lay perfectly still, her hands gripping the edge of the blanket. Very silently she stared up at the ceiling, thinking. A moment or two later, "Enoch."

"Yes, Ahavah?"

"You are a grandfather." She turned away from her husband, pulled the cover over her head, and sobbed as silently as she could force the tears back into her throat.

Enoch stared toward her silently, watching her as she turned away from him. He wrapped his arms around her, kissed the back of her neck, and shut his eyes.

⁂

While Enoch had every intention of facilitating Methuselah's transition from his house peaceably, Methuselah had no intention of spending any more time in the home he had spent the first 187 years of his life growing up in.

When the people from the village came to collect Methuselah's belongings, they sang his praises to his father and mother. They told the story of how Methuselah had become the savior of their village. Enoch offered the five visitors to stay the night, and fed them from his garden. The next day, after thanking Enoch and his wife for their hospitality, and finishing filling the cart they had brought with Methuselah's things, they returned from where they had come.

Enoch sighed to think of what had been broken by his son, and for a moment considered if his own actions might have changed his son's decisions. Completing his sigh, he entered into the silence that followed it, and remained there for the answer to his consideration. He reflected that though his absence had resulted in Methuselah accidentally stumbling upon the tool of his own self-destruction, anybody's best possibility must ensue from Enoch choosing to walk in Divinity on the one hand, and the nature of a man comes from the results of the choices he's made when not being controlled like chattel on the other. Returning to thought once silence had facilitated the reentry of the pure happenstance of Methuselah's self-obliteration in Enoch's conception, he concluded that while he did not like the results, the limits of being a drop in the river of God determined the outcome of other drops so much more than pre-known bends far ahead in the flow that by none, independently, had ever been experienced before.

⋅⋅⋅

Methuselah delighted to see the arrival of the remnants of the food he had harvested over the course of his life up until that point in time, along with the tools with which he had reaped. He withheld the tear that formed its natural impulse when he heard from those he'd sent that clearly the goodness in his heart had resulted from his father's own kind example over the course of his life. Methuselah thanked them for their labor, and promised them a stag for each of their families in the coming days.

He entered his home, informed a swollen-bellied Magatha of the arrival of his belongings, and promised her a thorough *celebration* once she had finished bringing them inside.

⋅⋅⋅

Storm had filled the night shortly after his wife had led Enoch to the home of her sister. Enoch followed her to Delilah's room, where the very young mother gently rocked the newborn child in her arms. Enoch entered cautiously, but with a sincerely grateful smile on his face as he greeted

Delilah, "Ah! So this is The Lowness of Humanity? Welcome to the World Create, little one."

Chapter 34

On the other side of the world, where no man knew, a sow suckled her piglets. In the distance a large buck ran by, leaping into the warm breeze and the bright sun that warmed it. A mile later, he didn't notice a gray wolf lapping at the water flowing through the forest; a silver fish jumped out and landed back into the current somewhere downstream from where she drank.

In the light of the sun, a bee landed on a daisy. The light wind tilted the flower as it passed around it. As though the breath of God, such was the air upon which the birds flapped their wings before gliding toward the horizon. Higher still formed a cloud.

Aloft in the air, two angels floated and drifted and flapped far above the unmanned land across the Earth from where The Garden had been planted. Here they enjoyed themselves to the fullest extent of their divinely-formed genitalia. They had not arranged this meeting, but finding themselves sharing air space, they'd decided to converse on their experience over the past nine hundred years. Their self-enjoyment was rather rigorous. While they joined together in conversation, a large, steady rain cloud formed that lasted for months as the two "caught up."

Upon concluding their discussion of whether it felt better going into the daughters of man, or the sons of man, and admitting that they'd experienced limited enjoyment in both cases, they paused and looked for a moment at each others' pair of wings covering over their feet. Then, from a distance, they uncovered their own feet for the other to see. Their phalli stopped from their self-enjoyment at the sight of the feet of the other, and each became very erect while they admired each other's toes. The rain stopped pouring, the cloud quickly evaporated, and they rose away from the lake over which they had spent the last several months hovering; they pursued the answer to their mutual question. They went to ask their Creator if It might lift, at some point in time, the singular prohibition that had been set in place long ago.

Chapter 35

When the roving giant came through their village, an alarm sounded and doors were locked tight. It seemed to take delight in breaking walls with its fist and plucking vegetables with one hand from gardens while simultaneously crushing crops through sweeping movements of its legs. It would knock trees over into front doors just for thrills, and snap the necks of any cattle unattended with the vice-grip of its hand. When it saw the pretty face of Delilah peering from behind a door in the distance, it decided it was hungry for the devastation of something else.

"Mother, I think it saw me!" Delilah was in a panic. She quickly barred the door after seeing the inbred creature stepping in the direction of her house.

"Stupid girl. Get back to your room. Now!"

Without stopping to verify if her daughter was right about the direction in which the giant was heading by unbarring the door, she went to find the biggest cutting knife in her kitchen. Concealing it under her belt, behind her back, she unbarred the door and took a deep breath before making plain to her eyes what evil might be walking her way. Twelve feet or so from where she stood approached the giant in question.

She smiled up at it as it pulled the door off its hinges one by one while smirking. It looked directly into her eyes. Its arm outstretched, slowly playing with the constitution of her property, she took the knife from her belt and, shrieking at the top of her voice, plunged the blade forward into the chest of the creature with the full force of her body. The handle of the knife found itself halfway into the giant's torso. Its eyes widened with shock, its hand slipped from where it had been holding the door moments prior, and the gargantuan being fell over from the inability of its heart to beat through the blade. The door still clung to one lone hinge at its bottom corner while it tapped backward against the side of the house.

Calling loudly into the dwelling that it was time to leave, she pointed her family toward the closest place on Earth she could think of that apparently had never been accosted by giants or Nephilim alike. At merely half a day's journey, she figured Enoch's home would welcome her family, given his family's debt to hers.

❦ ❦ ❦

Enoch was happy to take the men-folk, and girls who didn't mind swinging a hammer, alike, and set to work building a house for his sister-in-law upon the space of land in which he set his own home.

Initially, upon arrival, they were offered whatever place in his home was available to make their beds. The first night in Enoch's house, Lamech fussed and cried every time Delilah tried to fall asleep by his side. Wandering from where she was sleeping with Enoch's daughters, she saw an open, empty room and, not wanting to disturb the rest of the others in the house, she entered, closed the door, and began rocking her son so that he might sleep. Only a short time later, asleep he was. Delilah rose, stepped a foot outside of the room, and again Lamech woke and began to cry. Again she closed the door and rocked him, and again he fell quickly to sleep. It was not long before, resting her head against a wall, she was taking her own slumber along with her son in her arms. The following day, the same series of events occurred. Enoch's wife felt obligated to inform her why she'd not been offered the room at the onset. Swallowing her resentment, she decided that if this room was the only place Lamech would take his rest, then it would be in the room in which Methuselah had resided that a bit of peace perhaps would be restored.

Even after a house had been built for her family, Delilah found that while Lamech continued to fuss in the new home and could not be made to fall asleep, in the room in which Methuselah had grown up, Lamech was always easy into his dreams. Quite in love with his grandson, Enoch was happy to let Delilah stay in his house with his family, making every effort to see that Delilah was comfortable, having found her existence most tolerable in the room of the man who had raped her: his son. As the years began to roll forward, it wasn't long before Delilah left her son, at the age of three years, to take the room as his own and sleep alone, while she took her own rest in a room that had belonged to Methuselah's sisters past and present.

Over the next one hundred and ten years, Enoch delighted in raising Lamech as though he were his own son. Enoch taught him to garden, to build, and to help his grandmother, and everyone in both houses with whatever work they put their hands to, "Because, Lamech, as they are successful in the fruition of their labors, so too will you find fruition in the results of yours." As was such, Lamech was a joy to all his family and all who came and went from the house of Enoch.

❧ ❧ ❧

Lamech missed his grandfather when Enoch would take long walks, but, as he got older, Lamech enjoyed making himself useful to others and tended his grandfather's garden while he was away. When he had turned 113, he heard from his grandmother that his grandfather would not be returning.

He tried to sit in silence like his grandfather had taught him, that he might hear the voice of God guide him to understanding past his sudden sadness, but always too quickly his tears broke the silence and, while he lent his hand to make better the lives of his family, he found the months often brought him sullenness and despair. Then, shortly after he had turned 114, Lamech's grandmother gave birth.

❧ ❧ ❧

It gave Harratzarian great joy to hear the news that the wife of Enoch had been given a final gift from her husband before his parting: a daughter. So too did it bring joy to the whole of the households, not the least of which was Lamech's.

As much as it pained Lamech that the man after whom he'd patterned the behaviors of his own existence had parted from his life, just so did he pour his attention, smiles, and love into his aunt; the last gift given into *his* life by the direct cause of the cause of his existence, Enoch. Over the years, he watched her as a brother, was there for her as a friend, educated her as though a teacher, and was as close to a father as she knew. Her mother smiled upon their bond while her daughter grew. She was happy that Lamech was there for her as she saw the good-hearted, hard-working young lady she was becoming.

When Lamech was 126, however, he couldn't help but notice what a very pretty little girl his aunt was. When he was 128, her development into womanhood was becoming obvious. When he had turned 132 years old, he began to notice himself salivating, just a little bit, while in the presence of the beautiful young woman whom he'd spent the last eighteen years of his life pouring the love of his heart into.

He immediately filled with embarrassment, and his cheeks turned red at his thoughts of having spent most of a century and a half without companionship, and fully realizing how completely starving he was. Then, noticing the pull in his heart toward Light Within The Darkness, he found himself desperately trying to reconcile the enormity of his emotion with the tradition of his progenitors of finding kindred expression far removed from the immediate factors causing their own presence to materialize into existence within the world. Recalling the tale told him many times of how his grandparents had met at the river's bank, he never imagined he'd find the joy of his heart too close to home for the comfort of his mind, and his duty to the memory of the man who'd inspired him to be a man in kind. Feeling shame to consider the harm he may do to his family's legacy, Lamech resolved to ignore his impulses toward his young aunt, spend a little less time with her, and spend more time at market where he could get to know other women, and perhaps find one who would be more appropriate to feed his hunger.

The next morning, as he was setting out for other social climes, upon hearing his name called, Lowness Of Humanity turned to see Light Within running towards him. With a great smile upon her face, she threw herself into his arms, embraced him tightly, and wished him a good deal of fun wherever he was heading off to. Lamech squeezed her back, kissed her forehead, and wished her the same before letting go, turning, and walking away.

Chapter 36

They knew better than to bring Harratzarian news of Methuselah, of the adam who believed himself to be an ape, so Lashkantanktin asked her instead after Lamech. Harratzarian sighed heavily. "180 years old, and while he has... offered the fields many a fertility sacrifice, he still has never shared his fertility with a woman. I know he wishes to honor the customs of his progenitors, his own father aside of course, but the simple fact is she worships his presence just as he does hers. He pours his insanity so thoroughly into that garden every night that by each morning light, I cannot tell if it is he or the snails that have been occupying the garden by the rays of the moon. And by all means, *she* should be deprived of what they could be sharing no longer!"

"I hear you, Harratzarian, but he pays the price for the horror his father is, and she is still quite young. In due time they'll each find the light within kindled by another who would not co-create gargantuanism by the expression of their impulse to further adam existence."

"The light that is kindled from within them both shines from one to the other, just as Our Common Source considers Its infinity through Its knowledge of All. They deserve to share this light as surely as a Rose of Sharon deserves to know the sun's ray and the rain's kiss; the forces of the fibers weaving life existent funneled into the one flower, that the secret of creation's purpose may be properly whispered to the wind that allows the flower finally to breathe!" Finishing this thought, she stood abruptly and walked briskly from her friend.

"Light go with you, Harratzarian. May your heart know the peace of Perfection once more."

⟡⟡⟡

One day, Lamech's grandmother asked Lamech to go to market on her behalf. Though their farm yielded most of what they ate from day to day, a gathering of both families, as well as certain extended family, would be taking place in just a couple of days time, and there was much they did not have that they needed for the ensuing feast, "And please take Light Within with you. You'll need help bringing that much back."

"As you wish." Lamech could no more deny his grandmother's request than he could stop breathing.

From the depth of his heart, he issued forth from his lungs a sigh of resignation to the fact of his existence before starting out toward the marketplace with Light Within The Darkness by his side. In turn, the 66-year-old woman skipped joyously by her cousin's side to be spending her afternoon with her favorite person on the planet. Together they walked.

While at market, they began to gather the vegetables and meats not readily available in their own garden for the feast. As they surveyed the sellers to see what else they might need, a woman selling garments at a far corner of the market caught their eye. She motioned for them to come to where she stood. She beckoned them to peruse her wares. "Perhaps this belt for the lady? This shirt for the gentleman? Ah, but I must have the perfect thing for you somewhere..."

They took delight in all that the woman was offering, or more specifically, how the woman was offering it as they awaited whatever she would next pull from the bag within which she currently rummaged.

"Well, now! This is an interesting item... The two of you are already married though, yes?"

They stared at each other awkwardly and giggled a bit nervously. "No, no. This is actually my aunt. Far too close in family that it would even occur to us." Light briefly looked away from her nephew, not quite sure why it would feel painful that he had said such a thing.

"I didn't necessarily mean to each other." The woman had a look of concern on her face as she responded to Lamech. "And I certainly didn't mean to imply an idea that would be disquieting to either of you. Perhaps one, or both, of you have a spouse at home, and you are shopping for a larger family gathering." She gestured toward the fairly large quantity of food they were already carrying with them.

Lamech's cheeks became colored with moderate embarrassment to the conclusion he had jumped to by the woman's words.

"So it is understood. And indeed, we are shopping for a family gathering. Neither Lamech nor I, however, are married."

"Perhaps, then, this item would be appropriate to offer one or the other of you. Let me show you. Join hands!" Without waiting for them to respond she stepped forward, took the right hand of one, the left hand of the other, and clasped their hands together, holding them together in hers before commanding them, "Now, just stay just like that as I show you!"

She walked behind them and began wrapping a blue, red, and purple cloth around Lamech's upper wrist, around their clasped hands, and finally around Light Within's upper wrist as she rapidly spoke, "You see, this very special scarf is wound just so during a marriage ceremony as the initiator indicates that this entanglement is symbolic of the bond that joins two who love each other, just as the two so bind themselves to the choice of creating more capable of looking at their Self through the perception of what otherwise would be misconstrued as differentiation of being. So does the return to unity consecrate the formation of those who make the journey to returning. Amen. Amen. Amen. Or something like that..."

While catching only brief flecks of the meanings of the woman's words, what the two understood quite clearly was the feel of the one in the hand of the other, and it was not long before their eyes began speaking loudly to one another past the words of the woman spoken behind.

She began unwinding the scarf while their gaze continued to hold tight, much as did their hands once the scarf had been completely unwound and removed. Coming into his mind, Lamech slipped his hand out of his aunt's before thanking the woman for sharing with them her goods, linking his arm with Light's and walking them both toward the remainder of what they had to purchase before beginning back upon the path that led them both home.

After unwrapping the scarf expertly woven by Kleshala from the held hands of Lamech and Light Within The Darkness, Harratzarian was filled with joy in her heart to see that Lamech would not let them unlink from each other, even as he seemed torn between his desires to fulfill the shopping list of his grandmother, and to be as quickly as possible away from the eyes of the marketplace. She delighted to see them depart side by side.

❧ ❧ ❧

Still a mile away from where they lived, Lamech let go from him all he carried. He grabbed Light Within The Darkness around the waist, and he kissed her on the mouth. "Let us not speak of this again until two days after the gathering of our family is over." Then he picked up all he had purchased on Light's mother's behalf. Together, silently, they arrived home.

Chapter 37

Initially, Lamech's grandmother thought very little of seeing her grandson and her daughter holding hands; it wasn't so unusual, and their closeness had never been a secret. When it had become quite clear to her, however, that the belly of Light Within The Darkness was expanding in a way that mere food ingestion couldn't account for, as placid dirt under motionless water fallen into by a tree trunk, such were her emotions, the obvious settling itself firmly into the complacency of her thoughts.

Noticing the murk of her feelings all at once arise within, she remembered her husband's face. A smile arose to her own. She shut her eyes, sought a moment of silence within the entirety of her being, and heard the voice of over four hundred years of experience of life enter her mind and strain out all but what she had seen of love and creation in her time existent. Blood of her blood, she knew these people well; her role toward them was clear.

In the light of the sun, as they both held hands saturated by the brightness and warmth permeating the garden, Yofi Meikhil Aish Eloki stepped nimbly toward them such that they were not aware of her presence until she spoke. "Most of all, Lamech, I do not need to remind you of why the men in our family were particularly diligent in choosing for their self a wife who was as far removed from the closeness of their own blood as they were capable of discovering..."

❧ ❧ ❧

When Harratzarian had returned from market that day with the scarf woven by Kleshala's hand wrapped around her own arm, she found waiting at her camp her brothers and sisters-in-kind peering toward her from the large fire which they had encircled in assembly. Luciferous greeted her with the impatience of his own thoughts once she had arrived. "Where once from no intention of your own hand a curse was brought, nevertheless through you, upon the tranquility of being of this family, now you have chosen of your own free will to influence their choice toward dubious possibilities. Why?"

"Because they'd both already suffered enough from my needing one fine day to empty the contents of my bladder just at the worst moment possible! They were both born from Enoch's love uniquely, and have both shared a bond of that love uniquely from the day that Light Within was born. Fifty years he's spent trying to suppress what he could not run from; trying to deny himself truly in proportion to how deeply he's fallen in love with her. And she's spent at least as long looking at him as the only man whom time itself would stop its beating heart, that she could spend more moments with him. Knowing full well the sole reason it would almost behoove us to stand in their way, I resolved instead that they should stop suffering by their own hands, if only they'd place one of theirs in that of the other. I know those 'dubious possibilities' painfully as they seem almost the only possibilities this species of animal, adam, is capable of manifesting. If, as a whole, they persist in slitting their own throats accidentally anyway, if the same should happen here, at least this time the cut is consciously by *my* own hand, and the result is that two people share for a change what they ought to, and what is *genuinely* Godly, just as their father and his wife shared before them.

"You don't need to lecture me, Luciferous. These people write their own doom every day, without my help. Let us discuss what help we can legitimately offer to these who would shut their eyes to the light of the sight of their own salvation, just as the sun rises high enough for them to see by it."

With that she joined around the fire and sat by her brothers and sisters as they all began discussing what best to do, should a giant be born finally from the latest of the firstborn sons of Adam.

❧❧❧

"... which is how I know you could not have made this decision lightly. Where your father of blood hid from humanity, you have sought them for decades with your whole being in hopes that a mate would cross your path who you could share life and love with as surely as you have my own daughter from the moment she had been born. Your long and sincere self-denials and self-effacements have not gone unnoticed as you no doubt drove yourself quite crazy seeking to honor the memory of your grandfather, and what you wish your own father, my son, had respected as the tradition of our family since Adam himself found himself alone and solely create in The Garden of Divine Everlasting.

"I cannot imagine a man even with purest of heart who could share with my daughter the purity of what you apparently have chosen to share with her. I look forward to welcoming this new creation issuing from the depth of your beings. I've no doubt only love can come from true love touching true love, before which I stand."

From the corner of Lamech's eye, a tear whispered gratitude, reflecting the smile of his grandmother's face, indistinguishable from the smile upon his wife's face, the smile upon his face, or the rays from the sun making all life possible inside the garden within which they resided.

ༀ ༀ ༀ

In the one hundred and eighty-second year of Lamech's life, a great celebration took place in the garden first grown by Enoch. One month before the time Light Within The Darkness was expected to give birth, family amassed from all over East of Eden so that the marriage of The Lowness to Light Within The Darkness might be witnessed by The Eyes Of God through anyone who cared to see the union of the two to a life together.

As the firstborn of firstborns, coincidentally all male, Kenan, Mahalalel, and Jared were regarded as guests of honor, and stayed on the property in the houses that Enoch had built. All others made camp outside the gates of the garden, so that they would not have far to travel to join the celebrations within.

The smile of Light Within was as wide as her belly when, before their family, she spoke her commitment, and he echoed hers, that they would join to each other in life, create together, and support each other, be it with hand, head, or silence in whatever endeavor occurred to the other as being in the fullest sense Good. From the crowd amassed around them rose a loud cheer into the sky that mimicked what the two felt for one another as their arms reached instinctively toward each other's bodies, and they shared four lungs as though one breath. They celebrated what almost seven decades convinced them as truth beyond denial, and they delighted to share that truth, this day, with all of existence, which had played part in creating them as they stood side by side. Joy sang loudly and clearly through garden and encampment alike, and the two were grateful to take their rest together that night, honored in the continuing jubilation that awaited the near arrival.

❧❧❧

Through the rare convergence of over six generations of Adam from all over East of Eden, an opportunity of unabashed anonymity presented itself. The servants, who were made manifest as human anatomy, wasted no time taking advantage of these communities unfamiliar with each other, sharing together a common patch of ground for the sake of the revelry of their existence. As the masses arrived, so too did those once purely hosting Divinity Superseding Creation make camp outside of the garden now tended to by The Lowness. Should they be asked, each was ready with stories of lineage traceable to the origin of man.

As Light Within's hands found their way to Lamech's hips, and Lamech's hand to her cheeks, Harratzarian felt tears made seemingly of light fall down the sides of her own face while she watched, smiling, from mere steps away, gratefully in broad daylight. She felt an urge for Hardahor from her heart to her groin as she remembered the feeling of being complete. There was solace in the thought that as she existed, so too was he existent to be able to reunite with, once action in existence became clearer to her than leaving spears around while peeing, and encouraging those who would love each other to ignore the possibilities of inbreeding liable to lead to gargantuanism being created in their home. She sighed to ponder that a great deal of resignation to silent observation may be required before being returned to completeness of self, and then focused herself again on the faces of the young lovers whom she hoped, especially for the sake of her own ease of heart and mind, would continue sharing the joy they now felt as their lives unfolded to be experienced together.

The in-human-form-incarnate angels watched grateful that their influence could in some way cause great joy in people's lives, just as they'd experienced their influence cause great suffering in those of others.

❦ ❦ ❦

Two weeks after their commitment was made to be witnessed by all beings seeking to celebrate life, the other side of the festivities commenced with everybody attending in silence while the screams of Light Within The Darkness filled the air as harbinger of the new capability of perception almost arrived.

With a large forehead, but normal features, their firstborn, again a son, was named Rest, by Light, with Lowness' grateful acquiescence to his wife's choice. "From the pain that exists among us in creation, in this child we rest knowing that despite the storms of being that may arise loudly into our lives, the true love that brings us together will always offer a truth beyond the chaos where we may settle down and find comfort as the sun shows its face again between any beings in whom love exists." With that she rested her head back upon a pillow, Noah safe and warm in her arms.

Outside the house, Jared picked up an empty cup and shouted clearly to all those gathered round, "The boy is born! Let the festivities resume!" With that he grabbed a chicken off a nearby spit, filled his cup with crystal-clear water, and began to consume.

❦ ❦ ❦

The next day, as light woke roosters, roosters sung men out of their sleep, and Mahalalel shouted loudly from garden to encampment, "A new day has dawned in still the first day of the new one's existence. Raise your hearts out of slumber, and let merriment commence again!" So it was that people brought forth goats, chickens, and cattle to slaughter in honor of the newly-made life. Concoctions of juices and honey were rolled out in barrels. Fires were kindled. Before long, celebration was well underway so far as the eye could see. All shared with each other what was brought, the one family of Adam showing what nine generations of experimenting with foods had produced in innovations of pleasing the tongue for as long as the lives of conscious beings had subsisted on the lives of other beings with varying gradations of minds, just as *those* beings did of each other.

On a long, hot summer day, the jubilee stretched forth into the late afternoon when the far edge of the crowd turned silent. A man, followed by attendants pushing a wagon, began winding his way through the encampment until at last finding his feet to the garden's gate. Within the garden, Mahalalel, Jared, and Kenan had cups of honeyed apple cider raised to the Heavens in toast of the splendor of existence when Kenan saw the pale, husky figure of the man standing before the entrance to the garden, reaching his hand toward the gate to open it. "Not on your life, kid!" one of the three shouted toward the visitor at the threshold. They began quickly walking in the entrance's direction when Lamech, who'd been standing behind the three while they were toasting, looked up to see what his great-grandfathers in succession had begun moving so briskly to confront. Between their forms, on the other side of the fence, he saw a man he'd never seen before. He followed after to see what the commotion was about.

"It is my right as his father–"

"You gave up all rights to your father's garden when you lowered yourself to a common monkey and violated his mother. Good fortune your father was able to be man enough for both of you, and clean up the disgrace you brought to our family. Be gone, worm!"

"Jared? Why do you speak this way to any family who would seek celebration with us?" Lamech wished to know why the conflict was arising on the beauty of the peace of this otherwise in all ways blessed day.

"He's no family of ours. Go be with your son, grandchild. We'll take care of this... problem."

"But all here are family. What do you mean—"

"*Your* son? Lamech? Is that you?"

"Don't even know your own firstborn, chimp?"

"Your own firstborn? You mean, you're... Methuselah?"

"Yes, son. I've come to make you an offering of my hunt in honor of—"

"Don't call me son." Lamech's face began turning red as he took a step back from the face he never thought that in his lifetime he would see.

Lamech's grandmother began to approach the commotion from her house, as Lamech had addressed Methuselah.

"But you *are* my son. I—"

"You raped my mother *and* the love given to you by yours. Enoch is my father. You are as welcome here as a child of a son of God."

"I came to congratulate you on the birth of my grandson and—"

"If you wish truly to give a gift either to myself, my wife, or our child, we will never hear, let alone see, of your existence again. You are not welcome here. Please come, grandfathers." Lamech turned from Methuselah and began walking silently toward the house. Jared, Mahalalel, and Kenan turned from Methuselah and followed Lamech in kind.

As they walked, they came to Methuselah's mother walking toward the gate. Lamech reached his hand to his grandmother's shoulder and shook his head; the words not yet formed telling her she had no need to walk further. The old lady looked deeply into her son-in-law's eyes, made effort toward a smile that could not convince any of happiness, patted his hand, kissed Lamech's cheek, and then continued walking toward the garden's entrance. All four men turned to see the old woman face her son.

She stopped three steps from the gate and looked into Methuselah's eyes. Methuselah stared back at his mother. He began to smile and started to speak, "Moth–" before she quickly turned round from him and slowly started walking toward her home. A tear began to form at the corner of her eye as she took her first step away from her firstborn child. When she had arrived to where Kenan, Mahalalel, Jared, and Lamech waited and watched, she linked arms with Lamech and Jared, and let them support much of her weight while they made their way to the house that was Enoch's creation, brain to hand.

Methuselah, saddened, then moved to shame, and with it inward anger, gestured his hand to open the gate when a separate pair of hands grabbed hold of his arm and pushed him back. "Did you not hear their words? They do not want you here. As *we* honor the newborn Rest, we respect their wishes. You will not enter that gate, cousin."

"Do you not know who I am? I am firstborn son of Enoch. Descendent of Adam. Savior of the town to the southwest. This day my grandson was born!"

"We are all descendents of Adam here, cousin. All I know of who you are is that you are not welcome here. So, if you care about who you claim is your son, kindly do him the honor of leaving, yeah?"

Others from the crowd began stepping between Methuselah and the entrance to the garden. Methuselah spat on the ground and spoke to his attendants. "Being spoken to this way by these vermin is beneath me. Let us not waste our time or food on them further." With that, they turned from the garden's gate, a wagon filled with decaying animals of all kinds following behind Methuselah, pushed by his gaunt, pale assistants through the crowd, beginning a long journey back south and west from whence they came.

Mingled with the crowd, feet from the fence and where Methuselah had stood, Harratzarian began sobbing uncontrollably as Methuselah passed directly before her. "Miss, are you okay?" came from the gentleman beside her. But she was not okay, and could only sob and shake her head "no" as the humans around her put hands on her shoulders and back and attempted to calm her in every way they could while she fell to her knees, her face hidden as well as possible in the palms with which she attempted to hold back the two streams of water issuing forth from behind them.

When Methuselah was past the crowd, and clearly beyond the view of any who had come surrounding the house and land of Lamech's family to honor the life he created, Kenan raised his cup high to the air and loudly, joyously shouted, "Let our celebration of life begin again!"

Chapter 38

All were welcome to stay and celebrate for as long as they liked. Days turned into weeks, and in turn months, until finally, the only celebrants left were the great-grandfathers.

Jared tickled the tummy of his great-great grandson. Noah giggled, squirmed, and smiled up at him. "Well, old men," Jared spoke to his father and grandfather, "we do have our own gardens to tend. It is time, I think, for Lamech and Light to begin life without abnormal distraction. Shall we take our leave?" The old men smiled, nodded, gave due farewells and set out a short time later.

Lowness and Light Within The Darkness were grateful to have their home more or less to themselves. As they sat by the fire, Lamech ran his fingers over Noah's forehead and wondered. Might his son posses an intelligence that others lacked? Perhaps this physical characteristic was merely something temporary that would be grown out of.

As years went on, however, Noah's flat, wide forehead stayed a prominent fixture of his visage. Contrary to Lamech's hope, Noah did not seem imbued with an intelligence greater than that of other children as he grew up. Noah was five years old before speaking his first word, "Momma!" Although he was saying it to Lamech at the time, Lamech, in that instant, breathed a sigh of relief, since he had come to believe he may never hear a word uttered by his firstborn son. Several months later, he began to seem to clearly distinguish "Momma" from "Dadda," and again Lamech breathed another sigh of relief.

It would be some years later still before Noah was able to form whole sentences. Quicker than he was able to learn speech, however, he showed an aptitude for digging small holes, adding to them a seed, filling them in again, and repeating the process elsewhere. Though the capabilities of Noah's brain were clearly in question, his proficiency for holding a spade was not. It was often that when a flower he'd planted bloomed, he would pull it from the earth and offer it to his mother, or for that matter any other human being who might come within the range of his arm.

While Lowness and Light had created a couple more children together between Noah's birth and when he turned seven, Lamech, fully aware of the development of the brain growing behind the wall of his first child's forehead, decided that warmth and affection toward his wife might be preferable to copulation, lest a giant be born to their home. Long were the discussions for years about how best to proceed with their sexuality considering their circumstance, their love for each other, and the fact that both of them wished to create more lives upon the face of the world. In the end it was decided that while at the end of the night, most nights anyway, the two would return to the bed they shared, it was time that other houses be built outside the gates of the garden. The agreement was that any children born therefrom, as well as those partners in the creation of those children, should reside in said houses. It was also agreed upon that the children would be allowed to come and go as they pleased, and raised just as though Lamech and Light Within The Darkness had created them together. From forward on, any partners in creating life found would come from families unfamiliar, usually people found to be mutually attractive in the marketplace, so that no fear of gargantuanism would ever befall them again. So it was

Lamech and Light continued to have other sons and daughters.

⁂

One day, when Noah was twelve, as he was walking in the garden, his entire field of vision was filled by pure, white, light. As the light dissipated, a robed man stood before him, smiling. Noah looked around him quickly, found a yellow flower growing about a foot away, picked it, and offered it to the man in the robe. The man in the robe smiled wider.

⁂

One day, when Noah was thirteen, as he was walking in the garden, he saw a man, pale and husky, standing amidst a briar patch, grinning. He motioned for Noah to come over to where he stood, which Noah gleefully did. When Noah had finished skipping over to the man, he was about to say "Hi" when he saw the finger pressed to the man's lips that he should be quiet. Looking around rapidly, Noah found a white flower growing from the ground that he promptly plucked and offered to the man in lieu of a greeting. The man's grin changed to something more like a scowl that he immediately tried to turn back into a grin as he took the flower. He stared at it with apparent disbelief, crushed it in his hand, tossed it to the ground, and then began motioning with a crooked index finger toward himself. "Thank you. Come with me," whispered without joy to the boy's ear as he took a first step toward the garden gate. Noah felt very confused, but he followed behind the man with the long, pointy stick beyond the threshold of the garden.

They walked a bit farther, where the trees were many, before the man stopped and turned to Noah. "Do you want to know who I am?"

Noah thought about answering, then remembered that the man had motioned for him to be silent. He decided it was best just to look at the man without answering.

Unnerved by the way Noah was looking at him, the man became noticeably agitated. "Well, don't just stare at me. Speak!"

Noah responded, "I would like to know who you are."

"Good! Good. Noah, I, am your grandfather." Methuselah grinned widely down upon his grandson, as though he'd just informed him about his greatest accomplishment in life.

Noah looked up at Methuselah, a bit puzzled, and then responded, "Jared? It doesn't look like you."

The corners of Methuselah's mouth dropped and he responded dejectedly, "No, that's your great-great-grandfather. I'm your father's father–"

"Enoch? You don't look like him either." Noah frowned a bit.

"How would you know! I mean, no. I'm Methuselah." He again tried to contort his mouth into the shape of a smile.

"No. Daddy always told me that Enoch was his father. He never mentioned *you* at all."

"He knew not when I'd return from a long, exciting adventure. I'm sure Lamech just didn't want you to miss me." Noah smiled and nodded. Methuselah thought internally, *Wow. This kid'll believe anything.* "Listen, boy, your father still hasn't taught you to hunt, has he?"

"Hunt? What does that men?"

"What does that mean!" Methuselah stopped himself, clutched at his chest, and took a deep breath. He collected himself before continuing, "Hunting is what separates big, strong men from little boys. You do want to be a big, strong man, don't you?" Noah nodded yes eagerly. Methuselah breathed a sigh of relief. "Good. I just need you to promise me one thing, Noah."

"What is it... Grandpa?"

Methuselah's grin returned before continuing, "Just never, ever, tell your father that you've seen me, or that you're learning how to hunt. The next time he sees me, I want to surprise him with you and the first elk you bag, which you certainly won't find on your first day. Okay? You don't want to ruin the surprise, do you?"

Noah thought about trying to drag a large bag with a full-grown elk wriggling inside of it to his father, and the look that would be on Lamech's face. He could hardly believe that such a thing could ever happen, but if Methuselah told him he'd teach him how to put an elk into a bag, he had no reason to doubt. "Of course not! I promise I won't tell Daddy."

"There's a good lad. I knew you'd do the right thing." Upon his pale, well-fed face, Methuselah's grin was fully repaired and wider than ever, "Now, do you know what this is?" Methuselah held out his spear for Noah to look upon.

Noah nodded his head, "Of course I do. It's a walking stick! Though I've never seen one that pointy before."

"No. No. No! It's not a walking stick. It's a spear!" Grin again broken, Methuselah huffed, "God himself left this for me to find when I was more or less whatever age you are now, many, many years ago." Just as he finished speaking, a small bunny rabbit hopped out from behind a large tree. "Let me show you how it works. . ."

Noah was instantly spellbound by the beautiful walking spear gifted personally to his new grandfather by the Omni-Potent Common-Creator-Endlessness so long ago. He was even happier when the cute bunny rabbit appeared with such perfect timing, and a little, scrunched nose, for his new grandfather's demonstration. As Methuselah lifted the long piece of wood above his head, Noah thought to himself that maybe the spear stick would make the bunny jump upon its hind legs and begin to dance as though the trees made music for it to dance to, until it danced finally into a bag

Methuselah had waiting, much like the elk that Noah would one day hunt also.

Methuselah pulled back his arm, then after a brief pause, thrust forward and released the shaft into the air. The point hit its mark direct, and the rabbit was instantly impaled straight through; the spear's head showing clearly with a small bit of shaft on the other side of the small body it initially had entered.

Spear and rabbit lay together very still. It took a moment before anything made sense to Noah. Then, when it was quite clear that the bunny was far from happy, Noah's eyes widened and he began to shriek at the top of his lungs. Methuselah turned quickly toward Noah. Noah looked up at Methuselah, and his eyes widened more, and he screamed even louder. Methuselah started to take a step toward Noah and began to speak, "No–"

Noah instantly turned toward his house and ran back to the garden as quickly as his legs would carry him; tears streaming down his face, voice high-pitched and terrified all the way home.

☙☙☙

That night, Noah wept until finally falling to sleep from the sheer exhaustion of crying. "But why would he do that to the cute little bunny, Daddy? Why?" His mother stroked his head while his father rubbed his back. Lamech and Light Within looked at each other with heavy eyes as they tried to calm their hysterical son through the night. When, at last, he did fall asleep under the weight of his own tears, not fifteen minutes would pass before he would awaken screaming, followed shortly by another round of crying, until the cycle of his short-lived slumber commenced anew.

Over the following three days, through tears he was hand-fed. His parents rocked him in their arms in shifts, taking turns to comfort him. Then, finally, his sobs were slowed enough that he could lean away from Lamech, look him in the eye, and ask of his father intelligibly, "Methuselah is a bad man, isn't he, father?"

"Yes he is, son. Yes he is." Lamech smiled down upon his son to hear him speak a sentence rather than wailing toward him but a single word: 'bunny.' "But I don't think you'll have to worry about seeing him ever again." Indeed, Lamech didn't think Methuselah would try to see his grandson again; he counted Methuselah as too much a coward. *Besides,* considered Lamech, *if ever he should try, it will not be hard to hear the sounds Methuselah dreads coming out of my son from anywhere he may be.*

⋆⋆⋆

It was a week or so later that Noah played in the garden when a bright light filled the entirety of his vision. When the light subsided, and the garden could be articulated again, Noah was happy to see a familiar smile gracing a man in a white robe. "Grandpa Enochtron! I met a bad Methuselah while you were gone. He killed a bunny rabbit! And he said you were his father, and he's my real grandpa." Noah suddenly felt embarrassed that he had spoken the last part out loud. He frowned and lowered his eyes to the ground.

"He *was* Enoch's son, Noah. Though I think Lamech would tell you that Enoch was *his* father. But don't worry, Noach. Methuselah will never bother you again, and one day you will save *all* the bunny rabbits!"

Noah smiled up at the man smiling brightly down on him. Noah's vision filled to pure white light before, again, all he could see was the garden.

In the distance, Hoflan looked at Lemothta and asked, "What do you think it means that he keeps talking to the air as though someone is there?"

Lemothta responded, "I don't know. Maybe it's just another part of his 'condition.'"

They continued to watch in silence while Noah picked flowers for his mommy and daddy, and ran to the house to enjoy the company of his family for the night.

Chapter 39

One day, having tilled the garden the first five hours after the sun had risen, Noah took an ax from where the tools were kept and walked beyond the boundaries of the garden to where the trees grew. He walked himself a solid two and a half miles into the forest, found the largest, thickest tree he could find, and swung the ax into the tree as hard as he could. The vibrations hurt Noah's hands. It was hard for him to pull the ax out of the tree. When he finally did get the ax loose, Noah felt very tired. He was disappointed to see he'd only made a small mark where the ax had struck. Immediately he lifted the ax again, pulled its head back over his shoulder, and swung it into the tree. This time the blade landed a little below the initial mark he had made in the trunk. Taking all his strength to again extricate ax from tree, he frowned, discouraged that he had made a new mark rather than adding to the very small chip in the tree that had been created with his first swing. He sighed, drew back the handle, and lunged the blade forward exactly between the first two marks. He groaned, drew back the handle again, and swung. Without looking at where the blade hit, he immediately brought back the handle, and then swung forward. Again he swung forward, and again, and again, and again, and again, and again. Looking to where he had hit the tree repeatedly with the head of the ax, he was delighted to see that at least one of his swings had landed in a place originally chipped into the bark. Feeling something resembling satisfaction, he swung into the tree non-stop for the next hour.

Gasping for air and sweating, Noah looked to where he had been swinging. A large mark, about six inches deep, showed a clear gap where the tree had once been whole. Noah gazed at the gap in disbelief. He kicked at the tree and dropped the ax as his foot connected with the trunk; he cried a little that the tree was being so mean to him.

He fell to the ground and sat up with his back against the solid trunk. He sobbed into his hands for a moment or two longer. He thought about limping back home, dragging the ax behind him as he went, and then decided better of it. He simply couldn't stop now; *they* needed him too much. He stood back up, picked up the handle, and began to swing.

He thrust forward with all his might, one hour, two hours, three hours. After five hours had passed, hardly a break taken in between swings at the tree, finally, he heard a creaking sound from the spot in which the metal tooth that was the ax's blade had been swung. Hardly able to hold the ax up any longer, he dragged it with him to the side of, and away from, the tree as it teetered for several moments before finally falling from its inability to support its own weight.

Letting the ax fall to the ground and still regaining his breath, Noah threw his arms as far around the trunk of the fallen tree as they would reach and thanked it for finally laying down for him. He promised the tree to return the next day to play with it more as he stood up, picked up the very heavy ax, rested it upon his shoulder, and started walking back home, the last rays of sun kissing the sky goodnight.

Tartantuan and Triomvet looked at each other from where they watched a short distance from Noah. "Why do you suppose he just spent all day chopping that tree down?"

"Maybe it's just a new symptom of his 'condition'?"

"Maybe..."

They followed him home to where his parents and the rest of the household were preparing to partake of dinner. He replaced the ax unseen, though not intentionally, before joining with the rest of his family and taking his seat at the table. "What did you do today, Noah?"

"I played with a tree, Mommy!"

Light Within smiled at Noah brightly, happy that her son was happy. Neither his brothers, nor his sisters, nor his parents asked Noah to elaborate. After four hundred years of getting to know him, it was understood that so long as Noah was happy in his world, it wasn't necessary to know the particulars of what happened there.

❧❧❧

When Noah awoke the next day, he felt terribly sore throughout his arms and chest. He managed to get his chores done despite the pain, and once he had, he took some of the woodworking tools, including the saw, and put them in a bag. He sighed very deeply, considered he owed it to the tree not to have lied to it the day before, and struggled to lift the bag of tools up and over his shoulder. With the feeling of a small tree resting itself against his back, he walked slowly into the woods to where a very large tree lay in wait of his promised return.

He released the burden from his back with a grunt, his arm muscles aching at the weight's release; every movement felt like trying to open a door with a large, un-oiled, rusty hinge. With another sigh, he took a tool out of the bag and began to try to scrape bark from trunk.

It wasn't long before his "un-oiled joints" began to feel too uncomfortable for him to work through. "I am sorry, Mr. Tree. I came back today because I promised you I would, but I think I'd better come back again when my arms work better. I will sit against you now and rest, and then I will probably see you again in two or more days, so that you can help me to save the bunny rabbits... and the monkeys too... whatever those are." Noah did rest against the tree's trunk. He sighed deeply, let himself lie back, and listened to the birds chirp while feeling the warm breeze lightly brushing in waves upon his face. Apart from his upper-arm soreness, which was mostly released to the relaxation of pure experiencing, he felt very good, and happy. He stood up some time later and walked back toward home, leaving the tools behind to return to.

After two days, Noah felt much better. There was still residual soreness in his torso and arms, but he felt like he could lift the drawknife without it feeling like it was a small boulder. After greeting the tree upon arrival, Noah resumed attempting to remove bark from trunk. Without turning the tree over to remove bark on the underside, as the tree was much too large for Noah to budge, Noah had the would-be wood otherwise free from its outer coating in somewhere under three hours. Huffing a little from the work done, and proud of his accomplishment, he rested for a moment against the naked tree to catch his breath. Once caught to his satisfaction, next he removed a handsaw.

Knowing the shape he wished to see cut out of this tree, he began to saw at it lengthwise. It took some time, perhaps half an hour of abrupt stops to his attempts to start, before he had managed a good-sized notch in the tree. He was reminded of the time it had taken him to definitively chop merely a notch into the tree long before it had fallen only four days ago. Happy that the front of the saw had even a little bit of a track in which to rest, he paused for a moment, took a deep breath, and began to saw further.

He sawed, and he sawed. He sawed, and he sawed. He sawed, and he sawed, and he kept sawing until the sun was low in the sky, and he knew his family would soon be surrounding a table, atop of which would sit food. He left the saw where it stuck, about a quarter of the way through the length of the tree's trunk, and then went home to eat.

The next day, after planting in the garden, Noah returned to the saw in the tree. It was unexpectedly hard to move at first. It took great force just to budge the saw from where it was stuck in arboreal flesh. Once he had managed to get it free, he stuck the saw into the original crevice created and began through to where he had been when he'd ended the night before, even though up to that point, he was mostly sawing through air. When he did arrive, finally, to where he'd left off, his battle with the tree's trunk began anew. The hardest of it was regularly removing the saw and sawing from the other side of the tree, since the diameter of the trunk was thicker than the saw was wide. By the time the sun was low in the sky, Noah's arms were very tired, and he had managed to saw through three-quarters the length of the tree. He felt happy that the next day he'd most likely be able to finish sawing through the entire length of the tree. Before leaving, this time he removed the saw from the tree and placed it in the bag with the other tools, so that he may finish the last quarter of the first length sooner when he came back.

Indeed, the next day, not having to remove saw from tree, Noah had a much easier start to his work. The sun was still quite high in the sky when the top length of wood had been fully separated from the tree's trunk; Noah felt himself fill with joy to see what he had accomplished. Like he was a bunny himself, he felt the urge to hop and hop happily; to throw himself high into the air to say to the tops of the trees and The Spirit Of All that resided above them, "Look at me! Look at me! See what I have done! Look what I can do!"

Noah sat back down on the flat top of the fallen tree and looked at the strip of wood at his feet. He huffed and gasped for several minutes while he considered that his task was far from finished. He whispered under his breath, "The bunnies." He went to the tool bag and brought forth a hand plane. Between the saw and the plane, Noah began working the wood. From time to time he would bring out a small knife, or a different knife, to cut or whittle off something small and unnecessary. By the time the sun was ready to call Noah to dinner, he had mostly finished the first of many planks of wood he looked forward to crafting, so that the cute creatures everywhere would survive the fun ride Metatoch told him he needed to take the bunnies and gophers and butterflies on.

The following day, after a full week of effort, it seemed like this first plank might be useable. Noah went to the bag and removed the saw. He was grateful his muscles hurt much less than when he had first chopped the tree down, eight days prior.

Thirty-two days later, he smiled to see the pile of planks at his feet. One tree down, he decided to leave the tools with the planks, as he anticipated again borrowing the ax the next day.

Chapter 40

Over the course of more than five centuries of Noah's life, the question hung heavily in the mind of his mother. Noah was twelve years old when Light Within walked into his room to find him rubbing his hard penis up and down with his hand. Noah looked up at his mom and smiled. "Hello, Mommy."

Light Within immediately fixed her gaze up and held it to his eyes. "Hello, Noah. I'll come back later."

"That's okay, Mommy. I'm just making sticky come out of my pee-pee. You can stay, it feels really good..."

Light Within decided to speak before anything else came out of Noah. "Noah, my son, I want you to put your pants on immediately." Light Within made very sure not to sound angry as she spoke to her son abruptly.

"Okay, Mommy." Noah released his erect penis and put his pants on.

After briefly noticing the protrusion present below Noah's waist, Light Within again made very focused eye contact with her son. "Noah, it is customary, when making 'sticky,' to offer it to God amidst the crops so that That which makes life from us will be given to show our commitment to live, when not being shared with someone we would make life with." Noah looked at his mother with a puzzled look on his face. "Noah, when a man and a woman find that they love each other very much, they learn to share the... sticky... together." Light could see that Noah was on the verge of asking about this further. "You don't need to know just now how that works. But, when it happens, that is how babies are made."

"You mean Daddy let you play with his sticky, and that's what made me?"

Light Within smiled. "Pretty much, son. But when young men don't have a young woman to share their sticky with, it is customary that they give it to the crops to show that their sticky should always represent the creation and sustenance of life. Do you understand, Noah?"

Noah nodded that yes, he understood.

"And when you offer your sticky, please do it when no one is around, okay?"

Noah smiled up at Light. "Okay, Mommy!"

"Good." With that, without lowering her gaze until she was looking away from her son, Light Within The Darkness turned and left Noah's room.

❧ ❧ ❧

A couple of days later, while gathering crops for dinner that night, Lamech was walking from the outskirts of the garden when he arrived at Noah, who had his pants down, his hand around his penis, and his back to his father. "Noah!"

Noah turned to his father with his erection still in his hand. "Hi, Daddy!" He waved with his other hand. "Mommy told me to make sticky to the vegetables to show them I want them to grow, but only when no one is around. I'm going to pull my pants up now, since you are not no one, Daddy." Noah pulled up his pants, and then looked at his father. "Hi, Daddy." Noah waved again.

Lamech sighed. "Hi, Noah. From now on, just do it at night, after dinner, when no one is definitely present, okay?"

"Okay, Daddy."

"And please, just do it around new crops before their flowers have even budded, okay?"

"Okay, Daddy." Noah thought to himself: *My sticky has so many rules!*

❧ ❧ ❧

That night, when Lamech and Light Within The Darkness were cuddling before sleep, Light Within raised her concerns to Lamech after he had told her about his conversation with their son earlier that day. "Lamech, do you ever wonder what kind of woman will end up being married to our son?"

Lamech responded, "I often wonder if our son will find a woman who would take him as he is."

Light Within was silent for a moment before responding, "That's kind of what I meant, too..."

They spent some time talking about the possible realities of their son's future interactions with women late into the night. Finally, they rested on the fact that he was still very young, and the hope that he might become closer to normal as he grew older.

Several hundred years later, sharing an herbal tea alone together after dinner that night, Light again raised her concerns to her husband. "Lamech, do you ever think there could be a woman who would take Noah as he is?"

"My dear and beautiful wife, it seems that first he would have to spend any time *where* a woman is. The past hundred years he seems to have contented himself by 'playing with the trees' well enough, but perhaps some of his time might be better spent if we bring him to market to see if *any chemistry at all* might suggest itself between a fairly local unwed lady and himself."

Light agreed that it was not such a bad idea.

The next day, after his planting duties had been completed, Lamech stopped his son before Noah had the opportunity to wander into the woods. "Noah, your mother and I would like you to come with us to market today."

"Okay, Daddy."

Shortly thereafter, off they went.

Light Within guided Noah toward attractive young women, and Lamech tried to point things out to Noah in such a way that he'd have no choice but to notice the women in close proximity to those things. Every time Noah's focus was directed, however, it seemed as though his gaze would find itself past where his parents had wanted it to land, and straight to whatever large tree in the background was closest in view.

When closer-known cousins appeared with their daughters, Light attempted to introduce Noah to them. "Noah, this is Fariah."

Fariah stared at Noah's forehead for a moment before Noah spoke. "Hi, Fariah." Noah waved. "I'm Noah. Do you like trees?"

Fariah looked confused as she stared between Noah's eyes and forehead. "I... I suppose I like trees." She glanced briefly at Light before staring at her mother, and then finally back to Noah, who was smiling from ear to ear with a twinkle in his eye.

"I like trees too. I *love* trees. One day I'm going to use the trees to save all the bunnies in the world!"

Fariah's eyes shot up to her mother; Lamech had never seen a neck snap into a different position quite that quickly before. Fariah's mother spoke, "Well, we must make our way home to prepare dinner. You must excuse us, we don't want anyone to be hungry at home."

Light began to raise her hand to wave and say goodbye, only to continue the motion toward their backs, so quickly did they turn away from where the three stood. As Noah's gaze took to a cedar in the distance, he muttered toward his mom, "She seemed nice, Mommy."

Some conversations went better. Not every young woman was put off by Noah's expansive forehead. For the most part, however, talk tended to be stymied by the topic of trees, and for some reason, when saving bunnies was brought up, people at home seemed to get hungrier. As Lamech and Light stared at each other, they couldn't help but sigh together. "Perhaps our son is an arboreal-sexual," Lamech whispered to Light as they were leaving the marketplace. Light slapped Lamech hard enough on the arm to produce an audible "Ow!" out of him.

"Mommy, why did you hit Daddy?"

"Daddy had a very big fly on his arm that I was trying to help him get rid of." Lamech smiled at Light as he rubbed his arm.

❧❧❧

Later that night, it was decided that the time was a century overdue to see just exactly how his son was playing with trees, and perhaps rabbits, in the woods. The next day, once Noah's work was done, Lamech asked if he could join Noah past the threshold of the garden.

"Okay, Daddy."

Not three miles later, Lamech could not believe his eyes. As though ten giants, with a giant ax in each hand, had been chopping trees down for ten days without cessation, suddenly an expanse of emptiness appeared from out of the woods in which he had been walking. Where from the hands of giants he would have expected to see the bodies of trees nearly as far as his eyes could reach, instead he saw planks of wood covering the floor of the space of land that once might have been referred to as "forest." Lamech gasped to see the enormity of the clearing. *One hundred years of playing with trees!* he thought to himself.

"Noah," he began cautiously, "did you do... this?" He gestured his hand toward all his eye could see.

"Yes, Daddy. It's fun playing with the trees! Do you want to play with the trees with me, Daddy?" Noah picked up the bag of tools lying close to where the clearing began.

Lamech eyed the tool bag, then looked at his son's face in disbelief. "Noah, why have you done this, son?"

"To save the bunnies, Daddy." Noah said this as though it were the most natural thing in the world. "Do you want to come and save the bunnies and other cute animals with me?"

"Noah, what do you mean 'save the bunnies and other cute animals'?"

"When the fun water ride comes, Daddy. So that they can swim with me by standing on the boards when the water swims us and makes us go fun!"

Lamech stood very confused. "Noah, what makes you think there's going to be a fun water ride? What makes you think that making all these boards will help you keep rabbits from drowning?"

"Enotron told me so, Daddy."

"Who?"

"Metanoch. You know... Grandpa. Come play with the trees with me, Daddy!"

Lamech's face turned grave. "You go ahead and play, son. I need to go talk to your mother now." Unsure if it was wise to leave his son alone to play with the trees, he resigned himself to the non-immediate harm such "play" had caused over the course of the previous century, and began home to deliberate how best to proceed with his wife.

❧ ❧ ❧

While Lamech was discovering exactly how Noah went about playing with trees, Light Within The Darkness returned to market to meet with some of her sisters, aunts, and closer cousins to seek advice as to the problem of

Noah's interest in trees above women, and the lack of interest his tendency was to garner in the opposite sex.

"Dear, many who have no interest in the creation of new giants have taken to arranged marriages. Many have found this method to be a huge success in keeping their sons from raping their daughters."

"It's not like any of Noah's sisters are in any danger—"

"Nor was it suggested, Light! All I'm saying is that an arrangement, an agreement between families, might be the best solution for a son who would otherwise find difficulty in finding a mate."

"But what about love? We certainly don't believe in the wisdom of buying a young girl as chattel, and then forcing a life upon her that she didn't embrace of her own accord from the forces enabling her to exist as she is."

Light's cousin, Draeel, spoke up, "I know of a girl who'd most likely be grateful for the arrangement. She's only sixteen, but her parents are desperate to marry her off for her own sake, or so her mother says. They are from the line of the third-born son of Adam after Seth. I'm sure they'd count themselves humbled to receive a visit from the wife of Lamech."

"I'm still skeptical, Draeel. My boy should be with a girl who has joy in her heart for him; otherwise, they're both better off otherwise."

"From what I understand, this girl would be hard-pressed not to be better off from out of the house which she currently occupies. The dwelling is not far from here. Perhaps we could quickly visit now? Bring them a chicken from the market as a sign of good will? If you don't have the sense of good tidings you would want for your family, you lose nothing from the encounter, aside from the distress that builds up in a person from not giving freely enough to others."

Light Within nodded in agreement. She bid farewell to her aunts, sisters, and cousins, and followed Draeel's lead toward meeting a family she never had met before.

❦ ❦ ❦

When they arrived at the decrepit old house, Light's stomach tensed more than it already had been. On the walk from market, she was apprehensive with thoughts that she was even considering playing God with the lives of two people who through other means might find genuine affections on their own terms. When she saw the house where this would-be wife of her firstborn son lived, however, her heart couldn't help but sink, a small python seeming to slowly coil its way around her gut. The walls of the house all appeared to lean toward falling under their own weight. If not for the large tree at the back of the house, Light was quite certain it would have folded in upon itself, as it was the only stability that could be associated with this dilapidated lean-to. Vines and moss grew all along the outside of the dwelling. There was a gaping hole in the lower-left corner of the house where squirrels clearly came and went as they pleased; Light wondered what other creatures claimed access to this home as they saw fit. Light looked distraughtly over to Draeel.

Draeel smiled. "I told you the girl would most likely be grateful to leave this place." She took Light Within The Darkness by the hand, led her to the door, knocked, then released her. They stared at the door in anticipation.

They heard rustling and the murmur of a conversation within, just soft enough not to be discerned. A moment later, the wood of the door creaked open to reveal a pale, haggard young woman in her late twenties, leering at the two strangers as though gazing upon the deeply insane who should otherwise know better than to knock on doors that are not their own. "What do *you* want?" she snapped at them, turning her gaze directly into Light's eyes as she emphasized "you," insinuating that she may be persuaded to bite out at her visitors should they not give an answer capable of circumventing the gnash of her teeth, which was likely to afflict them no matter how good-natured their response.

Draeel briefly took the hand of her cousin again and lightly squeezed. She lowered her gaze as she spoke in a soft, but almost-cheery tone of voice, "Pardon our intrusion, Madame Chiantza, but we had heard that you sought a husband for your daughter. We meant no disruption, nor disrespect by our presence to you unannounced."

Chiantza stared at Draeel's averted gaze as she was speaking, then returned once again to the eyes of Light Within The Darkness, so fixated upon the shabbiness of the young woman. Light Within was taken aback by a second, much longer riveted focus. Holding this steady gaze constricted Light's heart where her belly had been before until, finally, after eternities of seconds had passed between the two of them, Chiantza's determined scowl loosened to a frown. Her eyes searched the ground after the corners of her mouth. Her own gaze averted from Light's sense of confusion, sadness, and concern. She looked up again at Draeel, who continued to keep her own eye lowered from that of the young women in front of her. "If you are here, it may mean the end of the suffering of my husband and I."

"Tranzaiel! Come here, girl."

From out of the darkness within the dwelling stepped a pale, very pretty young girl with matted, long brown hair, wearing a dress that looked like it had been fashioned out of a vegetable sack when she was about three years old, then stitched back together periodically over the following decade, and finally added to by a ripped-up dress that someone had thrown away, once she had thoroughly outgrown the original vegetable sack. The odor that came from her general direction supported the idea that this may have been the only garment she had ever owned, and that it was never washed, specifically for fear that it would disintegrate once touching water and disbanding the grime which now was all that truly held it together. Gazing at her, Light was struck by the one feature glaring out among all the others: she was truly beautiful. Her sight cast downward toward the ground as she emerged from out of the darkness, and very meekly she spoke, "I am here, Mother."

"You were wise to appear as quickly as you have." Chiantza left the question of what a slower response might elicit firmly in Light With The Darkness' mind. "Tranzaiel, these women are here to bring you to a man better in every way than your father has ever been to either of us. Would you like to go with them?"

Tranzaiel continued to look down at the ground. She seemed disinclined to even try to think of a response. It was merely a moment before her mother's voice cut through the point at which Tranzaiel might have spoken, even if she had been given to conceive reply. "As though it matters what you think. You may leave now." Without looking up for an instant at either Draeel or Light, Tranzaiel nodded closer to the ground in acquiescence before disappearing back into the darkness of the hovel from which she had initially come.

Light glanced over at Draeel. Draeel returned her gaze and smiled. They both looked up toward their "hostess," who now looked back and forth at both of them as she took a step forward, closing the door of the house behind her. Draeel and Light Within both took a step back; they too maintained their gaze. She took another step forward between them as she continued to observe the face of one, and then the other. "If you are serious about marrying my rat-haired, one-and-only child to a son of yours, or yours, accompany me, ladies, and we shall see if your degree of seriousness coincides with my desire to leave this world in better circumstances than I ever gave it while I have lived."

As they nodded and attempted to follow behind the young woman, they found she merely waited between them until they took the next step beside her. After no more than ten steps of attempting to maintain their natural impulse to enjoy a measure of personal space, and keep from her even a short distance, they finally resigned themselves to keeping pace with her rather than resisting her inclinations to take them on an apparently intimate journey.

❧❧❧

Chiantza looked from one woman to the other. "What is the lineage of this 'son' who would be married to my daughter?"

Light spoke up, "My son is the firstborn son of Lamech, firstborn son of all firstborn sons from the third-born of Adam, the line of Seth."

Chiantza stopped where her foot landed once Light had begun to speak. "You could have stopped at the name Lamech." She stared deeply into Light's eyes. "You do not lie? *You* are the wife of *Lamech*?"

Light couldn't help but smile to hear the disbelief of this woman suddenly seeming disarmed by the sound of her husband's name. "Certainly not. Perhaps you have heard something about the condition of my firstborn son?"

Chiantza continued staring at Light for a short time, mouth agape, before responding, "I have heard of your son born with..." she paused, "the large forehead."

Light again smiled, filled with joy to behold this youth's inner struggle to manifest as much respect toward her as she was able.

"My daughter is not worthy of your son, madame. We should reverse our direction now. Or perhaps I can lead you to the road straightaway—"

"With all due respect, if your daughter could love the uniqueness of my son in any measure, she would surely be welcome to my family."

"My daughter certainly possesses a uniquely kind heart. I have no doubt she would find love, genuinely, toward your son simply by virtue of the fact that he breathes at all. But, this does not negate the fact of inbred pond-scum from a long line of sibling-lovers we are from the throw-offs of the rest of the line of Adam. Our daughter is far too pathetic to marry your son. Please, let me show you the way back now."

"If I may be so bold to address you by your name, Chiantza, my husband and I broke a long-held tradition when we married five hundred years ago. That my son... has a large forehead, may be directly attributable to the fact that my husband is the grandson of my father." She paused and looked toward the ground for a moment before raising her vision back to Chiantza's watch and continuing, "Your lineage is nothing to be ashamed of."

"My house still is made of dogs in contrast to the great garden maintained by Lamech. It is a wonder my daughter is not a giant, given my brother's rape of me when I was twelve years old." Chiantza stopped and stared, now through anger-clenched teeth, deeply into the eyes of Light; Light did not look away. Chiantza continued to speak. "My brother always swore he would protect me from my other brothers; keep me safe from the 'marrying' of my sisters by my other brothers in turn. Many of my sisters have given birth to giants who destroyed their own homes before setting out to destroy the homes of others.

"Then, one night, when he was fourteen, he took me to a hollowed-out tree in the woods. He told me I needed to hide in there so that my other brothers wouldn't find me. He told me to turn around inside the tree, and to be very still. Then, when my back was turned to him, he ripped my clothes enough to force himself into my body before it could occur to me to fight back. He walked home after, leaving me alone and cold inside of the old, dead tree.

"When I returned home later that night, I took a knife from the kitchen and found him in his own bed, fast asleep. I snuck into his room, up to his bed where he lay, quickly grabbed his left hand, took it to the floor, and cut off his pinky. I thought it fitting that I take blood from him, as moments before he had taken blood from me; that as he'd done of me, I would take from him something that could never be returned. I kept that knife with me from that night forward. For the rest of my days, I would be the one to keep me safe from my brothers." She showed them the sharp blade hidden under her belt in the fold of her dress.

"Months later, when my belly began to swell, my parents forced us to marry; said it would be for the best. Building me a house and making sure I had food was the least he could do after what he'd already done. Dependent on my parents, what choice did I have? Though I swore that if I gave birth to a giant, I would toss myself off a cliff and into a river as soon as I became again strong enough to stand. Amazingly, my daughter turned out apparently normal.

"You must think I'm horrid for how you've seen me treat her and the conditions in which she lives. But she is born from rape and hatred between two siblings who wish sincerely to die. She can barely speak, and only knows to do simple housework. She is far too wretched a creature for the firstborn son of Lamech. Don't you see?"

"What I see," spoke Light Within The Darkness, " is a truly beautiful girl who is said to have a heart that might love my own son, despite his obvious... features. What I see is someone whose mother would like to see her acquainted with more pleasantness in her life than she has ever known before. What I see is that she would be no burden to my *happy* household, who I could accept into my family as a daughter regardless of whether she can accept my son or not.

"If you let me bring her with me, I can promise you a good life for her awaits."

Chiantza stared at Light Within in the eye. A tear fell from the corner of her own as her face held emotionless like stone. "Know, then, that if you take her with you, my husband and I will kill ourselves, as has been our wish since our slime of parents forced us to wed fifteen years ago.

"About three years ago, I heard my husband creeping from his room across the hall to my daughter's. I knew full well what he had in mind. I jumped out of bed, threw my full weight against him, forcing him against the wall, grabbed him by the balls, and twisted. I told him right there that if he ever forgot his own bed again, I'd twist them straight off as I rotated them another turn in my hand. He fell to the ground in tears. Then I showed him my old friend the knife and reminded him that I still know where his pinky is and how to give it some company once his nuts were off, if I hadn't given him enough incentive yet.

"I hear him with the sheep from time to time, but despite the pig he is, I know he's hated himself for so many reasons for what he did to me. From our father raping our mother, our family was born. If you really want her, we will be grateful to be free of this life in so many ways forced upon us."

Light Within stood with open jaw as the woman completed her tale. She looked deeply into Chiantza's eyes, two small stones fixed steadily in their scrutiny toward hers. "Surely without need to raise your daughter further, you'd be free to—"

"What freedom do you suggest from that enabled by the knife I have spent most of my life carrying? At least he's man enough to not wish to continue stealing from the sun."

Light within closed her mouth and gulped. "I promise your daughter will have no force toward my son, save for her own impulses. I promise she will have a good life in my house."

"I have no doubt she will." Half of a tear seemed to dew in the corner of her eye a second time as the corners of her chiseled mouth began almost to think about turning upward. "Let us return to my shack. I look forward to finally allowing it to collapse in on itself under its own weight."

Silently the three walked back, side by side, to Chiantza's dwelling.

༒ ༒ ༒

Arriving at the door, Chiantza pushed it open hard and shouted into the dark depths of the hovel, "Tranzaiel, get out here!" Barely a moment passed before the girl again emerged from the darkness, her face cast once more to the ground. "Look me in the eye, child."

Tranzaiel responded, "Yes, Mother," before lifting her head to meet her mother's gaze.

"You will walk now with these women. Give them any reason to regret your presence, and I'll give you every reason to regret mine. You understand?"

"Yes, Mother." She kept her face expressionless, and her eyes locked to her mother's.

"Good girl." Chiantza put her hands to her daughter's ears, gently turned her head downwards, and kissed her forehead. She raised her gaze back to her own, smirked, and then walked through the front door, slamming it behind her.

Tranzaiel looked bewildered. Light Within The Darkness walked up beside her, introduced herself with a smile, and offered her hand. Tranzaiel accepted it. Together, all three began walking, side by side, in the direction of home.

ᘓᘏᘓᘏᘓ

When Light Within entered her house, Lamech was sitting at the dinner table with his head in his hands. As Light approached, Lamech looked up at his wife. "We have to discuss Noah."

"Before we do, I have wonderful news." Lamech didn't know what to think as Light motioned and a girl entered. "Lamech, this is Tranzaiel."

Chapter 41

After forming and finishing a large plank, and cutting down a large tree, Noah returned home in the evening. His family, sitting around the table, hushed as he approached. He didn't notice the silence as unusual, and took the seat at which he typically sat for supper.

Tranzaiel, sitting beside Light Within and across from Noah, stirred in her chair a bit. Light Within The Darkness had spent the day helping her wash as though she'd never bathed before. It had taken more than three hours making sense of her hair without cutting it off altogether. Toward the end of the day spent living in the river and pulling incessantly at her tangles, Tranzaiel's old clothes were used as kindling while she put on a dress chosen by Light; the first clean and more or less well-fitting garment she'd worn in the better part of a decade. Tranzaiel stared meekly up from her plate at Noah, then turned her head for a moment expectantly up at Light. Again she looked back to Noah briefly, and turned again to Light. Finally she rested her stare straight ahead, straightening her plate without looking down at it.

Light Within spoke across the table. "Noah, there is someone joining us tonight who your father and I would like you to meet." Light glanced at Lamech, who tried to return to her a smile pushing past his uncertainty. "Noah, this is Tranzaiel." Light raised her hands toward the girl sitting beside her in order to make clear to whom she was referring.

Noah looked up at Tranzaiel and smiled. Tranzaiel nervously smiled back. "Hello Tranzaiel. Do you like trees?"

Lamech's hand went straight into the hair around his forehead.

Tranzaiel looked up at Light as though trying to find an answer to an important test concealed upon the woman's face. She looked back down to Noah, then answered softly, "They are very pretty," and smiled nervously.

Noah's face brightened and grew wide. Suddenly he found himself naturally drawn into her eyes. Tranzaiel felt a natural pull not to be stared at, considered following the reflex pulling her to look away, but reconsidered and held herself so as to let him look, and even enjoyed looking back. Then his eyes widened, and he continued to smile. "What's your favorite kind of tree? Mine's oak!"

"I... I don't really know. The taller they are, the more I wonder what it must be like to stand with my fingers nearly touching the sun; my hair dancing with the wind, a bird raising its family upon my shoulder." She still stared into Noah's eyes as she spoke. Light and Lamech shared each other's gaze as the girl and their son conversed. They told each other the amazement of a miracle without a word's utterance from either side of the table.

"Maybe tomorrow, you'll come play with the trees with me?"

Tranzaiel looked up at Light, who now stared straight down, motionless. Tranzaiel straightened herself in her seat. "That sounds like fun, Noah. I'd be delighted." Tranzaiel immediately stared back down at her plate.

Noah's face glowed.

After dinner, Tranzaiel and Light Within spoke. "You don't need to go with him tomorrow if you don't really want to. I appreciate you being polite, but humoring my son's obsession with trees is certainly not a requirement for your continued stay in this house."

"Forgive me, but life is suddenly moving rather fast. Am I not here to be married to Noah? Didn't my mother give me to you, that I would marry your son?"

"I'd be lying to you if I told you that that wasn't my hope. But I saw the spirit under which you lived. Your mother wanted you to have a better life, clearly. Given where you come from, I wish to give you the same regardless of whether or not you share affections with my son. Your will, your choice, is your own. A better life awaits you here, no matter what you choose."

"He is very beautiful. I don't know why I wouldn't choose to go with him tomorrow."

"What?" Tranzaiel's eyes narrowed. "Please, pardon me," continued Light Within The Darkness, "but even as his mother, who agrees wholeheartedly with you, I cannot help but acknowledge his... uniqueness. In five hundred years, I cannot recall anyone referring to my son as 'beautiful'."

"Not that I've been around many men over the course my life, Mom kept me from meeting almost any, but he's exceptional compared to the few I've met. He's simple, perhaps, but passionate. I think I look forward to getting to know your son better tomorrow as he shows me what he's clearly excited about. I'm just a little nervous, everything being so new to me."

Light Within stared at her for a moment, speechless. "Tranzaiel, if you really think my son is beautiful, and if you enjoy spending time with him tomorrow, there is something I'd like for you to do for me."

"Whatever you wish, if I can."

"If you sincerely enjoy the time you spend with my son tomorrow, I would like you to kiss him."

❧ ❧ ❧

The next morning, Tranzaiel helped Light within the house while Noah worked in the garden. As Noah was finishing his planting, Tranzaiel approached him in the garden. "Are you about ready to... go to play with the trees, Noah?"

Noah turned quickly to see Tranzaiel standing behind him. His face turned bright red, a wide smile filled his visage, and he stared at her, apparently unsure of quite how to respond.

Tranzaiel overcame her own nervousness to possibly help him past his. "Is there a place in particular you go to... spend time with the trees, Noah?"

Without letting go of her sight for a moment, a smile and blush hiding any other feature from his face, he rose his arm straight and more or less behind him, extended his index finger in alignment with the rest of his arm, and slowly nodded.

Seeing where he pointed, Tranzaiel began to walk in that direction as precisely as she could. Observing the sway of her hips once she had walked past him, after several moments of continuing his stare, Noah began running after her as soon as she was nearly out of his sight.

❧ ❧ ❧

Over the course of the next two miles, Noah followed closely and just behind Tranzaiel. Every so often she'd stop, point in the direction she thought to continue walking, turn her head without moving her body, and ask behind her, "This way?" Most of the time Noah simply nodded. Now and then he would raise his own arm and point, indicating a very slight redirection, of course. The final instance she asked, Noah raised his arm and pointed slightly otherwise than where she pointed. She redirected her extended finger, and as she did, she brushed Noah's hand with her own while asking, "Ah. This way?" Noah's face again brightened as though one of the pomegranates from his garden, and instantly his arm lowered, as did his eyes to the ground, and he stood motionless. Tranzaiel decided to step in the new direction without his confirmation.

Four minutes or so later, Tranzaiel stopped abruptly. She gasped in observance of the spectacle before her. Suddenly the forest fell away to the distance, and all around her stumps and planks of all sizes blanketed the floor where once clearly lived, as elsewhere, a wealth of pre-processed wood. She looked about her with wonder and awe while Noah skipped past her into his domain, stretched out his arms and twirled himself about before running to where she stood, taking her by the hands, and leading her forward into the clearing.

"I give thanks to each and every tree who has played with me." He almost sang these words as he led her further through a hundred years of his labors. "It is these to whom every bunny, and all the cute creatures of the wood, will one day sing in thanks for their lives saved by the sap of these giants, who do no hurt, shed, and made into boards!"

As Noah uttered these words, they'd all but stopped. Tranzaiel pulled her hands away from Noah and to her heart as her brain tried to reconcile itself to the odd notions raised by Noah, and the enormity of the space all around her. The confusion of her mind tried to make sense of the artfully orchestrated destruction, and the apparent explanation of what the speaker might call "reason" motivating her presence currently into a wholly alien circumstance. Eyes widening, she strained to return air to her lungs.

As Noah watched her place her hands to her chest, just above her bosom, and expel air in demonstration of her awe, he took these as exceptionally good signs of the fullness of her appreciation for his skill and efforts made in saving the whole of adorableness in creaturedom from otherwise extinction. "Tranzaiel... would you... like to... play with them with me?"

"Huh?" She was called from a great distance, from the other side of her mind, out of a trance induced by trying to reconcile many disparities in her conception of reality at once.

"The trees! Do you... want to play with them with me?"

"Oh? Oh! Um... How did you want to... *play* with the trees, Noah?"

"Wait here." Noah's face brightened once more and returned to being half-consumed by an ever-widening grin, "I'll show you!" Noah ran over to a tree at the edge of the clearing, close to where they'd entered. Several moments later, he returned with an ax in his hand. Taking the ax's neck up in his other hand, he stretched out both of his arms to Tranzaiel. He stood there for a moment holding it toward her.

She looked deeply into his eyes, glanced down at the ax in his hands, then looked again up to his eyes. "Go ahead. Take it," he whispered with reverence. He raised the tool an inch or two closer to where she stood, looking down at it as he motioned. He then returned his gaze expectantly up to her eyes.

Conflicted in her emotion, her mind suggested hesitation as unhelpful in an existence altogether unfamiliar. Glancing to the ax, then back up to Noah's eyes, she tried to smile as she reached out and placed one of her hands around Noah's ax. Noah's face shone elated when she took his tool into her grasp and pulled it toward her. He took hold of her free hand and yanked her forward. "Come with me!" As he began skipping with her in hand, she did her best to keep pace with his enthusiasm.

Moments later, straight across to the other side of the clearing, they stopped in front of a tree. She sized up its tallness. She felt the handle of the ax in her grip. She understood what was expected of her. She stood motionless. "Play!" Noah's voice broke the short-lived silence. She looked up as she recovered her breath from the run. She grasped tighter the handle. She cast her eyes back down toward the base of the trunk, and then raised her eyes ever so slightly. Redrawing in her breath, she raised the ax, sliding up a hand toward the head while she began to grip the other side firmly in her free hand. She looked up to Noah, who beamed back at her, looking like he was going to explode with joy at what was coming next. She breathed in, leveled the ax with her shoulder, breathed out, glanced a last time at Noah, inhaled while looking at the tree standing tall in front of her, and released her breath, swinging wood and metal toward the giant before her with all her strength. She felt pain from the reverberation of the strike that was felt within her stiff arms. Tool still in hand, she dropped it to the ground while she recovered her limbs.

Noah was giddy. "Again! Again!"

She rose her focus to the joy in his face, regaining herself from the pain that had just bolted through her. Her face turned red as pain became sudden rage. She lifted the ax once more, this time as though it were a feather, and with more relaxed arms threw herself toward the tree, leading with the blade, putting herself into it and through the tree, over, and over, and over, and over.

For the next five minutes she hurled all her being into the figure, large and casting shadow upon her while she continued chopping uncontrollably. The face of her mother, the face of her father, the three overused, uncomfortable, grime-laden garments she'd worn over the course of her entire life; hunger, fear, loneliness; being the pawn of the agenda of every person she had ever known; the pain that moments before had shot through her arms, and the unsympathetic smile toward her pain by some idiot bidding her to take part in the destruction of the homes of what he claimed to save through his mindless obliteration of *their* shelter, time and again she swung the ax's head at the face of every indignity, every frustration, every confusion that had woven the tapestry of all the life she had ever known since the moment of her birth. In the end, her last swing was to sever the neck holding up the head filled with every image, concept, and ultimately abuse that filled it to the brim, with little room for else to exist: her own.

The face of the ax cut deep and hard into the body of the tree. She attempted to pull the handle back, but the tree held fast, and her hands, now thick with sweat, slid free from where the ax stayed embedded within the tree's flesh. She fell back from the inertia of her energy disconnected from where it had been directed and landed upon the ground, weeping to release her power, finding her hands in the dirt below.

Noah was at first delighted that Tranzaiel seemed to be having so much fun playing with the tree. When she fell to the ground, however, and he saw the tears falling down her face and to the earth beneath her, he felt sad. He felt sad that she was now sad. He stepped over to her, bent down closer to her, and placed his hand gently to her shoulder. He found himself speaking to make her feel better. "Tranzaiel–"

As her shoulder registered his touch, she leapt up from under his hand. He stood up startled and found her eyes, and not much else, in his field of vision. He began to try to speak again, but as his lips formed themselves amorphous, seeking out a word from his bewilderment, a sensation unlike any he'd ever associated a word with before, he felt a pressure upon both his shoulders. Backwards he fell, until stopping hard against the trunk of the tree at which

Tranzaiel had been so frantically chopping mere moments prior. The handle of the ax leaning on one of Noah's thighs, his shoulders pinned to tree by small hands, he gasped to regain the breath he had lost amidst the fall.

She stared at this helpless boy under her weight for a moment. He barely had recovered himself enough to raise his head and glimpse a flash of her eyes. Suddenly, as his shoulders, he felt the rear of his skull knock into the tree. In a short span of seconds he'd felt two sensations that in over five centuries of existence he'd never felt before, and had no words to describe. In this instance, the second sensation felt of the pressure holding his head back upon would-be wood, was the unexpected and delightful force of the softness of her lips against his. He grabbed hold of his ax handle and braced himself.

Chapter 42

When they'd arrived home that night, Noah felt as though floating on a cloud pulled by the soft, firm grip of Tranzaiel. She had instructed Noah to let her speak when asked what they did when they spent time together. Noah was happy to let Tranzaiel speak; words were always so exhausting to form into together. That, and he liked to hear the sound of her voice.

When Light Within asked of her son that night at dinner how he'd enjoyed the day, Tranzaiel spoke up at once. "You would be pleased to know of the fun we had playing... with the trees." As she finished the statement, she glanced down and blushed a little. Looking back up to Light, Light Within smiled while giving a nod of her head. From there they ate in relative silence interspersed with casual, nonspecific conversation.

❦ ❦ ❦

Three months later, with the blessing of all respecters of the kind of party to come along every half a millennium or so, and those who saw value in the genesis of firstborns of firstborns since the birth of Seth, Tranzaiel was wed to Noah. It seemed as though all of conscious-capable creation rejoiced in unison. At the behest of The All *they* served, God's closest servants watched from an ethereal, distant vantage with joy. Those incarnate from service on high intermingled and further augmented the crowd. Harratzarian rejoiced that Noah was not doomed to cease the line of firstborns due to his peculiarities of formation. Luciferous was delighted to partake of lamb sacrificed amongst the throng. They all enjoyed the celebration of life continued between life to be, and life's cessation.

It was not long before Tranzaiel gave birth to a son. She reasoned he should be called Shem: for that there is a name at all is the fact The Existence has spoken Its own eyes into any and all called by different, but more or less the same, create by Its own breath. Again angels of flesh and humanity coalesced to celebrate the origins of existence maintained to the presence of continuation.

On the eve of the birth of Name, Tranzaiel made a request of Noah. "Noah, for over a hundred years you have had fun with the trees, that the bunnies will be safe from a water that never comes. Look at our son, Noah. Is he not cuter than a bunny rabbit?"

"Much, much cuter, Transi. He's beautiful!"

"Well, Noah, for me, for *him*, would you be willing to stop playing with trees for a little while, and play with us instead? I need your help even more than the bunnies. They'll continue to be all right, but we need you."

"Of course, Tranzaiel. I like playing with you much more than playing with trees. And I've never played with Name before. . . But, Transi, do you really think the bunnies will be okay?"

Tranzaiel smiled. "Yes, Noah. I think they'll be just fine."

❧ ❧ ❧

Two years later was born Enlarged. For when Japheth was born, enlarged had become their family by his presence.

Five years later still was born Of High Temperature.

Noah enjoyed finding ways to make his sons smile while they were growing up. His favorite thing to do was to catch bunny rabbits in the wood, then bring them home for a few hours to make his baby boys squeal with delight.

He also worked hard planting and cleaning. He did everything he was asked so that Tranzaiel was comfortable while she constantly watched over their sons. More than that, he delighted in bringing her forest flowers.

As years passed, and the boys grew, Noah found ever-greater joys in teaching them to plant and harvest. Tranzaiel spent more time tending to housework as Noah took more responsibility in instructing their sons to take care of their selves. Two decades more or less into the lives of each, they in turn met and joined with women in marriage. Before long these sons built for themselves their own homes and planted their own gardens. Their sons fully grown, Noah and Tranzaiel spent their days in daily housework before enjoying most of the rest of the time cuddling.

Shem was fifty years old when, one day, Noah was chasing a bunny through the garden. Noah saw the bunny slip through apparently unfamiliar feet, and stopped himself before crashing into what turned out to be a familiar guest, whom he had not seen in over a century and a half. "Tronenoch!"

The face of the Metatron reflected the favor The Creator had in Noah, pleasing in the sight of The Lord beyond all others. "The time has almost come of which we used to speak regularly, Noah. It is time to build the ark."

Noah looked down to his feet. "Is it... the bunnies, Metanoch?"

"Yes, Noah. Without you, the bunnies cannot survive."

Noah bowed his head lower. "If they need me... I won't fail them, Mety. I can't fail them!" He looked up into the eyes of the voice of God. "But Transi—"

"Your wife will understand, Noah. Now go. You have much work to do!"

The Metatron dissolved into light and air. Noah looked down twenty paces to his right and observed a rabbit biting at a blade of grass, crinkling its nose. *I'll tell her tonight!*

Tranzaiel took a deep breath as she stared at Noah in disbelief, "Our sons are grown now. I'll not try to stop you, if this is truly what you want. But I ask one thing of you: do not let your garden go to waste. Do not betray the duties you keep to your house."

Noah smiled. "I never have before. Oh, thank you, Transi! Thank you, and the bunnies thank you too!" He rushed up and embraced his wife, who received him stiffly. He kissed her cheek, then ran off to take his supper.

Once Noah had left the room, Tranzaiel quickly brushed away the solitary, small tear she had allowed to trickle down from the corner of her eye.

The next morning, Noah performed his daily tasks of residence maintenance quickly before removing a saw and an ax. He practically skipped the whole of the two and a half miles it took to find the clearing. He was happy to see it had changed little since last he'd left it a short five decades prior. Though trees and boards lay rotting everywhere he looked, he was delighted when a family of rabbits hopped away, around, and about the decayed lumber as he approached.

Tarzuncel and Havalon looked at each other in disbelief, shrugged, and continued their observations, recalling the century he'd spent here prior to his marriage.

As Noah began swinging his ax for the first time since the birth of Shem, Tranzaiel decided it best to visit their sons now. Arriving at the house of Name, she sent Name to gather Enlarged, who went for Very Warm in turn. Before long, all three were assembled at Shem's house. There, Tranzaiel told her sons of their father's fixation with joyously chopping down trees to the ends of saving the bunny rabbits of the Earth from certain demise.

Within each, a smile couldn't help but bubble up to hear of their father's intentions. Likewise too, they each in turn felt sadness at the full understanding not only of their father's simplicity, of which they'd all long been accustomed, but of the tricks his mind was capable of playing upon his sense of reality. Japheth broke the silence while his brothers couldn't help but squirm where they sat to hear such words. "We certainly must stop him, then, and lead him to a better and less dangerous use of his time."

"For half a century since the birth of your eldest brother, your father agreed to forsake his "boat building" that the three of you would be raised properly; that I may be supported in any way I might have a need. He fulfilled his duty to me faithfully, lovingly, and in so doing taught the three of you to become the men I am proud to have been the mother of. For over a century he 'played' with the trees before he and I had met. Long before I, or *my* parents, were born. Though I agree his time could be spent better otherwise, he's proven he knows well, and without much threat to his person, how to chop down, and subsequently begin to shape, a tree. I think, for the sake of our family, it might go better for us, actually, the opposite way of what you're suggesting. If the three of you were to help your father with his project, instead of having to wait another two centuries for him to get too old to lift his ax, die outright, or heaven knows maybe even complete the work of his intention, perhaps he would be able to complete his mission of 'bunny preservation' much sooner than if he were left to work at it alone. This way, the three of you could ensure your father's safety *and* bring him home to me centuries sooner than he might otherwise waste 'playing' with the trees."

The boys understood what their mother had said and nodded in agreement. Ham spoke on behalf of the three of them, "We will see to it our father is made stronger by the love you both have shown us, and each other. That both your minds should find rest from your worries, and free from them you shall be united in the fullness of your Love once more, your four strong men will take up where one has begun. The intention of our hands will complete our task just as true and quickly as the hearts in our chest will make able."

Their mother smiled widely through a short burst of tears to hear her son's words and know they stood for the love she had shown them over the course of their days alive. Shem and Tranzaiel walked home hand in hand after Shem had given word to his wife the plans he had set with his brothers. Ham and Japheth went to inform their wives as well before reconvening at the home of their parents, which stood adjacent to the dwelling still occupied by Lamech and Light Within The Darkness, Noah's parents.

That night, Noah was delighted to find his boys had come home so that they could all have supper together. Japheth informed him that in the morning, they would have another surprise for him still. Noah found it difficult to sleep that night between the excitement of spending another day playing with the trees, and whatever wondrous surprise his sons would present him once the sun awoke. He kept Tranzaiel awake in turn with asking her what she thought it might be.

"You'll know soon enough, my love. Let's rest now..."

Fatigue began holding her in its grasp as Noah tugged her ever away. "But what could be even better than having them here already? Maybe they've grown a new fruit in their garden and want to plant it in mine?"

"I'm sure we'll find out in the morning, my love. Do please try to rest now..." Finally, slumber ushered her toward the warmth of releasing from the day. While Noah begrudgingly allowed her to rest once she'd become unresponsive, he stayed quite awake, until at last he could rise with the morning light.

The new day started, the four worked together in the garden. What would normally take Noah half the day to complete took barely an hour.

"I need to begin my work elsewhere now. But what is your surprise for me before I go, sons?" Though tiredness had begun catching up to Noah, no less had he spent the early morning poking at his boys for hints.

Name spoke, "Bring us where you go for more work, and we will show you there."

For just a moment, Noah hesitated. He didn't know why. He recalled that of all those in his life he loved, Tranzaiel was the only one who seemed at all encouraging of his mission. But even that was up to the day she had asked him to stop. Asked him to stop that... that their boys would grow to become who they were today! Noah began nodding vigorously in agreement. "Okay. Okay! Come with me. I will show you the trees, and you can show me my surprise."

Ham, Shem, and Japheth nodded at each other knowingly. Though still concerned, they felt the warmth of their father's enthusiasm wash over them, and were satisfied they were doing something very good for him.

For the next couple of miles from the gate of the garden, Noah skipped out ahead of the three young men as they struggled to keep up with their elated father while carrying the weight of their satchels. Upon coming to the clearing, they gasped, much as their mother had half a century prior. "Can you show me my surprise now?" Noah asked eagerly whilst surrounded by his element. Without uttering a word, they each removed an ax from the bags they had kept the entire time slung over their shoulders. Now it was Noah's turn to gasp. He could not remember feeling a happier moment since their mother had kissed him, close to where he currently stood, all those years ago.

Chapter 43

Noah was delighted while Ham recounted that his mother had asked the three of them to help, so that the bunnies and other creatures could be made to be safe as quickly as possible. The four of them made no hesitation in getting to work.

The first day brought very sore limbs to the sons of Noah, but in two weeks' time they learned new strength, and by the end of the month were becoming adept at crafting planks and boards. When Noah described the dimensions Metatron had asked him to repeat ad nauseam, for the sake of the bunnies, until they were embedded permanently into his tongue muscle where his brain muscle was otherwise disinclined to hold, they nearly fainted. "Three hundred cubits?" Each had the same thought: *How am I going to explain to my wife that we won't be having any children for a while?* For the sake of their mother and father, however, they braced themselves for the work that was sure to take years, if not more likely decades, to come.

Between the four of them, a tall cypress became a matter of minutes, and its flesh barely days to form. The sons took a month off while their father continued to labor, to study with boat builders how best to smooth wood and cure it so that it wouldn't rot at the water's touch. They learned how to make pitch. They learned how to make new tools for better crafting the wood. Their father was delighted on the day of their return, and happy to learn new techniques of playing with the trees.

Ten years of daily struggle proceeded, and it began to look as though a bottom deck had begun to form. As time pressed further and further on, ladders were made from many of the trees, so that the sides of the boat could continue to be built up. After four decades of nearly constant exertion, most of the vessel had been constructed.

✦✦✦

Wanderers and passersby had found their way to the work site from time to time. They would ask with awe in their eyes, "What are you doing?" or, "Why would you spend your time making such a thing?"

Ham would simply turn to such momentary spectators and reply, "It is saving the bunnies and other creatures that is our mission," and then turn away to rejoin his brothers and father, who would not stop in their work during such instances.

Noah thought nothing more of it, of course. His sons and wife, however were not so fortunate to luxuriate in ignorance. The wives of the brothers, and Tranzaiel, would hear people talk whenever they visited market. The brothers would at times hear murmurs from passers on the road as they traveled home. Of course, there was also plenty of discussion to be had between families at night.

But despite a growing consensus among civilization East of Eden that Noah's sons possessed more than a little of the same affliction of mind that their father possessed, there was also more than a pinch of distinction to be had as the firstborns of firstborns down from the line of Seth. Although there was plenty of gossip among all of the human race, they never molested, nor deterred the first family of Adam from completing their task, "no matter how much inbreeding had finally corrupted their minds." The wives of the men took some small bit of solace in this fact as they persisted in hearing the chatter of the opinions of the rest of humanity over the span of the decades that unfolded.

As for the servants of the Divine who chose also to serve humanity, for their part, they warded off Nephilim and giants alike. There was serenity such that they were disinclined to wander in said direction anyway. To be sure, though, they thought it wise to post four shifts of two centuries each at each direction of an approach to form a five-mile perimeter so that any wandering by, especially at night when otherwise no one was present, would be dissuaded from destroying what was already built, as was the nature of the Nephilim and the giants. In this way, between the lineage the family held and the guard the angels of carnation kept, over the course of almost half a century, slowly the ark was allowed to be built.

They had worked tirelessly on the construction of the craft for forty-five years. It had strengthened their hands. Where once his sons had set out on a foolhardy task of keeping their father from wasting centuries of his life to the destruction and re-formation of trees to save creatures never in need of his help, now they embraced their mission to see the work of their hands through to the finality of its imminent creation. They stepped back together to gaze at this ark almost complete. Within them all was found a sense of joy that together, hand-in-hand, *they* had made their father's vision come true. While they looked on, so too did Noah gaze at them, unbearably grateful to see what his boys had become. He was humbled that they would dedicate, together, so much of themselves to see him complete his mission of saving the small, scrunched-nosed ones.

It was during this moment of enjoying the love and accomplishment shared between them that Tranzaiel stepped forward from out the trees that led into the clearing from the direction of their home. Looking for a moment past his sons, when he saw his wife approach from the far side of the clearing, Noah began to run to her with all his strength. Never before had she seen what they'd accomplished. Joy filled his heart that she would see now while he held her and kissed her cheek. He grabbed her, picked her up, and kissed her lips while putting her down. As she arrived softly to the ground, he looked into her eyes, and her into his. She sobbed. After she felt two tears fall quickly down her cheek, she pulled Noah to her so that he would see no more. She held him close. "Oh, Noah. I'm so sorry." She began to sob again, this time into his neck.

❧ ❧ ❧

When the five arrived home, Noah could not be dissuaded from entering the room once hearing his mother weeping within. It had been Tranzaiel's intention that her sons move the body before he had had the opportunity to enter. The sobbing of his mother's throat disallowed what small consideration Tranzaiel had tried to muster between the journey's start and the finish of retrieving her men.

"Daddy? Mommy, why is Daddy not waking up from your sad sounds?"

"Light, I tried to tell him–"

Light Within The Darkness held her hand up to stop the attempted explanations of her daughter-in-law. As she did so, her own voice strengthened. "I know my son well, Tranzaiel. Noah, Mommy is sad because Daddy will be asleep for a long, long time.

"You remember your very great-grandfathers, Kenan, Mahalalel, and Jared? You remember how long they have been asleep, son? So too we will make your father a very special bed that is never too hot, nor too cold, deeply in the ground. It may be that you become as tired as him, as all of them, someday, and sleep just as long. When you wake up from such a sleep, so will you find your Daddy awake to greet you."

"That will be a very long time, won't it, Mommy?"

"Yes, Noah. It will be a very long time." Light Within looked to her son's eyes and found herself a smile by them. She stood, stepped to him, threw her arms around him and held him for several moments, trying to hide her sobbing in his upper arm. When she was able to recover herself for a moment, she stepped back and took her son by the hand. "Come, Noah. Come keep me company while your sons make a good bed for their grandfather to rest in." Light Within nodded to Tranzaiel after catching her eye. She led Noah to the garden as Shem, Ham, and Japheth worked under the direction of their mother. While they sat together in the garden, a bunny hopped up to their feet, crinkled its nose, then hopped away again under a bush.

Chapter 44

The sons of Noah worked through the night, so that their grandfather would be buried with the rising of the light of the following day. They carried him out of the house, shrouded in the sheets that he had died in, and lowered him into the ground by their corners. Light Within stood weeping next to Noah, next to Tranzaiel, next to the side of the open grave as Enlarge, Heat, and Name shoveled the earth on top of the body they'd formerly called by the word 'Lamech.'

❧❧❧

As days passed, members of the community came to pay their respects. After placing stones on the grave, they reminded Lamech's widow, son, and grandsons what a good man Lamech had been to them. They brought animals and vegetables and useable gifts, so that the family would not need to work as hard for a time while they contemplated the loss of their loved one. Family came to help tend the garden. After a couple of weeks of mourning and arrangements, Noah's sons began to take shifts to make sure the tasks Noah would normally work were completed.

During this time, Noah spent his days with his mother, and his evenings holding his wife. As weeks turned into months, Noah's days remained the same: watch his mother work, and speak with her while it was light out, curl up with his wife in bed when it became dark. Aside from asking his mother if she thought his father was having good dreams, Noah spoke little. When his sons came to the house daily, they saw little more than their father sitting in whichever room Light occupied, frowning. Tranzaiel became used to the feel of his sobs into her shoulder at night. He did not mention bunny rabbits.

One day, Noah's three sons got together to talk about their father's state. They decided the best place to meet would be the ark, where they'd spent most of the past five decades toiling in play side-by-side with their father.

They gazed up at their work; what four novices could accomplish together. They contemplated what a seemingly foolish endeavor had produced from their desire that the completion might assuage otherwise apparent insanity. They marveled at the feat set in motion by the loving attempt at a fool's errand. They decided that even if their father could not be made to pick up a hammer, he could at least be forced more or less to his feet and pushed, if not carried, to where they stood now.

⋙⋙⋙

While his sons conspired to kidnap him to the great work of his hands, a testament to his irrepressible love of lagomorphs, Noah lay curled fetally in his bed, periodically sobbing. He wondered when he might fall asleep indefinitely, and if his dreams might bring him to the garden, where maybe he'd see Lamech once more. Tranzaiel walked into their darkened room, looked at her husband, walked to the bed, kissed him on the head, then walked out. Feeling dread, lethargy, and loneliness, Noah sobbed again.

He felt the place on his head where Tranzaiel had kissed. The feeling lingered through the darkness. Her touch continued, despite his loneliness. It felt as though she pressed her lips to him still. Strangely, the pressure seemed ever to grow rather than the natural dissipation he intuitively anticipated. In fact, the pressure on his head was even becoming uncomfortable. The touch on his head becoming even... warm. Noah's eyes snapped open. He became very, very still.

The warmth and pressure apparently lingering behind from his wife's kiss became even more than merely warm. The singular point on his head felt suddenly quite hot. He sat straight up and raised his hands to his head as hot turned to burning, and he felt the point on his head turn to a white light. This point lingered for a moment, then burst forth to fill his sensation of 'head' before finally overcoming the entirety of his field of vision.

"It's just me, Noah."

The blinding white dimmed itself slowly over a two-minute moment. By the slightest of degrees, the pure brightness relented to familiar vision. "Nochamet? Is that you?" Noah thought he saw the voice despite omnipresent radiance.

"Yes, Noah. It is time for you to wake up now."

"Why, Knockymed? I want to sleep, to dream with Daddy."

"The rest from your life will come as his, but you'll not find him from your bed. If you want your father's life to smile upon you now, Noach, your eyes must be open, and your bed vacant during daylight's hours."

"But my bed is warm, Knocky. What better have I to find outside of it?"

"The time I've told you of many times before is almost here, Comfort Upon The World. It is not only rabbits that will need to be guided past the waves, but also your sons; your wife. Should you succumb to your... perpetual rest to the emptiness you feel, your sons will rest as your father does now."

The room had returned almost to its accustomed lack of light. "I don't want Ham, Shem, and Japheth to sleep like Lamech! What do I do, Tronamet?"

"Just rise now, Noah. Finish the ark. You haven't much time."

"I will, Metty. I will!" As he spoke this final utterance, Noah's sight returned to normal. He could swear that as it did, he saw the ephemeral outline of an old man dissolve out of view while he rose to his feet.

❧ ❧ ❧

No sooner had he climbed to the top of his legs than did the door of the room open. His wife stepped in, holding free the space of the frame that shortly thereafter her sons appeared through, one-by-one, until eight eyes cast themselves upon two. No more than half of a second was given for those two eyes to speak, but speak they did.

Noah's lowered their lids, then he nodded, before walking through the space open directly in front of him without giving further indication by way of his mouth. His sons, and then his wife, followed after him. They found their way down the hall before, finally, Noah stepped out through the home's 'forward-facing' door. His sons continued through behind him, and his wife stopped at the threshold. She watched the passing of her men on their way to create their future.

❧ ❧ ❧

After eighteen months mourning the death of his father, Noah felt his muscles strain under the weight of the hammer where once such heft was barely an addition to that of his own arm. After days of soreness, weeks brought stability, and months brought strength to his old body, out of use for far too long.

Pitch had warded off decay and decomposition. The four were able to begin the completion of their project almost from where they had last left off. There was still much to be built, crafted, and assembled, but compared to the time already spent, they were practically through save for the 'finishing touches.'

With every nail hammered, with every plank smoothed, with every piece connected into place, Noah began to feel a little happier. He knew his Rontamet was adamant that the bunnies be saved. Noah's resolve bolstered his constitution while he kept the idea propelling him toward the completion of his craft. Also, he knew that if the bunnies could be rescued upon this boat, so too it was likely his sons, his wife, and his mother would require passage for the 'fun ride' soon to come. As was the way with work, Noah took the energies that weighted him previously with depression, and flung them away into the structural integrity of this ark doomed to save so many. Working hard so that these beings could continue their enjoyment of life, there came over the course of the next three years moments he shared with his boys that he could go so far as to call happiness, were he the sort of man to call his emotions by name. In turn, his sons were happy to see their father smiling while the last tasks of building the ark were accomplished over the final, few passing years.

Then, one day, the final nail was struck. The last piece of wood was covered in pitch. At long last, there were no more tasks to perform in the completion of their work.

Side-by-side stood the four men, gazing upon the enormity of the hollow vessel. Ham turned to his father and spoke the reflexive thought that had entered his mind: "Now what?" His brothers turned to look at him while their father maintained his gaze upon the creation.

"Now we wait for Grandpa Nochamet to tell us when to fill it with bunnies," he'd responded earnestly and resolved without taking his fixed sight from the labor of their hands. Ham, Shem, and Japheth returned their own stares back upon the craft five decades of labor had brought to fruition. Side-by-side, the four men stood before a work of incomparable magnitude and breathed in perception as they'd never worn it before: on the other side of a great life's work. They basked in the fulfillment of physical existence.

❧ ❧ ❧

That night they disbanded to return to their disparate dwellings. In the morning, they reassembled again with their wives at Noah's house. From there they brought their wives to see their work complete. After enjoying their mates' prerequisite gasps of its sheer immensity, they returned to prepare a small feast in celebration of the long-suffered endeavor come to fruition. All stayed the evening. Before the three brothers wished each other good slumbers, they congratulated each other on exorcising the idea of the boat from their father's system. They commiserated that in their lifetimes, they may never again possess such an opportunity for close quality time as they had had over the previous fifty years. Then they dispersed in the morning once more to their respective homes.

After his sons had left, Noah wondered how long it would be until he would know when the time was right to invite the small animals of the wood to take the fun ride with him and his sons on the ship he had just made for them.

❧ ❧ ❧

Four months after the celebratory feast honoring the completion of Noah's ark, Noah heard a light begin to brighten by degrees inside his ears. He didn't remember where he'd been a moment prior, as now all he knew was that everything was light. Through the core of his body, thoughts that were not his began to speak into his intestines and spine. "Noah, all life has begun to flow toward the ark that is your creation. Save a tenth of your garden for your family, and put the rest into the ark for food for your guests. Not only will the rabbits be taking this ride with you, Noach, but as well all their friends. You will also need to spend the next two months putting as much fresh water as you can into the ark, Noah, for your family and all the animals to drink. Finally, save as many living plants as you can. All the plants you know on land will not be able to survive underwater for the length of time the waters will cover over them."

"Okay, Nochnee. I'll start filling the boat."

"And don't worry about the animals, Noach. Just leave the door open so they can enter the ark as is best. You'll hear my voice from them telling you if they need help with food, water, or being cleaned."

"Okay, Metanoch. I'll start filling the boat tomorrow." As he felt his mouth try to voice this last utterance into his torso, light fled to its typical proportions, and he remembered where he was as he found his feet in the garden's center.

The angels who had chosen, watched apparent non-action dumbfounded. They felt strongly that something was definitely stranger about Noah that usual, but had no way of validating this deeply harbored suspicion.

❧ ❧ ❧

The next day, Noah arose with the sun. He emptied and cleaned one of the troughs for giving goats water, and began to drag it to the boat.

Tranzaiel, being awoken by the feel of her husband leaving the bed in the near-night, found herself unable to sleep thereafter. She silently followed behind Noah and watched his peculiar behavior with the goat trough. For the next hour and a half, she followed after Noah to see him drag it to where the ark, in all its enormity, stood. She watched while he struggled to open the door on his own, ultimately resigning it to fall under its own weight with a near-deafening thud. Then she watched as he began to drag the trough up the very large ramp leading into the vessel.

When Noah disappeared into the boat with the trough, she began walking immediately in the direction of the rising sun to her son Ham.

"I know your brothers and I thought building his 'saver of rabbits' would be enough to turn off his obsession. But now, it seems he's trying to furnish it, starting with the goats' source of water!"

"Mom, go home and watch what Dad does next. I'll get Name and Enlarged. Maybe he has a good reason for bringing a trough to that thing. . . and otherwise, maybe we can speak sense to him."

Tranzaiel sighed, hugged her son, and then set back out in the direction of her home. Ham set out in the direction of his brothers.

ᄼᄼᄼ

Upon arriving home, Tranzaiel saw Noah leaving their house with a large pot. She immediately felt pensive while she watched him carry the pot into the wilderness. This time, instead of walking straight to the ark, he walked to a flowing river about half a mile away from the ark, the banks of which were where his great-grandparents had met many centuries prior. He filled the pot with water from the river, then slowly began to carry it until finally again reaching the ark. Step by step he entered the ark, disappeared into the enormity of the vessel, and, several minutes later, emerged with a now-empty pot.

The rest of the late afternoon, Tranzaiel spent watching her husband fill a large pot, empty it into the bowels of the ark, and then return to repeat the cycle again. The sun hung low in the sky when her sons emerged from the trees while Noah was emptying the pot somewhere within the boat.

"I'm wondering how many troughs he took from the garden before I saw him take the pot. But maybe they're bigger than I think, comparing their size to how many trips he's made to and from the river. My legs are quite tired from following him all day."

"And you haven't tried talking to him at all?"

"No, Japheth. Honestly, I thought he might hear better if we spoke to him together. . ."

"Who are you talking to, Transi?" Noah emerged from the dark of the ship, pot in hand.

"Noah, honey, we were wondering why you've been bringing water to the boat all day."

"To keep the bunny rabbits and their friends from getting thirsty." These words came from him just as naturally as his family expected, at this point, that they would.

"Are the bunny rabbits... or their friends, on the ship yet, Dad?" Name ventured a question to seek sense out of the situation.

"Not yet, but Enochatron said they'd be here soon. That it was time to start making the boat ready."

"Noah, honey, how many troughs are in the boat?"

"Five."

"Dad, that's half the troughs for the animals. Don't you want to make sure your own animals don't get thirsty?"

"They still have water. The bunnies' friends will be here soon. I need to make sure they don't hunger or thirst when they arrive."

"Dad, we know you think you heard Grandpa's voice telling you, but you're taking time and water from your own garden now. What next? Will you start pulling up the plants from your garden, so that these animals might be fed?" Ham thought he'd try his own voice in dissuading his father from wasting his energy and losing what mind he had to an empty ship.

"Well, yes. Grandpametnoch said I should take nine of ten parts of the garden to bring to the animals."

"When are you supposed to do that, Dad?"

"Well, I was going to start tomorrow, when it's light out."

"But Dad, there are no animals to feed!" Japheth's patience had worn too thin. He'd crossed the verge of becoming animated when, catching Tranzaiel's field of vision, a strange, striped leg appeared out from behind a tree. She touched Japheth's shoulder and pointed. His overheated brain was struck cool with awe.

Ham's head turned as soon as he'd noticed Japheth's abrupt silence. Upon seeing the hoofed leg: "What the...?" Finally, Shem's head turned to enjoy what they all began appreciating.

Noah, catching on to the turned heads and the very few words coming from his loved ones, also looked toward the tree. He smiled widely. He walked down the ramp to the boat and stepped to the side. From behind the tree, slowly, cautiously, a striped horse emerged. It looked hesitantly side to side at the four people standing and staring at it. While it took its time approaching the ramp, it glanced behind itself and seemed to motion as though nodding its head. It raised and let fall its tail. Then, as it took another step forward, another striped, hoofed leg emerged from behind the tree. This leg was followed by another leg, which was followed by another leg, followed by another leg, and yet again another. As the first striped horse dissolved into the darkness of the ship's inside from the top of the ramp, seven other striped horses had emerged to slowly walk into the open from out of the cover of the trees. By the time they had crossed from tree cover to ark, thirty-five striped horses in all had passed into the vessel's belly. Shortly thereafter ran in fourteen lions from behind previous foliage cover.

Ham sprinted to where his father stood and yanked him into a run toward the direction of home, while Japheth took his mother's hand and slowly walked her back toward the trees. Shem nearly tripped over a pair of anacondas winding their way toward the ship as he followed, joining his family on their journey home as quickly as possible. He was hoping it was a good sign that both looked as though they each had a goat in the middle of their bodies while they slowly slithered by.

Upon arrival at their house within the garden, his wife and sons stared at Noah. "Why did we run away from the pretty friends of the bunnies?" Shem tried to imagine the pair of snakes he saw having a leisurely conversation with a group of rabbits.

Tranzaiel looked from her husband to their sons. "Well, I guess we had better start firing some large clay pots. Even if we bring the other five troughs to that boat, it won't be enough for our guests for very long."

The next sixty-one days were filled with work and excitement as Noah, Tranzaiel, their three sons, and their wives made preparation for 'a fun ride' on an ark filled with every manner of beast imaginable.

❧ ❧ ❧

Ligsbural and Harratzarian held the watch on Noah's family as the foreign animals found their way onto what they'd previously supposed as being a family's act of mercy, out of love, for Noah's 'unique' way of 'thinking.' Forced to reevaluate quickly the certainty of the opposite, Ligsbural ran quickly to fetch the next watch, leaving Harratzarian behind to monitor Noah and his family. Ligsbural expediently retrieved Luciferous and Tartantuan. By the time they arrived back at the ark, however, Noah's family, as well as Harratzarian, had already retreated to the garden. Nobody being present, Luciferous and company walked up the ramp of the ark to the vessel's opening. Greeted by a loud roar from somewhere within the hull, they quickly walked back down the side of the boat and in the direction of their village.

cĄɔ cĄɔ cĄɔ

That night, the humanity-clad gathered about the communal fire to discuss the day's revelations.

"Yes, when we thought he was conversing with himself about rabbits, the voice of God had caught his ear, while we were deaf to it."

"We have to warn the others."

"Zarnuchtron, Warmoot. You were the last to journey to the city of Enoch. How long would it take you to get to the rest of our people?"

Warmoot and Zarnuchtron shared a knowing look. Zarnuchtron answered, "It's been well over half a millennia since we joined you from Enoch. When we did return, it was by the watch of Enoch who, strictly speaking, was unsure of his own way as he was exploring. Perhaps if we could retrace our steps to the guarded gates of Eden, and then follow the sun as best we can remember doing at close to creation's beginning, maybe we could find our way there. I do not know if it could be done in less than a month, if even that quickly."

"Let alone find our way back with all of them in time." Warmoot finished his friend's thoughts.

"We either keep all the help we have and build with all our beings, or we send you two to possibly not find them at all."

"If we had more time, we could find them, but we don't. May I be forgiven for saying it, but what else are we to do?"

They all stood a moment in silence, horror-filled they could not warn their friends. It occurred to some of them already that perhaps even a full half of their own selves did not know what was coming for them next.

"But why would She not tell us that She was going to wipe life off the face of the planet? Is it just luck that we didn't find out by the drowning itself?"

"She left us to know the fullness of the pain of their existences. We must share in that pain just as them, if we are to succeed in assisting them past it to sewing seeds for themselves where they stand, so that the fertile soil beneath their feet yields what in another place and time they choose to walk away from."

"Take solace in this: if She had chosen, She could have hidden fully what is coming from our view. As it stands, we have an advantage the rest of humanity around us do not. We must build whatever we can as quickly as we can, and take as much food and fresh water as possible with us. These others, we'd otherwise choose to help to be otherwise, it seems they are not capable of understanding that after all Noah is right, and not a single one of them is not wrong."

Chapter 45

As they busied themselves making ready, firing amphora, preparing food, harvesting all manner of seeds they could think to, and collecting live plants in small pots, Noah heard the calling of bees from the direction of an old oak tree towards the center of the garden, "Nnnnnnnooooahhhh." He walked in the direction of the buzz accordingly.

At first, Japheth saw his father walking off and thought nothing of it.

"Nnnnnnnooooahhhh." The sound of his name grew louder as he grew closer to the tree. Finally, upon arrival, from a low-hanging branch hung a rather large hive; bees coming and going and crawling about it. Noah stood in front of the hive and spoke to it, "Did you call me?" Suddenly, thousands of bees poured forth from the hive.

From a distance, Japheth noticed a cloud of bees emerging from the tree directly in front of his father. He could hear the collective buzz from several hundred feet away. He called quickly over his shoulder, "Mom! Dad!" just as he took off running in Noah's direction. Tranzaiel glanced up from her work with the clay, saw her son and where he was running, stood from her work and ran toward her husband as fast as her legs could carry her.

The swarm hovered only a couple dozen inches from Noah's nose. A face, not inhuman, indented itself into the cloud they formed. Through the modulation of the numerous vibrations of their various buzzings, the mouth seemed to move, and apparently thousands of intonations sounded in unison as one, "Metatron has lent us his voice. We did call to you, for only two of us will be allowed aboard your boat, though more than two of us will be on board when you arrive. We will tell you more, but first, tell your son to come no closer, for we know our queen to be safe from you, not them."

Looking back, Noah saw Japheth running toward them, and his wife not far behind. Noah stuck out his arm, the palm of his hand out and up toward his son. "Japheth, come no closer. They won't sting me, but they might you."

Seeing the enormity of the swarm, Japheth stopped in his tracks at his father's words. He saw that his dad wasn't stung. He marveled. A moment later, Tranzaiel ran up toward Noah. Japheth grabbed his mother's arm and yanked her to where he stood, stopping her abruptly from running any further. "Mom, wait!"

Suddenly the swarm rushed toward and past Noah, flying all around him. They hovered between him, and his son and wife currently standing side by side. Then they encircled Japheth and Tranzaiel on all sides of them as a wall. Through the wall, Japheth could see a bee landing on Noah's earlobe, crawling up into the opening of his ear canal.

"Tell them they will not be harmed, for they are very afraid..."

"Japhy, Transi, they won't hurt you. They just want to make sure their queen is safe while I bring the hive to the ark. I'll be just a few minutes, and then they'll fly to a different hive, where they will await the flood." With that said, Noah walked to where the hive hung.

Japheth wanted to yell to his father not to touch it as Noah raised both his hands to the hive, but thought better of it, reconciling himself to the fact of being entirely surrounded by thousands of bees without the slightest sting from a one of them.

"Be very careful as you pull it down, Noah," buzzed the voice of God humming in his ear. "My queen and her selected drone, my brother, are in there." Noah loosened the hive from its grip on the branch as softly as he could, then began carrying it toward the ark as smoothly as his steps would allow.

When they'd arrived at the ark, the bees surrounding Japheth and Tranzaiel unfolded from them and took off in the direction Noah had begun walking almost half an hour prior. Tranzaiel moved to follow, but Japheth stopped her. "If they mean to harm Dad, we cannot stop them. I think we've seen enough to believe otherwise by now, though."

At the ark, the bee in his ear made his final requests. "Please choose us a spot away from where the bears will be hibernating through the storm." Noah found a suitable corner of the ship. "Now just hold the hive up to the ceiling and the walls." Noah did as he was told, then immediately heard the rush of the swarm of bees flying past the threshold of the opening of the ark. Quickly he and the hive he held were enveloped. A moment or two later, he heard their collective voice: "You may let go now." Much to Noah's surprise and delight, the hive did not fall.

All the bees regrouped once more, about a yard away from where Noah stood. As he turned to face them, the drone who had been riding within the opening to his ear flew to the rest of his brethren as again the cloud seemed to take on the form of a face. "We thank you for saving our species. We assure you at least some sweetness by our craft on your journey," hummed in unison the air generated from the pulsing of their collective wings before, amorphous once more, they all left the boat, leaving behind the hive containing their queen and her drone, well secured to the hull of the ship. Noah slowly followed in the direction the swarm flew, past a herd of deer, past a pair of tarantulas, and finally past a pair of drowsy grizzly bears, and once outside of the boat, began his short walk home.

❧ ❧ ❧

By the following week, the family had become quite accustomed to predators or other foreign animals stopping at the edge of the garden. A son would inform Noah, who in turn would walk up to the pair of tigers to assure them God had provided more than seven pairs of antelope, as well as other delicacies, over the course of the cruise. He would then thank them for not eating his family and point them in the direction of the ark. Or he would recommend foliage good for eating in the absence of something called 'eucalyptus' to the strange, fuzzy creatures standing on two legs, one with a baby in its front pocket. Or make a similar statement to a pair of anteaters as he had to the tigers several days prior that, "Yes, there are more than two ants on the boat," assuring them that he had watched several colonies of different types board personally.

When walking the piece of poplar containing the two termites on board, they assured him that the piece of wood would last at least two weeks into the voyage, and that by the time there were more of them, they'd hardly be able to make a dent through the hull of his beautiful ship before it safely made contact with dry land. In turn, Noah informed them of the ship's amenities and guests, extolling the virtues of the anteater's penchant for conversation. Not in so many words, of course.

Overall, however, two by two, seven by seven, drove by drove, the animals of the world found a comfortable home in the boat, well fed *before* they entered. Noah found great joy spending much of his days watching the beautiful, cute, and odd creatures of his Lord's creation embark, each in turn, and find their way to the most logically best possible place for the duration of their stay, fully of their own accord.

Meanwhile, as Noah often was called to ambassador and witness the seeming infinite diversity of Divinity's Life, his wife, their sons, and their sons' wives made ready for the journey. They spent all of two months drying vegetables and strips of animal flesh. They secured knives for when the dried flesh and vegetables had been consumed. Wood for making fire, and flint, and tinder. Large pots filled with water that later could be refilled with rainwater. The harvesting of live plants and seeds of every type from their garden and surrounding area, so that foliage would once again grow and proliferate upon the planet. Tools for repairing the boat. Bedding, clothing, pots and pans for cooking. Tools for crafting homes out of the boat once it settled, and later from new trees once they'd again grown upon the earth. Tools for farming. Needles, and threads, and a loom, and whatever knowledge in their heads that a millennium and a half of human existence had cultivated into them.

A relatively short distance away, the angels incarnate worked diligently, patching together a raft as big as they could construct. They dried as much food as they were able, and sewed as many bags as could hold as much of it as possible. They fired as many cups to catch the water as they could. As many large pots to hold as much fresh water as they could, and store what of the rains they'd need to. They crafted long poles, and wove heavy, long blankets frantically that they might have any refuge from the forthcoming deluge. And rope. They entwined many, many strands to make very thick, very strong rope, and they made a lot of it. In hopes of securing anything to their journey for as long as it lasted, as though it were the single most important of all of God's creations, they spent their time in constant, unending shifts of crafting rope.

Then, finally, one day in the distance, dark clouds began to encroach.

Chapter 46

They stood in the presence of The Heavenly Host; they had nowhere else they could go. They sat in the presence of The Heavenly Host; there was nowhere else they could go. They flew in the presence of The Heavenly Host, wings fluttering, wings still; present in the only place they could exist. They hummed to exist in service to Existence Pure Beyond Word, as the outermost skirt of immaculate light, created at the whim of Infinite Existence, begun with the ornament of conceived differentiation derived first for the obvious sake of pleasure alone if One would choose there could seem to be more. Given self-conception within the self-imposed limitation of only and purely service to what exists, before and within their Master, they asked and conversed with the answer between the beginning of the second millennium, and through almost seven-tenths of the way into it.

"The two of us met over the far-un-humaned bit of land and, conversing over the pleasures of existence you've given us to experience, we wondered if perhaps as you'd indicated at the start of our physical existence, you might allow us to share in the mutual enjoyment of each others' physical existences."

"As promised. You two will be Our harbingers to tell those as We made you. They will converge upon the place of the descendants of Seth, and know each other fully as desired for forty days and forty nights. When you have finished making sure that all of Our messengers and servants know, then you may begin with each other. They may begin with one another once the two of you have commenced."

Into corporate existence, in the year 1656, they flew their separate directions to deliver the message they'd been given.

Chapter 47

Finished and full, in all its enormity sat the ark. Sat and stood, its hull full of every animal that walked, flew, or slithered upon the earth or in the air. Gallons of water, acres of vegetation, dried meat, livestock, amphorae of seed.

Two miles away, Noah heard a hum that sounded like the softness of a bunny's coat: "Tomorrow it is time for your family to board." Then the hum was gone. Noah smiled within; the fun ride was about to begin.

❧❧❧

As Noah slept, two angels completed their task of informing all others of their kind the will of All they served. As the lesser of the two lights filled the clear, empty sky with its fullness, the two angels, having completed their task, gazed upon each other hovering in the moon's glow from a distance. At each other's presence, they ceased self-enjoyment in entirety, and ever so slowly floated in one another's direction. Their wings gleamed softly, shimmering in the cool night air. They admired one another's hardened nipples as they grew closer to the mutual satisfaction of one and a half thousand years, and more, of curiosity barring feet away from gratification of completion. They savored being drawn toward each other's perfectly self-contained selves that perfect existence would know perfect existence.

Within arm's reach, they stayed their progression of coming nearer.

They gazed into each other's eyes. Moon reflected sun, reflected eye, reflected individuation created by She Creator Master whom they served. Seeing His face in objectively Her eyes, they again drew clearer to see It fully in each other, in themselves.

Fingers touched, hands held, then ever slowly their hands slid up each other's arms. As they drew so close, eye never averting from one another, phalli stiffened, and vulva quivered upward deeply through to the inside of their selves. Hands around waists and upon shoulders, shortly before entering each other, as their lips touched another's for the first time, one's wetness, greater than the other, dripped down to the base of its quiver, and down from its body fell a single drop of its excitement. Shortly thereafter it landed to be drunk by the thirsty dust below, a kiss of rain that had not been tasted for quite some time. Quickly was this first taste followed by another.

Seeing the sign of the beginnings of their explorations of each other, at the sight of the two angels tasting each other's mouths, so too did the other angels slowly begin fluttering their way toward one another.

❧ ❧ ❧

The next day, Noah awoke to the sound of rain pattering softly on his front porch. With excitement and joy in his heart, he leapt out of bed, shaking his wife to follow after him.

He ran excitedly to another room where Ham slept. Noah shook him awake as well. "Get your wife! Your brothers! It is time to live on the boat!"

Ham was groggy at Noah's first shake of his shoulder, but came to attention readily at the news that he was to fetch his brothers to live amongst the beasts in a relatively small space for an undetermined length of time. If he had not seen an armadillo with his own two eyes, he'd not have jumped from his slumber to his brothers as though their lives now depended on locking themselves in with lions quite so quickly.

Noah ran to his mother's room next. "Mommy! Mommy! It is time to save the bunnies, Mommy! The fun ride is here!"

Light Within The Darkness sat herself up slowly, turned her attention to her son's gaze, and then smiled at him from behind a knowing sadness. In the gray of the dawning, Noah saw not past his mother's face while hearing her voice. "I will be ready for the journey shortly, my son. Make your wife ready now." Noah ran out joyously toward his own bedroom while his mother slowly managed herself out of her bed and toward her final preparations before the flood.

❧ ❧ ❧

Sacks and satchels had been prepared well in advance of the arrival of the now-pattering rain. With the last of the luggage to stow on the boat in hand, Noah joined his wife by the front door of the only home they had together known. Noah began looking up toward Tranzaiel to ask of his mother's readiness when the front door, left ajar, was beckoned open by the soft fingers of the outside's breeze.

There, several steps outside the door, stood Light Within The Darkness gazing outward toward the ground transitioning from dappled to damp, and the sky from which few drops deferred to almost many. After stepping past the threshold, Noah, standing beside Light Within The Darkness, asked, "Mommy, are you ready for the fun ride?"

Light Within turned to her son. As she stared at the one happy thought she had left alive lingering in her days, she forced a smile to her face. "Noah, my love, I will be taking the ride a different way. As these waters come, I wish to dream again by your father's side."

Tranzaiel's heart dropped to hear her mother-in-law's words. She knew what her husband was about to be unable to comprehend.

"You see, my child, I am very tired, and I need a very long rest." Before he had a chance to respond, Light Within threw her arms around him and held him tightly. After a minute or two had passed, she stepped back, looked into his eyes, then took a step forward and kissed him upon the forehead. "You are my children, who will step forth once more onto dry land where none other are deemed worthy. Take good care of each other, and treat my grandchildren to do the same!" Light Within's tears, now falling, could not be discerned from the drops of rain wafted over her face by the lightly rising wind while she slowly began to step backwards, keeping her gaze fastened to her son's.

Tranzaiel nodded as Noah, whom Light Within stared upon, stood dumbfounded. Tranzaiel took Noah's arm and began to pull him in the direction of the ark. Light Within turned and took two steps toward the garden where Lamech had been buried five years prior. Noah, several feet from where his mother walked, being pulled in a separate direction, turned toward her and shouted, "I love you, Mommy!" Light Within turned, blew a kiss to Noah, touched her chest over her heart, then turned from him and continued to walk.

The sound of the rain kept the sound of Noah's sobs from being carried far while they began the short journey through the trees.

⚜ ⚜ ⚜

Through the falling rain, Light Within The Darkness walked to the grave of her husband. Beside it was a gap in the earth that she had spent the month slowly digging.

She kissed the stone that marked the place her husband was laid to rest. She then turned to the hole she'd crafted to a depth several feet below the surface. Slowly she lowered herself toward its bottom, finally releasing herself into a shallow mixture of water and mud below.

She lay down into the mud, the water risen almost to her belly, face feeling the drops from the Heavens. She squeezed herself between two boulders she'd rolled into the hole by using planks as levers. She pinned herself down as adequately as she could between the large rocks. She found the length of rope hung with intention toward the hole's head.

The rope broke free from the muddied wall at the behest of a slight tug; she winced as small bits of dirt and clay fell to her face, quickly to be wiped clean by the waters from on high. Then, taking the rope in both hands and closing her eyes, she pulled as hard as she could. At first it did not budge. Her eyes opened. She struggled with it. Raised her torso up, and then with all her might yanked down. Through gritted teeth she tugged, and she tugged, and she tugged. Gasping, and grasping, and grunting, barely she could elicit even a budge. For minutes she wrestled to pull down her contrivance set above.

She stopped. She took a deep breath. She closed her eyes again. She relaxed, feeling the drops of rain on her face for several minutes. Then, her eyes flashed open before closing them with a simultaneous heave through the entirety of her thin, frail form to muster every bit of strength she had within, a roar let free from the depths of her chest and, at last, down fell the rope with the drops of rain.

As release quickly overcame her, Light Within The Darkness was given leave to dream by her husband's side forevermore.

Chapter 48

"Come on, Noah. We're almost there." They were all but soaked as they wandered amidst the foliage and the now-steady rain. Noah had to be led by Tranzaiel. His mind was not present while his legs acquiesced to the pull of her grip on his arm and the feel of her motion beside him. She guided him through the drops falling down from and between leaves. Together they continued onward.

Not long after, they came to the place trees met clearing. The ark loomed high and large above them. The rain began to fall from steady to hard as their feet found the floor of the ramp leading into this shelter from the waters above.

Once inside the boat, with flint and tinder Tranzaiel lit candles and lamps to see by. Noah just stood at the top of the ramp, staring at the darkness within until it lightened by Tranzaiel's efforts. She walked over to where her husband stood.

As she approached him, the feet of her sons and their wives on the ramp could be heard. Tranzaiel was eager to greet her family and welcome them aboard when she noticed what Noah was standing in front of. Several feet away from Noah was a massive pile of seeds. As Ham, Shem, Japheth and their wives arrived at the top of the ramp, they too noticed the seeds their parents were staring at. They too stopped to ponder.

"They could only have been carried here by the birds," Japheth broke the silence. "None of these are local to our area."

"To keep the plant life from where they came from dying out altogether," Ham finished his brother's thought.

"Grab some empty pots and fill them with these seeds. No doubt the birds will carry them back when it's all over."

"And how long can we expect to be on this cruise for?" An unfamiliar voice came to them all from behind, on the back of their mother's direction. Everyone turned to face its origin. All, that is, aside from Noah, who continued to stand still and stare silently.

They peered toward the heavy rain, the opening in the vessel, and saw a man—tall, old, pale, and soaking—slowly dragging his legs behind his walking staff, up the ramp. He reminded them all of a rat standing on its hindquarters that had just happened to wash up on a shore, that just happened to be the entrance to their boat.

"Who are you?" Name asked the question of the old man before his mother had time to bring the sound to her own lips.

"The direct cause of the cause of your arising, young man." He spoke through a high-pitched wheeze as he addressed them, "I knew he was building something special. They called him crazy, and worse, stupid. But I began to watch from a distance. The building was incredible, but when I saw the animals come, I knew just how stupid *they* were. When the rain began to fall, I knew just how brilliant he was. Of course he's brilliant! How could my grandson not be?"

Ham and Shem turned toward each other's eyes and spoke the word simultaneously. "Grandson?"

Tranzaiel gasped aloud. "Methuselah?" A bolt of lightning striking nearby revealed the top of the staff, which had supported him for a lifetime.

Noah had turned by now to see the wrinkle and scar-infested face that had murdered an innocent bunny rabbit with that spear so many centuries ago. Just before Noah's mouth opened, Methuselah extended his unburdened arm, "Noah, wait!" To no avail, for shortly thereafter his voice loudly filled the ark as a continuation of what he had began to say so very long ago. Wordlessly, Noah expressed the terror his grandfather had infused into his veins. Noah pointed at Methuselah and let forth a scream, shriek, and howl somehow simultaneously.

The three brothers again caught each other's eyes briefly before walking in Methuselah's direction. He tried to raise his voice above Noah's as Ham, Shem, and Japheth closed in upon him. "Wait! Stop! I'm your great-grandfather. I should be on this boat with my family!" One took hold of his staff as the other two took hold of either arm, and they dragged together this unnecessary weight back down the ramp and several feet away into the torrential downpour from above. They set him down gently and laid beside him his spear, then walked back up into the vessel. Once inside, the sons and wives together raised the ramp of the ark into the side of the boat while Tranzaiel held Noah close, stroking the back of his head and reassuring him that the bad man would never, ever harm a bunny rabbit again.

The rising ramp several feet off the ground, the brothers and their wives could hear a thump against the boat below, accompanied by a voice penetrating somehow past the rains of the near fully-brewed tempest. Methuselah beat the butt of his spear against the side of the ship. "Damn you, Noah! If I could I'd put a knife through your heart, just like I did fourteen years ago to that little cunt Magatha! Bitch of a wife wouldn't open her withered legs that last night of her life. Then that ungrateful town exiled me, just so that I could humiliate myself by being denied my right as your grandfather to be spared the coming waves, you ungrateful little shit? You earned what's coming for you, you–" Eventually his voice was drowned out completely by the torrential rains, the resound of thunder, and the snapping shut of the barrier, forevermore in his life between them, that had been the ramp of the ark, converted now into the hull of the ship. The springs of the Earth burst forth; the sound of the waves against the side of the boat now replaced the banging of the back of his staff, and the last of Methuselah's stifled cries.

Harratzarian watched from behind a tree as the ramp of the ark closed. She found solace that her spear was soon to find lasting rest upon the ground. Hoflan pulled at her arm. "Most surely, now it is time to go."

Chapter 49

From their work together, they'd fallen and fastened tree beside tree. For sixty-one days, cutting down trees and tying them together with rope was most of what any of them did. The rest of what they did, primarily, was gathering food and pots of water. All but eight worked tirelessly at any given moment. Two watched over Noah's house, two over each son. If they were awake, they worked.

When they saw Heat leave for his brothers, Triomvet left to warn the tribe, and Childreth followed after Ham; Hoflan and Harratzarian stayed behind. Hoflan followed after Light Within and reunited with Harratzarian at the ark upon being given no reason not to. Once Ham, Shem, and Japheth were on the boat, Harratzarian and Hoflan, having seen the closing of the door of the ark, joined their brothers and sisters at the raft. United, they all huddled together for warmth as the love made by their brethren above crashed in waves down upon them.

Initially they'd propped the thick cloth they'd woven up with poles. They'd hoped these odd little tents might be enough to offer some shelter from the rain. Though the cloth was thick, however, these "tents" quickly failed and did nothing to shield them from perpetual wetness. Realizing what was coming quickly, they feverishly sewed the cloth together as a way to hold themselves fastened to the raft when waters might get choppy. They did their best to secure pots filled with any kind of food they thought would last. They tied the thick blanket-tarp to the ropes around the edges of the raft. They left themselves lengths of rope to wind around their arms, to make it harder to be thrown about once they began to rise off the surface of the Earth. They held each other in anticipation of the waters to come.

In villages all around them, the people were concerned that they could not remember the last time it had rained so hard.

⚛⚛⚛

Up above them all, vigorously, the angels in the firmament made love to one another. As they mutually filled with orgasm, sheets of rain fell upon the people below. At every climax, the sound of their ecstasy was the thunder, as lightning filled the sky so that all the world should know the joy they were bringing to each other. Unceasing they wished only to be filled, and release, and they knew that this was the singular desire of All that had created them in this moment, and they obliged happily. In the name of their Father, they rained over the Earth.

⚛⚛⚛

To the East, in Enoch, began to fall the light patter of rain. In the camp several miles to the west of town, the incarnated servants entered their tents while the rains slowly began to fall harder.

Seven miles north of the camp, Casarta walked alone, meditating and enjoying solitude; she manifested a small cloth tarp above her head, made of the same material of the tents in the camp.

Gendlebleth had decided to take a day for himself in the city; he sat beside the reflecting pool in the city's center. As rain drops began to cast ripples upon the water's surface, he smiled. Gendlebleth loved the rain. He contemplated that he may return to his tent, with any luck, soaked, before his outing was through. He welcomed the thought of feeling cleansed.

Toward the outskirts of Enoch, Cain sat contemplating his unique loneliness. It had been centuries since he'd noticed the townspeople murmuring frequently that he didn't much seem to age, every time he was walking by them. His great-great-great-great-grandchildren would bring him food, wine, and news from the city, but he rarely left his house during the day. He even pondered the value of maintaining the knowledge of his family amongst his far offspring's offspring, considering the whispers they must have to live their lives amidst as they carried out their days on his behalf. He contemplated his children long-since past, as well as his wife. A tear fell from his eye and down to the floor below. He listened to the echo of its fall on the roof of his home, *and* the ground outside of his door. His heavy heart sighed and breathed its way out up through his lungs and passed his lips. The rain fell steadily harder.

Casarta sat upon the ground in the wilderness. She decided this could be an opportunity to meditate and focus. She considered that she could hold herself sitting and dry for perhaps two full days, should the rain last so long. She widened the canopy above her head as she welcomed the stillness and tranquility of her one focused manifestation, and the sound of the rain.

Two hours later of rainfall, the water fell quite hard on Gendlebleth's face as he leaned his hands back against the side of the pool. He thought about the miles and hours it would take to journey from where he sat, to return to camp. Knowing a solid three-hour walk in clear conditions, he resigned himself to another brief hour or two to shining waters before making his way home to dry.

In a central, large tent in camp, a handful of the incarnated began discussing supper for everyone in the evening. They decided a stew would be in order to warm their tribe through the damp of the night.

A cup of wine in one hand, Cain softly wept into a handkerchief in the other. He considered how many centuries he'd lived, then uttered a soft prayer that his death might be swiftly forthcoming. He brought again to his remembrance the image of his long-departed wife. He wept more.

An hour later, water poured down in sheets. As Gendlebleth felt drops of water begin to sting his skin, he brought forward his head and tried to open his eyes to a bolt of lightning peeling the sky in two. Through squinted sight, he saw the early hours of the afternoon were covered almost to night. He considered that with skies this dark, and clouds this heavy, he was best off beginning a very long walk home to the shelter of his clan, and rest from waters that hurt. He sighed at his naiveté earlier, thinking the rains were nothing more than a blessing to him on this occasion. He decided that further enjoyment of rain might best be experienced closer to home, barring arrangement for a room at the local inn; he wasn't accustomed to carrying money or sheep with which to barter.

At the house of Cain, the rain beat mercilessly at the walls and against the door. Water fell as lead upon his roof. So was echoed within his dwelling the sounds of despondency he felt assailing his heart, as for centuries he'd sought shelter within *it*.

While preparing supper, the carnalized angels began to doubt the integrity of the large, thick tent surrounding them. They gave thanks the wind was still mild enough that the stakes were not torn loose from the ground to which they clung, despite the fabric shaking violently by the waters pelting it from all sides and seeking rest upon the roof.

Out in the wilderness, Casarta remained quite dry under a rather large, rectangular covering of tile of her imagination's devising. She heard the water pouring from its edges all around to the ground below. She could detect the ground slowly absorbing the water as the rest of it was felt creeping toward her. Then, beneath her she felt an even odder sensation; as though far below where she sat, she thought she could hear the fibers of the Earth being ripped apart from itself. The thunder surrounding her paled next to the low rumble she heard building a pressure she sensed, but did not understand. So clearly the ground shook until, now knowing fully she must move and take to the sky, her eyes opened just as the underground springs broke forth to the surface. She was too late.

The waters overcame her. The pressure bursting forth pushed her swiftly as a flood rose all around her. The force of the water took her too suddenly for her to have time to think her "ceiling" away before the water rushed her quickly into it. Her head knocked hard against very solid tile. Her consciousness was lost.

No more than three miles along his journey back to camp, Gendlebleth was overcome by the waters bursting forth.

In the camp, the fires under the pots were unceremoniously snuffed. The cooks could not think to seek the tent's opening before swimming had already involuntarily begun, and being pushed hard to the top of the tent by the water that had brought them there. They had to focus to take one more breath before they could even consider finding a way out of the water by swimming downward to the greater openings of the tent, or trying to push past each other through the holes in the roof of the tent that were designed in size only so that the smoke of cooking fire had a place to exit. Similarly, the others in *their* tents found themselves quickly tangled in the cloth of their dwelling and unable to move, let alone swim to an escape from these rapidly-formed watery cocoons. Those who happened to be outside were overcome by the water quickly. Those thinking through the suddenness of panic began diving toward tents to untangle their brothers and sisters at once.

Far above, the angels reveled in the beauty of the absolution of God.

Down below, the dams broke forth, the springs beneath the earth broke forth, water fell almost in waves from the sky, and the crash of the waters overcame the city of Enoch. As its citizens added their own tears to the waters silencing their cries, Cain shed a single tear of joy that perhaps, at long last, his dearest prayer was finally answered.

❧ ❧ ❧

High overhead, through ever-pouring ecstatic sheets of water, a comet three miles wide careened downward toward the Indian Ocean.

❧ ❧ ❧

As above, tongues tasted tongues, and tongues tasted genitals, and bodies moved in fluid rhythm with other bodies, feeling as deeply into each other as either could; below, those of their own kind who had eaten from the Tree of Knowledge gasped for breath as tongues tasted water, throats filled with fluid, and the flood was all their bodies could know before going limp to the waves. Most lives—human, animal, giant, and Nephilim alike—were ended within the first thirty minutes of the waters washing over the face of the Earth. East of Eden, a large raft was beaten by the water of the sky and the waves of the flood. Periodically flipped over as easily as spun around, its occupants clung to ropes and each other alike in an effort not to be lost to one another into the depths drowning out the lives of all the world. Those who could make it to the tops of tall trees were granted an extra two hours, at most, of existence. Those at the tops of mountains' tallest peaks lasted an average of three days. The last goat's life was snuffed a week into the waters. Two days later, there was not a bird that could not resist the urge to rest its battered, rain-ravaged wings. The water offered a final rest to all.

She did not know after the water had filled her unconscious lungs that the current had dragged her well under the waves for miles, pulling her down to the flood's bottom where once had clearly been defined the surface of the Earth. Also unbeknownst to her lifeless form was the large boulder the waves had managed to roll over her right foot, pinning her to one place where she otherwise would have floated off with the swiftly-moving underwater stream. There, in the silence of the watery tomb of the world, Casarta's eyes snapped open.

Chapter 50

Feeling the pain caused by the boulder pinning her foot to the floor shooting up her leg, through her spine, and finally into her brain, her first instinct was to scream out the shock recently hammered upon her head. So easily responding to her instincts, she found herself gagging on a world filled with water, her lungs already expanded mostly as far as the water filling them would force. Her eyes widened in response to her terror while her mind awoke to the nightmare. Brain racing, she identified her wish to breathe, then considered the space surrounding her mouth filled with air rather than water.

Instantly a bubble surrounded her head. Her lungs contracted and water poured forth through her lips and nose. She gasped inward and choked on the water still remaining in her lungs, while water mixed with snot ran forth from her nostrils.

She considered the space all around her body surrounded by air, at which point she fell to the ground, several inches below, screaming with agony to feel her ankle twist further by the gravity of the rest of her body pulling backward from where it was stuck. As she screamed, she continued to choke. Pushing herself up by her hands, she got herself sitting upright, then breathed outward through her mouth as hard as she could to expel the waters left before gasping again for oxygen. She next blew out through her nose to clear her nasal passages, so that she could attempt to breathe at all normally.

After hacking and coughing and blowing excess moisture out of her esophagus and sinuses for the better part of five minutes, she felt as though she was breathing more or less regularly. The only severe discomforts that now lingered were in her chest, her head, and of course her foot. Focused ever on air surrounding her body, she expanded the space filled with air and envisioned a baby elephant on the other side of the boulder. She next imagined the baby elephant pushing the boulder off her foot. As the large rock rolled away and to the side of her, again she screamed with the fresh sensation of her mangled foot and ankle pulsing throughout the entirety of her being. Past the pain, retraining her focus on the space around her filled with air, she recovered herself with every subsequent gasp. Her mind cleared to the point of more than sitting in agony: she could breathe.

❧ ❧ ❧

After resting in her pain a moment or two, she began to look around her. Under water, under cloud, it was terribly dark. She considered illumination, and her vision could penetrate several feet around where she sat through the waters surrounding her. Six feet or so to her left, she saw a body. *That poor fool. There must be so many bodies down here.* Thinking thus, she gasped when his eyes suddenly snapped open. She couldn't be sure, but she thought she saw him motion his hand toward her.

Filled with pity and dread, she tried to stand up to walk to him, then instantly fell back hard against the ground, screaming. She thought her foot full and healed. The pain was still within it, but she could use it, stand, place her weight upon it without her weight causing the pain that still afflicted it. She walked toward the man, expanding the air further outward as she walked it with her as quickly as she could to where he lay. Light, air, and foot balanced in her mind, she pressed forward.

When her bubble of oxygen penetrated to his lips, water poured forth from his mouth, and then his nose, and he shortly thereafter feverishly began to gasp a breath. Filling the space surrounding him with air, Casarta dropped down to the ground, suppressing her cry while she lost focus on the wholeness of her foot, and the darkness again surrounded them. But they could breathe.

Chapter 51

He dreamed of water collapsing his roof down upon him; the feel of water filling his lungs. He drank his suffocation greedily; joyfully coughing, then choking, then releasing to the fullness of the cavity in his chest expanded and unable to move out the water. Then, light. Moments later, the face of what must be an angel to greet him in his death. So light in her arms. But then he was no longer floating, and upon cold ground the joy of suffocation emptied past his lips. Then, darkness. Perhaps his rest had come.

Until he awoke in darkness.

The sound of lungs screaming themselves empty of every drop of their suffering. Then, in a low light, eyes noticing his. Then perfect darkness once again, and silence.

⁂⁂⁂

He again woke in silence.

"You are awake again?" A soft, female voice. Subdued. Cautious.

"I am." He feared he may not be dead. However many questions in the darkness, his choice to withhold his voice further was a conscious one.

"I could hear the pace of your breathing change. It was so subtle, but I've been listening to your breath for what I suppose are hours."

Silence.

"My name is Casarta. Your breath has been distracting me from the pain of my crushed ankle, for which you have my gratitude. How is it you are not dead?"

Weakly he hissed a bemused thought through his lips. "Happy my breath could ease anybody's pain." The rest of his words past irony: "I was cursed many centuries ago by the voice of my father, the direct son of God, for killing his son, my brother. The words were beyond my understanding that day, but it seems I am held to seven full lifetimes of existence for originating the crime of dismissing the earth holding the breath of our Common All-Just Creator." More than sixteen hundred years of wishing his own death for the pain of exile his action caused within and without, he sensed he could moan his anguish five lifetimes more without cessation, but he also observed that his story was a short one. So, he stopped.

"You are... Cain?"

Who knew his story that they could identify his name by his tale? His wife and her father had perished long ago. His children did not speak of what little they did know in their life. "I am." He breathed. "How is it we are not now inhaling water? I remember a face the color of pomegranate seed after water filled my lungs out of breath. Are you some manner of angel?"

Casarta thought, and there was light. The plants in the water surrounding them seemed to glow. The light was soft, gradual. It did not hurt Cain's eyes as he made out her shape before detecting the ruddy color of her face. "Rather, the daughter of angels. Shortly after your parents conceived you, my parents ate from The Tree. Soul divided from soul. My parents were not born from the one from One, yet became as they had briefly in their despondency and pain upon realizing two. Before you killed your brother, my father raped my mother. I am the only one of my kind. By my thought, water is pushed from water that air has entered. By my thought, we can see each other now."

Cain marveled to hear her story while his mind returned to a time long since past. "Your father... he is not Gendlebleth?"

"*Ha!*" Casarta was surprised to hear anything resembling laughter involuntarily push its way through her, at this of all times. The utterance was sharp, and it was brief. "Sorry. No! No. The dear sweetness of that beautiful, broken-hearted one. I am not his daughter. I had forgotten he blames himself for your brother's murder as though he'd committed it himself. But there are many more than he here, and he has never known but the separateness of his true other half, like all else aside from my parents. No, my father is Lousitous."

"We are surrounded by water," he gazed around him, "are the rest of your people drowned?"

Casarta frowned. "I awoke filled with water and pinned under a large rock. By my light and my air, you are all I have known since losing consciousness from the waters. I do not know how long ago. Though we did develop an understanding of the capabilities of the minds we possess in the image of yours. Be so kind as to allow me silence for the time."

Cain did as Casarta spoke.

She closed her eyes and noticed her own mind. The air encompassing them both within water held from water all around. The light held in her thought. The pain by movement and involuntary dynamic of her physicality. Her ever-shifting placement of focus to remember each as simultaneously as mentally possible.

She allowed the light to fall away from her focuses, maintaining visualization of her shared room of water walls. She turned her attention away from her pain, to her recollection of Gendlebleth's face. She observed her lungs fill, allowed the pain, observed the room allowing her lungs to fill. She let her thought seek Gendlebleth.

She saw from outside her body the room held created by her mind while she asked herself past and into the water *Where are you, Gendlebleth?* Her mind raced through the water. It came to a ring of concrete she recognized as the pool at the city's center. Her mind moved further, a half-mile or so. She saw a body dragging back and forth, moved across the ground by conflicting current. She remembered elsewhere her body breathed close to Cain within a room of water held from water. Her mind touched to Gendlebleth's head. *Please think me you are alive, at least through this unceasing suffering that had been the bulk of your existence.*

She felt his eyes twitch in his skull. She felt his brain tingle with anticipation of response. She felt his lungs contract against the water filling them, his brain alight with pain to try to respond from immutability. While she felt him strain against himself and the impossible to resist, she felt him lose consciousness from the strain, and took her exit from him with the answer she sought. Through miles of water she allowed her mind to snap back to her physical self without thought, remembering the room that surrounded them as she journeyed back to her coarser self. Her eyes opened. She brought light once again into the chamber.

"I found Gendlebleth. At least, I found that he is alive..."

"So you can... think him here to us?"

"It doesn't quite work that way. What I think is created, but it goes away if I don't sustain the thought. You have no idea how difficult it was to maintain this room while dividing off my focus to find that Gendlebleth was merely alive. If I hadn't remembered this room existed while finding him, your lungs would be quite filled with water again, and this time without hope of it ceasing your existent pain."

"How is it I breathe, if this air is not permanent?"

"So long as I think it, it is here. Should I stop, it will not be long before water quickly takes its place. Up above you could breathe real air to take its place, but we have no boat."

"But you could think us a boat!"

"To be quickly overtaken by water and storm, yes." She frowned.

"Wait, do you sleep?"

"Of course I sleep."

"What happens if you fall asleep?"

She paused. "You cease to breathe until the waters disperse... and so do I. Until I wake again."

"And how long has it been since you last slept?"

"Given that it feels like I've been awake for eighteen hours, I'm guessing it's been closer to six or eight while you slept."

"Can you conceive live creatures?"

"I can. That's how I got that boulder off of my foot, in fact."

"Dolphins!"

"Pardon me?"

"I've heard merchants from a faraway land speak of some kind of sea animal called a 'dolphin.' It's said to be a very large sort of fish, except sometimes their heads emerge from the water to breathe air. If you can conceive this room into some sort of sea chariot, it could be pulled by dolphins, and then you can find Gendlebleth and have the dolphins take us to where he is!"

"I've never seen a dolphin, but I've seen enough fish. I can attach a really big fish to our room and have it follow my mind to him. To all of them. Perhaps several big fish."

No sooner had she spoken than the ground beneath them was turned to wooden planks. She sat in an odd-shaped seat that conformed to where she sat, her leg supported in a sort of long box. Short walls appeared, making their room a cradle containing a pocket of air. Two very large fish appeared before them, tethered to the box. The glow of the light now seemed to be emitting from the fish. Casarta closed her eyes, and the fins on the fishes' tails began to sway in large, sweeping motions back and forth. The box in which they sat began to lift from the ocean's floor. The nose and backside of the box became pointed, and the sea chariot began to move faster and smoother by the fishes' pull.

Cain marveled while he watched water and fish pass by all around. He trembled as occasionally human bodies were passed while en route to recover a body *not* dead. Casarta remained still as the large fish batted back and forth, the ocean surrounding them with their tails. She felt as though her own mind sought after Gendlebleth once more. This ride went on many minutes before they stopped in front of Gendlebleth's motionless body.

"Can you stand?"

Cain hadn't thought about it much since expelling water from his lungs; there really wasn't very far to walk to, or much room to rise. He began by stretching his legs back and forth. Slowly he rose himself to his feet. His legs felt wobbly at first, but he could stand. He turned to observe Gendlebleth's body, face turned upward, otherwise supine in watery space, bobbing with the flow.

He looked back toward Casarta. She pointed her finger forward. Cain returned his sight to Gendlebleth. A pocket of air had formed around him. Save for the water beneath his back, several feet above the ground, Gendlebleth was in dry space. Cain walked up to where his old friend floated. The water that still supported Gendlebleth made dragging him into the boat far easier; Cain bent down to him, wrapped his arms into Gendlebleth's, and pulled. The man had made it on board.

Gendlebleth lay on the wooden floor, motionless. Cain stared at him expectantly. After a moment, Cain looked to

Casarta. She held her hand toward him, palm out. Cain looked again to his motionless friend lying on the floor.

Cain's shoulders rose and lowered with a long, heavy sigh. While his sigh was releasing, water shot straight up, out from Gendlebleth's mouth. His eyes snapped open. Trying to gasp inward for air, Cain heard him clearly gagging on the water still saturating his lungs. As he was writhing and choking, Cain immediately thought to turn Gendlebleth over on his side. Once there, he took himself the rest of the way to his hands and knees so that gravity would aid him in expelling the remainder of the water forth from his mouth and nose. A sort of dry gargling turned into a wet hacking and wheezing, his chest expelling the last of the water contained within. Again he gasped inward, this time successfully inhaling oxygen. Interspersed with deep, small coughs, Gendlebleth breathed.

He stopped there, drinking in the air, re-engaging his lungs for some time before looking up and about him. He didn't understand why Casarta was reclining, watching him. He noticed a small school of fish swimming by behind her. He marveled at the wall of water and began following it around. Quickly he came to Cain's shins close beside him. He looked up to see the old victim of his friendship. He began to shake. He wanted to weep. He wanted to freeze. He shook.

Cain didn't understand what emotion had seized upon this being, so long ago his friend. His fear told him that Gendlebleth must now dread to look upon his lowness after having taken his word horrifically wrong, using it to conceive murdering his own brother where he was meant to humble himself before life as it was. Cain felt his upper lip begin to tremble, and then looked to Gendlebleth's eyes. Meeting his gaze, instinctively he extended his hand to Gendlebleth.

Gendlebleth continued staring back up into Cain's vision. He glanced down at Cain's hand, then back up to his pupils once more. He found his hand instinctively rising up to meet Cain's. Face to face, eye to eye, they looked deeply into each other. *For he offered his hand, perhaps he could forgive me inspiring him to murder his brother. For he took my hand, perhaps he could forgive me blaspheming his word as I twisted it.*

From beyond the sea from which he had so recently been dragged, water welled up within his eyelids. From eyes long-since dried where the flood had too forced his submission, also within eyelids the promise of a new flood began to fill. In each other's eyes, they both saw the life of Hebel dismissed by their own hand. Sharing perfectly the same pain, they embraced.

Chapter 52

"Casarta, what happened? I'd ask about any two things together not making sense, but nothing about this makes sense. Or does it?"

"All I know is that where before the land was dry, now all seems to be sea. I thought Cain otherwise should be dead, but he explained to me that he appears to be cursed to live seven very full lifetimes. What you're standing on, and in, is what I could think up, with Cain's help, to allow us simultaneously to breathe and to be transported to where you were, so that we could get you breathing again."

"Was I very far from where you woke up?"

"Yes. Especially since my foot and lower leg is broken. I thought a way to walk on it, but the pain was still too strong to maintain it for a long distance."

"How did you find me?"

"I focused on you as though when we try to relay a message by thought. By focusing on you, I was able to see where you were. After that, it was just a matter of considering the big fish follow my connection to your location."

"Have you found any of the others yet?"

"No. Not yet. You were the first, because you came up in conversation between Cain and I. You were obviated, so I started with you."

"Casarta, your mother!"

Casarta immediately became annoyed with herself that Antagnous hadn't been the first person to reach her thoughts. After a moment of initial chastising reflection at her realization of neglecting the obvious, her eyes closed abruptly. She remembered the face of her mother while considering their shaped bubble attached to the fishes.

⁂

Antagnous' body hung in the water. The chariot stopped next to where she floated, rocking softly in the gentle undercurrents. Gendlebleth took hold of her ankle and pulled her in, Cain helping to steady her so that together they lowered her unhurriedly to the floor. They turned her onto her side. Casarta's eyes opened and she considered their room a few feet larger than it had been before. Then, her focus rested squarely upon her mother.

Antagnous lay motionless until, all at once, her eyes snapped open while water fell from her mouth. She tried to inhale, choked on the substantial amount of water still filling her lungs, forced more water out by a belabored push through her esophagus, then continued to hack and wheeze and wrestle control of her breathing function to the point where air might flow freely into her without consideration or annoyance of excess fluid. Gendlebleth attempted to comfort her arm and shoulder while she battled away the unwelcome waters within.

When the worst was over, she rose to her feet by way of hands to knees. After glancing quickly around, she rested her gaze upon her daughter while wiping watery snot away from her nose and onto the drenched shirt clinging to her. "Where is your father?"

At once Casarta's eyes closed shut, and soon they were brought to a man floating upside down. As Gendlebleth motioned for Antagnous to assist him and Cain in securing

Lousitous inside without him landing on his head, he began to recount events as he knew them.

"Have we been so offensive It would wipe our slate so clean, torturing us in the process? I thought things were going well. We haven't even had a major calamity here since Cain invented homicide. No offense."

"None taken," Gendlebleth and Cain responded to Antagnous simultaneously. Gendlebleth noticed immediately how readily he responded reflexively. Cain shot him a glance upon realizing he'd responded in concert.

Casarta felt something new and unpleasant as she heard her mother's words and began to think for the first time about why she was rescuing her friends and family from being otherwise indefinitely drowned.

"Casarta." Casarta was pulled back to the present moment by her mother's voice, her father just beginning to choke on the water being pushed involuntarily out of him, "we need to find the others!"

Casarta was at a loss for words. Antagnous picked up on her hesitation. She became very aware that their safe passage and protection from the waters was contingent on her pain-filled daughter maintaining focus past joining voices, and that whatever her level of fatigue would slowly grow. Ceasing her own speculations, refocusing her own racing and divergent mind, Antagnous picked the first face and name that came to her so as to direct her daughter back to the present. "Let us start with Darius." Gendlebleth nodded in agreement as Casarta let her eyelids lower, a third large fish appeared beside the others, and Lousitous began gasping up oxygen with greater frequency than the thin wheezes that had followed toward the end of particularly long inhalations.

The chariot raced through the water. As they dragged Darius in from off the sea bed, Antagnous spoke the name she'd already made ready. "Next, Lemisslept."

Casarta's eyes shut and the chariot's floor grew around them; they had more space to move.

Lemisslept secured aboard, Antagnous spoke the next, "Telnaxson."

Those who'd recovered their lungs spoke together as the fish pulled them all through the water. They agreed to contemplate those who were still missing together so that Casarta could readily bring her mind quickly to them all. Their sole focus became to round up their half of the incarnated, separated from Luciferous' camp as they were, before Casarta could no longer maintain them all from her own exhaustion. Though Antagnous herself believed she could recount all clearly from memory, she had no choice but to concede her memory could lapse momentarily, as any human's.

They comforted the newly saved from the water in turn as three prepared to accept the newly found gently upon their ever-growing vessel. As their numbers increased, the majority sat in meditation so as not to distract Casarta's already burdened mind. After Telnaxson had been pulled on board, Cain sat a few feet from Casarta in silence, watching in awe. As they awoke, those who noticed Cain nodded toward him as they were informed quickly the circumstances in which they all now found themselves.

Ternaddain, Handoroth, Darwith, one by one were recovered. Slowly their room grew, and more very large fish were added to accommodate the ever-growing submersed vehicle.

Caldas, Taolith, Lajiel. Casarta began to grow visibly weary.

Randolfy, Gernow, Ceaslar, and at last none among them could recall one of their band who was not recovered safely. Antagnous turned to her daughter. "You have been recovering us for hours, focusing on our accommodation without cessation the entire time. My daughter, have you ever focused into being a manifestation for so long? It is time you rest!"

Casarta dragged her eyes up to her mother's from out of circles around them the color of coal. "But if I lose focus, you all will drown again."

Lousitous stepped beside Antagnous, "Daughter, we have spent some time discussing as far from your meditation as we could on this now very large raft beneath the waves. Take us to the surface, where there is air. We will make of ourselves a raft. It is time *we* support *you*."

They all nodded in agreement while Casarta rolled her eyes over to match those of Lousitous. "But what, father, of Cain?"

Gendlebleth stepped forward this time, "We will support him as we will you. It is the least we can do, given what effect I... I mean, we have had upon him already." Again they all nodded in agreement.

With the last will in her being, she turned her attention to the eighty-five mammoth fish at the front of her ship. They flapped their fins, swished their tails, and up they rose higher and higher through the sea.

Floating plants, fish, and bodies just beginning to bloat and be nibbled upon by other fish, rushed by on all sides of them. Until, finally, some many minutes later, all at once the school of eighty-five fish turned nose downward as the top of the raft pierced the surface of the sea.

Casarta did not dare to close her eyes while she directed her gaze toward the nose of the raft. It continued its momentum forward out of the flood, rushing into the air as the large fish disappeared below the water and out of tangible existence. Up rose the raft above the tumultuous waves, when at last she uttered, "Are we out?"

Turned to her, Antagnous, Gendlebleth, Lousitous, Cain and twenty others to respond in unison, "Yes." They dropped seven feet down to the waters' surface below. She wrestled her eyes not closed while she envisioned a raft large enough to keep her band afloat as rain and wind and rolling hills of liquid expanse pushed her conception of steadiness for all held in the vision of her mind's palm: rope to grab hold of while planks expanded large enough that stumbling could not be into the greater waters' grasp. On a small island they stood, fell, and rocked afloat as sheets of water spurned on by torrents of wind pelted their soaked bodies from all sides. They scurried as quickly as their footing would allow to one another through the storm.

Hand grabbed hold of hand. Legs interlocked. Hard they grabbed. Tightly they held. Over each other they climbed. A latticework of bodies up toward the heavens, they turned their faces in defiance of the doom of humanity. The cascade barraging them, twenty divided into ten surrounding Casarta, and ten surrounding Cain.

He felt hands grab hold of ankles, hands grab hold of wrists and shoulders and hip as he was pinned atop those lying about face-up to the ravishment of the heavens assailing them all. The waters almost caused him suffocation yet again as he closed his eyes to the barrage. Then, no more rain pelted his face. His eyes opened into the eyes and smiling, bedraggled face of Gendlebleth where he'd expected rain to be. "Sorry, my sir, but I'll not have you suffocating at The Lord's life-giving bosom again." With that, Gendlebleth and several others lay atop of him and interlinked with the bodies making the raft's "floor." His breathing was not as he would choose, free, but he thanked his benefactors that he might this way breathe at all, if in the end he must awake either way. He thanked God for the first bit of mercy he had known since he had taken his brother's life, here amidst the flood.

Likewise, Casarta felt herself bombarded to the boards, and finally lifted up to the lattice of bodies spread across the floor of the raft while the space where she had rested was covered over by bodies bonding together amidst the downpour. The rain filled her mouth as she screamed in agony at the pain in her foot and ankle. She envisioned it set and protected, wooden boards supporting them all as she was secured to the flat plane they had made of themselves now below, and to all sides of her. One, two, three they arched above and atop her, absent her leg. Her mother's breast descending to the other side of her head as she heard her voice: "Rest now, my child. It is done," and all at once leg rested free, wood departed from underneath, and Casarta relinquished her mind to her exhaustion.

They floated together, in unity, amidst the storm and waves.

Chapter 53

Sheet after sheet careened down into their faces, letting too little air in and causing too many moments of choking on the rain they would keep at bay. Over the course of hours they'd pass out from oxygen deprivation, only to wake up a short time later coughing out water, not so unlike they had when waking initially from the grand drowning of all by the flood.

Having not expected comfort, and finding none to lose now, they began flipping over onto each other, noting the wisdom of the approach they had taken to in any way try to protect the lungs of Cain and Casarta. Belly to mouth, they turned themselves to garner any protection from the fluid world, then locked ankle to hand, arm-in-arm to keep together floating once what little breath could be protected was ensured. One atop to other, midriff to face, able at all to breathe, they continued bobbing atop the flood, half the surface space of when they'd begun.

Hours later, Casarta's eyes opened.

The fire shooting through her being from her ankle carried up into her body while her foot was blown by the wind and tossed by the waves shaking them all. She immediately set it with her mind and surrounded it with a box stuffed with feathers to immobilize it. Then, she remembered the rain.

A canopy formed above them all. A raft arose from below the waves. It carried them over the waters and into the air.

Casarta retracted, then reached her arm from beneath her mother and Androda to Antagnous' arm to squeeze it. She gripped, patted, and ultimately shook her mother's shoulder until Antagnous' groggy face met hers. "We're safe from the rain for now."

Antagnous looked from her daughter's visage to see the large wall above them all, glowing. She rolled off her daughter and onto Dernothsis, Landolo, Joshan, and Lemisslept, holding tightly to one another. "No water. No water!" She spoke to each awake face she saw as she tried to untangle them, to be able to find a place to stand that was not on her friends. All around her they started noticing that the storm had abated from them. They began to unweave. They began to try to get to their feet.

Antagnous found her footing and yelled for all to hear, "We're safe! We're safe! Get up! Get up!"

So many opened their eyes. So many awoke. In turn they let go the grip of their hands. In turn they untwined arms and legs, rolled off one another, and stood.

Cain's lungs were free to again drink of the air. He inhaled greedily, coughing and almost choking on the life so fully returning within him.

Much like Cain, Casarta gasped in joy once Mentildeth rocked himself from her to free her lungs' inhibition. She watched while all around her they rose. She was happy that for a moment, they need not suffer this flood and storm. She turned to the side as Caldas and Remblelok disengaged and crawled from beneath her. She considered the floor below her to rise into a chair that would keep her comfortable and allow her to sit up, much as she had formed for herself in the "chariot" beneath the waves.

When most had untangled and risen, some still lay on the raft's floor. Those closest to them noticed and tried to shake their brothers and sisters awake, but they would not open their eyes. Moments later, the sound of small water slapping and falling to the wooden floor of the raft, and coughing, and hacking as the last of them woke from suffocation, though this time lungs less than over-filled to brim with the waters commanded by Whom they all served.

While she watched these last recovering from being drowned again, she felt an emotion rising to her face. She felt the rain of angels beat upon the roof of her mind, and her fingers rolled inward to tighten into fists. Her visage grew redder as her thoughts raced. The skin tightened around her ankle along with her stomach, and her lips descended into a scowl. Through her body and lungs was released a scream that shook the raft on which they all stood and sat. Water crashed down through the ceiling upon them all. As the water touched her, soaked her instantly through, her focus returned to roof and raft once more.

The shaking stopped, their immediate worries departed, they all turned to look at Casarta. She reciprocated the gazes surrounding her everywhere she looked.

"I became angry. All humanity, or for how far and wide away I do not know, was just murdered by what had created it to begin with. And how long are we to suffer unceasing waters above and below? You are my family. Now every time I waken from my exhaustion, I will get to watch you choking on the will of a *Creator*? Being tortured? For what? Choosing to help people It decided to slaughter outright? Then why not kill us too? Put us out of the misery we no longer have the purpose for!"

Antagnous looked softly upon her daughter's face. Her heart sank while she thought about what her daughter found herself waking to.

"Maybe it was to cleanse away all I contaminated." Many eyes looked up to see Cain speaking. "You said it yourself. We don't know how far these waters stretch. Maybe all that I have touched has been wiped clean, so that those surviving where there is no water may maintain their lives hereafter without the blemish of my mark upon their heads. God's mercy be done upon humanity!"

"No, Cain." Gendlebleth continuing *his* responsibility to the wrong *he* had committed. "It is not Her way to torture one who has wronged thus. If She has wrought this death, it is by their hands, not yours."

"What could they possibly have done to warrant mass annihilation?" Casarta responded, and again the raft began to shake. It dropped a foot before evening out.

"Casarta," Cain hoped to ease her mind, "whatsoever the case, we do not know how widespread this flood, nor why it is here. More than anyone, I loathe being surrounded by death. But please, until we know, let's focus for now on getting through it."

The raft stopped shaking.

Lousitous stepped forward. "It would be too much to say we *need* food, if being drowned is any indication. But already our stomachs tell us we would like to eat. Even still, we can suffer further starvation, but perhaps for Cain such a hunger would be more maddening to his mind."

"And we don't know what it would do to his body to not eat, even if he won't die by it." Antagnous followed up Lousitous' line of thought, "For that matter, we don't know, ultimately, what it would do to ours."

The raft resumed its previous elevation and remained level. "I'm open to suggestions, but even if I thought into existence food for us all to eat, it wouldn't make it to your stomachs before disappearing."

"We have plenty of food below us." Lemisslept spoke up, "You could think us a great net, and we could go fishing."

Antagnous followed her up, "Or, if we were under the water, like when you found us, we could simply pluck the fish out of the sea as we like."

"We could encase them in air onto our boat." Gendlebleth hated that he was the first to speak probably the most effective method for bringing the fishes to their death. "Get beside them, extend the raft around them; lunch."

They all looked at him, then at Casarta. She nodded. The raft descended.

Without so much as a splash through the rolling waves, a depression opened beneath them while the raft lowered into the water. Surrounded by oxygen, five invisible walls made an inverse fish tank minus the glass. Fish swam all around. Casarta had but to extend the "walls" of their underwater raft, and fish fell in, at times by the school. Within two hours they had as much fish amongst them, flopping about, as they could imagine eating. Then up again they rose, out of the water and into the air, a massive ceiling high overhead, a source of light, and protection from the wrath of the joy of angels.

"But how will we cook them?"

A large fire appeared in their midst. Without a stick to skewer a fish upon, Lendlelan grabbed a fish by the tail and slowly held it out toward the fire. Closer and closer she drew, respecting the heat she supposed to come from the flames. Nearer though she drew, however, she persisted in feeling no heat. Finally she walked her hand holding the fish straight into the fire. Nothing. The fish flopped about uncomfortably within her hand, but felt no more cooked for the light surrounding it.

Casarta, noticing her friend's arm in the flame, as well as the lack of grimace upon her friend's face, returned her full concentration to raft and ceiling. The flame dissipated. All eyes once again turned to her.

"Perhaps, daughter, your projected fire cannot burn?"

"But how will we eat our fish, if my thought of fire cannot cook them?"

Gendlebleth grew very uneasy. He watched from feet away as Lendlelan smacked the head of the fish hard against the raft, She rose from one knee, made sure the fish no longer moved, then bit into it and chewed. Gendlebleth looked away, instantly bursting into tears. Then he ran to the side of the raft and threw up.

Well, he thought, *at least she had the good sense to make sure it felt as little pain as possible first.*

⚓ ⚓ ⚓

Mouths covered in blood and scales from fish, picking away bones, guts, more bones and scales at their feet making the raft slippery to walk upon, they all felt sated, if not a little disgusted with themselves. Their stomachs told a tale animalistically gratifying, while their heads painted a fuller picture of a duality all too human. They thanked Casarta, and began again discussing as she stated the obvious from her contemplations.

"What must be of the others? Shall we again descend to find more bodies to release water from? How far would the journey take even to find one?"

Gendlebleth, recovering from his nausea after the three bites into a dead fish he had been able to take, responded, "We have to try to find them. What has it been? Three, four days this water will not stop pouring forth from the sky? And perhaps it is drier where they are, and if we find them, we find land. We must try!"

Lousitous spoke next, "Are we to be pulled again by a school of large fishes under the waters? Casarta, already from half a day of maintaining focus, you look very fatigued."

"But we must try, and I can go several more hours awake. Then we can raft again as we did when I slept before. What choice do we have? If under the water is the only way we have to have a creature to follow my mind, then so be it."

"Look down below!" Cain said this excitedly, looking down from the side of the raft.

Gendlebleth raced over next to him. "Yes, everybody, come and see!" More ran to where they stood.

Casarta created the wood to rearrange itself to convey her to the side of the raft. Planks reformed up into the chair as supports behind her fell back into the floor, until finally she was there beside them all. "What are they?"

"I believe those are dolphins." Cain felt a happiness he hadn't felt in a very long time to be able to identify the silver beings in the water to those around him.

The dolphins breached the surface so high that they almost flew into the raft as they soared into the sky, and then back into the sea.

"I can conjure more of those to follow my mind."

"Let us meditate as one, Casarta, to discover the others together."

"Farfrouth, I love the idea, but they will only follow my mind, and my mind will be able to find them readily enough on its own."

The raft lowered to a foot above the highest wave, ceiling emanating light maintained above, and at the "front" of the raft, one hundred dolphins appeared, tethered to the raft by long, golden cords that attached to bridles of gold the dolphins wore around their faces. Casarta closed her eyes. The dolphins began to swim. The raft began to move.

Ten and a half hours later, Casarta's eyes snapped open, and the dolphins disappeared. "Dolphins, their minds are so complex. They already know where they are."

"Are they... all suffocated, choking without cessation upon the waters of life and salt of our beings, as we were before you found us?"

"I don't know that yet. All I know is that they are all together, and very far away. But the important part: Regroup together, please. I am about to pass out." With that, she gripped the sides of the chair in which she sat while her mind turned entirely to raft and roof, focusing on the cramping in her hands from her grip, and that upon which she clung.

They briefly looked to one another, then Chothran took Randolfy's hand, and they began entwining and lying head to foot upon the floor of the raft. Quickly all others did the same until a new raft was made atop the old.

Cain felt arms take him off his feet by ankles and thighs and shoulders down to those below him before feeling the warm suffocation of bodies above him; assurance that despite the weight on his chest, he would breathe through the storm.

Casarta suspended the back of her chair above the floor of the raft while two entwined below her to fill the hole in the floor of the new raft. She felt hands gently take hold of her all around. She let the conception of "chair" go. She felt herself rested slowly upon the bodies below. So too was the raft lowered the last foot to the waves. While she felt the rocking, swaying, and upheaval of God's Will upon them all, she felt simultaneously her own body cocooned over by the body of her family, genetic and extended. As her mother covered over her face, she released to her fatigue. They were at the waves' mercy, yet united beyond its consciousless destruction, once again.

Chapter 54

She awoke. They awoke. They untwined upon the boards of wood. She made sure her foot was set and motionless.

"The minds of the dolphins are complex. Though mine were impermanent, they still could communicate with those around them, who knew much I did not. Their complexity was actually exhausting for me..." She became quiet for a moment, looking toward the foot of her extended leg. She looked up again and toward Cain, "You are hungry, yes? We should go fishing."

"No more hungry than you must be. If the way is still long, there is no need to delay our journey for a hunger that can wait. Perhaps it would be best to eat after waking tomorrow?" Cain looked around toward the others, all of whom nodded affirmatively. Gendlebleth's nod was more subtle for the lack of freshly killed fish he'd barely been able to chew any of into himself the day prior. The thought of trying to eat more was enough to allow him to also nod in agreement.

"There is not a one of us who cannot wait a day to eat raw fish unceremoniously murdered after such a feast we... enjoyed... yesterday. Should be more satisfying a meal for the wait, in fact," Randolfy concluded, and Casarta nodded.

As Gendlebleth's stomach gurgled its bile, he sighed to think he may have no choice but to eat the next day, if not but for the sake of his stomach alone.

The raft lowered, dolphins appeared, Casarta closed her eyes, and the raft began moving in a particular direction. The others sat, many crossing their legs upon sitting, and closed their eyes as well.

Cain remained standing, watching them all in wonder, curious that they seemed to know how to move together. Meanwhile, joining them, to him, was not intuitive. After observing them settle into sitting simultaneously, he spent some time walking around the raft amongst them. He walked to the "head" of the raft and watched as the dolphins swam, often leaping out of the water, gilded silver beings almost playing in a united mission to bring them all to what destination he knew not. He sat there at the vessel's edge, created far from the raft's center, and let his legs dangle over between cords, his feet lightly touching atop the waters rushing below. He cleaned his soles in such a fashion for some time, letting his eyes run with these conjured beings bringing them all, glittering in what little sun the downpour above allowed; more likely merely the distant reflection of their illuminated ceiling.

The raft maintained its height, a foot above the highest crests, and so the raft gently swayed over them as their height changed. It dipped up and down as though it rode upon them itself. As swells periodically appeared amongst the upheaval of the storm, a gargantuan wave suddenly towered over his watch and broke upon the ceiling holding at bay the waters of the angels. The result of the tidal wave was further cascades off the barrier above. The raft dipped down to keep in with the waters below as the rest of the wave safely fell off the sides of the "roof," but Cain immediately felt it in his best interest to retreat to a more centralized location upon the raft. Mesmerizing as watching from the bow was, upon grasping hard to the cords tethering the dolphins, he'd decided such a close proximity to the edge might too easily allow him to be thrown from the sole island holding him from a desolation he could not fathom agreeing to willingly. Half-soaked from the spray caused by the raft entering into the roll of the tsunami, he lay as close to the middle of the raft as he could, between those sitting calmly, serenely with their eyes closed. He rested, regaining his breath as his trousers returned to a more tolerable damp.

He felt the raft rise and fall under him. He heard the waves, the rain, the wind, the storm from every direction. He felt warmth from the bodies that surrounded him. There was a peace here, riding the rocking of the waves.

Cain opened his eyes. A flat glowing, twelve feet above him. He gazed into the solid, warm illumination. Sleep was hours away. He had no desire to ride the sides of the raft again. He began to sit up. He looked around him. He crossed his legs. He closed his eyes.

Cain's mind was filled with the sound of the wind and rain, the feel of the swaying of the raft over the waves. He felt the slowing and evening of his breath. He thought about the discomfort of his soaked pants and shirt; how damp and soft and raw he felt. He was filled with guilt, as though so many were dead now because of his brother's life lost at his hand. He thought of so many bodies floating under the sea amidst houses and tools. He thought himself into one of the houses. A family floating around a dinner table. He saw a little girl, upside down, turned by the water's current. He saw her face, her eyes snapping open to meet him. His own eyes snapped open. He was startled.

He considered the images that had just flooded through his mind. He stood up and began to walk around. He looked at them all sitting in such peace. He thought more about the images that had disturbed him while trying to sit as they sat. He heard the storm while he pondered. In very wet pants, he walked some more about them, observing storm and dolphins past the edge of the raft.

He wandered back to where he had been sitting. He sat again. His legs folded, his eyes shut. His mind once more filled him. The sensation of the wood, hard against his bones and flesh. The motion of craft following the crests unceasingly. The guilt of death. Contemplation that perhaps, if not for his own hands, dry land and living people might otherwise have occupied far below the imaginary wood that held him. He felt the desire to squirm out of stillness. When his mind began to contemplate piles of bodies drifting in the currents beneath him, the sensation of his eyes about to snap open percolated within him to the edge of action when he heard a voice: "It's not because of you." His eyes and body did, at that point, jerk to attention.

He looked around. Still none stirred while the raft rolled over waves, and onward they floated. He'd felt his life disturbed. The voice was unexpected, albeit seemingly friendly. He closed eyes again.

He tried to keep his mind fixed to the sound of the rain crashing to flood, and the thunder that rolled with frequency. He attempted to focus solely on the feel of oxygen blessedly filling his lungs freely. Even his legs pressed against the floor was a possible perception with which to maintain his mind. It found its way back to the pain in his heart, however, carried with him for well over a millennium and a half. He saw his brother, lifeless and bloody at his feet. He saw the bodies of the people of Cain lying dead all around him in the city center while he stood in the reflecting pool, then floating, the last feeling the filling of their lungs to the brim as his had been when he'd spent too many hours drifting, gagging on what his lungs were too expanded to release. . . "But you breathe now, and their deaths are not your fault!"

"Who are you?" he screamed into the vast space of his own head, his voice echoing back into himself from all sides.

Then the reply from that point within: "You don't recognize my voice? It's me. Gendlebleth. Of course."

Cain's eyes again snapped open. He took a deep breath. Looked all around him. Several sitting figures over sat Gendlebleth, still and silent upon the swaying raft. Cain stared at him while contemplating the events recently unfolded in his own brain. He straightened himself after several minutes of staring and pondering, then closed his eyes once more.

He waited. He continued to wait. "Gendlebleth! Are you there, Gendlebleth?" *Where is he? Do I have to be filled with my self-generated dread again to hear him? Where is he?* "Gendlebleth?" he shouted into his own mind, but received no response.

Then, he paused. Just a moment of quiet. Letting go to the sounds of the rain, wind, lightening, and thunder. Waiting. A moment of patience.

Then he thought *How nice.* Hearing again the sound of the rain. *But where is Gendlebleth's voice? Did I just make it up in my head?*

"No. It was me."

"It is you?"

"It is me."

"How is this possible?"

"Just a little concentration is really all it takes. Kind of like the way you can blow out a candle, and your breath goes from your lungs to the flame. Same basic concept."

Cain was perplexed but intrigued. What struck him in particular was the voice returning to him. It sounded as though he were imagining his own voice coated in the voice of Gendlebleth. It almost felt like he was the true origin of both voices, like he was making up the voice of the other.

"Why are we all sitting like this? Before you spoke to... er... into... with me, all this sitting did was to obviate the pain of my wrongness."

"Yes. That is why I'm speaking to you. I understand, for like you, I am filled with pain. But I do not do this to mire in my disgrace. Quite the contrary. Noticing how filled with loathing I am for my inadvertent inspiration of you murdering your brother, I've learned how to allow it to exist in me without having to focus ever on it. For example, here I have the opportunity to bring my focus back to the rain and wind outside. Or if I can't help but be reminded of my despair for my first attempts to help humanity, so miserably failed by me, I have learned how to allow it to be while I exist not just as *it*. It helps to be able to identify that part of myself, and then notice that I am noticing it with a different part of myself, and then attempt to resign myself into infinite potential independently of the original parts of myself I initially discerned and separated apart in my conception. After a bit of practice, sitting allows me to escape the horror in some small measure, really. I suspect it could help you similarly over time..."

Gendlebleth's voice faded away in Cain's mind, leaving him in something of a daze while he'd tried to follow what his friend had been communicating. He found his confused brain drift naturally into the rain and wind. He found himself absorbed further beyond the wind and rain, hearing beyond even that the beating of his heart. He thought briefly about opening his eyes and walking around. He remembered he had nowhere else to go. He allowed his mind to drift into his heart's beats along with the dance of water and air. His breathing slowed. Time apparently elongated between inhalations. He sensed a growing illumination past his eyelids, much like their "ceiling" above the raft. He found letting go of his physical identity followed naturally while he experienced a depth he did not know where or how, or have the conception to think to ask. His breathing fell to almost imperceptible. Silence became more. Deeper into he became. He released to where he "went."

Time was meaningless where his mind evolved past his mind. "She is about to request us make the other raft. I don't relish disturbing the first peace you've known since... But the alternative would not do."

Cain recalled from out recollection of what Creation knew of his truth. His focus returned to his breathing, now quickening to perceptible from out and with the universe to his own. He became again distinct, and took his time opening his eyelids. Eyes open, he looked upward to see Gendlebleth smiling down upon him. After matching Cain's gaze for a moment, he looked over. "He's ready." Those closer to them began intertwining. Cain shortly noticed that those farther away had already begun to. He stood, then lay down on those who filled the spot where he'd been sitting moments prior. Others covered over him. Gendlebleth smiled lovingly above him once again while he descended over his head.

Onto the waves they crashed together. Together they were a raft upon the tumult. Together they released their minds and bodies to sleep after a day and a half from when they'd initially woken.

Chapter 55

Slumber was not easy, tossed and turned upon the ecstasy of the angels and the will of All-Creator Common Presence. In and out of sleep they rose and fell on the waves, tossed and flipped over in the milieu. Yet, in and out of half-dreams and no dreams, their consciousnesses attempted, and to some measure succeeded, in recuperative regeneration and ease of their common pressure of being. They kept eyes closed and held to one another as passively as possible to regain energies as well as possible until, by the will of Casarta's mind, her creation woke them from attempted rest more or less simultaneously.

Into the air, six feet above the waves, they untangled and stood. Those who had drowned during the night spit excess water from their lungs and rose to meet the others. Cain was grateful to have his own lungs to himself again.

When all had arisen, Casarta spoke. "It is time to go fishing once more."

Gendlebleth tensed and restrained a recoil in light of his disturbed stomach begging for any morsel.

They plunged back down and under the tumult of the water's will. Quickly enough, fish fell onto their vessel. They took them up in turn, clubbed them upon the raft's floor, and ate them on the spot; their stomachs grateful for sustenance by which they could sustain human processes. Cain requested Casarta conceive, briefly, a tool he could descale with before eating his own raw meal. Casarta was happy, briefly, to assist.

On their way back toward the surface, as Gendlebleth stared at the dead mackerel in his hand, something green caught the corner of his eye. "Casarta! Stop the raft, please!"

The raft paused its rise toward the surface. Fish still in hand, Gendlebleth ran to the side and looked down into the water. "Casarta, can you lower the raft back from where we are, to where we were about seven feet ago, please?"

The raft reversed its course to descend a short distance. Gendlebleth's eyes grew large. "A little closer to that, please?" Gendlebleth pointed. The raft, along with their pocket of air, moved up next to it. Gendlebleth reached his hand into the water, grabbed hold of the mass of seaweed, and pulled it onto the raft. He looked at it, sniffed it, then took some into his hand, raised it to his mouth, and took a bite. "Oh Good, Gracious Lord! Oh great, Divine merciful bounty! Thank You for remembering your humble servant and putting upon my path sustenance for my body that doesn't make a living brain-being suffer by my hand! My stomach is quenched! Oh, thank You! Thank You! Thank You!"

Casarta felt in herself a natural repugnance that any could give expressions of gratitude toward their maker from this far beneath the water where dry, fresh air ought to be. She was glad, however, to see her friend so happy.

"If any would like salad with their fish, please come partake of this feast!" Many took a piece of seaweed to try. Most decided to leave the majority to Gendlebleth to enjoy, as they'd all had their fill and more for a second meal of fish, for the time. While Casarta raised the raft back above the waves, Gendlebleth ate almost greedily of the salty leaves piled at his feet.

Again in the air, just above the height of the water's reach, Casarta resumed allowing her mind to lead the dolphins pulling them all in the direction of where the rest of their tribe must be. Again most of them sat to calm themselves, focus their minds, and pass the time. Again Cain contemplated the moments he was given to spend.

Cain sat as the others had and closed his eyes. Wind and rain. His breath. Waves. His ears heard. His flesh felt. Salt in the wind upon his nose. He anticipated a feeling of body falling away, a heightened sense of unity. He anticipated perhaps feeling unforgiven and guilty for his crime upon his brother. He did not anticipate his head falling forward ever so slightly, and his reflex to return it to its previous position.

Three times his head began to lean forward an inch or two. Three times he noticed he did not even need to think to return it upright. He felt himself fighting a neck refusing not to go limp. His eyes opened. Almost immediately he let go a loudly audible yawn from his diaphragm. He was confronted mercilessly by his unbearable desire to sleep.

Cain began to tense his muscles to stand, so that he could wake himself up and return to sitting. Then he thought better of it. Instead, he rearranged his posture to supine. His head rested on his arm. Sleep overtook him quickly.

Gendlebleth heard the movements of Cain; perceived his absence of mind. He opened his eyes. He saw Cain lying down, resting. Gendlebleth yawned. He looked around at the others. Kendelklept opened an eye and stared at Gendlebleth. Gendlebleth shrugged, lay down, and was glad to find his mind flowing easily into sleep after so much half-to-not rest soaking in the tossing of the waves.

As Kendelklept spread his body out on the floor of the raft, so did Lousitous and Handoroth take notice. So others began opening their eyes at the sound of so much movement. All felt tired. All recognized the wisdom of sleeping while free of the flood's violence. As Antagnous lay down to rest, she vowed a better configuration surrounding her daughter, so that she may rest better as well once *her* exhaustion commenced.

As the angels above joyously created the waters of the flood, the incarnated servants of the divine below slept together harmoniously, grateful for a little bit of genuine slumber.

૭⟆ ૭⟆ ૭⟆

Lemisslept awoke. She saw Randolfy sleeping beside her. She saw more resting beyond him. She sat up where she lay and looked about, all the others still sleeping. Casarta sitting, eyes closed, to the side. She felt rested. She folded her legs, closed her own eyes, and observed.

Darwith awoke. His process was similar. He was rested. He closed his eyes and sat.

Shortly the rest in turn came to.

Cain awoke and could not fall back asleep. He sat up, saw some sitting, others waking up and observing. He decided to stretch his legs for a few moments; watched the waves from the side of the raft, watched the others, watched Casarta. Finally, he wandered back to where he'd originally lain. He sat. He closed his eyes. He focused upon his breath.

Wind, rain, the rolling of the raft upon the space over the waves as though the waves themselves. He returned his mind to his breath. He noticed his breathing exist in the tumults and tranquilities surrounding him. He felt his mind turn toward his remorse. His breathing grew heavier in anticipation of images of death, the lingering thought that the world may not be so thoroughly engulfed in water if not for the action of his hands so very long ago. He turned his mind to Gendlebleth's words: that the Creator Of All would regard destruction of everything due to Cain's malfeasance alone a pettiness far past anything within Its scope. But his own hands did sew the first blood taken away by another; taken away no less by a brother. What could this water be, if not the cleansing of that stain of blood embedded to the ground by his solitary handling? But he arrived here, and there were so many others when he was made to believe that he was the very first after his parents. Surely if that was a lie, perhaps his was not the first rise of brother upon brother. The image of his hands before his face, an ever-lighter shade of crimson, barely noticeable save for that he knew the darkness of the color he'd carried with him for so long. The slipperiness as one passed over the other. But by a single degree lighter now than he'd seen more than a millennium and a half before. Somewhere in between, it occurred to him to remember his breath, and more the next five seconds he followed with his breathing. Then the sound of rain and wind. His thoughts were beginning to speak and appear of their own accord when, with a sort of suddenness, a light scuttling, the creaking of human joints. The movement of feet. His eyes opened.

They all knew apparently when he did not. They joined arms. They locked legs. They formed an orb of bodies around Casarta, making themselves two deep around her. They piled atop him, all interlocking everywhere. Embracing for their lives. Tying together into a vessel of flesh and what wet rags still clung to them. Wood and roof vanished. Tossed upon the waters, they floated at the mercy of wave and storm once more.

❧ ❧ ❧

In another place, ropes still held, mostly, ten days tossed upon the sea. Tightly they held to each other under the tarp. Grateful only some food had been lost, and no one was absent among them in the moment that some trunks of the trees had broken free. Today their raft had only flipped over in the water once. They had even been flipped back over quickly enough that only five of them had briefly drowned before coming back to life. They held to the binding ropes and each other. Passing time without measurement. Eating remaining food sparingly. Feeling the crash of waves over them again and again. They breathed barely through water-soaked covering, but they were together, and *above* the waves, and they *did* breathe.

⚬⚬⚬

Soaked, and tossed, and clinging to each other with their lives with renewed energy. Sleeping came less, as they'd already rested, so they hung to each other tighter, more consciously.

Casarta rested more fully, more loosely within a cocoon of her people surrounding her, trying to lace about her rather than on top of her. In dreams she fell and flew through the clouds. Around streaks of lightning, extended moments of escape from enclosure in her mind gave her the rest that her brain needed from focus through the storm where she had come to live, detached from the anger she otherwise wished to allow to consume her. She would not let her family be submerged due to her rage, however. Her focus toward the others was her love for them all. She took refuge and refreshment in thoughtless flight. Rest in between waking recollections of the will of all that otherwise inundated her.

Eight hours or so later, awake, she pawed at her mother's face. A hovering barrier from the rain above, the solidity of the form of wood above the waves below. They floated in between the wrath of existence upon the unwanted. They untied their selves.

Casarta, sitting familiarly, down they all rushed below the waves. In but an hour's time, fish and kelp enough to satisfy the hunger in every belly; all inherently grateful to partake of existence's bounty despite such time of turmoil.

Only an hour later, above the waves, low above the waves, again they hovered.

Casarta, finishing her fish, turned her attention to dolphins and the direction in which the others must be. Her eyes shut. Concentration spoke their fate for her.

Gendlebleth formed a pillow of seaweed and allowed his full stomach to take his mind's hand into slumber. So too did the others pile the remaining fish for a brief snack later, before recombining, and then allowed their bellies to tune out their brains. Sleep came welcome to them all.

When they awoke, they meditated. Cain walked the raft, saw what could be seen, infinite variations of water's might. He joined them after his promenade.

His breath. The surrounding world melting off to the caprices of his mind. His breath briefly. His mind; remorse and dream. Remembrance of his breath. The nodding of his head into relaxation as he struggled again and again to return his focus to his lungs' inhalations and exhalations. He remembered when he first sat, his self-hatred and the horror of his hand's blasphemy and its results. He remembered the revelation of self-dispersing into existence as is. He remembered that perhaps there is more to the suffering of all existence than merely the wrongs of his own actions. He remembered the surroundings all around him. He remembered to notice his own breath. He felt grateful for such progress over such little time.

He remembered to notice his breathing.

He opened his eyes. He thought about walking again. He knew there was not very far to go. He had had all the sleep his body would allow. He was not tired. He closed his eyes. He turned his attention to his lungs, his nose, the feel of inhalation, the feel of exhalation. His mind went to the storm, flooding, death. A breath. Another breath. Thoughts. He let them pass. Focused on sound. Focused on breath. The rolling raft. The feel of his head on his neck. The air through his nose. Thoughts. His damp trousers. His breath.

Another four hours later, the rustle of the others informed their formation against the storm.

High above, the angels made love, cascading forth from them as they joined in altitudes reaching from cloud to stars. Down fell to Earth their passion as lips and loins explored alike, seeking sensations unto themselves of the joy Creator Eternal thought with which to equip their journey in service to The Most High. They delighted in serving so Infinite Will, and carrying out Its desire, pleased them all to no end while they pleased each other. The winds howled their delight, lightning and thunder enjoying electric surges from whence heightened touch expressed most exuberantly. Together they sang a choir of ecstasy that their gratitude might be pleasing to the All-Encompassing ears dwelling on High.

As The Lord commanded, so was Its will fulfilled.

They untwined. A handful spit briny water from their lungs. They submerged and fished and harvested. Careful this time to gather only according to their needs before becoming, once more, the raft, with bellies not desperate, they strove to ensure no life was lost in vain.

Then, above the waves again for repose and meditation.

Cain sat and noticed his breathing. He felt damp and trapped. Breath. Death. Breath. Letting go. Dampness. Rain. Rolling. Responsibility for humanity's demise. Breath. Suffocating stillness and boredom. Breath. Breath. The feel of the wave's will below. "Gendlebleth! Are you there?"

"I am."

"Why do we spend all our time sitting when we could be talking?"

"We sit this way to remember closer where we came from before we ate the fruit. But we can talk, if you want to."

"Yes, please."

Cain opened his eyes and searched around to find where Gendlebleth was sitting. He stood and found him blinking where he sat several feet away. He walked over to him. Gendlebleth smiled up at Cain. Cain offered him a hand to his feet. They walked closer to the side of the raft, though still a hundred feet or so from the edge, so as not to be thrown off.

"What do you want to talk about?"

"Is it really okay to talk? I mean, won't it be distracting to the others?" He tried to whisper against the sound of the rain in the asking.

"This far away from them, the rain may well be louder than our voices anyway. But despite that, our voices are part of their remembrance should they make it to their ears beyond the storm."

"If they're hearing us talk, that's not remembering. That's being present."

"But you do not know what it is like to be devoted to serving Absolute independent of differentiable self. She Is All that's happened already. Ideally our voices would blend into the harmony of time all-encompassing. But if not, we are a moment remembered as it is, along with the rest of eternity surrounding us infinitely. We are a manifestation of Its entirety. What is there to distract?"

Cain felt suddenly silent. He sat down and closed his eyes. Gendlebleth followed suit.

Soaked through. Huddled together. Clinging, shivering, and prey to the storm, the raft rose, fell, and was perpetually assailed by the waves while they waited through days of darkness, at the mercy of the will of The Divine.

Remembrances of the last sixteen hundred years was a wonderful respite from the constant gloom. "Ah, but the first time Seth discovered a butterfly! Tartantuan and I were there for that one. How he chased that beautiful little creature. Its colors were..." "How about the first time Enosh made love to his wife? He was so tender with her..." "When Noah hammered his thumb, then dropped the hammer on his foot, and *then* slammed his fist into the tree with anger!" "Yes, if we hadn't been so concerned with his pain, we would have laughed away our cover!" They refrained mostly from remembering Methuselah. They were grateful for more than a millennium and a half worth of stories with which to pass the time.

In a moment of solitude, Luciferous was surrounded by companions exhausted enough to give over to slumber, but he was alert and could not sleep. He sat still under their tarp, let his eyes close, gave in to the thrashing of their raft and selves from the wrath released by their Common Creator All-Loving Endlessness. He let himself be aware of it washing, pouring over him; waves rolling them all violently. So also came into focus his breath. His heartbeat. His stillness amidst infinite processes containing infinite processes he had no control over whatsoever. It was, though by his own hand along with others, almost miraculous he was still on the side of the waves he was. He exhaled.

He inhaled. It was more difficult breathing under the tarp, but now he was used to it. It was automatic. He let himself go to it all. He remembered.

Sometime beyond non-conception, his companions awoke and began to shift. They started to converse beside him, letting him be to what they supposed an unusual sleep.

He slowly recalled himself. He slowly opened his eyes. His body felt fatigue, but before releasing himself to rest, he had for his companions one story to tell.

❧ ❧ ❧

Casarta's eyes opened. She squeezed and poked and wiggled, but intuitively many began to come alert regardless. As had become accustomed, so now started the routine of the day.

They caught fish and seaweed as close as possible to their needs: a breakfast meal, a meal after sleep, and a meal after meditation.

After waking, rather than going straight into meditation, Cain tapped Gendlebleth on the shoulder, and they walked together around the group and discussed. As they looked over at rain and convulsing sea, Cain questioned Gendlebleth, "This quiet sitting that can allow a recollection of unified existence itself, do all people have such a potential?" The corners of Cain's lips quickly drooped downwards. "*Had* they all such potential..."

"Keep hope. We're still here. She may be true to the core of Her words, but She is not cruel. If we are still here, someone must still be alive somewhere. And yes. If we have the potential to remember as we do, it is a human potential, much, if not more, as you have been touched in the experiencing."

"If mankind had spent more time sitting, perhaps they'd still be alive... Why did you never teach me to meditate when I was young, Gendlebleth?"

"We hadn't learned yet ourselves. Frankly, it wasn't until we followed you, and we had so much free time on our hands, that it occurred to us to as thoroughly explore the nature of our own minds."

Cain watched the sheets of water cascading down in the distance; the violence of the waves so close below. He turned back toward Gendlebleth. "It's hard not to be angry." A tear began to well up into his eye's corner. He suppressed more from developing.

Gendlebleth took in his friend's emotion and gazed solidly into both his eyes. "It is so hard not to be sad. I pray that when I have helped truly, I will be able to settle past the harm I have done. It helps in no small measure that you do not hate me."

Cain shook his head. "If two lifetimes has taught me nothing else, surely it is that my hands will not profit by holding to hatred. It was what was within me unchecked that caused it, not what came out of you. Perhaps, like you, I can strive to bring blessings to any who might survive this. Otherwise, if none survive, at least I can pass a very long life in good company."

Gendlebleth smiled and nodded as he felt his cheeks grow a little flush. Cain motioned toward the wood beneath their feet. Together they sat down, shut their eyes, listened to the rain, and felt the air in their chests.

ᐱᐱᐱ

A little raft, trunks of trees tied together, was assaulted mercilessly by crests of water and wave after wave of cascading rain. A raft of servants bobbing and flipping. Damp, cold, often suffocating, and increasingly hungry at the mercy of endless water and whatever moments fatigue might set in briefly to better pass the time. Oxygen deprivation would lend itself to a temporary cessation of the dreadful time perception as well. For love of adam, they endured the torture that no human body could otherwise survive.

Above, a host of angels consummating love of their Lord; singing from their selves as closely as possible to the gratitude they were sure Their Creator must know by perceiving Its own existence and all the infinite ways in which It self-manifested. Their love cascaded upon the world below.

Their love cascaded down upon a cciling conceived by a rouge-fleshed woman also contemplating a raft to hold more servants still meditating on The Source of All and how humanity might be assisted by them should any have survived, and a team of dolphins to pull such a raft rapidly over the ever-surging waves of The Great Will's upheaval.

Twenty-seven days of resurrection and travel had passed when, by her light cast from above, Casarta could see the form through the dolphin's eyes. Automatically, with no command from her mind, the dolphins disappeared once they touched upon the raft of the tree trunks and rope. Seeing her own raft would soon collide with theirs, she raised them all ten feet into the air.

Those meditating felt the differences of rhythm and returned to themselves. As their eyes opened, they were delighted to see the waters so far below. They found the sensation of floating really very pleasurable.

Beneath, they felt the barrage of the rain upon their heads and backs cease. Though the waves still rolled tumultuously, a certain joy slowly filled them at the realization that the perpetual waters from on high might finally be coming to an end. Their muscles were mostly atrophied now from so little movement over most of four weeks, and their skin soaked, pruned, and delicate. They moved their limbs as they could, however. Hands trying to untie ropes holding the tarps together while others made their way toward the edges of their covering, hoping to pull themselves out from under the water-logged barrier between them and sky.

Casarta lowered them toward the raft below. She conceived a wide staircase to lead down from the edge of their raft to the edge of the one beneath. By now all had risen. Casarta pointed to the raft's edge where she'd envisioned the steps, and the hearts of everyone on board lifted and felt lighter to realize they'd be reunited after so long a time apart from the rest of their tribe. One by one they turned their first footfall toward the way to speedy reunion. Behind them, Casarta's chair followed, carrying her across the raft as the planks rose to lift her forward. While the rest went quickly to the steps and carefully, though with haste, started down them, Antagnous and Cain waited at the raft's edge for Casarta to catch up to them.

A few steps down the stairs, and Gendlebleth looked back to see his human friend looking behind as well. Gendlebleth received a sensation, and then turned and continued to be reunited with the fullness of his clan.

When Casarta arrived at where Antagnous and Cain waited, she smiled. "You certainly had no need to wait for me, but thank you." Antagnous at one side, and Cain on the other, they began down the stairs side-by-side with Casarta. The portion of the steps beneath her rose to carry her to the next, while the rest of the step on which her partners walked remained still. Two steps down, and the raft behind them disappeared. She felt relief not to have to contemplate it any longer for now.

Under the glow of Casarta's ceiling, the first to arrive on the new raft perceived easily the forms lumped, huddled together, and rapidly wiggling beneath the expansive, well-woven tarp that covered almost all in sight. Immediately, despite the chaos of the waves tossing the raft beyond possibility of balance, they worked together to begin peeling back the edges of the enormous covering.

Casarta watched from the steps above, and conceived great eagles at each corner of the raft. They rose from out the water, straight into the air, and carried the raft with them as slowly they ascended. Three feet off the rolling waves, and as the raft continued its rise, so too did her staircase follow its edge with it. All still upon the stairs continued their journey, ever on a more even keel.

They worked quickly to untie the ropes' connections to the tarp around the smaller tree trunks at the edges of the raft. A few minutes of working together revealed their brothers and sisters. A waft released with the opening. They were soaked through, and terribly pale and pruned, but they were together at long last.

"Be prepared! It won't be long until you will need to tie it back again!" Casarta admonished down to them from not too high above. Word was passed on, and it was understood as minimal unfastening revealed reunion all around.

Much embracing and smiling. Tarp was pulled back until, shakily, everyone stretched atrophied legs to standing, and together they stood around.

As Antagnous, Cain, and Casarta stepped upon real wood not concocted by the imaginings of mind, stairs vanished, and the raft rose higher away from the waves that might disturb them. Twenty feet into the air they ascended. Casarta's chair walked as though upon legs over the raft, keeping her own leg immobile and her self more or less comfortable, now eased from burdening itself with thoughts of wooden planks or stair or dolphin. Her current focus felt far simpler.

They hobbled apart to make way for her as she approached Luciferous.

"Pardon me not rising to greet you properly. My foot was injured during the initial flooding. My recollections of you come from a very far place, but I know we have always looked to you for leadership. Lately, circumstance has commanded I take such action myself."

"Then we are in good company, Casarta. You have no need of apology if somehow you have led us to reunion under unfathomably unfortunate circumstances otherwise. We must have much to discuss of your journey and apparent abilities. Simply put, you are a wonder to behold."

"I thank you for saying so, though it has been my focus in coming here that has kept an anger deep below my surface from ruling me entirely. Though I am much too exhausted now to give it mind, I have little doubt that when I awaken, I will need assistance refocusing my self in such a way that I will not let it take over the vivifyingness of my thought that you otherwise perceive now, amongst other things, as the ceiling above you sheltering us all, for the moment, from the deluge pouring down. Before I make clear the consequence of my mounting fatigue, the preparations we have need shortly of hastening, please inform me, for the sake of my mind upon waking, if you know if it is possible that any human life that is not Cain's has survived these waters that it has been a strain for us in our immortality to have been able to rise above?"

"Simply put, marvel of us all, yes. The ninth generation of Adam, Noah, has managed to build a great vessel in which to house not only his own wife, but also three sons, their wives, and every land and air dwelling creature that would call this world their home."

"Thank you, Luciferous. This knowledge is enough that my hatred will be quelled long enough to seek your guidance of focus, after I should awaken more or less refreshed several hours hence of my coming slumber. In the meantime, you will need to prepare us for a few more hours below these coverings, secured together again to your raft, so that we may be the victims to the violence of the waves while I sleep. But, when I awaken, in between the time of my sleeping, I will be able to take this raft not only high from the waves, and keep us sheltered from the storm, but also I can take us to restock the food that is beneficial to consume for the sake of our bodies. Now is the time to prepare for us lowering back to the waves, however."

"Casarta, your news is most welcome, for the last of the food we had stored with us ran out four days ago, and we have been suffering the physical pains since."

With that, Luciferous instructed them to make ready the raft.

"One other thing, Luciferous. When I fall asleep, this chair supporting my leg will vanish. If you have rope, or cloth, and maybe even a piece of wood, I fear my leg is having difficulty healing while I sleep otherwise..."

Luciferous saw to it Casarta's leg was splinted and wrapped tightly. He was happy some of the wooden poles he had initially hoped to hold tents to the raft could be put to good use of any sort.

Casarta's parents slept beside her on either side after a struggle to find a place under the tight, heavy wetness of their mutual covering. More than any other moment since she had awoken pinned below so much water, Casarta felt immobilized, as though her leg had little fear of suffering more for the passion of the waves. In point of fact, once they had managed to secure the tarp to the edges of the raft, all of their kind shared the same covering, lying tightly side by side beneath, with little room in between. Those who had journeyed the previous four weeks beneath the thin layer hardly separating themselves and the storm, noticed little difference save for an accentuated lack of space with which to stretch. For those who had been accustomed to banding together while Casarta slept, however, they were relieved and overjoyed not to have to cling to one another as though the cost of letting go might be the ability to breathe air for a time only Their Lord could know, which assuredly promised to feel like a full measure of an eternity.

The wings of the eagles beat slower, and the raft lowered gradually to the constantly aggravated sea below. Casarta relinquished her mind to sleep, and the barrier above them vanished. Half experienced as they had for a month. Half were relieved not to need to clutch to each other for the sake of their lives. All together, all were grateful here, being beaten down upon and thrashed by merciless waves, to be united once more.

Chapter 56

She awoke with the rain beating down over and around her. A thought later, the rain had stopped. Next she felt the upheaval below her, thrashing the raft about indiscriminately. Another concentrated focus of mind, and her environment was at peace. She was grateful to awaken beneath wet cloth, no matter how rank the stench within, rather than heavy bodies. She was grateful not to have to form a full, flat vessel in her mind. Now, she looked forward to being free of what little layer of suppression was left. She was happy to hear and feel the rustle of bodies beside her.

While they awoke, those who weren't asleep Luciferous made a point to direct in untying the thick cloth from the middle of the raft. Soggy, fragile fingers groped around in the dark, estimating a center of the raft. Slowly, and with concentration and patience, they began to untie knots. Casarta cast light into the rope itself, and it became far easier to find both center and knot. Still their fingers did not find it easy to locate ends and untie wet rope from heavy, soaked cloth. Over half an hour or so, however, and it was done.

Leaving edges intact, they crawled out through an opening made centrally. "The security of our covering is best assured if we keep the edges tied tight, and make a section of its center loose for entrance and exit. It's not the easiest way to cover over ourselves again, but nothing about this is easy, and it should prove to be more secure. We can widen the ties on the center with far greater ease of access. Casarta, did you say that you can arrange for us food?"

Her red lips smiled. "Indeed I did."

The eagles descended, the raft went to the waves. A thousand dolphins appeared tethered to the raft. Surrounded by air, the raft dipped below the water.

All looked about in awe; half their party had never been below the surface of the tumult in this way, the other half was unaccustomed to being pulled below by dolphins. The raft ran alongside a school of tuna and slowed to keep pace. Casarta expanded the air bubble not only to surround the fish, but the large, extra measure of raft she added with her mind for the fish to fall upon. Ternaddain motioned for Luciferous to follow along beside him. The mark where true raft differed from false was clear as they began corralling the fish over the line, with the help of the others, onto the real wood of the raft.

Casarta repeated this process twice more before estimating with Luciferous the food they'd collected to be enough to last about two days when stored in some of the bags that had previously held the vegetables that had been lost to the waves. Casarta took them to a patch of kelp for Gendlebleth's sake before returning them above the water and into the air, on the backs of giant eagles once more.

Serenely in the air, Casarta, along with everyone else, collectively took a moment simply to breathe before beginning to eat. Just for a moment, they all felt like the weight of the Divine Will was not crushing upon them to motionlessness. They prayed their gratitude as their feeling of relief into the sky alone surrounding them before partaking of the meal Casarta had been able to make possible. In slow bites, their starvation was alleviated, and relief slowly began to give way to contentment.

"Over the days we've grown accustomed to sleeping predominantly while Casarta gives us shelter from the violence surrounding us."

"Telnaxson, I am sure many of us could use a slumber non-inclusive of the feel of the will of The Divine upon our persons. I am sure, likewise, if your sleep patterns follow Casarta's awakeness, you will likely enjoy a good sleep yourselves. Frankly, I likely will join you all shortly. I believe I owe our Casarta a conversation before I do, however."

With that said, Telnaxson bowed agreement with Luciferous' statement and went in search of a place to rest along with the whole of the tribe. Meanwhile, Luciferous turned to where Casarta sat upon a chair of her mind's invention, leg well wrapped from hours before, and walked to her. As others found their tenuous, supine comfort, Cain lay in a place close to Casarta, within easy hearing of their conversation, upon the soaked layer of cloth that made for nominally softer reclining than the drier raft of Casarta's mind he had become accustomed to.

"So, Casarta, more than a half-millennium ago I'd heard of your abilities, but I had no idea your strength of mind and what wonders it could conjure!"

"This strength you see, I myself did not know was in me before the flood came. Over centuries I've carefully cultivated focus of thought. But as to the enormity I have maintained over the course of the last month, I have become powerful beyond measure of where before I believed my limits to rest. And my mind's strength stretches still. I'm contemplating adding more space onto this raft while I'm awake, much as I did when we were underwater to catch fish. This way they can have more room to rest and stretch themselves about and around, when they are not asleep."

"And what about you, Casarta? What do you do while they are asleep? Will you merely sit there, focusing your thoughts on the maintenance of the size of the raft?"

"Up until now, I spent this time meditating my mind into dolphins to find you all here. I need to maintain us above the waves, barrier above us. It occupies far less of my conception, but I suppose I can meditate while everyone else sleeps. I'd walk if not for my foot. But Luciferous, before I brought us here, my anger began to posses me. It was through the focus to reunite us that I was able to keep it away. Even now, however, I feel it wanting to return into me."

"What makes you think you haven't sent it away through your focus to be here?"

"Because so vividly it seemed, *seems,* so right to me. Like what I *shouldn't* be able to understand is why everybody on this raft doesn't hate what created us all right now."

"Hate our creator? Would you suggest we begin by hating ourselves? Such is the wisdom of despising one's own origins."

"But *It* sets us apart from *It.* It makes us to suffer Its will when we have done nothing against It." An eagle vanished, and the raft began to tip toward the corner from which it had disappeared.

"Casarta! Focus, please."

She remembered four eagles at four corners, and they resumed levitating level. "Like that. It is easy to lose focus surrounded by this cruelty and death toward what was. 'Its divine will.' Where would you suggest I rest my mind as we wait for this, Noah, and his family to hopefully find dry land again someday?"

"Upon your family, Casarta. Rest your mind upon your father, your mother. Rest your mind upon this band of eager, impetuous fools who took the opportunity to taste knowledge, not knowing it would lead itself to ignorance of all the forms Her will would take. Rest your mind with our striving to do right by a creation doomed to know its own dissolution and inevitably of pain, no matter how kindly Our Common Mother smiles upon us. I know you did not choose this differentiated perspective of Infinite Creation, but before in our blindness, we manifested our ignorance of how to exist. We did choose to be here, and thus chose to create you among us. Rest your mind upon the fact that we must live to see them rest upon solid land and create the world better than it had been. Or rest us all below the waves if we, who created you, are so hateful to you as you find Our Common Oneness, which we all serve."

A tear filled her eye while she contemplated the love she felt for her family filling all over the raft. She stared into Luciferous' gaze. "But She created you too for the fall. She set us all apart from Her, knowing our pain also. But I have nothing but love for all of you. I will set my mind upon the safety of you all. And then, should we ever see dry land surrounding us again, and far enough to run to, I will be setting myself apart for a time that I may be furious by That which would create this, without further disturbing you all who I do love as my family, and wish to see through this time securely *above* the waves."

"We would regret your departure for however long it would be. Thank you for taking care of us in the meantime. We must wish for you, as we wish for them, the joy of existence they embody, unique in their capability of perceiving infinite distinctness in an existence without end."

"Here, surrounded by so few possibilities, I regret that joy is one manifestation of my mind that at present I am not able to conceive. Be that as it may, toward the ends of your joy, I have so little to say that I think it best I focus on this manifestation holding us aloft and, as you suggested, rest my mind in the focus of our bodies' well being. I will tell you all when we must descend to the waves once more. Perhaps you, as well, would prefer a time of rest between now and then."

"Thank you, Casarta. Much as them, I am confident that one day life will shine happily in some mode of common understanding that will allow an existence in creation all around perceiving true."

"Maybe, but right now the only understanding the corpses making up most of the whole of humanity surrounding us seem to possess is the decaying of flesh, and the feeding of fishes by it." With that, Casarta snapped her eyes shut and began to recollect the eagles beating wings in unison at the four corners of the raft.

෴෴෴

More or less, they awoke simultaneously. Those who had been traveling with Luciferous looked about with wonder. They had kept themselves cooped under the scant and barely effective shelter for so long, they scarcely could remember the feel of fresh air, cool against their perpetually dampened skin though it was. They walked about, marveled to be so high in the air, and grateful to be sheltered so substantially from the storm.

Likewise, those who had followed Cain East of Eden were grateful to have the feel of real cloth, real wood, and real rope beneath their feet. Cain was happy to be able to dangle his feet over the edge of the raft without worrying about falling off. They were grateful not to consider the inevitability of clinging together for survival.

More than all the wonders that safe harbor of unification brought was brother to brother, sister to sister, sister to brother, and grand reunion of beings who had chosen to be created together, returning to each other. Meditation was joyously pushed aside for conversation. New stories were welcome after a month of recollecting shared experience. They eagerly engaged together to reveal to one another what over a millennium and a half had shown to one group, but not the other. Two weeks suddenly passed quickly, as so many played a seventeen-century-long game of catch-up.

Under the cloth and onto the wood. A few hours conversing and resting, being ravaged by the storm as Casarta re-energized once achieving exhaustion. Fishing and harvesting every other day. A proper sleep, once stable above the waves and below the barrier. Conversation and recollections shared between old friends, and group-wide. A common pattern to wait and see if the storm would ever abate was soon established.

"But we witnessed the creation. What do you mean, there were people where Cain wound up?"

"All we can tell you is that there were adam all around and traveling through, from places not just The Garden."

"Yet Cain lives?"

"It seems when Man cursed Created, Our Common All-Loving Uni-Being Endlessness took his word to its literal-most extreme and granted him seven lifetimes, the like your Methuselah lived, in the process. As near we can tell, anyway."

"That I should live with the murder on my mind and in my heart indefinitely, for being the first to create such an abomination."

Gendlebleth recalled a bunny rabbit from his first days on Earth and began to sweat. "Actually–"

"Yours is not quite equivalent, Gendle, it was not... in your image."

"What?"

"Well, this poor rabbit hopped up to me and–"

"And it has little to do with your own case."

"But I would never have–"

"The point is, he lives a long life with knowing of his mistake, just as you live a long life with knowledge of yours."

"And for all of us, may we learn to do well by our future actions, as we have learned through our ignorance how not to harm again!"

"So it is." They answered in unison, save for Cain, who marveled at their simultaneity. He still wondered what Gendlebleth's rabbit had to do with his brother, and then considered the clothes he remembered his parents wearing, and thought better than to ask anytime soon. His friend's guilt suddenly seemed more obvious, the sweat barely dry on Gendlebleth's forehead.

They continued to converse.

So many stories to tell. Tales of civilizations unknown. Histories of lineages. Recollections of different people in day-to-day life and how their lives unfolded from them. Humanity transmuted to the voice of God, and humanity drowned in flood rather than dying from hearing Its whisper, save for one. Humanity learning from its own trial-and-error, building atop the lessons that life unfolded naturally. Casarta, and self-observation of mind.

They'd heard the stories long before, when Enoch had returned from Cain several centuries prior, but Luciferous was able to connect with tales of meditation from his own experience only days before. On some level they all did. As they gathered together for an experiment, they marveled at the gifts Holy All-Encompassing had bestowed upon Casarta; the lessons she had to teach them, the energies she willed within her own being, the focus she not only could choose, but chose for the sake of the greater physical well-being of them all.

Lajiel directed them simply, "Close your eyes. Let All swirl within you. Notice where your mind goes. If it is particulated from All, open yourself again to All. If the particles appear larger than The All, forgive yourself as you open yourself to All again." With that he was silent, sat, and joined them as they allowed their focus to follow the natural results of allowing the whole beyond particular things.

❦❦❦

When they awoke to rest without slumber for the sake of Casarta's alleviation of genuine exhaustion, they were grateful to their state of allowance as they released themselves to the turbulence all around: storm and wave.

❦❦❦

Until she awoke. Then, food. Then, sleep. Then recollection and awe of particulars: wind, rain, the dangling of feet, light. Then, meditation.

"Focus on your breath. The feel of breathing in. Breathing out. The feel of transition in-between. The difference from one breath to another as you allow your breath to come and go without controlling; without trying. In through the nose. The feel within the nostrils connected into the lungs from out of the air all around you. Release from lungs. Through nostrils back to our common, shared source of life. And again. Where your mind is. Always on the lungs or back to the lungs. The heart fed by the lungs. The fullness of breath. Focus back and only to the breath. Forgiveness for wandering in focus from your breath. And back to the breath again. As you are able, become centered in your breath, and see where it will take you. Return again to your breath when you find your perception a place other than *it.*"

After, as they rested below the tarp while Casarta slept, the howling wind made them all smile.

❦❦❦

"Focus your mind to the All. Let your mind grow silent beyond itself as The Entirety knows silence in Its only frequency. When calmed, tuned, 'silent,' if comfortable in the tranquility of recollection or a step before, consider one of us from Cain. Where calm enough, consider one of us from Created, and observe."

They began to learn about their own minds. They were grateful.

The time came that Casarta set to sleep. Two hours of waiting and resting passed. A familiar feeling stopped. The waves convulsed as much as ever, but water ceased to pour down upon them.

Lousitous whispered to his daughter, "Casarta? Have you awoken?" But she was fast asleep.

Chapter 57

"Argee'el. Ginsheriel. Come here. No need to stop your enjoyment of each other. No need to move. But fix your attention on Me as it is already. My will has been done. You, My hands. Without you, I still Am. With you, it is. Now slow. Stay as you are, but slow. Slow. Slow by degrees. Slow."

So, hardness to softness, one into the other, into the other, slowed. By degrees they focused their attention fuller on the action of their bodies, where before they had released themselves fully into the other, into dissolving between the two. Focusing on their own action, now they too broken further away from prior unity, noticed the result said action had on the others' state of being. Slower and slower their action, as per the command of their Creator.

"Good. Good. Now each of you pairings pick a direction and spread your wings, each pairing a different direction than the others, and continue flying until all of you coalesce at the same spot when you reach each other once more.

"Now go! Slow by degrees, ever as you continue, until you are about to stop as finally you reach each other again!"

While the wings of all the angels pushed aside the air simultaneously in perfectly opposite directions, a mighty wind began to blow over the face of the Earth and the waters below. While ever-gradually they slowed their enjoyment of each other, off they went toward the time they would meet each other again. As they left, the rains falling from them slowed and began to cease, starting at the spot over which they departed from two-another, specifically, more or less directly over the ark Noah and his sons had built.

c‌ﻬ‌ cﻬ‌ cﻬ‌

They unfastened the middle of the covering that vaguely sheltered the whole top of the raft. Ding poked her head out. She hollered forth her gratitude toward the sky. A long, middle-pitched intonation, something like, "Whooooooot." A stretch of breath toward the heavens until she had to inhale again.

Awake, those around her felt the absence of the accustomed downpour, and also thought Casarta had awoken, but it was more silent now. Those surrounding Ding began to peel back the covering little by little while she untied, as they would most days, but enthusiastically now, catching a glimpse of pure blue overhead. One another nudged one another. One by one, presuming Casarta before their focus shifted from supposition of inner-mind to present perception of what was, an electricity began to ruminate while they waited for the work of the others to be completed, for their eyes to see what their ears clearly knew: a revelation of clear sky above.

When the middle seam was opened, they began to emerge. They held on tightly to the tarp, for the real threat of being bucked from the raft continuously remained. Still, they had to be careful not to step on the others while they made room away from the center for everyone else to emerge through that solitary opening. But one by one, they crawled out and into the vastness decidedly friendlier than it had been mere moments ago. They smiled and laughed. The covering was kept secure, and they continued clinging to it and the ropes where otherwise they'd embrace, but a surge of joy passed through them all despite the upheaval of the waves beneath the raft.

Casarta, who held a place central on the raft for need of exiting easily due to her still-mending leg, was awakened by a ray of light. She felt confusion not to feel rain falling upon her face. As she opened her eyes, pulling back the lid muscles slowly, there, in all its grandeur, greeted her the sun.

❧ ❧ ❧

The raft hovered safely over the caprices of the waves. They all gathered to discuss.

"How long was that?"

Many from the group answered simultaneously, "Forty days."

"The world seems covered over with water. Not a peak of a mountain in any direction."

"And it's not dropping off immediately."

"No doubt that wind will have its effect..."

"But how long do you think it will take for the waters to recede and evaporate? How long till the occupants of a raft will find release?"

"However long it will be, we'll be here as long."

"You'd think at least the waves would settle."

"I think they are settling. Just give them another three weeks. They'll calm again."

While they deliberated, what became clear was that aside from as much saturation, they were likely going to follow a similar daily routine of gathering food, sleeping, catching up, and meditating. Until the waves settled, the covering of the raft would contain them, and no tents would be pitched. They were grateful, however. Now at least they had hope of seeing land again; of sleeping soon beneath the stars.

Casarta inquired as to whether or not they were hungry.

cbo cbo cbo

After twenty-one days the waves became comparatively calm. The tarp was mostly dry, and many marveled that the swaying of the sea actually inspired them to slumber rather than question the knots of the ropes around the trees making up the raft. Twenty-one days after that, they fixed their poles under the woven fabric in such a way as to make tents upon the raft.

Casarta breathed a sigh of relief to be allowed freedom of mind. On the other hand, Casarta's freedom of mind left a great deal of mind unfocused and surrounded by the waters that had drowned out every animal, tree, and human being previously alive. Not long after her focus unfixed did the desire for fixation on the unfair done to so much life, apparently on a whim, begin to occur to her. While she no longer had to worry about causing everyone in the raft to fall and drown again in the waves below, suddenly fires began to shoot up from the waters all around them.

"Casarta." There was no urgency or agitation in Luciferous' voice. "Be so kind as to focus here for just a moment, please." The flames subsided and vanished.

"Your mind. I know accepting anything surrounding us as good is almost impossible at present, but do please take notice that this water ultimately will give life. This sun will grow food, vegetation, most likely even again trees. And what was destroyed will be regrown in the image of a good we have not yet seen or been able to imagine. But It knows that good, what it will be, and how best to create it. At the least, we know that Comfort rests upon that boat, and the family of Comfort will potentially rebirth all of humanity. From Rest, from peace, will the seed of the Eternal Self be reborn to see Itself in All Its creation. Rejoice!"

"Couldn't get it right the first time and circumvent this much death from Its omnipotence, eh?"

"She did get it right the first time. That boat is the proof. A remaining seed of all that is right to rebirth life above water absolutely. The thread of continuity. A long culmination of existence, that a seed could remain capable of giving Her creation the fullness of life she wanted it all along to be. If not for this death, She could otherwise not fulfill the intent of Her creation as it is about to be."

"Isn't this a lot of speculation? Isn't he known for his limited capability of thought?"

"And strength of gentleness and kindness! The best of humanity, and an ability of faith to guide him there. Along with a family of goodness in the image of their father, and the strength and goodness of their mother! You are new in this life, but we have served Her and have insight into the ways in which She works."

"Even if you are right, She's torturing Cain and my family and tribe, never mind the rest of the death fertilizing soil far below our raft for your so-called 'seed.' How do you expect me to reconcile myself to this too-simple life, before my mind conceives something that might cause us more problems than fire from water?"

"As for the sake of us, your family, you focused with your being on keeping us in the air. Perhaps now would be a time to focus on the wholeness of your own being. See your foot and ankle whole, Casarta. Feel yourself and your surroundings inside and out. Let your mind rest here and now. For the sake of us, if not for you. When we touch ground again, then if you wish to wander with an active and unsettled mind, none of us would deny you your solitude as you would explore your turbulence on your own, and on a healed foot for the practice."

Seeing Luciferous' wisdom, Casarta nodded, sat, closed her eyes, and focused. She visualized her lower leg whole and healed. She screamed in pain as it set itself.

The whole of the tribe looked over to where she sat, leg outstretched. After the initial scream, she sat still. They continued watching her intently for all or part of five minutes. She continued to sit, motionless. They carried on with their conversations, promenades, and respective meditations.

Her foot set, Casarta brought her attention solely into it. She directly experienced its pain, the feeling of it rapidly repairing despite her perspective's illusion of slowness, the wood beneath it. The tingles, the numbness. Release as it was filled with light and finally dissolved into the whole of all else. Part to whole, Casarta remembered what they all knew. She released to the time that passed on into eternities. She rested into the tranquility of apparent non-differentiation.

When she opened her eyes, she could lay down for her slumber without need to move her leg.

Seeing her lay backward down for her rest, Lousitous found a remaining cloth bag and arranged it under her head for support from the hard, otherwise uncomfortable wood.

❧ ❧ ❧

She awoke to the stars shining above her. Several moments later, she heard the voice of Cain. "Are you hungry? I can bring you a fish."

"What? Were you watching me sleep all day?"

"I've learned I become more sensitive to what goes on around me as I meditate. I heard your eyes open and your breathing quicken. You fell asleep so early, I thought perhaps you would be hungry when you awoke. So, I decided to meditate by you."

"A fish would be very nice. Thank you." She felt herself smiling as she spoke. The world under water drifted away beyond the kindness of the man. She arranged from out of the wood a chair that kept her leg just as it was, but allowed her to sit up. Shortly thereafter, Cain presented her a fish. She smiled at him, and then began ripping into the dead creature's flesh with her teeth. It was good to eat.

"If you keep falling asleep during the day, you'll miss the light of the sun."

"I'd wake just to take us all hunting for more food beneath the water's surface. But after the last three months, I'm still readjusting to sleeping when everyone else is too. A few hours of meditating with the stars, however, and I'll be closer to waking with the sun."

"I'll be happy to meditate alongside you, but after a long afternoon of sitting, I'll be surprised if I don't quickly fall asleep."

"Perhaps a short time talking before you fall asleep, then?"

"That I can do. Though I'm not sure we have much in common to discuss."

"By now we've both woven in and out of the thread of existence enough to understand each other well enough on the particle level. But let's start with the basics. Here we are on a raft. We're surrounded by the conscious, singular choice that death would be preferable for *Its* creation. Surely you can't be happy bobbing up and down upon this sea of genocide?"

"You don't do light, do you?"

"I'd love to, but it's hard for me just now."

"I killed my brother. I've lived to watch my wife and children die. Then lived longer to watch their children die. Then their children die. Until finally, living longer still, the last of the generations from me I have seen drowned simultaneously as my own lungs filled with water. I won't tell you I'm happy about any of this. The thought that so quickly enveloped my mind, however, is that I had caused all of this myself. Which, I know, isn't right. But if there weren't many, many more people like me, I don't think we'd be having this pleasant conversation atop a raft that neither of us ideally would be riding upon."

"If there were more like you, they'd have stood aghast at the sight of themselves and done better by their lives for it."

"The time of several lives lends one little choice but the obvious vision of one's own face, at some point. But then, consider even how much worse than I they must have been, if Our Common Maker saw it fit to bring them to this common end."

"They couldn't have all been so bad as to warrant this."

"My experience tells me She's nothing if not just. If the stories of Methuselah show humanity at its worst, I shudder to think the shades of evil that lean toward him across adam's spectrum. Our town of Created sounds relatively calm compared to the rest, closer outside East of Eden, but what person's hand is so clean of wrongdoing that taken as a whole, perhaps this was the better option to letting the unpleasantness *we* create go on existing?"

"You think so little of your own species, you condone this kind of death of it all?"

"I was only the firstborn among them, and already look at what strange a beast we'd become. Or even if elsewhere already there were others, still, as I've lived with my own deeds, how much worse the deeds taken all together?"

"And yet She did see fit to let life go on existing. The ark this man, Noah, built would re-birth life across this world, including humanity. Was their life too spared a mistake, as you view humanity's grim potential?"

"They tell me he is good as others were not, if a bit simple. Perhaps we simply were predisposed to thinking too much, and that alone was the flaw that necessitated our doom."

"His children are said not to be so... simple. What of them?"

"Mankind reborn to an exception of goodness contrary to what otherwise blights those with similar image to my own. The future of humanity is lucky to have such people unblemished by inherent wrong as their future progenitors."

"It is difficult for me to imagine those eight people left alive are the only of all of humanity who could be described by the word 'good.' Furthermore, it does seem a tad hypocritical to me that That which created you all to begin with would lower Himself to your self-proclaimed level, and kill as basely as you say you all are inclined to. Like you all were made in the image of It..."

"Odd that you would criticize what is so much larger than ourselves, what you know experientially that you, yourself, are a part of inherently. It left them alive. It left us alive. Perhaps now the right foundation to make this world what it was intended to be, is where it is supposed to be. Or at least, the allowance that life's best elements deserve a second chance."

"You sound like Luciferous. He couldn't simply have done it right the first time? Are we all so deserving of being thus tortured? Drowned, starved, dehydrated, and left to the release of our own minds to stand floating from Earth for how long? Do we really deserve such cruelty? Is Our Creator really so flawed?

"Forgive me, Created, but if I do not settle to meditation now, I shudder to think what my mind may make manifest. You're welcome to sit with me, but my mind ingrained, at this point, is clearly the safer choice for us all."

"As you wish," was all he said. Together they closed their eyes. They sat, and they remembered that where one ended, one began, and the difference between their regarded self and that which created them was a far more blurred line than usually their eyes were prone to admit.

Before releasing his sense of self thus, a single thought crossed through Cain's head: *What did she mean dehydrated?*

Chapter 58

"How many days has it been?"

"One hundred and eighty-five."

"Six months?"

"Yes."

"Plenty of water to drink. Plenty of fish to eat. Plenty of time to catch up with each other on the last millennium and a half."

"Plenty of time to meditate."

"You know the upside of this little journey? Gives us plenty of time to rest from the pains we were born to alleviate."

"It is nice not to have to worry for a few days. Especially now that we're not perpetually being drowned..."

"Hey. Do you think they're okay?"

"Who? Noah's family?"

"No. Of course *they're* fine. She saw to that personally. No. I mean, *them*."

"Either drowned or floating hand-in-hand, I'd imagine. It's hard for me to believe that somehow they knew to build a raft of their own."

"At least the waters are calm for them now."

"Hey. The love in their chest burns as surely as the love in ours. Through tears till smiles, we find our way back to one another. She wouldn't have let us come if it wasn't meant to be."

"Still, I can't imagine her pain through these waters, too deep to support life."

"Nor I his. But when we meet again, we will have served as we were made to. Through their joy, and unto ours. Remember the taste of the fruit?"

"In my memory. It was so very long ago."

"So too the moment passing now, when we arrive there later. Through their joy, and on and into ours."

Chapter 59

"What is that over there?"

"Over where?"

"Over there." Tishna pointed toward what she saw.

"I don't see what you're pointing at."

"Doesn't that look like a small point of rock, there in the distance?"

Argnel squinted and strained his eyes. "I think I see what you're seeing. But it could just be a distant wave top."

"Not unmoving! Casarta."

Casarta opened her eyes. "Yes, Tishna? You want me to bring us to where you are looking?"

"If you would, please."

"A welcome distraction." Dolphins appeared at the side of the raft. For the first time in months, they pulled the raft over the water rather than under it. The golden cords attached from the dolphins to the raft allowed them great distance from it. The cords were tied to rings on the thin beam of wood Casarta thought as grafted into the side of the raft, so as not to splinter the real wood. Water rushed by while hundreds of conceived dolphins swam in the direction of the vague point in the distance. The closer they got, the clearer it came into view.

A thousand feet away, all at once the dolphins disappeared from the side of the raft and reappeared on the opposite side, pulling the raft in the other direction.

Everyone was jolted, some tumbling dangerously close to the side of the raft rushing toward the point mere moments prior. The dolphins stopped the raft's motion in the one direction, and then began it very slightly in the other before disappearing seconds after they'd emerged.

Picking themselves up from the edge of the raft and catching their bearings, all looked expectantly at Casarta. "While I was looking through the eyes of some of the dolphins, I realized what we were looking at. That is the top of a mountain. If I hadn't stopped us, we would have run into it. Our raft broken and stranded on the top of a mountain didn't seem like a good idea to me, especially if this means the waters have begun to dissipate."

They all looked to the now-large rock clearly jutting out of the water's surface. Joy filled them to see earth, any earth, separated off from water at long last. Luciferous spoke up. "Casarta, can you keep us in proximity to this mountain, so that we can watch the waters lower in relation to it?"

"I can," she answered, "but I have another idea that might serve your aims better..."

❧❧❧

Luciferous agreed that Casarta's idea was best, but had a request for her before they got underway.

"I see no reason to give praise for such destruction that I regard as absolutely pointless. You understand that, right?"

"I do, Casarta, but I'm not asking for your sake. We feel strongly that *we* have a reason to express our gratitude, and *we* would be grateful to you if you could facilitate this for us, without us having to swim for it in the process. Besides, it'll give you something to occupy your mind for some span of time. How many of us do you think can fit on that rock, anyway?"

"I don't suppose the ark could be drifting much farther in the near future. Nor do we risk running aground anytime soon. I do appreciate a new place to set my focus for a short while. One way of passing time being equal to another, if this is a form of love my family wishes to express, I see no reason to deny you, so long as you have no request that I should practice in kind."

"Nothing could be further from my mind."

"You do know I can listen in on your thoughts if I so choose, right?"

"In that case, even if such a thought should occur to me, I certainly won't burden you with it!" Luciferous smiled at Casarta.

Casarta sighed, and a small boat appeared next to the raft. She and Luciferous boarded the boat. As though of its own volition, it sped through the water toward the peak of mountain poking up through the unending sea. The boat slowed and stopped directly next to the rock.

As Luciferous found his balance out of the boat and onto the ground, he requested of Casarta, "Perhaps the others would prefer a slightly more leisurely pace to and from? No doubt, though, I thank you sincerely for the feel of solid ground beneath my feet."

Casarta nodded. As Luciferous prostrated himself before All that he was not, and uttered gratitude aloud and to himself, it occurred to her that after seven and a half months of nothing but water, feet upon solid ground must be a pleasing sensation to them all, regardless of homage paid to a Creator that delighted in genociding Its own creation. As Luciferous arose and spent a little time feeling rock upon bare toes, she smiled to be able to facilitate his feeling the slow return of the world to him for the first time in terribly long, and the feelings of joy and hope such stone upon the soles of his bare feet must engender. She watched with her own gratitude while he spent another half-hour meditating upon the ground before rising again, finding his way back onto the boat, and nodding toward her that he was ready to return. Back at the raft, he bowed to her and said simply, "Thank you," before returning into his encampment of fellow angels enfleshed.

Shortly, Randolfy appeared separate from the group, "He said there was comfortably only room for one on the mountaintop for now, but that you will bring us there for our own time, as you can."

Casarta nodded deeply to Randolfy. "And happy to do so." She smiled meekly back up at him, humbled now to be able to give such a gift slowly but surely to the whole of her tribe. Randolfy stepped carefully into the boat, and Casarta focused on a smoother, calmer ride to bring her passenger to the first experience of solid ground he had had for a very long time.

⚭⚭⚭

Luciferous, Randolfy, Higderon. One, two, three, she brought them to earth and back. Four, five, six to and from: Slesheron, Harratzarian, Tritictus. Antagnous and Lousitous; Casarta felt overwhelmed as the sun cast color across the sky. An evening meal accompanied by the gratitude of the tribe, and she found her way to dreams.

She arose with the sun, with the others. She arranged a sort of boat for herself and fifty others to gather fish and seaweed beneath the surface. Once food was brought back to the raft, she began shuttling again to and from the mound of earth sticking up from the rest of what was fully submerged beneath water. With some spending an hour or more with dry land, after bringing ten to and from, she was ready for a short meditation before sleeping until the light of a new day.

The next day, one by one, twelve made the journey. Each expressed gratitude toward Casarta for allowing them a dry voyage to dry land, for thankfulness to see their past passing and a proverbial new day dawning upon the whole of the world.

A bit more gathering of food the following morning, then Casarta brought Telnaxson, her first passenger of the day, to meet water-free earth. Gratefully he disembarked and felt rock under foot, cool and steady. Looking back at Casarta, he asked, "Has there been this much stone exposed the last three days?"

Casarta looked at the mountaintop closely for the first time since she'd begun bringing them back and forth. It hadn't occurred to her that the waters really were receding. Now that she was looking at the exposed ground, however, she couldn't help but see there was in fact more area exposed than there had been when Luciferous had touched his foot to it just three days prior. "No. At least, there wasn't when we first got here. I'm pretty sure not quite that much yesterday, either. Though I really didn't pay as close attention to the exposed area yesterday."

"Well, I thank you for giving me plenty of space here for myself, but you might consider on your next trip bringing two. There is more than enough room for two to give gratitude and appreciate this occurrence fully and simultaneously."

"Thank you for drawing my attention to what is so fully in plain sight. I think the others will be grateful to arrive here more quickly, too. It shall be done!"

Telnaxson enjoyed his time with solid stone. He lay on his back, he lay on his stomach. He prostrated, he stood, he walked, he danced. He took of his time as he liked, and then he was taken back to the raft when he was ready for others to take their turn.

As conceived by revelation, on her next journey out, she took both Lemisslept and Ardrojaxt with her to the small island that was the mountain's peak. Two there, two back. Then Jurngosset and Tartantuan. Bizcoyoth and Kleshala. Zarnuchtron and Childreth. Two there, two back. Two there, two back. Two there, two back. Two there, two back. Two there, two back, and with the sun gone from the sky, light too was all but gone from it, and she was ready for rest: meditation, and then slumber.

The next day she first brought Isston and Chothran to the rock. As they embraced its solidity, Casarta made a point to assess how many could comfortably fit upon the singular bit of dry land they'd found, and saw that still, two was a good number. Having thus noted, she continued to observe that while they enjoyed the firmness and thanked the possibilities of the future, she could have ready two more by the time Isston and Chothran were through. She considered that this way, in shortening the time of travel, it would give others their opportunity more quickly, over the course of a day, to have their turns, and in so doing reduce the need to make everyone wait as long. This in mind, she called to her cousins, "Hey! I am going to gather two more while you pray. I will be back soon." They nodded. Casarta returned to the raft.

At first, as Casarta approached, they did not know why she had returned with an empty boat. "If I take two back with me, then bring two more there, if you don't mind waiting in the boat a few minutes, I think I can get more of you the contact and contemplation you all who have not yet gone are anticipating, over the course of a day."

They nodded approvingly of her wisdom. Esajah and Caldas boarded the boat to be taken to where their feet could feel unmoved. Upon arrival, they waited barely another ten minutes before Isston and Chothran were ready to return. Esajah and Caldas disembarked as Isston and Chothran boarded. They were brought back to the raft as Esajah and Caldas were left to worship. Darwith and Gernow stepped on board, and their journey to solidity began. Upon arrival, they waited thirteen minutes before the positions on boat and island were swapped. Again the routine repeated.

Two there, two back. Two there, two back. By the end of the day, as Velendtrenda found her foot back on raft,

Casarta had doubled the amount of beings able to pay their respects, much as she had done the day before. This day, before her period of rest began, thirty-six more had gone there and back. The next day, thirty-six more still.

On the seventh day, while Avalon and Figget disembarked, Casarta saw the water had dissipated enough to allow three visitors, which she promptly left the island to gather. Three there, two back. Three there, three back. From sun-up to sun-down, Casarta had made over the course of the last three days an average of eighteen trips each day with a fresh set of passengers to the land. Eight days, nine days, her mind tirelessly rowing.

Three there, three back. Four there, three back. Four there, and the tenth day promised near completion of each incarnated servant paying gratitude for what had created it also creating a continued existence to behold. On the eleventh day, Casarta brought three boats of four to and back. After the fourth of the third group had stepped off the boat, she returned to the far side of the raft where Cain sat, his feet dangling in the water. "Forgive me for not asking you sooner. I know how they long to revere what creates a new beginning for them all, though I cannot yet fight winningly my despondence for what has passed. But in it all, you I did not ask. Cain, would you like a few moments alone with the protruding peak of the mountain? We will be leaving soon, and I cannot tell when we may have occasion again for dry land."

Cain paused. Spending days watching Casarta shuttle her people to and from, he'd given up hope that she would consider him. He was delighted to find that she had. "I would like very much to feel solidity beneath my feet once more, if you would be willing to allow me the time."

"Of course!" Casarta smiled. "Step in."

She brought the boat to the island. He waited with her until the other four had finished. He then got out to allow them to get in. She promised to come back as she set out to return them to the raft.

The rock immediately felt cold beneath Cain's feet. He felt comforted, however, by its unyielding support of his person. Though small waves splashed up at its side, he was happy to feel the lack of movement beneath him. When his eyes were closed, not even the faintest illusion that he stood in a place which drifted remained. This, in turn, sparked an idea.

Cain sat down upon the rock and closed his eyes again. He heard the gentle slapping of water against stone. He felt the breath in his lungs. He reveled in the stillness of existence in the moment of time he currently inhabited. There, in that moment, he sat. There, with that stillness, he became. Every breath took on the lightness of gratitude while he inhaled the serenity of being. Sometime later, with a deep exhalation, he opened his eyes.

He opened his eyes into the staring watch of Casarta waiting in her boat, several feet away in front of him. He smiled at her. She returned his smile. Slowly he began stretching his body outward from its sitting, until blood returned to his limbs well enough that he could bring himself back to his feet. He took a moment to stare around him at the placid fullness of water covering the Earth. He walked around the rock for a couple of minutes, looked down at the brown stone beneath him several seconds more. Finally, he brought his gaze back to the boat and Casarta sitting in it, waiting patiently for *his* return.

As he entered in, she said, "You were sitting for what felt like two hours. Longer than six times the length of time some of them embraced their experience upon the ground."

Cain felt himself begin to blush. "I'm sorry. I–"

"No, no! It's not a complaint at all. I have never felt you so at peace."

"Maybe if ever I was, it was two lifetimes ago. But even then I doubt it. I have heard many times now the stories of how humanity came to be. You come from beings created without need of earth, but earth, it is almost all of me. Honestly, I don't think *I* had any idea how good it would feel to reconnect with ground after spending the better part of a year so far removed from it."

Not knowing how else to respond, Casarta bowed her head slightly in acknowledgment of his words before starting the boat back to the raft.

Upon arrival, first Cain stepped off. Then, he offered his hand to Casarta to help her back onto the raft. Though she did not need it, she was happy to take his offer of kindness up to the firmer ground. Again she bowed toward Cain, this time in gratitude, before turning her attention to converse with Luciferous. "All have paid of their acknowledgment and love of their Creator. It is time to seek out the ark, Luciferous." As she spoke these words, the boat that she had conceived that day vanished, and a vast contingent of dolphins tethered to the raft suddenly appeared, apparently prepared to take them all, and the raft, anywhere they wished to go.

"But did *you* stand upon the mountain's top, Casarta?"

Casarta was caught off guard by Luciferous' question. As her attention shifted to an appropriate response, seventy-five dolphins disappeared from the side of the raft about which they had been swimming back and forth in wait. "Luciferous, believe me when I tell you I will need a greater space to traverse than that rock provided, the next time my foot touches solid ground."

As Casarta's eyes held a perfectly still gaze, dead center to Luciferous' own, it became Luciferous' turn to be knocked out of balance by the words of the other. While he contemplated whether it was warranted to fathom a reply, two hundred dolphins appeared where before seventy-five had left. Many hundreds now abounded, frolicking as their tethers would allow. Casarta sat and closed her eyes. Luciferous searched his own mind. While he pondered the girl before him, the raft began very definitely to pick a direction and move.

Chapter 60

This sensation felt familiar to Casarta. Gazing through the eyes of any one of twelve hundred dolphins towing the raft, she felt relief letting her physical existence be led by her intent certain to find its way to her goal without knowing where, but only what, it was.

Every so often she'd remember the graft of wood woven into the side of the raft holding the metal rings, securing tether to harness to dolphin. From the creatures of her own supposing, she heard the thoughts of those that occurred naturally, beyond the doom of the terror of the flood. She'd converse, with those swimming by, of what they'd seen. She'd hear and send to those at a distance the thoughts that let her know her direction was true. The distance was long. It could be years, for all she cared, to finding her mark. Her mind's freedom to seek brought joy to her heart amidst a torrent of distress that they'd all been created for the sake of merely experiencing misery without mercy. Through the liberation of focus without known direction or time, she was happy to frolic and be led for the sake of those she loved, without need to think otherwise. She was released from considering the purpose of her own being made to be victim of the cause of her creation, the victim of the desolation of others she would otherwise perceive.

It had been a month, now, that Casarta had focused her mind on the intent of finding the ark containing Noah, his family, and the rebirth of the world. The sun was high in the sky when, pointing upward, Telnaxson shouted loudly for all to hear, "There! Look there. Everybody, look there!" Casarta's eyes snapped open.

The dolphins disappeared all at once while she raised her gaze to the heavens. Sure enough, there before and above them all, was a sight to behold: A raven flying overhead, to and fro.

"How long has it been?"

"Two hundred and sixty-three days."

"Casarta, do you know how close we are?"

"The dolphins had been telling of a strange sort of whale, much, much larger than any they had ever seen, beached close by. I would be surprised if we are more than two days away."

While Luciferous, Casarta, and the others conversed, Cain came over thirsty. He dipped his hand in the water and brought a sip to his lips. Immediately he noticed a change: the water tasted particularly salty today.

He was startled by the taste, but his mouth was dry. He continued to drink. He became sated, but there was discomfort to the drinking. No longer distracted by thirst, he began to return his gaze again toward the sky, toward the beauty of seeing another living creature taking naturally into the air after so long.

Glancing over for a brief moment, he noticed Casarta sitting with eyes closed. Most of the others held their eyes fixed to the bird above. Luciferous, Antagnous, and Gendlebleth instead watched intently upon Casarta as she sat. No dolphins appeared. No movement of the raft. Cain wondered why she would choose now to meditate. Finally, questions unanswered and put aside in mind, he brought his sight back to the raven above.

She flew aloft above them, so far over the face of the water. She could see the raft from her place in the Heavens, flying back and forth. As she turned back toward the direction she had come from, she could see far in the distance over the shining reflection of light spread seemingly infinitely into the horizon. Seventy miles from where she'd come she saw, small in the distance, the speck upon the large rock that had been her home for more than the last eight months. Wings spread wide, she glided in that direction now. Casarta's eyes opened.

"The ark is three days away if we take our time about it. There is no rush. Neither people, nor animals are going anywhere for a little while. A great deal of mountain is showing, but this water is more than far from gone."

"Casarta, would you be so kind as to call forth your dolphins? Let us journey half of the way, and then discuss what distance to maintain. I recommend we consider amongst ourselves, and discuss fully once Casarta can join us." Casarta bowed her head, and then closed her eyes. Dolphins, tethers, and the ardent splashing of water commenced much as before. The rest watched the raven until it was beyond sight, and then sat to fill their minds with their own thoughts, or lack thereof. At night they spoke together about the few and probable options they'd conceived before falling asleep. The next day, Casarta brought them further.

As the sun set, the dolphins disappeared and the raft slowed rapidly. "Any further, and we run the risk of being seen. If any of you can see there a speck against the horizon, that is the top of the mountain.

They squinted and followed where she pointed, but in the rapidly dimming light, they thought more or less similarly that any speck they thought they saw was likely as not merely a figment of their desire to see. So, in turn, they resigned themselves to the possibility of its appearance in the coming day.

They awoke to the sound of a bird croak overhead. They looked above to see the black body and wings passing by while it glided effortlessly through the air.

Cain held his head high, watching for so long as the bird could be seen in the sky. Once it was out of view, he rolled over and pushed himself up to his legs. He walked over to the side of the raft to take a drink. It seemed slightly saltier than the day before. He turned to Drawsonen, sitting close by, "Drawsonen, have you noticed the water taste different over the last several days?"

"We all have, Cain. We didn't want to bring it up before you did, though."

"Bring up what?"

"It seems the less water covers the earth, the more minerals and substances decaying get mixed with the water. It is easier for us to suffer the salt water, or simply extreme thirst, as the waters continue to abate. For you, however, we took the few remaining pots we had that weren't thrown from the raft during the storm, and filled them with as much water as we could as soon as we noticed the water would likely soon be undrinkable to you. We think we have enough to last you twenty days comfortably. If you ration well, maybe it could be a forty-day supply. Perhaps slightly more. Keep drinking of the sea until you can no longer, and when that moment comes, we are ready to give you what we have."

Cain considered briefly once Drawsonen became silent. "Thank you. I am grateful for your foresight, insight, and the kindness you all have shown me over the course of this very long journey."

"For us, we have a debt perhaps we can never repay you. You are welcome to whatever service we can provide for you. We have great amends to make for so, so long ago."

"You have no need to apologize for the action of my own hand. But thank you for all you do for me."

Drawsonen bowed his head toward Cain, then looked up again and into his eyes. Cain smiled, and then made his way toward where Luciferous and Casarta sat together.

"Then it's settled."

"Yes."

With that, Casarta became still and the water began to open beneath them. Well below the level of the surface above, the water closed over them, surrounding them in all directions. Large fish appeared at a side and began to swim. Through the water the raft was pulled, Cain imagined, in the direction of the ark.

Cain enjoyed watching the water pass. Fish flew by from time to time. Thankfully, bodies no longer floated frequently, or now at all, about them. He found the rays of light penetrating the water everywhere soothing. Simultaneously, the rush was a rush, and yet it was calming watching it all pass. So much had been destroyed, and yet now, in this moment, all that encompassed him was life.

୧୬୧୬୧୬

The raft slowed and came to settle. A few hours later, darkness set in. Slowly the raft began to rise. Water displaced over them, swelled below them, and finally the fresh air of the evening greeted them above. In the moon's light, they looked about at each other's faces. In the moon's light, they looked up from where they sat and stood upon the raft. There, one hundred yards above them, the back of the gargantuan boat.

They spent a moment gawking before the sight of the colossus perched upon the side of the mountain. Then, the raft began to move. They all at once heard the sound of Casarta's voice in their minds. "This close to the ark, we must not speak. During the day I will submerge us again, so we can discuss your surveillance." Soon the raft came to a stop. In the light of the moon, they could see the ark no longer. Only the mountain's face and peak were visible to them, the ark somewhere behind it. One by one they contemplated the soft breeze of the warm night, the full moon, and how much mountain was there risen before them. One by one they shut their eyes against the soft, bright light to await the rising sun in silence, and dream.

ϟϟϟ

When the sun of the following day pierced Casarta's eyelids, immediately she pictured the submerging of the raft upon which they all slept. Beneath the raft, the water flowed outward. As the raft descended, the water held as walls on all sides of it. Until, finally, the water formed a three-foot-thick roof above them, at which time Casarta sat in repose waiting for all to awaken who had not yet risen from a supine posture. One by one, in turn they did.

Many had already resumed standard consciousness with the sun. More still felt the coolness come over them with the water as it occurred to them to arise in this reverse aquarium. They stood and sat up within short times of opening eyes. The rustling of the others brought more up still. Throughout them all, it happened very naturally to awaken simultaneously. Before long, none slept, all alert to discussion now that again they were reunited, albeit at a slight distance, with all life upon the planet.

"It was built to withstand what we just had no choice but to experience. There's one well-latched door which, when opened, is a sort of window on the left side of the boat. Otherwise, it's only the main opening."

"So, they can't see us. But might they come out of the ark, just to have fresh air and walk about a bit?"

"That's unlikely. They'd let heat out quickly on the one hand, and possibly animals on the other."

"So, they're all but blind up there. Still, I should keep us beneath the water. Unless you're not concerned with them hearing us?"

"Unless we sat quietly all day. Though it is nice to continue swapping stories."

"And Luciferous, it is nice to be able to... practice focusing my mind."

Both Luciferous and Cain couldn't help but immediately appreciate the wisdom of her approach. "It may be good to have time to walk upon the mountain and watch the flight of the bird ourselves, from time to time. So long as you don't object to periodically allowing us the sky, we probably are better off ensuring we will not be heard by any watching the raven fly from the ark."

Casarta was relieved to continue to have distractions from her emotional center.

They sought food, keeping close to the mountain beneath the water by day. In the mornings they could see what recess of water had transpired by night. They would awaken to the sun and watch the raven fly. To and fro, no place particular to enjoy landing, they watched a creature that was not them with admiration for the grace knitted out of the fabric of eternity soaring through created existence, and gratitude that life already begun its slow seep out from the odd-shaped wooden seed that promised the rebirth of all the world waiting patiently above. When they needed food, or looked again to converse, below the water's surface they'd descend.

Chapter 61

Jawrldrook and Honoth thanked The Creator of firmament and rock alike for the feel of firmness beneath their feet. Slowly they felt their bare soles upon the ground, so as not to speak their presence to the wind and any open window it might divulge their presence to. Up above, the raven swirled on the thermals carrying it here and there over the waters of the Earth, never too far from the sole source of a perch, should its wings have to do much more of the work.

Step by step, slowly they climbed toward the gargantuan, hollow composite of wood holding the life of the world within, now planted on the earth, waiting for its chance to open to the created and begin its sprout. After two hours of scaling, finally they came to rest under the very long shadow cast by the boat. They surveyed its side, decided they could see the cracks of the only place it could open out, and nestled as close to the boat as they could come. They both remembered the size of the ramp well. Overhead, a raven circled the sky.

❧❧❧

"So we hunt for as much seaweed as we can, and wrap it in those blankets?"

"They'll be up there longer than a few weeks at this rate."

"Yes, a few blankets' worth won't be enough, but we will bring them more."

"How many pairs of shoes do we have left amongst the lot of us?"

"Five."

"And we probably won't see another pair for another century, if not two..."

"I think I can cover your feet while you climb the mountain. Might get a little more life out of your real shoes that way. Cut it to a half-dozen decades for a lucky pair of you."

They smiled down at her. "I like the way you think, Casarta."

❧ ❧ ❧

Cain cupped his hands and dipped them into the water, reluctantly. He brought liquid to lips. Upon it touching tongue, he spit it out immediately. The day had come of which Drawsonen had spoken. He sat pondering the salt on his mouth still lingering, and his slight thirst. Slight compared to what he knew it would become. He contemplated asking for water, knowing that with every drop holding thirst at bay, he was one drop closer to a pain he'd never experienced before. He decided that the time to ration was now. He sat and closed his eyes. When he was truly thirsting, this, he decided, was when he would ask for a drink.

Day passed. Night fell. He felt weak while he observed the lethargic dryness of his tongue and the arid futility of his throat swallowing nothing. He decided water must now be sought. He opened his eyes. He stood. Energy failed him, his tongue dormant in his mouth. He gazed around him.

"Drawsonen..." his throat barely uttered while he searched in the thin moonlight to find his friend. Taerna looked up to where Cain stood. "Wa... Water." Cain lowered himself back down to where he had been sitting, propping himself up on his arms.

Taerna was not sure why he had specified Drawsonen when they were all prepared to bring him water, but he knew the sound of thirst all the same, and went quickly to fill a small vessel from a bigger vessel, and returned again to Cain's side.

Cain lapped at the cup like an overheated dog, taking in many little sips through a throat that seemed to have to re-learn how to allow the cool liquid in. He wondered how much worse the feeling would be when the day came he would have to go days, if not months, without a drink. He was grateful to have the taste of life-essence now soaking into his mouth. He was as grateful to its Creator as he was to the hand offering it. He looked up into the eyes and face. By the moon's light, he was glad to recognize Taerna. "Thank you." His word was weak, but true.

"You are ever welcome, Created. We would see you never suffer, had we such the luxury." He smiled down on Cain. Cain drank in the light, past his ever-present inner conviction that he hardly deserved it. "Are you hungry?"

"I am."

"We have been drying some seaweed to take up to Honoth and Jawrldrook. I will bring you some."

Cain's lips felt sore at the thought of their moisture being absorbed into the dry plant stuff. "No."

"What?"

"The moisture from my mouth will go into the seaweed. I'll need to drink even more, simply not to be in pain."

Taerna understood. "Give me just a moment. I think Takla might still have something." He walked from Cain and returned several moments later.

Cain felt a smooth, almost slippery roughness enter his hand. Holding half of a fish up to the light of the moon, he rejoiced. As he bit into its soft flesh, his mouth remained moist while he gratefully chewed up the creature's body and took the masticated protein into his own. "Thank you."

Taerna beamed downward toward his face. "Most welcome, Created."

Cain lowered himself onto his back and drifted off into slumber almost as quickly as his eyes shut.

⁊⁊⁊

When Cain awoke the next day, he asked of the nearest available body, "Tomolin, where is water?"

"Son of Mankind and Living, there below those blankets you'll find a cup, several actually, next to the water we have saved for you. Please, drink more than you did yesterday, unless you have no choice. The waters are parting quickly now. Perhaps fresh water is near at hand. In the meantime, allow yourself the strength to rise to your legs while we seek to discover your optimum contentment."

"I will drink more than I did yesterday. But still, I am in no rush to deplete the fresh water you have been kind enough to put aside for me."

"So long as you can rise to your own legs and enjoy the feel of light on your face, together we will figure out the best next steps, should what we set aside run out."

Cain rose to his feet, enjoyed the light pouring through the water above and the fish journeying through the water all around.

⁊⁊⁊

Argnel, Jurngosset, and Randolfy unloaded heavy tarps filled with pounds of seaweed, half-dried, onto the place where the mountain met the water. Casarta whispered into Randolfy's ear, "A hundred eagles could bring this up the mountain so much easier than three bodies made male after Adam."

Randolfy whispered back, "The sound of wings, the dust of earth, the unlikely but unknown opening of a door. And what if any of those inside have learned to see through the eyes of the raven? As unlikely as they could accept the servants of All Created, how much more so the unexplained appearance and disappearance of animals thought since dead?"

"I doubt highly they have discovered sight through the eyes of another. Though I appreciate your predisposition toward discretion. I can at least push or pull."

Randolfy smiled. "That you can." She stepped out of the canoe-like boat and onto solid ground while the boat disappeared behind her. Together they began the hours of pushing, pulling, and climbing the seaweed up the mountain.

❧ ❧ ❧

"Discreet removal of these blankets will be no trouble at all. I won't even need eagles to fly them out." She winked at Randolfy.

"Thank you for bringing us food. We shudder to think of our mouths to quickly fill with the taste of dust for no water, but we will enjoy what moisture remains in these plants before they dry to the point our distress returns for the imminent, genuine lack of drink." Just as these words left Honoth's lips, they all felt the gentle sprinkle of mist on their faces accompanied by a subtle darkness, as though a wispy cloud had passed over the sun. Together they looked up to see twelve wings fluttering toward them, liquid-like in motion, in unison.

They were very still, save for the flow of their wings, while they descended with each other toward their incarnated brethren discussing the circumstance at hand. With one voice they thought into the minds of their former compatriots, "Our Common Creator All-Encompassing is as well All Merciful, as you all are aware. As is such, we are here to assist in this instance. You are going to want to go back to your raft and fetch at least two cups..."

cⰔ)cⰔ)cⰔ

Casarta's initial greater impulse was to make sure Honoth and Jawrldrook had cups, though she wanted to linger. She, Argnel, Randolfy, and Jurngosset bid the pair of angels farewell and hiked down the mountain. Casarta brought them back to the raft, and then went to fetch a pair of cups that waited beside the stored drinking water.

"But if we bring them their cups now, it will be dark by the time we return." Randolfy cautioned.

"But if we don't bring them cups now, they may have need to drink without them." Casarta looked Randolfy dead in the eye when she spoke.

Randolfy acquiesced and the two of them took to a boat, and back up the mountain. "You don't need to hike up. The sight of the angels..."

"Is there a way I should think as I look upon the servants of Our Common Omni-Being Endlessness?"

Randolfy found himself without a response. Side-by-side they hiked again up the higher half of the mountain, until they came once more to their friends. Casarta held the cups out to Jawrldrook and Honoth while she resumed staring at these two angels joined, as it was, at the hip. While staring, her own groin quivered. The obvious, after more than a millennium and a half, became clear. She had no desire to look away, and became even redder of skin tone while she watched the angels in union. Jawrldrook, Honoth, and Randolfy all stared at Casarta's staring, uncertain, as the pair of angels enjoyed each other with the greatest stillness they could muster for the sake of their Lord.

"Well, we have our source of water. We have our cups. We have enough food to last us something like two months, if it all dries out well."

"And it is getting dark. Casarta, can we head back now? Casarta?"

It took her name being spoken the second time before she looked up to Randolfy. "Casarta, we should be getting back." She nodded. Still, she had a great deal of difficulty keeping her head turned away from the coupled angels as they began their journey back down. While they turned to leave, Jawrldrook, Honoth, and the angels moved closer toward the ark. They got as close to it as they could, just under where the ramp, the door to the ark, would extend out when it was opened.

In relative darkness, save for a slender moon and the light of the stars, Casarta brought herself and Randolfy back to the raft waiting a few hundred yards away from where the water met the earth of the mountain. Vividly in her head was the image of the angels, and the acute awareness she currently had of her own body. Now, not only for the sake of being alone with her anger did she find herself desiring to be away from those she cared about. She knew that when the time came, she would have much to explore in her mind that she dared not with her family surrounding her.

❧ ❧ ❧

Cain learned to whisper drops from his cup slowly over the course of a day. Seaweed he stayed away from entirely; the taste of the raw fish kept his mouth moister, and the lesser saltiness prolonged his tongue's cravings for water. Otherwise, he sat observing land or sea or, with eyes closed, his own mind, from morning to slumber. He had never been so acutely aware before how important breathing through his nose really was, for the sake of not immediately drying himself out. Specifically, now he was mindful of his genuine thirst, careful to sip throughout his waking time so that the put-off pain would not accumulate too deeply to the extent of his inability to will his own body. Though he did sleep more while his body learned its functioning upon minimal moisture.

✦✦✦

Cain awoke to the raven in the sky circling. Looking over, he saw the mountain, tall, looming above him. He sighed to himself as he felt the dryness of his mouth. His cup, half-full, sat within reach of his arm. He took it within his hand and brought it to his lips. He took a sip. He put it down and lay back again. The raven's curved glide. The now-tall mountain loomed, dwarfing him.

Within the context of what touched the sky, Cain watched the passing of time. Around the bird, around the sun, around the blue. Time was a perpetual arc, never quite returning to its own beginning, but often something so close to it.

There was no longer need to submerge the raft. The waters had receded so far that the mountain was again a mountain, not merely an island or a berg of stone. So far below the ark, there was now no risk of their voices carrying that far upward on currents non-existent blowing toward the sky. Sipping from his cup on occasion, Cain followed the course of the sun as from the horizon it arose to well over his head.

He opened his eyes. Held his hand between his sight and the sun. The raven spun through the firmament. Around and around the speck of black. In spiral up above, it seemed to become bigger in Cain's mind. He wondered that a constant concentration could make his sight bend. He closed his eyes. He thought of the lone bird patrolling the skies. Suddenly, he could see as the bird saw. Mountain and ark, and raft so far below. All the people sitting and standing and walking, and even himself laying down. Then, there, in the distance a dead tree sticking up through what still covered over the earth below. He felt so tired. His desire to land overwhelmed him. Cain's eyes opened. The raven still circled, but it was indeed bigger to his sight.

He sat up and watched as its crossings over the sky became longer, and the raven itself grew clearer. Many around him watched already. Those otherwise occupied were tapped to observe simultaneously. Eyes opened and heads turned toward the sky.

In the distance, finally, it came to land. Though the tree was dead after the waters had suffocated it and prohibited light to touch what leaves once grew, it still stood strong enough for a single bird to find its rest there. Together they knew it would not be long now before their feet would touch upon flat earth, after so long floating above it.

"We must prepare the raft to be far from here and broken apart, before water no longer holds us."

Casarta shut her eyes and contemplated how far to go from their brethren on the mountain. She would consult soon for the perfect place, but for now, she knew the wisdom of simply creating distance.

Chapter 62

Jawrldrook saw it first. "Honoth, has the raven turned white, or do my eyes deceive me?"

"Looks gray to me. Smaller than the raven. We didn't see the raven return to the ark last night, did we?"

"No. It went off into the distance, toward the horizon. Then it did not return."

"It's a dove."

Jawrldrook and Honoth looked up. "Thank you, Logosel."

"And the raven landed safely atop a tall tree that had good rooting, despite its suffocation by water."

Honoth sighed. "And thank you, Theeisel."

"Very welcome. Would you like more water?"

They both sighed together. This time Jawrldrook responded, "We are quite sated, thank you. But we've told you many times now, we are happy to ask when we thirst."

"But we want to make sure your cups are ever full. We'll make them ready for you. We'll just—"

"We know what you'll just," Honoth cut off Logosel. "We can see clearly how eager you are to please. Now, if you'll be so kind, we are eager to enjoy the sight of this beautiful manifestation in silence."

Theeisel responded, "To serve you is our pleasure. But should you thirst—"

This time Jawrldrook cut it off. "You two will be the first we tell. We know just how happy the two of you are to assuage the possibility of our being parched." He smiled widely as he spoke this, and then abruptly turned his back to them beside Honoth, who had already refocused his attention toward the newly discerned harbinger of what was to come.

⊱⊰⊱⊰⊱

Casarta enjoyed a new sensation: gazing through the eyes of this dove, high above them all. She felt it seeking ground; worms. *Poor thing,* she thought, *the only earthworms alive must still be in that boat.* She enjoyed with it the soaring, despite feeling the hunger simultaneously. She experienced its ecstasy of freedom after so many months not reveling in the air on its face, let alone the sensation of the sky taking it into her bosom and holding her safely over the earth as time fell away, her mind only existence aloft with an occasional remembrance of what fleeting captivity remained far below.

But, as she went to and fro, and around and around, her hunger grew. While she saw no place upon the earth to land, she flew nearer and nearer the ark, knowing she would need to set her foot down eventually. As sun began to descend below horizon, she knew fatigue must eventually follow, and only one place surrounding could offer rest simultaneous with a meal. Faithfully she returned to an outstretched hand, kind and gentle despite the darkness and captivity it receded into. She acquiesced to her physical needs despite herself. Casarta's eyes opened.

"Where did it go?"

"It didn't go in the same direction the raven went, did it?"

"Maybe it found a different tree still standing?"

All around her Casarta heard them talking about the dove, wondering where it went after just one day of being seen.

"It returned to the ark."

All heads turned to where Casarta sat.

"It was hungry, and tired, and returned to the shelter it has become accustomed to. It wants to fly free and find its own firm footing away from captivity. But there was no ground for it to land. Lacking options of food for it to eat, it returned to the ark."

They marveled. They became deeply grateful that such as Casarta could result from such a beginning as created her. They were thoroughly thankful she was among them. They began to contemplate their own capacity to see through the eyes of another being, and many sat to meditate, contemplating the creatures near.

Luciferous, Casarta, and the others interested in such conversation decided on the proper distance from the mountain to wait before the waters dried away to leave them only in mud. While Casarta moved them all "far enough" as determined by consensus, they unfastened logs unnecessary for belongings and personal space. They floated to the agreed-upon place, closer of quarters but excited for the inevitability of ground beneath their feet so soon to come. Into the night they sat, talked, ate, meditated, and finally slept, until dawn.

෴ ෴ ෴

Days passed that they waited to see the return of the small bird to the sky. Hours after sunrise they would stare still at the large, brown object, speck-like as though some sort of queer bird itself, perched upon the mountain. They looked to Casarta for confirmation.

Her eyelids remained lowered while she focused on her friend through whom she'd soared. Her eyes opened into darkness. No window to shed light. Some room, she supposed, within the ark. She felt for these creatures so neglected without either window or flame. She wondered that they could live in such desolation for so long without dying of depression. Then, she heard a chirp. Then another chirp in response. Somewhere she heard a song. Before long, she was listening to their conversation echoing off the walls. They were shrouded in darkness, but they were not alone. They reminded each other of that incessantly. Casarta's eyes opened.

"The dove is on the ark. I think it will not be flying again today." Indeed, it did not. Nor the day after that. Nor the day after that.

᪥᪥᪥

Dawn was breaking, though the sun could not yet be seen, as Cain awoke. For two days, no bird had been sighted in the sky. Cain propped himself up on his elbows, surveying the tightly packed raft all around him, watching as others slowly came to their wakening.

Since the excess logs had been shed, Cain had taken to sleeping near the water pots so that he would not have to step over the others to take a drink. He stood, dipped his cup into the pot to retrieve water, and then sat back down with his legs folded. While he slowly sipped, he contemplated the slight saltiness which this water held, as he had done every day since this had become his only source of drink. Three more care-filled sips later, he set down the cup in front of him, closed his eyes, and felt the air fill his lungs while the sounds of existence filled his ears, and his eyelids lightened to feel the rays of a newly rising sun, a breeze caressing his cheek containing the salt lingering upon his tongue rising with the inhalation soon to be released from his chest.

He sensed no tension, nor heard murmur toward the sky above. Past a dove unpresent, he allowed himself to blend into the day and be at peace with the incapability of action about which he sat. When his tongue bade him notice, his eyes opened, and he sipped.

He stood. He stretched. He sat. He sipped. He closed his eyes once more. Light led to peace. Led to dissolution. Led to awareness outside and inside his body. Detachment from, and attention to, need. For water.

Eyes opened. Harrington passed him a fish. As Cain took a bite of the raw fish, he felt his thirst diminish gradually from the moisture of the fish's flesh. After two bites, he supplemented that moisture with a sip of water.

He finished the fish, stood, stretched, sat down again, and closed his eyes. He rested his hands in his lap; left palm face-up resting on right palm face-up. The tips of his thumbs very lightly touched. A few minutes of sitting, and a feeling like claustrophobia began to tighten within him. He was not hungry, but a little tired from blood flowing to stomach. His mouth was not arid, but thirst somehow lingered in thick mucus. He became acutely aware of how little space he occupied while surrounded by so many. He began to feel encroached upon. He investigated and stayed with that feeling until it felt, finally, unbearable. With an inward gasp of air, his eyes opened as they had many times that day.

Cain rose to his feet; stretched. While he stood with arms reaching past his head, he looked around at the others sharing this raft with him. Much meditation. Much consideration, conversation filling the air. Staring up toward the mountain peak, toward the heavens, seeking any small speck seeming to fly. A tension surrounded him surely while he arose; speculation. Past it all, he raised his own hands high into the sky as they would go, taking in a deep breath from the air around. Releasing next, lowering arms and letting out. Then, he stretched.

Then, he slept. He dreamed of meditating on a bird soaring high overhead.

When next he awoke, it was to darkness but for the stars lighting up the firmament. He quickly found water to sip upon, so as to combat the dryness that had accumulated in his mouth while he'd dozed.

Once awake: meditation. Contemplation. Conversation. Another sip, another sip, another sip. Life on the raft. He considered it had been some time since he and Casarta had last spoken, before falling asleep again.

❧ ❧ ❧

Seven days after the dove had first been sighted, it was discerned to have reappeared.

Casarta spoke without opening her eyes, "I see light. He's taking me to somewhere. Everyone, watch toward the sky around the ark." All heads and eyes did as Casarta had commanded. After moments of hushed anticipation, indeed, very high above them all, most could almost see a speck seem to issue forth from the larger object which they knew to be the ark. Casarta felt freedom throughout the entirety of her being again.

❧ ❧ ❧

It was the ever-present sensation of seeking. The desire not to return to the darkness. To find a place to land, independent of the confines that had kept her otherwise well-fed. She thirsted now for any safe landing in the light that would allow her to keep her freedom.

High in the air she began. Around and around she flew, lower and lower toward the ground, scanning the face of the Earth, still maintaining its crust of water. Scanning and searching for her liberation into all else existent. Round and around, lower and lower she flew, observing the reflection of the sun off the face of the water. Nearer and nearer the raft she came, passing it by after the course of her various rotations around the mountain. Round and around, but then, she felt its very small brain's exhilaration. *Could it be?*

She swooped down toward the distance. *Yes! Perhaps my foot will take hold here! Yes!* Gently she set herself down upon the very small branch sticking out through the water's face.

Grabbing hold between toes, she kept her wings open to the air while she tested her weight upon the dead tree's finger. The more she let it try to hold her, the more surely she sank toward the water out from which it poked. Frustrated, she grasped it in her claws and pulled it out of the water with her toward the mountain.

She flew, the small branch held tightly, until close to where the mountain met the water's edge. She landed. She rested, laying the branch upon the hardened clay. Then she jumped away from it. Closed her eyes and stood in the sunlight. She was warm. She was still. She was free.

She glanced over at the branch lying in the sun, dead and limp with the water bloating what of it still clung to itself. She closed her eyes again, enjoyed the light of the sun.

ꗥ ꗥ ꗥ

After a time, brief hours of two, three, or five, the breeze began to blow cooler. Casarta could hear them wonder where the dove had gone. She could feel its stomach desire the worm she had no hope of finding today. "Look to the sky," she spoke. From behind the mountain she rose up, careful with the brittle branch in her beak that had dried with the warmth from on high. The bird had had its own thoughts upon the initial plucking. *Perhaps if he sees there is little water left, he will release us to the freedom of fresh air while the rest dries.*

With the sun beginning to set in the sky, upward it flew in hopes of delivering this message to their would-be savior. They watched in gratitude while it flew off to bring its plea, not knowing what gingerly it carried upon the tip of its mouth. As the last rays of light disappeared below the horizon, the dove landed in Noah's outstretched hand.

He took the brittle olive branch from the dove and pulled it back inside. Stepping away from the window, he handed the branch to Ham. As he took the branch from Noah, it easily snapped with barely any pressure. He caught the two halves and examined them upon his upturned palm, "An olive branch. It's completely dead, but also brittle from being dried out."

"Do you think that means that the water has dried from the face of the Earth?" Japheth asked excitedly.

"I think that the fact the dove returned probably means that it didn't find a place to land. Though it could be that it just couldn't find any food. Let's give it one more week, then try again, and go from there."

They all nodded agreement, except for Noah, who just looked back and forth, and then fed the dove and returned it to the dark room when they had finished speaking. Though the dove did not understand their conversation, Casarta did. The dove merely understood that the kind hand had brought it food, but ultimately placed it again into the dark place it dreaded.

Casarta opened her eyes and looked about her at the others. "We can expect one more week without seeing another bird." They nodded acceptance, then returned themselves as before to the passing of time. They had become used to abiding the will of the fleeing moments of water.

Water. He drank sparingly, but still had his energy and moistness of mouth. In between sips, the flesh of fish eased the pain. The meditation made it manageable. He eagerly awaited the opening of the ark. The return of a clear, clean stream.

Peering over the side, mud became clearly discerned to the perceiving eye. "Casarta, would you be so kind as to manifest a dry pole, please? Maybe one the size of four men in length?"

She nodded. "Hold out your hands above you Luciferous."

He did as she commanded and there appeared, leaning between his grasp and the raft, a twenty-foot shaft of wood. He thanked her, and then dipped the stick into the muddy water below. The more substantial amount of the stick was untouched by the water.

He placed his hands below the center of the stick. "Would you mind, please, leaving only the bottom ten feet?" So it was, still very much of the staff untouched by water. Luciferous raised the stick out of the water, observing how much was actually wet. Not much more than half of the stick had apparently touched any sort of moisture. "If even five feet of water holds us afloat now, it is likely a high estimate."

Randolfy spoke up. "We will have to dispatch these logs soon, so that there is no sign of our raft when they leave their boat."

Luciferous responded, "Yes. We should find where the water finally settles to flow; a river. Casarta. You'll help us when the time comes?"

"I always have." She was happy her mind would be filled with activity in the days to come. Her sorrow still wanted to be explored. Keeping her mind from it was her greatest challenge daily. She was grateful between the return of the Earth's surface and the present moment, in which there was much to keep her focus engaged.

Daily, Luciferous measured the shallowness of the water. He started using the poles with which they set up tents on the raft when the water became shallow enough. Daily, the waters had receded more. About three feet up from the ground, beneath he spoke, "Soon we will need to depart from these logs that have sustained us. We are coming to the time we must stand upon our own two feet. Are you with me?"

"To what end, Luciferous? Will it not be as easy for Casarta to move these logs once we are fully grounded?"

"We just don't know how quickly they'll be out of the ark, or where they will go..."

"That dove will be released again in four days."

"Look over there." The thick, dead branch of an overturned oak had claimed its place in dry air, its root structure beginning to show through the murk some several feet away.

"He's right. It has plenty of places to land now." Casarta spoke up again, "And I know its longing for freedom. By the time it is released, it will not be a long wait for surviving worms. Besides that, I will feed it from my own fish rather than allow it to return to the darkness that twice now I have felt it crave the liberation from."

They stared at her while she spoke, contemplating the ramifications of intervening in the life of a bird.

"Have you considered the consequences of retaining it here prematurely, if it is inclined otherwise to return to the ark? What of the effects if they should open the boat early as a result? Discover us before we have time to set our post appropriately away from them?"

"It behooves us, then, to move these logs sooner than later, doesn't it? While you all await Our Common Creator's glory in the form of Its creation, I've had the opportunity to feel its confinement, and its ecstasy in freedom from it. We can accommodate easily enough your concerns for adam, but I won't allow you to make this creature suffer needlessly when otherwise you clearly have the opportunity to make its life in every sense better."

Luciferous heard Casarta's words penetrate and reverberate throughout his sense of self-reason. He walked through his brothers and sisters to the edge of the raft, sat at the raft's edge, his feet dangling in the muddy water, then lowered himself off the logs.

A sensation he had not felt for a very long time: feet on the ground with much, but not all, of his body submerged, head well into the air. "Three states at once! The embodiment of experiencing three disparate states simultaneously. Oh, that we are created of such substance that we are capable of appreciating such a thing!"

The others observed as Luciferous stood in the water covering the surface of the Earth, and it now barely rose to the level where most human beings would have the small recess they referred to as 'navel.' So observing, they began in kind to lower themselves to the water from the raft. Some even jumped straight in, overjoyed to be capable of sharing collectively in such an experience.

Watching with a mild confusion the exuberance with which the others thrilled to again be otherwise but dry, eventually Cain shrugged. The only conclusion he could come to was to join himself in the revelry at hand. He approached the side of the raft, lowered himself down much as Luciferous had done moments prior, and allowed himself to slip easily in. There was something very comforting in the feeling of engulfment by water, especially when it was chosen rather than forced. He also appreciated the feeling of toes squishing in mud. After so much time married to the raft, he leaned against the raft, hands upon it, then let himself experience immersion; drifting with the water. Sunlight above, warm water holding him in its embrace, he released himself to being the tanned and soaked piece of leather stripped off the face of humanity, fully submissive to The Whole of That Which Had Created

Him, which made clear by now, after more than a millennium and a half of experience, in no uncertain terms, that It would make use of him precisely as It saw fit to the exclusion of the will he had been offered when life had begun so very long ago. To the kiss of the sun's fire, and the power of the whole of life-giving, suffocating water, he released. The particles called "children of the Earth" would sustain him to whatever fate the marriage of sky and sea, in all their life-maintaining glory, had in store for him, even if it meant the freedom of choice in life once more.

Casarta stood. She had stretched her muscles over the months as she could. After the immobility of her leg for the sake of her bone's mending, her position well set for some time, she'd began the long process of flexing her sinews until they responded to her thought as well as did her external creations of mind. Several weeks prior, a climb up much of a mountain spoke the results of her constant efforts at keeping her mind focused when concentrating on augmenting the raft had become irrelevant. Through the eyes of the dove, she'd remembered her previously outstretched leg. Freedom was walking into the woods, away from her tribe whom she loved, away from the last vestiges of humanity clinging to existence for the sake of their own meager lives, on her own to scream from her soul every life silenced by the waters that had not been allowed to live to the point of a breath in their lungs, let alone making of the lives of others something better than the common horror they all had come to share. Freedom meant release from the past to the question of the future. Upon landing on Noah's hand, and opening her own eyes, freedom meant keeping her ankle all the more limber to walk her to her process of return. For all her journey, awaking pinned beneath destruction's wave, holding together all her tribe, and feeling the longing for the rebirth of the world to be free, she spoke on behalf of the freedom of that life. All those around her took to the water in acquiescence of her pleas. Moved to what must come next at the behest of her word, she stood.

She stood, then took one step forward. Slowly she made her way to the edge of the raft, and then sat down, dangling her bare feet in the warm, shallow water, watching the entirety of her tribe wade to the strength of her voice. Beside her, Cain leaned against the raft, obviously content in the sunlight. To her other side was a rope holding together logs, a complex knot securing their temporary home. Cain, severely weakened by malnourishment and dehydration, nonetheless looked fully at peace. She hadn't the heart to dissuade his bliss. She thought to the others that they should take a moment in gratitude, and then begin to loosen the other side. They took their moment, and then waded around the raft. As they made their way over, so too did she rise once again to the tops of her legs and carefully feel the stretching of her healed ligaments over to the other side to watch their progress. Together, they all began to unbind. They had furiously tied tree trunks in groups of threes months ago, when it was all about to begin. Now, they worked the knots loose slowly, with the painful struggle of the tips of their fingers.

Randolfy had an idea. He climbed onto the raft and searched the large pots holding the last of the drinkable water. He found one that was empty. He dragged it to a far corner of the raft and smashed it against the hard wood. He took a broken piece, walked to a rope, and attempted sawing it with the shard. Sure enough, the strands were cut through with comparatively little effort. He invited the others to take tools, and before long many had a broken piece of pottery in their hands. When the pot had shattered, Cain's eyes had snapped open abruptly. He watched their work attentively from the other side, where he stood in the water's warmth.

Strand by strand snapped. Log by log fell away from the rest, floating free from immediate purpose. As it disbanded, Casarta scooted backwards from the edge, continuing to stretch her legs while she watched the fairly quick progress they were making. A quarter of the way through freeing its binds, Hoflan bade them all stop for a moment before turning to Casarta. "Casarta, this water does not flow. Will it not look suspicious when finally the waters dry from the surface of the earth, and all these logs and ropes have such close proximity?"

"The ropes are easily enough thought away as drifting from what has been destroyed. By the time the waters are gone, they'll be half-buried anyway. But as to the logs themselves..." As her voice fell away, her eyes closed. Suddenly seven hippopotamuses appeared on the side of one log, grabbed it in their mouths, and began to push it away from the raft. Those in the water waded and swam out of their path as quickly as they could while the hippos began to carry the log from them. Then another seven appeared at another log. Again, everyone scattered. This time everyone made their way to the side of what hadn't begun to be untied from the raft. Sure enough, shortly after they'd finished regrouping, another pack suddenly appeared at the side of each shorn tree trunk not still tied to the greater whole. In unison they took the disbanded quarter of raft in the same direction, out of sight once the enormity of spectacle had set in. Hippos out of view, they all turned to Casarta.

"A hundred miles away. I'll have plenty of time later to find a steady stream to deposit them, if it is still necessary. When water flows again, it will be easy to make right anything still amiss."

Hoflan nodded, shaken by the awesome force created via Casarta's mind in response. He walked around to the other edge of the raft and began again sawing at a rope. The others silently followed suit. Three by three, the logs broke free into the last lingering remnants of the flood.

❧ ❧ ❧

Three large trunks remained floating upon the shallow water in unity. Upon them leaned Cain, stood Casarta, and sat what supplies had withstood the flood and time, prominent among the rest being the last of the water tolerably free of salt. The others, much as Cain, looked up at Casarta in anticipation. Slowly they all felt themselves begin to rise. Most naturally inclined to their knees as the rest maintained their balance upright upon their feet. The water fell away to reveal a new raft. The middle three trunks arose proportionately while the raft emerged from out, and finally atop, the water. Then, it lowered down to rest once they were all out of the water again; the three tied trunks raised just a step above Casarta's creation.

"We have done this before, but this time we will not suffer as we did. Here is a refuge for others who need it when I sleep. There is mercy with feet touching ground and heads all well above water. Soon water will bring us no annoyance, but now, where once we were tortured and drowned, we will be at worst discomforted as so quickly beyond that discomfort, the joy of the world will be returned to us once more."

Hearing her words, feeling the solidity of her creation beneath them, they could not help but to be filled with gratitude. They watched while she sat and closed her eyes. They knew they now had several hours to rest, and that soon it would be her turn to rest. She knew it would be a kindness in the coming time to find slumber during the day. They all took solace in recognizing ever-lowering levels of water, and that dry land would soon utterly negate an old, albeit comparatively luxurious, practice.

Later that evening, when she changed her position to supine, wearily they entered the water tired, but ready for their midnight wade. All, that is, save for Cain, who was allowed to continue to rest upon the unimagined logs, not far from where Casarta took *her* slumber. As grateful as they were not to be overcome by the capricious whims of waves, so much more was their gratitude to save Cain more suffering than even still they knew he must endure.

Chapter 63

In her mind's eye, light suddenly permeated. On the cusp of imminent freedom, she took flight. Down below, she knew she was there, she knew she could find a certain, safe place to land. Likewise, she knew the genuine impulse of the bird she embodied. With gratitude in her own heart for the sacrifice her tribe had made in honor of freedom and the sanctity of life, all life, that they all served supremely, she also felt quickly within the entirety of her being the exuberant joy this dove experienced, now setting sight on a safe place to land far away from the help of human-shaped hands. Though a water-logged, rotting half of a tree trunk protruding from the water, it would be a far kinder home while she would wait to detect the movement of a small fish.

Her awareness raced upward toward Noah, waiting by a window, sad, resigned. Casarta had no wish to continue to touch his mind. She returned back to the dove, happy. So filled with joy to be, after so very long, free.

She sat there for a moment, allowing the sun's light inside as well as out to wash over and through her. Then she opened her eyes to the raft she kept create for her people. Knowing little from far further a distance than she had seen by, she almost sang in the telling of what had come to pass.

Shortly after Casarta fell asleep, Cain slowly walked the few feet to the three pots still upright toward the center of the three logs still held together. Gazing within, two looked to be completely empty. The third had, apparently, little to offer. He sighed and dipped his dish into the remaining vessel, retrieving a mostly-full cup. As he sipped the sweet saltiness, he savored the elusive moisture, knowing that soon he would be at the mercy of his weakened body. As he sipped, grateful for what he had, he prayed for the fatigue to overcome him quickly and lend itself to numbness. As thoughts of the pain set in, he remembered his brother and considered his future to be a small price to pay.

Believing he could stretch his water out another two days, he rested.

❧ ❧ ❧

So, he struggled with his thirst. In and out of sleep, craving the taste of moisture to his lips and upon his tongue. In and out of consciousness, in between he would drag himself to the brief, salty tastes remaining of what was still left before giving deference once more to his fatigue.

Finally, inevitably, the small bit of something resembling fresh water ran out. All that remained was the rapidly drying bottom of a large clay pot, and a rapidly dehydrating Cain. He crawled back down to where he had grown accustomed to lying, closed his eyes, and anticipated the tortures of being without water to slowly rip through his flesh.

He opened his eyes again, the smiling face of Darius hovering several feet above him. "We have been watching your water supply. No need to speak, I've become rather good at hearing thoughts clearly if you direct them at me. You couldn't be suffering too much yet. It can't have been more than a few hours by now..."

Cain thought in response: *Just tired, so far. You all have been without water for months now. How are you able to have energy, let alone not be crippled by pain?*

"The meditating helps. Really we're constantly in pain, but between fresh fish and fresh seaweed, we at least maintain enough moisture to subsist adequately."

Cain considered momentarily: *My friend, are there still fish?*

"Fortunately, there seems to be no shortage there."

Please bring me one.

Darius returned a few moments later, fish in hand, headless, gutless and partially deboned. "I did the best I could to clean and get rid of the bones from this thing with one of those broken bits of pot. Hope it's to your liking."

Cain pushed himself up to a sit before taking the small fish from Darius' hand. He pushed his lips to the fish's tender flesh, feeling the moisture against his dryness. Immediately he indulged his instinct to lap at it with his tongue as though to drink it into himself rather than devour. His teeth felt slivers of meat separate into mouth, but his tongue searched out most the cause of moisture while he found himself automatically sucking more than chewing. It was then the thought rose to his head. Through half-dried tongue he gasped the words to Darius to accentuate the urgency of the fulfillment of his thought. "Darius, can you bring me... a full fish with a head, please?"

Seeing Cain with the lightly-gnawed piece of fish in his hand, Darius had an unpleasant sense of where this would lead. Darius considered that it was, after all, where they had all found to wet their throats in desperation, and he took it as his solemn duty to bring to Cain what he requested, having concluded thus all on his own. Along with the whole fish, Darius offered also a shard of clay previously broken from a pot, an apt tool for the job at hand.

Cain hesitated when he accepted fish and shard. He stared down at the fish weakly wriggling in his hand, gasping at the gills, eyes bulging at his. He considered his thirst not yet severe enough to warrant it. Darius' voice entered his ear. "And in a couple of hours you will feel drier, cracking in the throat, and the fish will be in your hand once more. There is no joy to be found here. Merely, when the pain is great enough, you now know how to suffer otherwise through it. There is no rush. Wait until you are ready."

Cain closed his eyes, putting down fish and clay a few inches in front of him on what remained of the raft. Not an hour passed before he opened his eyes again, took clay, and pressed it hard down upon the fish's neck. What liquid within didn't fall quickly to the wood, he turned swiftly up into his throat. Immediately he was soothed. He gasped in gratitude as the blood of the fish absorbed near instantaneously into his over-dried body. He angled his gaze up to Darius, who still watched over him. "Thank you, my friend."

Darius nodded. "I will bring you three more. They should serve you for the day." Darius turned toward the other side of the raft, where a pile of fish gently flopped close to its edge. Toward the other end of the tree trunks upon which Cain recovered himself sat Casarta, cross-legged, close-eyed, obviously sustaining them all mostly dry atop the appended greater raft.

"Are not the waters too shallow now that we can accumulate so much food?"

"She's not only maintaining the integrity of a dry place for us to rest and enjoy better during the day. She's searched out schools and big fishes, and basically herds them straight to us with bigger fishes, dolphins, and now even large, fish-like things of her mind's creation, with baskets for mouths, as she sees fit. She says soon the muddy water around us will be too shallow to herd the fish; that soon the basket-mouths will be given wings upon which to fly from where the water will remain deep. When rain returns, we will drink from rivers. Until then, when harvest returns, she will keep us alive with the fish who are so many, until the rabbits make quick work of copulating. And, if God sees such a mercy fit, perhaps rather than rabbit blood, It will instead send masturbating angels to drink from!"

Cain could swear the corner of Darius' eye actually sparkled as he spoke. He was grateful he hadn't the energy to produce the facial expressions he was certain he wouldn't be able to prevent, had he been less fatigued. "Should we be given to drink water again, mercy has been done unto us indeed." Cain contemplated the poetry of the punishment of having to drink blood as the price of taking it from his brother a millennium and a half prior. Still worn, but with his throat well soothed, he lay back, shut his eyes, and prayed implicitly he would not dream of blood while he slept.

Chapter 64

Leaning up against the ark sat Honoth and Jawrldrook. "They sure did leave a lot of seaweed."

"A good thing they did."

"Yes, it is good we have something to eat."

"Theeisel, Logosel," Jawrldrook hesitated, "a cup of water, please."

Honoth sighed. "Fill mine too, please."

"As we serve above, so too is our joy to serve you!"

Without urgency, Jawrldrook and Honoth received their cups. Both sipped a bit of their water, glanced over at each other, then put their half-filled cups to the side. They folded their legs, closed their eyes, and let what was wash through their perceptions as their time unmoved flowed on.

☙ ☙ ☙

Since the water had receded to ankle-high, they had taken to allowing themselves to nod off while sitting cross-legged at night. They leaned against each other's backs so that there was no fear of waking up wet from falling forward during the night. During the day, the sun baked them into a thin layer of coagulating mud as the water all but evaporated off.

Casarta had filled two large clay pots with water with the help of her large-mouthed flying fish. Then she filled those pots with fish so that Cain would not thirst, and excess fish would not be wasted when she brought them piles of fish daily. They all looked forward to onions, figs, and beans as they quelled thirst and hunger only so far as necessity called them.

Two weeks later, the Earth was damp, but dryness was imminent. Instead of extending a raft off the three large logs, now Casarta had but to fathom a dry floor of wood. She had discerned where water had leveled to sea, and a supply of fish was maintained regularly.

While the sun dried away the waters, Casarta listened to the minds within the ark: *Let me look, Dad. Yes. It looks almost all dry. Let us give it another three weeks for the earth to harden.* Casarta opened her eyes.

"In three weeks, they will be opening the door of the ark."

Luciferous spoke in response. "The day after tomorrow, the ground surrounding us will be fully hard enough that the heavy pots will not sink, nor will our feet become stuck in clay. Casarta, that would be a good time to move the last of the tree trunks, yes?"

Casarta nodded affirmatively.

Two days later, after everyone had arisen from slumber, seven rhinoceroses appeared. They separated off and began rolling one of the trunks away from the rising sun. Immediately, seven more rhinoceroses appeared and did the same, following after the other seven. Still another seven appeared, twenty-one rhinos making their way away from the tribe.

"Where are they taking them?"

"Where there is flowing water," Casarta answered Randolfy.

There they stood. A few pots filled with salt water and fish. A few empty pots besides. Many blankets. A few remaining poles. Some rope. Some pottery shards for cutting.

"If they see any of it after we are gone, they will simply think it is some remains from those who were murdered by God in the flood. They won't think much deeper than that; they're not that smart. Any fish flesh will be eaten by the insects soon set free from the ark once we dump out the water before leaving, after the ark's door has been opened." Casarta answered as though they had asked aloud the questions many of them were contemplating regarding what Noah's family might think about any remains they'd find once the site had been abandoned, and whether or not to carry the bigger pots away with them.

All looked up at Casarta, not knowing quite what to say.

Casarta responded again. "It may not be a kind thing to utter, but it is an accurate assessment. Noah's family were not chosen for their overwhelming intelligence, and their intelligence does pertain directly to your mutual concerns."

Considering that nothing productive could be created from arguing the point with Casarta, Luciferous quickly turned to his tribe after his pause of thought. "Casarta clearly has considered the finer points of what is soon to come. All the same, I suggest breaking apart the heavier vessels we won't want to carry with us when the moment comes to retreat and maintain our distance from them." Dazed by Casarta's assertions, they nodded agreement nonetheless with Luciferous' detail on how best to proceed. Simultaneously, Luciferous considered the conversation he'd had with Casarta long ago, and took strongly into account how her anger must still weigh upon her mind. He breathed in gratitude that no one thought to argue with her the intrinsic good and value of humanity.

Besides the initial awkwardness of navigating Casarta's passive frustrations, something new and exciting was being felt by all of them. Now every one of them had an acuity of awareness that whether in three minutes, or three weeks, the door of the ark was about to open. They were soon to retreat to other grounds, making way for the family on board to have space for *their* world—but more than that, the rebirth of life into created existence was imminent. As though a bolt of lightning flowed through them and paused at its apex, so was the feeling of anticipating the fall of the door that would precipitate all the actions of their existences thereafter.

❧❧❧

They reveled at the feel of dry, hard dirt beneath their folded legs. They reveled at the feel of standing, walking, *running* without getting wet. They passed the time in joy that soon the purpose of their existence would have the opportunity for fulfillment again.

Meanwhile, Casarta, while relieved not to have to expend her thoughts on the maintenance of her people's physical comforts, simultaneously was deeply frustrated by having nothing with which to occupy her mind between the present moment and the time in which she would be free to set off and explore the churning depths of her inner-most revulsion at all she had witnessed. She would wake up from nightmares of being trapped in a clear box, upside down, dangling from one foot while dead bodies floated by all around her, promptly sitting up and opening her mind to fill with the sound of the breeze and the conversations or thoughts of her companions; the solidity of the ground beneath her; the entrance of the air within her. Perception of the present moment was ever the only respite from everything she did not want in her head.

When not in meditation, she would seek conversation in the hopes of finding a preoccupation to help her not fall automatically to her inclinations toward utter despondence and fury. Trying to navigate herself in the limited form at her disposal, she kept her self-processing mostly to Luciferous, her mother, her father, or Cain, so as not to disquiet the entirety of the tribe to no productive end. "You took the life of your brother and know what that feels like. But *It* just took every life but for that boat, you, and us. And they're revering It still. As though It's a good thing!"

"There was no word for rape before your life's conception, Casarta. Parents with the purest of hearts were immediately broken by their humanity through acts deadliest to our innermost core. We have no choice but to live off death in some measure. And there were good people in my town, I know without pause of consideration. However, if the majority carry a burden such as I, the knowledge of harm to one's family, close blood, let alone distant blood, all ultimately from the same marrow, She did them a service by ending the misery in them that I have borne for more than a millennium and a half. What mercy to see the eyes of death, and yet know my pain still? Though beings of service, who among you would not wish to return home? Even you, now, Casarta, are driven chiefly by your desire to see your own pain pass."

"Should my life be so long as yours, Cain, I may see reason to murder. But where I stand now on the other side of life lost, and before the wisdom of life reborn sheds the possibility of new light, I am at a loss to see the wisdom of predetermined annihilation where wisdom otherwise could be planted by Her gentle, intangible hand on initially well-designed brains. Why go through all this to end it? To start over with traumatized, poorly-made people, all with the foresight it would be here thus? It doesn't add well!"

"I can't fault you your anger. You might ask your parents, who I think once asked something similar."

Promptly she sat down to meditation on the sounds surrounding her, and the feeling welling up that she knew too well would turn to images of rage if she did not bring her mind to a fullness of the present.

"We are not given to know the whole of Its intent, probably until at least we fulfill our self-imposed mission and join into unity once more, daughter." Casarta had seen wisdom in Cain's advice. Antagnous continued, "What we do get to know is that just as certainly as Adam and Eve were created to eat from the fruit of the tree of knowledge of good and evil, so too were we. Before declaring Light existent, It knew already we would choose once knowing there could be choice, and all it entailed. Just as It knew that giving us all the same knowledge, the other angels would choose otherwise. This was not a punishment. This was the inevitable consequence of making the choice we did. And soon, also the consequence will be to seek serving them again, beyond this suffering our choice entailed."

"But you were not given warning the pain you would suffer; the torment of them you would watch firsthand making that choice!"

"No, but from our ignorance, the first choice we made was questioning Her choice. All *we* knew was from watching them eat from knowledge. From that alone we made a choice: that we could ask a question. So, He offered us further insight by allowing us to make ourselves in *their* image, the only way we could understand this creation genuinely; the only way we could know what they really are, let alone find a way to help them. And in that moment, all of us, every one, even those who hadn't initially questioned what was done to Adam, mankind, and Eve, living, were given no choice but to make a choice. We chose to serve Its creation. Those who did not eat chose to serve It directly. But we were all created only to serve It one way or another; there was never choice in that. And with our choice came that choice's consequences, also what *we* chose. Having eaten the fruit of that particular tree, we know now what we did not know then. What we still do not know, yet, is the feeling of returning to our self, and perhaps then once more serving It as we did before, but with the knowledge of having been as we are now. So, to me, the future looks well that our opportunity awaits past what has been. What I know is that unpleasantness is behind, and together, we will strive to bring something better for it to them."

"You may have been born only to serve, but that is a choice I *can* make!"

"Perhaps," her mother smiled down upon her, "but remember, It too knew of *your* existence and what *you* would bring to Its creation before It spoke the light into being."

The sentiment penetrated Casarta as deeply beautiful, while simultaneously she conceptualized a sort of entrapment that made her prone to anger. Immediately she sat down and watched emotion flow within her, breath enter her lungs, and the cool breeze touch her neck. She let what was fill her.

❧ ❧ ❧

"Your mother speaks it as well as I could, Casarta," Lousitous began his response to his daughter. "Cain, who has more claim to the suffering of creation than any of us, speaks forgiveness and gratitude. As to the rest of us, we chose the form of service we seek now only to become adept at. You will not find one here who will encourage your swell of concept based on unprocessed emotional conviction. The time you yearn for on your own, I think, is wise."

"I'll not have you starving, Father."

"And for that, we are all grateful. But when the moment does come that you can dig into this darkness you carry, digging deeply enough, we all have experienced the only genuine conclusion you can come to. And I'll await your return just as surely as for the sake of your self, I now await your departure."

Casarta looked warmly up at her father's face. While in her state she couldn't imagine reconciling her mind with their Common Creator, the thought of her path first having to lead her into her own darkness rang true. The fact was, being left alone with her anger had thoroughly been her desire for months, but it was having it uttered aloud by another that offered her even a nod to peace with her current inability to wallow; the fullness of the picture of pain her mind wished to paint being the perfect terror she had literally awoken to find herself drowning in. She bowed very slightly to the wisdom of her father's words, sat, and enjoyed the feel of stillness surrounding her, light chatter floating around and by her ears, and the air finding its way to filling her lungs before being released back out again.

Casarta sat down beside Gendlebleth. "Casarta! I am certain we will be thanking you for millennia to come, but thank you so for saving us and seeing us through the worst calamity of adam we can imagine witnessing, so personally we have been afflicted by it ourselves. There are no words for the gratitude that swells within to have your company so directly."

"It is no small flattery you give me, dear uncle amongst our tribe. While you humble me with your praise, however, you also bring to the sight of my mind what so often is at its forefront. You speak of the horror and abject torture we all simultaneously experienced as if it too were an honor to suffer. How can you reconcile immeasurable pain with a persistence toward joy, after observing That which you held yourself with no desire but service to decimate Its own creation at the cost of those surviving being spared no nightmare whatsoever, and even denied the mercy given all others besides: death?"

"Niece, do I call you now? As apt a title as any, and again a title filling me with honor to utter it. My joy, simply put, comes in you, as you were the redemption amidst nightmare otherwise so complete. And even still, in you, born of first calamities, *is* the mercy we were given. After that, the waters diminishing daily, the seed that is that ark, and the unknown life that must spring accordingly is mercy besides. I think our only regret, you who saved us all, is the pain you have been made to suffer that you, amongst us all who did choose to witness these consequences, did not choose."

"I think, Uncle, neither too did these humans."

"I remember, once, Luciferous having a similar conversation with Creator Undifferentiated Absolute."

"And now they are all gone, Gendlebleth!"

"Not all, beautiful child." Gendlebleth pointed toward the mountain's top.

"Not the same! Not what was..."

"The promise of Its creation in all its glory. One seed, or one garden, they are at one point the same. And that seed—all you have seen is how He created that seed, there. That is the foolishness of our choice; we did not know the seed that She had created there already. The Hand whose same movement created us as well. I cannot fault your impulse, nor am I here to tell you we do not seek union with our self and release from this place. But to be created in fullness of perception like them of Her creation in its fullness, for us; yes, it is an honor for which ultimately we *are* grateful."

Casarta felt her face grow redder at her good friend's words.

"Just as we give glory for the flood which has created that seed, Its creation of which still we are yet to be aware, so too from the fullness of our gratitude that we were not made to suffer as we would have been without your presence, so too do we give Glory to It for you."

"You, who have struggled within as though you are Cain yourself, do not see all we, *they* have suffered by Its hand as blasphemous?" She did all she could to temper the emotion welling within.

"By Its grace, even that disgrace of my own mouth finds its place. I have no doubt I have not seen my last thousand years of suffering. Nor have I doubt that after it all, I will be returned to my other half. It creates Its interior as it does. I complete my intention ultimately as I do. The difference between us is my action in order to determine fully by consequence to where ultimately I must succeed, for I exist at all as I am."

"Then what's the point of your existence, if it's already known before you begin?"

"Them. Who otherwise would not be served unto where they will be. I can try forever. They are unique unto time."

"A lot fewer of them these days."

"And as they've never been before."

Casarta sat down. Perception filled her as drop by drop, she emptied of her anger.

"You've known all along you have to be alone with yourself for a time, Casarta. We all believe in an inevitable conclusion to your pain, just as we all wish no longer to see you in pain. Until you can allow yourself to experience it, however, even if we are right, you'll have no way to come to that conclusion."

"So I meditate and strictly focus my thoughts, Cain."

"You know there's not a one of us ungrateful that you've saved us from a worse fate, right?"

"If I cannot save the dead, the least I can do is not leave the perpetually living for dead."

"Thus our lives speak gratitude."

Cain bowed his head to Casarta. Casarta bowed in response to him. Together they sat, closed their eyes, and meditated. Together they envisioned the fulfilling of light.

❧ ❧ ❧

At the far end of the world, the angels founds themselves flying mutually, keeping perfectly still in each other, all arriving together in the same place at the same time. They shook, quivered, and joyously ached as they arrived and awaited word from on high. Slowly, drop by drop, water fell to the sea below while they focused intently upon their stillness; their fullness in each other, and what within *was* released as simultaneously they did not motion, save for the gentle, persistent fluttering of their wings.

Upon arrival, upon stillness, they heard The Voice. "Prepare yourselves now. Together, all at once, it will be yours to penetrate deeper, push, and hold together. Three. Two..."

Chapter 65

Noah was six hundred and one years old. The year was new. No rain could be heard for months. Not even a breeze whispered to any seeking to hear. Jawrldrook and Honoth were quietly sipping at their cups of water when a sound came to Jawrldrook's ear. "Hey. Honoth. Do you hear that?"

"Hear what?"

"Listen."

"It sounds like creaking."

"Maybe a gust of wind upon a loose board?"

Suddenly a shadow began to fall over them. The creak became loud. They became motionless as they were suddenly enveloped in darkness. A moment or two later, a deafening THUD, and their vision became fully impaired.

While they continued to sip from their cups, a pair of angels lying perfectly still in each other beside them, just as they were before the ramp had fallen, Honoth and Jawrldrook thought to each other, *Well, time to get back to work.*

❧❧❧

Almost two months later, Jawrldrook and Honoth heard a sound upon their "ceiling." First a footstep. Then, another. A pair of footsteps. Multiple footsteps. Faster, multiple footsteps. Like the beginning of the pattering of rain above their heads. Then, a stampede of a multitude stomping quickly over them. A rush into the sky as the light of the high sun dimmed by the whoosh of flapping; thunderous beasts continuing too close a parade.

⁂

Casarta looked through many eyes. She felt the light fill her mind before she looked to see. The feeling of sudden liberty. A peace of waiting the last few moments in fresh light. The exhilaration of starting into a run, a skip, a gallop into the fresh air unbreathed for over a year. In the midst of it all, humans.

She turned her attention to feel the freedom of a thousand birds flying, unrestrained simultaneously. Again her attention found itself staring at Noah and his family. Instead of concurrent release, she found herselves eyeballing a mound of seeds in the middle of the place Noah and his family were standing around. One by one, the birds would take a seed or two into their beaks before flying off into the world. Casarta felt the rush of freedom as they arose into the blue, singularly and in small groups, each ever so slightly weighted by the responsibility of carrying the fate of land-based vegetation, and thereby the food supply of those above water, as they made their way otherwise uninhibited. When each fulfilled their task of planting a seed, then real freedom set in. Casarta detected in some instances very long journeys to their true liberation.

Casarta also marveled that a pelican could carry a koala, as they made sure native creatures returned to their true homes safely.

⁂

Tens of thousands of seeds retrieved, Casarta eventually felt the ecstasy of thousands of wings flying off in different directions as ever more filled the skies. Tigers, lions, and panthers of all types running free among drowned, knocked-down, and then dried forests. But freedom it was, into light, with infinite dirt beneath their paws upon which to play. Rabbits by the hundreds being chased by wolves. Deer, zebras, horses' hooves bounding over boards to arrive into the horizon. Giraffes stretching toward the sun. Sloths, anteaters, and snails making trails at their own pace. Kangaroos hopping. Polar bears tumbling. Hippos rampaging. Squirrels, and lemurs, and gerbils, and boar, and spiders, and gibbons, and mantises, and penguins, and lizards, and snakes, and platypi. Surging through her, top to bottom, the liberation of the world. Waves of release. The ecstasy of birth from out the seed. Until light. Only light. Waves upon waves of light. As through tens of thousands of eyes rushing in unison from out of darkness within which they had been stored, into the view of infinite creation upon space enough to roam, filling their optic nerves that had starved for oh-so-very-long. Without conscious volition, a smile extended to the ends of her face.

All around her close-eyed, sitting form, stood the angels who had tasted the fruit, and Cain, staring toward the mountaintop in awe. The birds bursting forth in droves flying out from the mountain's top in every direction, blotting out the sun before light shined forth after them once more. Dust rising in a growing line as they all anticipated what soon would be much larger to meet them, gently rising into the air toward the top of the mountain, slowly spiraling around it. Dust seeming to rise higher as it rounded lower. Dark forms within seeming present. Sudden breaks as the dust discontinued its line and began to rise in a ring expanding toward them. It appeared to rise higher as it stretched further. Anticipating eyes followed moving forms down the mountain for a very long time while they wondered what would run past whence reaching the bottom. They marveled as the loop grew thicker before thinning out finally as the last of the animals took their places behind the first of the animals, and the spreading loop began to thin and dissipate where it ceased to be created.

About an hour after the first traces of dust could be discerned around the mountain, actual animal shapes came almost into focus. A blurred stampede of black, gray, brown, orange, and yellow, shrouded in dust, and moving nearer and nearer, bigger and bigger. Many feet coming to visit, albeit momentarily. Until not a ring, a line. A row of dust and feet and forms. Minutes away. And there before it all, the brethren of enfleshed servants of God, and Cain.

As the rush of feet, the thunder of stampede, and the dust of the ground rose into the air, Cain began to feel a very natural uneasiness inside himself grow. As he looked around at the blissful, smiling faces anticipating the return of all life with joy in their hearts, Cain couldn't help but become acutely aware of his material self. Though drowned and almost twice as old as the longest-living man, the idea of being stomped upon by two thousand different animals held little appeal to his concept of body, despite being fairly certain that still, at this point in time, he would not die.

Closer and closer they came. Dust, thunder, form. Until, at last, confluence was imminent. The first of all creatures to reach them, a squirrel. It ran between their legs, over stones, past them finally, and away. Following not so far behind it, a fox.

Much like the squirrel, the fox dove between and around legs. Unlike the squirrel, a gazelle was close behind. As was a lion, a cricket, a zebra, a rabbit, a kangaroo, a platypus, a gorilla, and an armadillo. The crowd began to scatter in movement in an attempt to let the creatures by. A toad, an ostrich, a bonobo, an elephant, some beetles, a zebra, a chicken. Frantic feet falling. And, much as he'd feared, there Cain stood watching a leopard charging right toward him. He began to flinch, and then forced his eyes to stay open; if it was going to try to eat him, he could at least attempt to wrestle it away. Up went his hands to protect himself as the leopard leapt into the air. Then, down came its front paws, down came its hind paws, about a foot away from Cain's head. Floating in mid-air while it continued up over Cain's head, and finally behind him and on the ground again.

Cain stared confusedly at the stampede still charging toward him. "Well, you didn't think I would let them hurt you, did you?" Casarta walked toward where Cain stood from a few feet away.

"What?"

"There's a big rock surrounding us right now." Casarta arrived by Cain's side, "I made it invisible from your perspective, so that you could watch their liberation. To them, however, it's a perfectly solid, very large rock." A gazelle, a llama, and an aardvark ran in succession around the place Cain and Casarta stood.

Cain looked into Casarta's eyes. "Thank you." Then he turned again to watch the tide freed from the boat, by her side.

ᘓᘓᘓ

Giraffe, capybara, groundhog, scorpion, mongoose, wallaby. One after the other, until a slow-settling dust cloud was all that remained. And then, all heads turned around to watch them run off, chasing, running from, enjoying liberation, into the distance.

"But what about the ones that only eat plants?"

"There should be more than enough seaweed in the waters until the harvest comes..."

Chapter 66

"ONE!"

At the word, in unison, they all pushed into each other as deeply as their common anatomy would allow. Collectively, involuntarily, a loud groan emitted from them all, vibrating their immediate surroundings at the exact same frequency, impacting a pattern of very small ripples woven into the concave shape formed in the sea below.

"Ommmmmmm…"

And when they could hold together no longer, collectively, release. The newly-receded ocean below rose half a foot. From their exhausted and wholly satisfied genitalia poured forth all at once, all colors of the Light's spectrum as a fine mist covered over the whole of the Earth. Again in unison, though now all separate, they slowly rose toward the light above.

So very slowly they rose, as so very slowly the very light mist made its way to coalesce on the other side of the world, carrying the colors of the angels with it.

⋯⋯⋯

Save for a small variety of animals Noah and his family would personally keep for food, the whole of the ark had been vacated by their saved guests. The rush having passed, Noah and his family stepped out into the calm and sunlight, down the ramp, and onto dry land. Looking about at the desolation all around, Noah remembered his father and mother, and sighed. "I'm hungry."

Ham gazed around. There were dead trees, but not many here at the top of the mountain. He considered the firewood within the ark that remained. He enlisted his brothers to build a fire outside of the ark. Quickly they chose a hoofed beast to slaughter, made quick work butchering out a steak, and roasted it over the flames for their father. Seared, fresh flesh at the ready, Noah was sated while his sons finished butchering the animal properly for their own meals, as well as those of their wives and mother. When at last they put their own cuts over the fire, the air was filled with a scent that pleased them all. As the scent filled the air, so too a light mist began to creep slowly up the mountain.

Shortly after they had all eaten, they found that they were surrounded by a very thin layer of condensation. The vapor was all around them and slowly moving to cover also over them. Feeling the very light spreckles of moist light kissing their faces, they saw a spectacle they'd never seen before: Rainbows crossed in every direction between them and the sight of the sun. Suddenly, throughout all their ears, they heard a voice speaking clearly: "Never again will WATER blot out all life on this planet." And then the voice was gone, leaving just the now-large, single rainbow overhead. Noah nodded without raising his sight from the view of the ground. "Thank you, Metatron." Shortly thereafter, the rainbow began to fade away and the mists receded from them, leaving pure sunlight once more.

ᔔ ᔔ ᔔ

After the dust had settled, a light layer of mist fell around them. Looking up toward the mountain's top, a rainbow spread across the sky and filled their common view.

"God spoke to that dimwit, but not to us? Couldn't even bother warning us to build our own raft?"

"Of course not, Casarta," Luciferous responded to the girl, eyes unremoved from the full breadth of color above. "If ever we are to succeed, we must know the fullness of the pain of their existence, which they in turn must learn to overcome if ever they are able again to plant for themselves the garden of The Most Holy Eminence Existence Itself."

Though impressed by the beauty surrounding them from above, Casarta considered how quickly the harvest would come that she could spend a few moments alone. She gave due reverence to Luciferous' words, respecting him and his chosen servitude, but simultaneously felt the urge to vomit upon considering the dynamic of creator and created alike. She held her tongue and prayed the next several months would bring fast fruits. Moments later, seed rained down into soil from birds passing by. Mist departed, and the sky returned to blue.

༺ ༻ ༺ ༻ ༺ ༻

On the other side of the world, they fell. As from the fullness of their physical existence they'd found the capability of the experience of fatigue, they descended down to the ground without awareness of bodily sensation as hard they crashed, all together, upon earth, sea, and each other. Merely, they knew satisfaction as they had not known before their bodies were capable, rest coming upon them unbridled by thought of any measure or sort.

Falling into deep, blissful repose, the last of the rainbows left their genitalia, and the sky became clear all the world over.

Chapter 67

Noah's sons gathered up the remaining seeds not taken by the birds to regrow the rest of the world. Together they loaded up their cattle with whatever tools and possessions they could, and together as a family, they descended the mountain. Ham took his father by the hand. Tranzaiel took Noah's other hand. Between the two, he was walked downward while he saw the world numbly from behind his eyes.

At the bottom, dead dry wood, with very little good for building. But the sky was clear, and the wind blew warm. An uninterrupted slumber later, as the sun rose, after slaughtering a goat and preparing enough food to last until the following day, Ham, Shem, and Japheth took several donkeys up the mountain back to where the ark sat, and set themselves to taking from it wood to build a new dwelling. Returning the next day, the boys knew it would take much workable lumber to create shelter. They knew it would take many journeys up and down the mountain, and a great deal of labor. They were greeted at their return by newly hatched chicks, and their father staring at the ground beside the chirping baby chickens.

Shem walked to his father and placed his hand to his shoulder.

"They're gone, Shem. Daddy, but now Mommy. She was supposed to be on the fun ride too, Shem. But Mommy's gone. And the fun ride, it wasn't fun." Noah began sobbing, wetting the ground with his freely flowing tears. Beside him, Ham's wife was spreading the seed put aside to feed the fowl.

Shem saw the wet earth so close to where the chicks ate. He bent down and picked up a seed. "Dad. Dad, look at me!" Noah did not move from the spot over which he wept. Shem took Noah's hand and pressed the seed he held onto Noah's palm, turning his father's hand in the process toward the sky, that his father would see it. "Dad, look at this seed. If The Lowness or Light Within The Darkness were here, what would they tell you to do with this seed?"

"Mommy or Daddy? They would say to plant it. To make it grow into a plant for all of us. They'd say 'you've got to do to the seed what you want it to become!'" Noah suddenly brightened. He stood up and plunged the seed into the ground where his tears had landed. Then he sat back down, and again broke down into tears.

Shem stood and walked over to where their reserve of seeds sat in pots, waiting to be planted. "Japheth!" he shouted over to his brother, "We need to bring water from the stream. I have an idea!" With donkeys and water pots, the brothers sought fresh water and returned several hours later. That night they spoke with their mother.

The next morning, Shem approached his father with Tranzaiel near, a small clay pot of wheat seed in his hands. Still Noah wept. "Dad. Dad!" Noah did not budge.

Shem took his father's hand and pressed a pinch of the wheat seed into his palm. He then turned his father's hand upward so that he could see the seed in his hand. "Not only what your father and mother would tell you, *my* grandparents, Dad, but also what your family needs to live." Noah's head snapped sharply up to meet his son's face.

"We need food both for us and the animals. But also we need lumber to build the houses before the rain comes again. We need you to plant a garden while we build; otherwise, we will have to join Grandpa Lamech and

Grandma Light Within The Darkness in the long sleep. Not just myself, my brothers and our wives, but Mommy also." At which point Shem motioned over to Tranzaiel, who was near and easily within sight.

Noah gazed up to his wife's eyes, pausing for just a moment. Then, just as earnestly, his gaze found his son and he rose to his feet. He flung the seed from his hand, then turned to Shem. "Water!"

A wave of joy passed through Shem. Then, coming back to himself, he ran over to where the water sat not far from them. He filled a cup, then brought it back to his father, who promptly splashed the water approximately to where the seed had landed before uttering, "More seed!"

Shem ran over to the pot of wheat seed he had left where they'd sat moments ago.

"Wait!" Shem stopped where he stood. "Where's my rake? This dirt shouldn't be so hard!" Shem ran to where the tools were placed. He found a strong rake. He knew that soon, they'd need a plow.

"Here, Dad."

Noah took the rake, and then got to work scraping at the top soil of the earth. Shem walked to his father and placed his hand on Noah's shoulder. Noah snapped around to him. "What?"

"There is seed there, where we sat. There is water in those pots, there." Shem pointed. Noah nodded grimly, then turned back to his work.

Shem walked away toward his brothers. He wanted to smile to see his father working beneath the sun again, but couldn't fight away concern for his obvious inner turmoil. Together he and his brothers set upward to gather building material. Together they knew they would be giving their father more to plant when they returned.

Twenty miles upstream from where Noah's family collected water, camp had been formed by the possessors of the bodies that had refused to die. During the days, Casarta sat in meditation, keeping track of the brothers' location on the mountain, whether they were in vantage to be able to see the camp, and camouflaging it in their sight when they otherwise might. She kept track of the camp of ten who were always ten miles between them and where Noah's family built dwellings, thinking into them if they risked being seen so that they could hide behind decaying trees when the need arose. Lastly, she kept track of the minds of Noah's family, reporting to the group what the scouts could not know by their close watching through sight and ear alone. Particularly, she felt deeply for Noah's sorrow, raising within her her own still repressed anger for the genocide she could not conceive as having been necessary. Otherwise, she made sure they all had fish and seaweed in abundance as they strove to find ways to plant any food at all, and on occasion hunt a stray bunny rabbit.

After all the animals, Noah, and his family had left the ark, Jawrldrook and Honoth had followed at a safe distance behind, but always within eye-shot to bear witness. Shortly after, others had taken their places, and they'd reconvened with the rest. They recommended scavenging the ark for seeds that had fallen and been forgotten, scattered on the boat's floors, especially in the aviary. Seeing the wisdom of the suggestion and the need for food, Luciferous, Hoflan, Antagnous, and Trelsonfer fashioned bags and began climbing up the mountain in search of said seed.

Up the ramp and through the entrance of the ark, light shined through, and indeed there were some seeds scattered on the ground, wedged between boards. The further into the boat they went, however, the darker it became. When it became too dark to see, Luciferous sighed, at which point illumination came to them all. A small ball of light hovered before them, brightening all directions. "You're welcome," was heard in all their minds, spoken in Casarta's voice.

Through the boat, they collected. Finally coming to a large room, the floor covered in dry white feces, among it they could find seed to add to their bag. Fortunately, the shelves where the birds had sat were not as coated, and contained also many types of seed. They spent hours scouring the rest of the vessel. When finally they exited, night had fallen, and Casarta ended her light for the clarity of the stars. The next day they returned to their camp, a small bag of the treasure in hand.

Meanwhile, Casarta had seen the seed they'd gathered. She conceived their success mimicking a wild garden that would feed them all, well enough that she could soon take her leave of them. Past her thoughts of their well being without her, she sensed Cain would miss her. Stranger still, she sensed somewhere in herself that she would also miss Cain. That aside, she knew too quickly that most of her being would devote to the attention of why she needed to leave. She felt relief at her impending freedom.

❧ ❧ ❧

"You want me to do what to who, now?"

"You are My lips to stutter. Surely We know I was not unclear."

"Forgive me for sounding like Casarta, but it does strike me as a cruel message to send. To anybody. Ever."

"And yet, most Devoted of all embodying Us, you need an explanation to obey, for you are not an angel, but one created from *their* image and so in need of Our Mind. If you do not send precisely that message, he will never ponder himself in relation to the world, and thus never fulfill Our will that Our creation be done."

"Of course the future, as now, is Yours. Ever presently through me, Thy will be done."

Having spoken accordingly, Metatron shifted focus from All-Source to the point known as Cain.

꣠ ꣠ ꣠

"You all have plenty of food to eat now. You don't need me!"

"What about keeping watch?"

"They were keeping chronicle of the blood of Adam and Eve long before I could look through the eyes of another being. And for that matter, before *you* were born."

"But we could be detected so much easier without you. We could not see as much."

"And again, as they were fully adept at remaining hidden amongst the masses for centuries, so too will they elude these eight, very much as in times of old. It isn't like they don't know how to do this."

"What about me missing you? Here I am, left an immortal human among angels. You're as close to a friend as I can imagine having in this world."

"My family will take care of you just as they did me. It isn't as though I won't miss you, either. But if I don't leave now, there's no telling what my mind will conjure. What I do know, however, is that it's spent more than a year and a half waiting to express it."

"But, Casarta—"

"Goodbye for now, Cain."

That said, Casarta, with a small bag slung over her back, turned away from the encampment and all within it, and focused very closely, exclusively, only on the existence immediately around her while she began her intention of a very long walk away from them all.

When she had strode three hundred feet out, as he still stared at her, Cain heard a voice fill his head: "So as *they* came here to learn on your behalf of *your* pain, it seems as they do, you come to learn of theirs."

Cain answered the sound aloud. "This voice is in my head, as would be Casarta's. Who is speaking this?"

"I Am sent to give you a message. There is no greater offense can be offered, one to another, than to rise up against another to the other's cessation. Though in every case this is utterly revolting, even more so that *he* was your family. Here you stand that you were the originator of sin. That is the crown you wear. That yours was the first of all sins, Cain, you have lived through the flood as you have, watching all your own progeny perish. And yet, if you have lived three of the seven lifetimes bestowed upon you, in Its eternal wisdom, already these two lives beside were cut too short."

Throughout all of Cain resonated his mother's shrill, all-encompassing wail from over a millennia and a half away. Where he stood, he began to shake throughout his being's entirety. His heart pounding upon his chest was singular and acute, while the rest of himself went numb save for the rush of blood flooding through his shell in response to the palpitations of his torso. He thought his heart perhaps beat also in his skull.

The Metatron spoke to Cain's eyes, radiance evaporating away to an old man with a long, white beard who bore a resemblance to someone he had met terribly long ago. "I am as your great-great-grandnephew would appear to you. And What I speak on behalf of knows I have no love for delivering this message, and that otherwise, I would not augment it thus. Being Its voice, It must wish this statement made too, for It knows the nature of what It created, a nature that demands capitulation: As one who once wasn't personally regarded as one and the same as Her, personally, I see no justice in prolonging your suffering so apparently indefinitely. Somehow, by keeping you alive even past the annihilation of your own progeny in the flood, your life must be of benefit to *them*."

Cain's heart rate slowed, his shaking reduced to a murmur while heat returned to his extremities. "Of benefit to who?"

Enoch's form dissolved to light and finally away from any view of Cain's eyes, hearing, "In all things, She has Her reasons." Then all voices of the Metatron were gone. Cain was left to stare at the trees after the path taken by Casarta.

Chapter 68

The time for reaping was near at hand. With a little help from his sons, Noah had planted plants yielding seeds and trees of every kind that bear fruit with seed in it. In his garden, Noah had made to grow the beginnings of every tree that is pleasant to the sight and good for food. In the midst of this garden on the brink of harvest stood Noah. Noah wept.

There stood in his head the face of his mother. There stood in his head the face of his father. The rain. Many fewer bunnies than his mind had envisioned on a ride upon the water which, by none of his standards, could he consider to be "fun."

Noah stared at the faces of his parents. His tears fell upon a fallen apple and penetrated to the seed. The seeds met the salt of Noah's tears and receded into themselves, away from the water carrying it as the fruit decayed around them.

Day after day Noah toiled in his garden; watering, digging, cutting. When the bulk of the work was through, he would stand amidst his work and weep. Day after day, working and weeping. All around him the garden grew.

One day, after weeping, sullenly he walked to the shed where grapes were kept; he desired food. Despondent and suddenly overcome with a moment of ravenous hunger, in the relative darkness of the shed, he grabbed a large handful of grapes and barely chewed as he took them as quickly as possible down his throat. They tasted odd to him, but before hesitating on account of taste, he took another large handful and inhaled them almost as quickly as he had the first. Definitely, the taste was off. *Are these bad?* he thought. *Maybe if the grapes have gone bad, if I eat enough of them, I will sleep forever as Mommy and Daddy do, and be with them in a long dream.* Quickly he began to thrust handfuls of turned grapes into his mouth accordingly.

When the grapes reaching his mouth started tasting good to him, he stopped. "Yur not to poison grapes!" he said aloud to the grapes. He threw the bunch currently in his hand down to the ground and turned back to the opening of the shed. He took a step toward the door, stumbled, and fell on his butt. "That didn't hurt!" he noticed happily. "Maybe the long sleep that doesn't hurt is coming. I'm tired." Noah stood up, then stumbled his way back to his own bed and fell face-forward down upon it. Sleep overtook him quickly.

☙ ☙ ☙

Noah awoke the next day with a throbbing head. He remembered eating the bad grapes the day before. He remembered he had fallen on his butt, but that it had not hurt. He noticed that his butt did hurt now. As he found pain in trying to roll himself out of bed, he wished he had more bad grapes to eat, to take away the pain in his head and on his butt. A rare idea sparked into Noah's mind.

Noah walked down to where the grapes were kept when he was done with his day's work. He searched each bunch for a rotten grape, but none were to be found. So, Noah filled a large, wide trough with grapes and left them behind the shed, away from easy sight, to rot in the sun. Every day after his work was done, he would test a grape from the trough. Much to his dismay, however, after three weeks the grapes were not turning bad the way he'd hoped.

They just looked funny, were dry, actually tasted good, and in no way took from him any of the pain he felt from any given second to second. While he enjoyed eating the sweet, funny-looking little things, he was frustrated that what he was trying to do clearly wasn't working.

Again he entered the shed, and then opened a window to let light in to see by. He looked to the spot he had taken the grapes from off the ground to begin with. He saw a purple stain, and a small pile of yeast spilled down from where a bag on a shelf next to the grapes had a small hole in one of the corners.

Noah seemed to remember that of the funny-tasting grapes he ate, they did seem already squishy. He bent down, pinched up a small bit of yeast and stuck it on his tongue. He couldn't decide if it tasted similar to the squishy grapes or not. What he did decide, however, was that if he mixed squishy grapes with yeast, either it would make him not hurt, or it would make him dream of his parents for a very, very long time. He was happy, whatever was about to happen.

Noah brought the trough from behind the shed to inside the shed. He emptied the raisins into two very large buckets and set them by the door. He spread a layer of yeast over the bottom of the empty trough. Then, he filled the trough with bunches of grapes. He knelt down and started squeezing the grapes between his fingers. This hurt his fingers, was taking a long time, and made him frustrated, "Get squishy quicker, grapes!" He didn't want to get dirt in his grapes, but he did want to show them who was boss. He took off his shoes and began stomping up and down on the grapes angrily. Soon he had a song about it: "Up I jump. Down I stomp! Up I jump. Down I stomp!" As Noah sang and stomped, Japheth walked by the opening of the shed.

"Dad? What are you doing?"

Noah stopped where he landed. He stared his son in the eyes. He felt wet grape between his bare feet. He had to think fast. "I'm making special Daddy grape juice."

Japheth stared at his father for a moment. He considered how happy he looked for the first time in a long time, and that whatever was on his feet probably wouldn't kill him if he actually did drink the juice. So, he shrugged. "Okay, Dad. Have fun making your grape juice."

Noah felt relief as Japheth looked like he was about to walk away. As Japheth did turn to take his leave, Noah stopped him. "Japheth."

"Yeah, Dad?"

"You see those two buckets by the door?"

Japheth saw two baskets filled with small, wrinkled, weird-looking little things. He cringed his face, looked up at his father, and nodded.

"Try one."

Japheth looked at Noah, dumbfounded.

"They are sweet grapes kissed by the sun for three weeks. They taste good. Try one."

Hesitantly but obediently, Japheth reached down, picked a raisin from the bucket, put it onto his tongue, and then chewed. The corners of his mouth rose from a grimace to disbelief as he found himself inadvertently enjoying the strange little thing. He returned to his father's gaze and nodded approvingly.

"Please take those in to your mother and brothers, and sons and daughters, and enjoy. That is what happens when you leave grapes in the sun a very long time."

Japheth thought it was odd that his father was suddenly doing weird things to grapes. He liked the results so far, and really it wasn't any weirder than so many other things he'd done in his life, so despite his natural inclination to question his father's actions, he just said, "Okay, Papa." Then he picked up the two buckets of raisins by the handles and turned to leave.

"Oh, and one more thing, son."

Japheth turned back around and met his father's gaze.

"Please leave my juice trough alone, and tell your brothers to leave it alone too."

Japheth paused again, then again shrugged. "Okay, Dad." With that, Japheth turned a last time and walked away, out of sight.

Noah breathed a sigh of relief. He then resumed stomping and singing.

⌘ ⌘ ⌘

Noah left the yeasty, stomped-upon grapes in the darkness of the shed alone for a full week before drawing out the peel of a crushed grape and tasting it. It tasted like bad grape juice, but not quite like what he had remembered eating.

He waited a second week. The wet grape skin tasted closer. Almost as he'd remembered, even. He decided to wait one more week to be sure.

A week later, the taste was very much as he'd remembered. He decided the time was now to eat the rotten grapes. By the handful, Noah dug through stems and seeds and plunged the wet grape skins into his face while the juices ran down his arms.

He had been at this for minutes when at last the thought occurred to him to cup his hands into the trough and drink the liquid, which was easier to consume than skins pinched off stems one at a time. Ten minutes or so later, a familiar numbness began to set in.

Hearing a commotion coming from the shed, Shem poked his head in to investigate. There Shem saw Noah, his head hidden within the trough. "Dad?"

Noah quickly raised his head out of the trough. He tried to snap his head toward his son's face, but found he needed to turn his whole body around in order to make eye contact with Shem. Rolling himself around, Noah fell back hard and familiarly on his buttocks before figuring out how to meet his gaze. "Hello, Shem."

"What are you doing, Dad?"

"Oh, Shem. It's wonderful! I mix grapes smooshed with yeast, and let them wait for three weeks, and they give me the most amazing feeling! Here. Try!"

Noah cupped his hands, dipped them in the trough, and then held them out toward Shem. Shem smelled the sour juice from across the room as he viewed his father presenting toward him. The obvious thing in his mind was to refuse his father's offer, but he seldom had the heart to turn his dad down. He thought, instead, he would play along to a certain point beyond which he would not pass. "It's fine, Dad. I can use my own hands." After Noah shrugged and slurped up loudly what he had in his hands originally for sharing, reluctantly Shem cupped his own hands together, reached them into the trough, and drew a small bit of the liquid into his mouth. What slipped between his lips was mostly unpleasant, but there was enough taste of grape to the mixture that he could keep it down. "I'm sorry, Dad, but it just tastes like bad grape juice to me."

"You must drink more!" Noah suddenly became uncharacteristically agitated. "Drink until you feel it. Then tell me what you think!" He closed his remarks by punctuating his words with his index finger pointed and placed against Shem's face, between his nose and his right eye.

Shem was taken aback and confused, pausing before responding, "I will drink as long as my tongue allows, but no more. It does not taste good to me. But if you want me to feel something, I will try." With even greater reluctance, Shem again cupped his hands, lowered them into the trough, and handful by handful, began to drink.

Three minute or so passed of Shem barely tolerating repeated small quantities of the obviously bad grape juice past his palette at the behest of his father. Feeling absurd for having gone along with his father's simplicity, and in this case insanity, for as long as he had, finally, he stopped drinking. He placed his hands on the edges of the trough and lifted his head. "Dad, look." He looked into his father's wide, expectant eyes, "I can't drink anymore."

"You feel it?"

"No, Dad. It doesn't taste good to me. I can't drink anymore."

"But you have to drink more. Until you feel it!" Noah's eyes had a wideness with clarity of veins that Shem was unaccustomed to. For the first time in over a century, Shem actually felt nervous around his father.

"Dad, look. I love you, I just really don't like the taste. But if you're enjoying it, I'll just leave you to drink it, if you want."

Noah began to calm. "Okay. I don't like how it tastes too. I like that it makes pain go away. If you don't like it, I understand. I'll stay."

"Okay, Dad." Shem slowly walked out the door, out of view of his father, and toward the house.

❧ ❧ ❧

It was a warm summer evening as Shem walked away from the latest variation of his father's unique mind. Uncertain of whether he wanted to share his experience with his brothers, or even with his wife, he decided to walk in the light of the moon to clear his head. He enjoyed the sweet fragrances of the fruits on the vines and in the trees, the flowers all around him, while he sauntered through the garden. Ten minutes or so of leisurely stroll later, his thoughts drifted airily from the matter on his mind to the sudden sensation of lightness in his body. His head wobbled a bit upon his neck. His gait felt less need to keep a straight line. Shem felt freer, like dancing to the rays shining upon him from above. He pinched himself and barely minded the self-inflicted sting. Shem remembered the bad-tasting grape juice. *So this is what Dad meant.* He went off to tell his brothers immediately.

❦ ❦ ❦

Noah sat happy upon his backside, laughing. As his sons drank as much of the foul juice as they could stomach, one after the other, he pointed and giggled, "You look just like a goat. My family farm. My sons drinking from a trough, just like horsies." Noah was overwhelmed with joy.

Beyond the utterly unpleasant taste of the liquid, one by one Ham and Japheth both felt what their brother had described to them. Despite their own father resembling a donkey to them, they could relate, and soon all four had found the floor, rolling around and laughing together.

❦ ❦ ❦

Over the days of the summer, the three brothers and their father "played with the grapes" after their day's labor had been accomplished. They played with the amount of yeast until they struck the right balance. They made sure to pick only the ripest grapes. They learned to pluck the grapes from the stems before placing them into specifically made "troughs." They maintained that the feet were still quite handy for crushing while they considered new tools to invent, to aid in obtaining the juice. Then, they thought to strain the skins away from the juice. They noticed that the longer they let the juice sit, the better it seemed to taste. They also noticed the way the wood used in making the troughs contributed to the taste, as well as the kind of grape chosen.

By the time the grape harvest had ended, most of the grapes were turned to the juice now stored in various wooden troughs and clay pots. Already the brothers were talking about new ways they could experiment with the harvest in the coming year. Noah was just glad he had a lot of the special juice available to help make the hurt inside less. He was also happy that the juice did not taste as bad as when he had first eaten the rotten grapes, which now seemed like a long time ago.

As the days passed, however, the boys began to become more concerned after the welfare of their father. Noah seemed to drink more and more every night. Ham would try to bring his father's drinking of the wine up to him, but Noah would become agitated. "Just drink more and shut up, and you'll feel better like me!"

Ham, devastated, went back to his brothers. "I think Shem and I both agree that him drinking that much wine isn't good. Winter is sad anyway, though. If it distracts him from thinking about Grandma, isn't that for the best? Let's just stay out of his way, and maybe when we harvest in the spring, we can talk him away from it." Ham was not convinced his father should be allowed to continue drinking, but likewise he could not think of a better approach to take.

As spring finally did near, Ham, Shem, and Japheth worked hard that the garden would bear fruit in the summer even more copiously than it had the year just past. Noah, however, had become less inclined to work as his habit of drinking wine had strengthened.

Midway into the season, when all the fermented grape juice had run out, Noah was more easily dragged to the garden to toil. At first he was very irritable, though. Noah picked up a hoe and began working the soil. Shortly thereafter, however, rather than working the soil, Noah just angrily pounded at the same piece of ground over and over again, howling at it in frustration, until finally he dropped his tool and fell to his knees, weeping. His sons rushed to where he knelt crying into the softened earth, "I want more wine to make the hurting stop!"

"With your help, we'll plant even more grapes than last year, Dad. That way you'll have enough wine to last all year long."

Ham glared over at Shem while he spoke. He knew that his brother merely wanted to see their father not in pain. He did not agree, however, that ensuring his supply of alcohol was a good way of doing it. He watched Shem and Japheth help their father to his feet and into the house.

Shem and Japheth left the weeping Noah in his room, where he stayed and wept through the rest of the day.

❧ ❧ ❧

Every day, for a week or so, Ham would ask his father to come out to work in the garden. After seven days of coaxing Noah from his place of despair within the house, he finally agreed to come out and help Ham and his brothers to do the work of planting and tending to the garden. "Come on out, Dad. The grapes will not be as numerous, not so healthy, without your love, care, and experience tending to them."

Begrudgingly, Noah knew what his son said to be true and put his grief aside so that the grape harvest could be at its fullest, and the yield of wine plentiful enough to last to the harvest thereafter.

Shem and Japheth were happy to see their father rejoin them in the work. Noah picked up a tool, and together they continued to make the garden flourish.

Chapter 69

East of Eden, but West of Nod, together all of Noah's family had come to plant what remained of the seed of the ark to yield fruit and vegetables, good things to eat from just about all the world over. Over the course of the flood, Noah's sons knew their wives. Before the ark had settled on the peak of Mount Ararat, Canaan had been born to Ham and his wife. Though despondent, Noah took some solace, over the course of the journey, in the face of his grandson. Canaan looked nothing but happy. Somehow he saw, at any given time, his parents' happy faces shining forth from that of his grandson. Sometimes he saw his own; before his father or mother dying, before his mean grandfather in the woods, his own face when it had no reason to be sad, before all the rest of the bunnies were killed by the fun ride except for those they'd saved. Noah felt inside a time when all he could know was happiness in life, for in that time, that was all he could know. His new grandson had made him happy, just as would his other grandchildren who followed shortly thereafter.

Now Canaan worked beside his grandfather in the garden. Picking and eating new berries as they were barely ripe. Playing with the wrong end of a shovel in the dirt. Chasing bunny rabbits hopping about, ever out of his reach. Through the pain constantly consuming him, past his desire for the grape harvest to begin from the second his last drop had been consumed, somehow within him, a ray of joy pierced through it all at the sight of his grandson "working" by his side.

Over the course of days turned to months, this single, penetrating shaft of light he could cling to. Over time, the work itself could be the distraction. His body felt better for the fresh air and the sun. He ate again with his family. Though he lived begrudgingly despite the depression, every action did make life hurt less, and his children's children did allow him to remember that joy was an experience he had touched, and perhaps even could touch again. All around him, the garden blossomed beautifully while the depth of spring transitioned into the summer's more omnipresent light.

❧❧❧

Labor and pain. Then the labor that turned the pain away, or off, or out, or into something even resembling pleasure. The light that filled the days seemed to last so much longer now than the nights serving as blank canvases for memories and nightmares. But even in the nights, warm blankets and warm embraces and kisses from his wife filled the greater part of his sightlessness through to the brightening sky.

The days of summer passing, Noah remembered through his pain that in life, joy too existed. Though as the summer drew on, the grapes on the vines plumped. He sincerely enjoyed the solace his family had brought back into him, and yet he knew a more instant cessation to his ever-present pain was now very close to fruition; even but a squeeze and a few weeks' wait away.

While his eye sustained its fascination with a grape, so too did those of two of his sons find him: Ham and Japheth.

"He's always in pain, Ham."

"I have seen him smile of his own will since working after the spoilt grape juice ran out. You ferment those grapes, you're taking his family away from him, and he from his family. Don't do it, Japheth."

"You would have him suffer without hope of it stopping? You know our father's brain works differently. How many seasons of working in the field and harvesting will make him forget how much he misses our grandmother? How much he misses our grandfather? The bunnies that didn't come on the 'fun ride?' That he ever met Methuselah at all?"

"The bad grape juice will cripple any chance he has at genuine happiness. Please don't do this to him!"

"My brother, if he didn't look at that grape now as though his life depended on it, surely I would not. But I do not have it in me to allow him to continue in such pain. I ask your forgiveness, but I cannot abandon him to this misery when I have it in my power to help him bring it to an end."

"My brother, I respect what you are saying, but it will be hard for me to forgive if you take away his chance for true and genuine happiness."

"Then, my brother, forgive me for wanting so to see the end of his pain."

With due respect, mutually they parted.

❦ ❦ ❦

In the six years since they had landed atop the mountain, they had vigorously planted and tended to the land. Seeds from all the world over they had carried with them in the ark. Whatever remained after the birds had carried them off to all corners of the Earth, they dutifully planted and tended to. All types of flora conceivable bloomed in their garden now. In the heat of the summer, there flourished everything they could imagine good to look upon, as well as good to eat.

Central within this garden, Shem and Japheth picked grapes.

ᐧᕹᐧᕹᐧᕹ

"It tastes far better than it did last year."

"Yes. It's even enjoyable."

"I forget mostly what it feels like."

"I seem to remember it's like becoming the wind. And then it's harder to walk and speak, but easier to be happy."

"Shem, we shouldn't tell Dad. Ham's right. He's been doing a *lot* better since he started working again."

"Ooh. I just started feeling it. Have you started feeling it? I don't feel emotion as strongly in my chest."

"I do feel more relaxed. My mind still works, though. It would be wrong now to tell Dad that some is ready."

"I'm just happy to feel this lightness again. It's like a long season of work has declared itself culminated and satisfied. It is good to be here with you, brother. If you say Dad is better now without this, I will not argue with you."

Just then a faint sob floated upon the warm summer breeze and into their ears.

"Tell me you didn't just hear that."

"I certainly haven't had enough to drink, not to walk. Let us follow it."

Not too many steps later, they spied their father sitting beside a young fig tree, weeping softly into the wind. They looked at each other.

"Ham may wish our father greater health, but clearly his pain has long to go before leaving."

Japheth nodded affirmatively toward his brother. "Dad, come with us. We want to show you something."

After making their presence known to their father, with hands comforting him upon his shoulders, they led him off to a place his sorrows could not follow.

cⱥ‧cⱥ‧cⱥ

Ham was dismayed. Two weeks of a father preferring his bed to the work of the field. His nights spent withdrawn, drinking with his other two sons, if not all alone.

For Noah's part, he was happy not to be at the mercy of the will of his grief; to have command by any measure over his own tears; to have a way to part himself from the pain of loss otherwise always present.

His wife hardly enjoyed sharing a bed with her husband as he spent his days and evenings fleeing his emotions. She kept a separate bed specifically for such occasions, almost every night as time wore on. She was grateful, however, that he had found a means toward any measure of peace.

cⱥ‧cⱥ‧cⱥ

One night, toward the end of the summer while Noah drank alone in the shed where the wine was kept, he spotted a rat enter and stare at him. His eyes made contact with those of the rat. He squinted. "Oh no, ratty. You not gonna bring disease into my home and poop on my garden! You can find other people's food to eat!"

With that, Noah picked up a nearby candle and held it out toward the rat. "If my parents can die, and all the bunnies not on my boat can die, rat, then so can you!" Noah took the flame in his hand and started running with it toward the rat, who immediately ran off squealing.

Noah ran after the rat, following it into the garden. When he saw it run under a bush, an idea came to him. Noah ripped off the branch of a nearby willow and stuck its end into the flame of his candle. It had the desired effect.

Quickly as he could, Noah stumbled over to the bush he'd seen the rat run under, and stuck the flaming branch under the bush.

The rat ran out quickly and over to a different bush. Noah immediately pursued after the rodent, again plunging the flaming branch under the rat's cover. When he did, Noah failed to notice the previous bush had quite thoroughly caught flame. This process continued another six bushes and two trees before, hearing the commotion, Japheth came out to see the fires being set by his father running through the garden like a mad person waving the flaming stick, which by now was starting to set other trees and crops on fire, since the flame of the branch itself had become fairly large and was being wildly flailed about.

"Ham! Shem!"

Everyone came running to the garden. They grabbed any water they could—where the cattle drank, slop that would have been fed to goats, their own drinking supply—and threw it over every flame they could. Their wives ran out with their thickest blankets to suppress the smallest flames. Japheth caught the blazing branch by the end Noah held, and wrestled his father to the ground before rushing the branch to where their family's drinking water was kept to be put out. After extinguishing the branch thus, Japheth went back to where he'd forced his father down moments before to find him passed out upon the dirt, no longer a threat either to garden or rat. He and Ham dragged him into the house together, so that he wouldn't breathe in any more smoke.

Frantically, all night long they battled the flames that had been set by the drunken Noah. As the sun rose the next day, it revealed the smolder and destruction of over half the garden, and much of the ripe crop that had been ready to be harvested. The women wept, as did Japheth, his face held in his hands while the light slowly filled the sky. He felt his brother's hand upon his shoulder. "What do we tell Dad?"

"The truth, Japheth."

"But Ham, he'll be in even more pain. He'll just want to drink more."

"Yes. That is true. And since the grapes were one of the few crops not burned to the ground, and the wine shed completely untouched by the flame, he'll certainly have plenty to drink. But we're not going to let him be alone while drinking from now on, are we?"

Japheth shook his head. "How can we let him drink again at all, Ham?"

"What are we supposed to do, Japheth? Lie to him? Fight with him? Let him howl in agony all the rest of his days? The one thing we can do is make sure he doesn't do this again. So, when he goes for the cup, we will be there with him. Want to take the first shift?"

His brother's head sunk even lower.

Chapter 70

A month passed. They replanted what they could. They harvested what they could. They made sure that at all times someone knew where their father was, and exactly what he was doing. Most days, though, what he was doing was the same.

Noah woke up every day hating himself and missing his parents. Noah woke up next to a cup and a deerskin sewn together so tightly it could hold wine. Outside his doors, the fruits of the world were reduced to what was left to be grown forevermore as the 'specialties of the locality.' Despite that, there were still many good things to eat, and the rest of the world had yet to be explored.

As the days turned into weeks, Noah's grandchildren grew. Where once Noah had always his sons or his wife by his side, the time came when Canaan was old enough, the age of twelve by their determination, that he could be set to watch over his grandfather while his father and uncles spent their days working in the fields and garden.

Canaan wished he could be outside in the fresh air and the sunlight, but he also knew that watching over his grandfather was very important. Be that as it may, it was very difficult spending that much time doing little besides occasionally refilling his grandfather's cup and handing it to him. Nonetheless, he fulfilled his service admirably, and knew that after all, there was no greater way apparent to ease the sincere suffering of his grandfather, whom he deeply and intrinsically loved.

In the evenings, after returning from cultivating the garden or hunting in the land, the brothers would relieve Canaan, taking turns watching their father, a different son each night.

For her part, Tranzaiel would spend the days occupying her time mostly away from her husband. She'd tend to the needs of the house, spend time with her daughters-of-marriage and the upbringing of her grandchildren. She even spent time beside her sons, tending to their garden and animals. Whatever was useful over the course of the day or night that could keep her distracted from the plight of her husband, she welcomed to occupy her time. Few and far between now were the times he called out for her. When he did, however, she'd dutifully come. Each time the same: simultaneous welling up within her the gratitude that he hadn't forgotten her, and the sorrow to see the light of joy no longer present in her favorite friend's eyes. As she lay by his side, holding his sobbing form, stroking his head, she found somewhere inside of herself any happiness at all that she could by any measure ease his pain. She saved her own tears until after departing him, generally stopping quickly thereafter to her own room or one of many favorite secluded spots in the garden.

Ham, Shem, and Japheth worked. Together they labored and toiled, that their fruits would be plentiful and much. Apart from each other, they lay with their wives that they may be as the fruits they cultivated and multiplied themselves, that soon their nieces and nephews too would have someone to marry, that again the Earth would be populated. Together again, they joined in gatherings of meals and tending to their father. Going whichever way the spirit moved to teach their children and cultivate their families as they would, in this way, they lived. In this way, they coped. In this way, they passed the months. In this way, they cultivated the memory and continuance of life, carving out from the marble of renewed existence every conceivable opportunity for joy, despite the wails of their otherwise great father sobbing ever in the room containing the bed he kept himself almost exclusively, drunkenly, loathe to leave.

Though Noah would stumble to the daylight briefly, or dance to the song within him moving his ever-wobbling form to the breeze of the evening air, it was seldom long before he found himself greeting earth upon hands, knees, and sometimes face. At such times, either of his own immediate preferences, with tears in his eyes, would be to crawl whimpering back to his bed, or to be half-carried there after being lifted from where he landed by some member of his family shortly thereafter.

☙☙☙

Not long after Canaan had turned fourteen came a sudden sun's summer heat. Though Noah's depression had not eased over the preceding two years, life's routine wove around him and allowed him his new nature to be where he lay apart, though somewhere physically as a center of them all. But when the heat of the summer arose that year hotter than any of them could remember feeling, mixed in with his traditional regularly sprinkled sobs throughout the entirety of the day, now emerged past wine-soaked lips a new phrase: "My skin is on fire! My brain is too hot! Where is my mommy?"

It had already occurred to his sons to make tents outside to be in cooler air than thicker walls would allow, even before their father had begun his latest bout of wailing. Once the shrill cries began, however, promptly they made him a bed in a tent, a cup and skin placed close beside him. Likewise they set tents for themselves, their wives, their mother, and their children as well.

It was three days into their new community of tents that amidst an already hot summer, higher still the temperature peaked. Canaan had no reason to stay in the tent with his grandfather. Ham had instructed him to supply Noah's tent with a large measure of both wine and water. Having done so, Canaan stayed close enough to his grandfather's tent that he could hear, should Noah call out for something. He removed his shirt in the hot sun and found the shade of a tree, whereby he could rest and pass the time otherwise feeling the oven the sun cast of the earth. He had no concern for his head upon the tree's trunk; he knew his grandfather's voice well not to be subtle.

Though Noah's tent was in-shaded, nonetheless, the extraordinary heat of the morning was penetrating. In the comparative coolness of the early hours, Noah's breakfast of wine made him once again sleepy by mid-morning. The sun reaching closer to apex an hour and a half later, however, Noah awoke.

His clothes stuck to him from sweat. The surrounding summer had pierced into his tent, and he felt as though he wished to rip his skin off for the severity of the heat. He reached out his hand, grabbed the cup holding the water without looking, then sprayed it forth from his lips right after it had found its way to his tongue, "No. Wine! Only ever wine!" He threw the cup against the tent's side, then grabbed the other cup beside him, immediately drinking greedily. "More!"

He turned to his side to see three full skins of wine lying beside a large bucket filled with water. Noah grabbed the nearest skin to himself, uncapped the top, and drank from it liberally. As though inhaling every drop, he suctioned the liquid down his throat quickly into his stomach. Emerging from the skin's opening, he stopped to heave air back into his chest, spending a minute gasping into the oxygen surrounding him like a fish on the sands of a beach, desperate for water to find him. When he found his breath again, he let out a large belch, declaring both liquid and gas happily his friends.

The wine had cooled his throat for a moment, left him the temporary feeling of hydration. But even still, though slight, he felt thirsty. Having returned to normal breathing, he took up a second skin, this time lessening its contents by merely half in a single gulp. Again he gasped heavily to regain his breath. Again he belched. This time satisfied, he reclined on the side of his bed. From the half-empty skin, he filled his cup. He began to sip. Feeling as though nearly roasted, fermented grape would begin to dribble down his throat, only to evaporate midway to his esophagus. Nonetheless, the wine had its desired effects. Throat wet with wine, his cup found its way safely to upright on the ground as between heat and drunkenness, he slipped again into slumber.

When Noah awoke an hour and a half after, however, he began feeling his throat almost too tight to swallow with the heat stabbing everywhere through him, even more surely than before. Clumsily he knocked over his cup and its contents in search of wetting his dryness. Now annoyed, his eye fell upon the half-consumed skin. He was only too happy to guzzle what little, to his sensibility, remained as certainly as he would have had his way with the cup by his side to begin with. Tearing the top off the last full skin, he ingested as though the wine itself was the oxygen he denied himself in the process of drinking. Then, with the tent spinning, he collapsed to his back, the heat overtaking him, and he gave into an intoxication far beyond his body's ability to compose to waking.

A half hour past mid-day later, the sun barely on the other side of its apex, the heat being greater than any living human could recall, Noah's eyes snapped open. Soaking in his clothing, inundated by compressing swelter, his throat closed in upon itself, sealed by dryness. His hand caught the empty skin dropped to the ground, close by his reach.

Raising it to his lips, not a drop to dampen his thirst. Noah began to flail about, rolling himself over from his bed, dropping down onto a knee, and then over upon his side.

Flailing even more, Noah maneuvered himself up upon hand and knees so that he could dizzily crawl to the next empty skin, and the next, while the world around him gently but persistently decided to turn enough that balance upon all fours was inch-by-inch a formidable challenge. Still, not a drop of wine to be had. Letting go a long roar from the bottom of his chest, Noah gathered the fortitude to trek the half-yard to where the large wooden bucket of water sat. His constricted neck being his master, he plunged in his head and slurped the water into his dryness. Inhaling as he drank, quickly the direction of suction shifted and, raising his head back out, a spray of water sent a momentary mist into the air. As he landed on his back, Noah hacked on the water still clinging to his lungs, while air was harder to internally absorb than ever.

Noah shrieked, and shrieked, and shrieked again. Hacking interspersed with gasps interspersed with shrieks, whines, and sobs as he beat his hands upon the ground while his body would not listen to the directions he wanted it to go in, and the world nauseatingly still turned.

Not too far outside the tent, Canaan heard the commotion of his grandfather, and it frightened him. Canaan ran from the sound as quickly as he could to where he knew, despite the heat, his father and uncles worked as best they could out in the fields.

Meanwhile, back in his tent, Noah felt as though his clothes were suffocating him. Frantically, his fingers sought out the edges of his garments and tore at them upon the discovery. He ripped open his thin shirt, tearing it from the barrel of his old, drooping belly, bending his arms backward that one hand might find the other arm's sleeve, tightening the garment's grip upon him while he pulled it off, maximizing friction caused to his arms in the removal.

He forced himself forward, once again on all fours. He leveraged himself up and, wobbling upon his legs, got himself close enough to the water bucket to fall in front of it. Noah again dipped his head in, slurping desperately, but this time slower, causing less water to make him gag but only occasionally choke. Rising back up to his knees, he splashed water onto his chest, which dripped down to his pants causing itchiness, sloshiness, and general discomfort in the heat. Again with maximum friction due to the water's unwillingness to lubricate, but quite the contrary without any attempt to unfasten, Noah struggled his pants off himself until finally they reached his ankles. At which point, he fell backwards upon his butt.

In hot, angry, drunken awkwardness, he flailed about like a fish plucked from the ocean and tossed now on the sands of the blindingly hot desert moments after being taken from the water. It was difficult for his old, fat, withered frame either to bend up toward his ankles, or to bend his knees up far enough for his hands to reach his trouser-cuffed feet. So, like a turtle on the back of his shell trying to reach for freedom from his feet's uselessness in his ankle's bondage, he rocked back and forth with all the energy he could muster, coupled with the frustration that came to him naturally. Just as he struggled, exposed, in this most vulnerable of positions, Ham entered the tent.

Initially, seeing his father in this exquisitely unusual position, taken aback, at first all Ham could do was giggle while his brain ran frantically to catch up with what his eyes were seeing.

Hearing his son's laughter toward him, steam rose to Noah's cheeks and he began shouting at him through slurred speech, "Whats donkey's shit-butt a problem with how hot and pain and hatred I can't get my legs free? You ever love yer Daddy? Let my legs free, helping please!"

Ham jumped back to his senses as he heard his dad's deep frustration, seeing how much he strained simply to have a chance of controlling his own legs. He helped his father's bunched pants and undergarment off his ankles, allowing Noah half a chance to try to rise to his feet once more.

"Wine, Ham! Bring wine more! I have out more wine, and is dreadful thirty!"

"No, Dad. I'm not going to bring you more wine. If you're thirsty, I'll bring you some water."

"Screw yer otter shit bag. Wine!"

Ham was shocked to hear his father speaking to him in a way he had never heard before. As Noah continued intensely struggling to raise his completely naked form to his feet, Ham turned toward the water bucket. "I will pour you some water. It will make you feel better. Cooler."

Having almost risen himself to a balance of standing posture, Noah fell down again, but this time upon the makings of his bed, landing squarely upon his already bruised posterior. He began sobbing. Ham handed him the cup of water freshly poured. Noah sucked it down quickly, then returned the cup. Ham refilled it. Noah drank this one only slightly slower. Ham poured him another. Noah felt better by the end of the third cup. Ham poured him a fourth. Noah dumped the cup of water on his head and down his body, turned suddenly and sharply to be lengthwise with his bed, and fell heavily backward, simultaneously closing his eyes and passing out. Ham caught the cup from his father's hand before it had a chance to hit the ground.

Rising up, cup held, there stood Ham staring down at the fat, but shriveled, naked Noah splayed out on the bed below, limbs hanging where they'd landed. Noah's fully bare form was apparently entirely comfortable for any eye to see. Staring at his father, Ham shook his head. Anger and sadness welled up inside of him. He decided then it was time that his father continue his life without wine. Just as this thought passed across his mind, he heard footsteps coming over grass in his direction. He exited the tent to meet his brothers and and his son.

"Dad, I got Shem and Japheth like you told me."

Ham looked his brothers cold in the eye; first one, then the other. "His drinking stops now."

"What happened?"

"He's a drunk, slobbering mess who thinks wine his friend over water on this, the hottest day we've ever known. He's passed out in there, totally naked after throwing a fit that I wouldn't bring him more wine to 'cool him down.' He was so drunk he couldn't even stand. Water's become contemptible for him to drink. He swore at me, Japheth. Our sweet, loving, kind father swore at me."

Japheth's face melted down as though under the heat of the sun. "I don't know what to say."

"Say his drinking stops now!"

Shem responded, "His drinking stops now. He's going to be very confused when he wakes up. We should cover him."

"And overheat him? He's going to be sick for water as it is. And the extreme heat will just waken him quicker. . ."

"The summertime cloth Mom has woven is super-thin. Let us dip it in the cool stream water and drape it over him to cool him and cover his nakedness, so that we don't have to worry about his likeliness of being confused and running around naked when he awakens." Japheth nodded approval toward Shem. Ham sighed.

Shem and Japheth walked off and came back about fifteen minutes later, soaking-wet cloth in hand. "The stream water felt wonderful, like it is melted directly from snow."

"Ham, is he exposed on his back?" Ham stared at Japheth, annoyed by his question, and nodded. "Shem, we should walk in backwards, with the clothes on our backs so that we can cover him without having to look at him."

Shem nodded affirmatively.

Really? Ham thought to himself as he watched them throw a long tunic over Shem's back, and a shirwal over Japheth's, both soaking wet. They walked backward into the tent, covering over their father's nakedness. Once the clothes were over Noah, they positioned the long tunic so that it covered him like a blanket. They then worked the shirwal over Noah's ankles and halfway up his legs. They figured that when Noah awoke, he would have an easy enough time pulling the pants up and putting on the tunic. They hoped that after he awoke, he would emerge from the tent clothed accordingly.

Almost six hours later, they were relieved to discover they were correct.

They awoke from a shared, warm summer nap to a beautiful sunset over the field. They heard the confused and awkward shifting of their father within his tent.

"S... so... so thirsty."

They heard him pull up his pants. They heard him wrestle himself up from supine, take two steps to the water, and slurp gratuitously from the bucket. When he had finally stopped, he burped loudly before consuming air back into his chest. They heard him fall back onto his bed and groan.

"Dad, we're outside," Shem spoke first. "Are you okay?" Noah groaned again. "Do you mind if we come in?"

"Yes. Do you have clothes on?" Japheth blurted out. Shem hit his upper arm with the back of his hand. Noah grunted. They looked to each other, one to another, and nodded.

Ham held back the opening of the tent for Shem to enter, followed by Japheth, before entering himself.

As Shem entered the tent, Noah's eyes widened and rolled forward in his head enough to see his son's face, followed by Japheth's. When his youngest son entered the tent, he sat bolt upright. "You!" He extended his arm and pointed at Ham. "Have you brought me more wine yet?"

"No, Pop, I'm not bringing you more wine."

"That's fine. Canaan is gooder at fetching it for me, anyway. Have the boy bring me more wine!"

"No, Dad. No one is bringing you more wine, after the way you acted earlier today. Certainly not Canaan."

"Did my penis offend you? Your not getting wine offended me! Have Canaan bring me more. Now!"

Shem and Japheth looked at each other as Noah spoke to Ham. Neither had ever heard their father speak in such a way before.

"Dad, after the way you've acted today, I told Shem and Japheth not to give you any more wine. My son *certainly* won't be bringing you any wine."

"Fine. Then let Canaan be the lowest of slaves to his brothers, if you won't let him serve *me!* God bless Shem, and Canaan can be *his* slave! Let Shem always be welcome by Japheth, and Canaan can be Japheth's slave too! May Canaan only ever marry of his own sisters, and never of his cousins like Shem and Japheth's children will, so that Canaan's children will be just as stupid as me. Now get out!"

"Dad—" Ham tried to speak.

"I said leave!" Noah slammed his head back onto his pillow and closed his eyes, listening while slowly he heard his sons leaving his tent.

Chapter 71

"Well, they've conspired that he should marry his cousin anyway..."

"That's not the point, Lengner. He's crushed that Noah has betrayed their relationship in such a way, and for absolutely nothing he's done wrong toward his grandfather. All of humanity starts anew, and this kind of bitterness, resentment, and fear is placed into the world by the word of a man once so good and noble of spirit? It's just not right. After all that trouble, such trouble should come to exist again, no less by the word of the very man who saved them all. It seems as though a waste."

At Antagnous' word, Luciferous spoke in response. "They all carry with them the death of the world, just as like as its salvation and resurgence. Uniquely amongst them, Noah and Tranzaiel, the deaths of their parents. But for Tranzaiel, this is not such a hardship. They all are destined to pass down what has made them; death in greater measure than any who come after could possibly know. But Noah, not so impersonally, has known the loss of his parents harshly. It is natural he would take hand in creating his grandson in his own image."

Antagnous replied, "Luciferous, the image of *The* Creator gives them the capacity for choice. Humanity's potential rests solely in their opportunity to choose wisely; to love one another rather than to inspire hatred and resentment amongst each other. So many should not be affected so adversely by one man's poor choice not to rise above the pain in himself."

"But for that he was not created by the poor choices that conceived him. You know how his brain is, Antagnous. Are you really going to tell me *he* had a choice?"

Antagnous frowned and bent her head toward the ground. After a pause, she said, "No. It just doesn't seem fair."

"No it doesn't, Antagnous. But, unlike his grandfather, *he* does have the capacity to choose. Let us more than pray, but work that when the opportunity comes, he chooses wisely. The fate of the potential of humanity may turn on Canaan's wisdom in deciding when the time comes. Indeed, most of them can freely choose giving each other a hand up, rather than a push away, when faced with choice. We must work that they find the strength within to embrace Our Creator's Creative Consciousness, rather than the dissolution of self from self in the ignorance that they cannot look at another without seeing their own true face."

✿ ✿ ✿

As though they had a world to populate, Noah's sons had many children with their wives.

When Arpachshad and Javan were born within a week of each other, and already Gomer was preparing for a long journey to explore the lands around, Luciferous held a meeting amongst all those servants of their Lord incarnated that they might too serve Adam-kind. "The land of the world is large, and before long they will be many. In the beginning, it was relatively easy to blend into the lands of Cain, and likewise watch over the lands begot by Seth. Though through our pains we had earned by our own merits, it was relatively simple to recombine our numbers for the two groupings. Tonight, however, it is wise to decide how best to watch over; how best to try to serve them to highest good, now that they will be spreading far and wide shortly."

Lemisslept responded, "We should watch how they develop, and aid as we can. Let us divide ourselves in groups of twenty-two or so and watch over them as best we can. When each has populated an area to several hundred, it should be a simple matter to mingle amongst them and offer suggestions pointing them to their place in Greater Unity as creates their highest potential. Until then, we will watch them learn their newest natures, and follow their greatest and most potential-bearing creations of being. We will study, that we may be effective in assisting them in any way they might believe to doubt the fullness of the good so easily it should be theirs to exist as. We will work, that they might be returned in identification to their own, genuine Divine nature."

"It is a good plan, Lemisslept, but should we really be so divided from each other?"

After Luciferous had asked, this time it was Gendlebleth who responded. "Knowing the loudness needing conquering of my own mind, with joy let me answer: Casarta taught us well to focus on the minds of each other. Should the need arise for one another, or even regrouping, let us maintain our practice and be prepared to reach out thought to thought, mind to mind, as we find we have necessity. We can even test the physical limits of our practice, should they exist, and alter course in accordance to experience's lessons."

Luciferous nodded agreement. "Tricky things, though the caprices of a mind might be, that we maintain honesty in practice, already we know our capacity for inner-connectivity most well. As they divide and become, we must keep track, learn, and assist as our mission commands. Diligent in our practice, our hearts will flow, and our minds speak. We will join each other again." As he spoke, a new thought occurred to Luciferous.

All around the fire, twenty miles from the dwellings of Noah and his progeny, they nodded and buzzed in agreement to the warmth they felt growing in their chests. They all relished the possibilities present to begin pursuit of their mission in such a way as they hadn't before.

That night, once Luciferous retired to his own tent, he lit a candle. He sat upon a mat where he'd become accustomed to quieting and focusing his mind. Luciferous lowered his eyes and recalled practically the first sight he could remember that had beheld light refracted by joy to his physical capability with which to see. The face brought to the focus of his inner vision, he spoke into the release of allowing his mind to flow where it would go: "*Lucisity?*"

Chapter 72

Many a day he thirsted for a drop of wine. Many a day he wept. Many a day he craved the pain go away.

At first he brooded, stomped, and even stormed when his sons would not bring him a cup of wine. He begged of his grandsons and granddaughters, but to no avail. For years he would try to steal a handful of grapes and crush them in some dark corner of a room, utterly forgetting the necessity of yeast. He was watched closely, however, and always the next day the dish containing the small puddle of grape juice had vanished, causing Noah to further sulk.

The anger distracted him from his greater pain, however. After the first year of wallowing without drink, Shem finally convinced Noah to pick up a shovel. He worked barely two minutes before throwing it to the ground and huffing back off to his room. The next day, Noah walked over to the shovel all on his own and worked a full half-hour before letting its weight drop from his hand, and slumping back to his gloom and solitude for the rest of the day. Inconsistently at first, but over time, Noah began working once again in the garden in between ineffectual attempts at making for himself even the slightest taste of what would numb the pain automatically, without the benefits that came as a result of the sincere efforts that would otherwise more truly lead him away from it.

It did take years, decades even, that the pain of loss in the memory of love moved more to the background of the capricious focuses of his mind. As he was turning seven hundred, however, one could claim that more often than not, Noah was a happy man. It had taken a great deal of time for emotional scar tissue to cover up the deepest of wounds, but even that first two minutes of shovel in hand had shown Noah that work, too, could bring his mind from the pain, even if he could not find there the ease of numbness; in conscious suffering, the automatic pain found no easy place to rest. A century later, it had almost flown away altogether.

Noah did feel the pain of loss until his dying day, however. Amplified by his mistrust of the living he loved most deeply who would not obey and help him anesthetize, over time, the work that kept his recollections of loss at bay gave way to a body inevitably growing old. At the age of nine hundred, he could barely work long with a tool like a spade. He could barely carry into the field a handful of seed, let alone a bag filled.

Three hundred years after the flood, however, the world had begun repopulating. While he aged, he found himself more and more surrounded by his progeny. He could recline in a wooden chair made by his great-great-great-great-grandson, and watch his great-great-great-great-great-great-grandchildren playing with each other all around him. While he sat in his chair, he thought how wonderful it was that the person who came from him, who built him his chair, also liked to play with trees. He was delighted to see the young ones chasing bunnies, giggling, petting their soft fur. He felt deep gratitude that Tranzaiel was still there by his side, holding his hand. She was happy that the pain was secondary to the joy he felt by life again. Likewise, she was grateful when the day came that she knew he could not suffer any more. She was grateful she lived to see the day she could find her own rest, without fear that her own long sleep would cause him to pass with a heart agony-filled. The day Noah's own long sleep came, her final happiness was giving him comfort and love out of the suffering his very long life had provided.

After the flood, Noah lived three hundred and fifty years. Nine hundred and fifty years from the time of his birth, Noah felt very, very tired, as though he required a very long sleep. "Transi, if I napped for a long time, maybe hundreds of years of your life, would you forgive me?"

Noah had been sick for a month. Lying in bed the last three days, though he seemed better than he had in that month, it was clear the toll the illness had taken on him, and how fatigued he really was. Tranzaiel smiled down on Noah. She rearranged her position so that she could lay his head in her lap. She gently stroked his forehead as she responded to his question. Her face beamed down upon him. She rolled the meaning of his words around her mind like a fine wine, overcome with joy that he was asking permission from her, out of his love, that his suffering may be allowed to end. As though sipping from the cup, she spoke, "My love, you deserve to rest as you like. Should you sleep for the next two thousand years, I shall enjoy watching you dream as though you will never wake, even as if I were kissing your lips for all eternity. If you are so tired you would rest for the next seven centuries, with joy in my heart, I will have nothing but happiness for all you have brought me since we met: love, our children, and then theirs for all the generations of the world. Sleep as long as you like. You have nothing to be forgiven for. I will be forever happy, even unto the day you wake."

"Transi, I love you."

"Noah, my husband, I love you too."

Tranzaiel leaned over to kiss Noah on the forehead. He felt the warmth of love wash over his heart, and his mouth naturally form a smile as his final breath left his lungs. His eyes held the image of her face as though for hours, days even, until it seemed to fill with pure, bright, crystal-clear white light. "You are ready to join your parents, great-grandson?"

"Metanoch? Is that you?" Noah felt the same warmth of love filling him as he felt held in the same position, but now he was looking up into his great-grandfather's face. The elderly face seemed to grow younger by degrees while the light faded to somewhere behind his great-grandfather's visage, and all around them. Above, in the distance behind Enoch's head, he could see the tops of trees.

"You may rise to your feet as you like, great-grandson; no strength will fail you here."

As Noah rose up from his great-grandfather's lap, he found himself sitting up in a wide, open field surrounded by beautiful trees of all sorts. He looked around in awe while he slowly stood. "How did we get here, Enotron?"

"I am here to grant you a final wish you did not even know to ask, Noah. In human life my name was Enoch, your great-grandfather. But I sought after my own divine nature such that I was made as a connection between my own true true natures. In tones progressive from high to low, as a willing servant ultimately to myself, I communicate Its voice that others as I was may hear. So, different now in nature to as I was, I am now called Metatron. The simplicity of your brain is what allowed me to speak so fluidly to you in so many ways, without killing you. Hear now, as you couldn't before, Our voice."

"Wha–" The question Noah was about to ask was cut off in the time it took Metatron to apparently open his mouth, and music to touch upon Noah's ear. The vibration and oscillations emitting from The Metatron utterly filled Noah's spirit. In the music, there seemed words, and yet Noah could not distinguish any. As though little symbols of color and light filled the air, surrounding his head and entering through and into it on all sides, he came to understand them as notes while they turned to bright white, and suddenly he was looking at a ridged, domed shape.

Gray, then pink, then turned to bright white as the notes bombarded it and it expanded in front of him. He watched lines of light being drawn within it where what looked like nets were far simpler before. Suddenly a great deal of netting took shape into interwoven patterns almost resembling making a cloth to him, in some ways, as he watched and began to know somehow this was called a brain, and further, that it belonged to him. The bright white notes and lines were his brain becoming more than he'd known it to be. Enshrouded in Metatron's symphonic vibration, with self-perception as he'd never known it before, he looked back at the entirety of his life.

He saw himself formed with a far simpler brain that belied complexity while he'd developed. The love his parents had shown him. The extraordinary love his wife had shown him. His cruelty to his son and grandson despite the love they'd shown him, juxtaposed to his inability to be otherwise through the great deal of pain he'd suffered by his inability to understand, let alone reconcile himself with, the deaths surrounding his life. Not even realizing the toll on his being that all on Earth died while he lived. The realities of the evils of Earth, why his simplicity had made him immune to those evils, and thus chosen to see human life past them. The toll his apparent insanity and realization of the sentence passed on all life, let alone the journey to reestablishing it, must have taken on his family, and the extraordinary love his sons had shown him all throughout. The bravery it had taken Ham to try to act truly toward him, even knowing he could never fully understand. All the pain, all the joy, and the unequivocal fact that never could he have been anyone except who he was, throughout it all.

He wished to weep, except that the fullness of him was perfectly balanced now, and that he did not really have a body. As though he had eyes, he opened them. All around him a beautiful open field. On its outskirts, beautiful trees of all different types. By his side a man, not too young and not so old, about his own age, smiling at him. "Thank you."

"Don't mention it. Questions answered, and faculties understood, just one thing left, yes?"

Noah nodded in agreement and smiled. "Again, I thank you."

"Happy to serve. You may stay here as long as you like. Call upon them as you wish. The light waits for you to become when you are ready to pass to the final truth of us all."

Noah nodded. Metatron disappeared, and in his place now stood Lamech and Light Within The Darkness. "Mommy! Daddy! I can speak to you! I can articulate my love!"

"Yet you know that we heard it loudly in our hearts as we lived, son." They spoke in unison, and it made Noah smile. He hugged them, one at a time, and as a family. He conversed with them, telling them all about the flood, his life, and his wife and children. He asked them all he could want to know. As though years passed, they spoke, sometimes one at a time, sometimes in unison. A feeling filled him that they were there to be called as he chose, and he no longer needed to miss these who it felt could never be apart from who he was. They all embraced again, and then his parents vanished.

He looked all around him at the different, beautiful trees, giddy at the idea of 'playing' with them; he laughed. In the distance a bunny rabbit hopped along, stopping occasionally to crinkle its nose. Then, he had one final thought.

There Tranzaiel stood before him. Her arms stretched out to him, he took her into his, kissed her deeply and long, and then smiled at her. They conversed at length of their lives, all he didn't know, all she hadn't been able to say. They made love for what felt like millennia, giggled, kissed, talked more, kissed more. Looking deeply into each other's eyes, they told each other wordlessly that they loved each other. They took a deep breath together, held each other's hand and looked forward, side by side.

A single point of pure light shined before them. Toward the middle of the field, hand-in-hand together they walked toward that point of light. With every footfall it grew bigger, until all there was was the light through which they walked. The warmth of her love and the love given him by everyone he'd ever known surrounding and filling him, Tranzaiel dissolved away as he continued to walk. Until, finally, he too dissolved away into Light, that which He and All had always truly been.

The last of his breath having passed his lips, Tranzaiel could feel his body had life in it no more. A single tear passed from her eye down onto his forehead, while the relief of the burden of his pain laid down washed forever away from her. Later that night, she would have time to mourn the loss of her best friend and companion, awaiting the moment she would meet him again when, before too much longer, her own long sleep would arrive.